LAND GIRLS

The Promise

Roland Moore is the award-winning series creator and script-writer of the BBC1 period drama Land Girls. He's delighted to be able to expand on that world in a new series of novels for HarperCollins.

His lovely wife is a great source of support and his son often comes up with helpful suggestions – even if they mostly involve laser beams and robots.

You can find out more about Roland on Twitter @ RolandMooreTV, Facebook www.facebook.com/landgirlstv-book/ or at www.rolandmoore.tv.

ROLAND MOORE

LAND GIRLS

The Promise

A division of HarperCollins*Publishers*
www.harpercollins.co.uk

Harper*Impulse* an imprint of
HarperCollins*Publishers*
1 London Bridge Street
London SE1 9GF

www.harpercollins.co.uk

This paperback edition 2018

1

First published in Great Britain in ebook format by
Harper*Impulse* 2018

A catalogue record for this book
is available from the British Library

ISBN: 9780008204440

This novel is entirely a work of fiction.
The names, characters and incidents portrayed in it are
the work of the author's imagination. Any resemblance to
actual persons, living or dead, events or localities is
entirely coincidental.

Set in [illegible] by Palimpsest Book Production Limited,
Falkirk, Stirlingshire

Printed and bound in Great Britain by CPI Group (UK)
Ltd, Croydon CR0 4YY

To Rafał with lots of love. Always proud of you and your wonderful imagination.

Prologue

As the young girl with red hair reached the street, she was surprised to see her mother, Margot Dawson, standing outside their house. Of course, she had seen her there hundreds of times before, cleaning the step, chatting to neighbours, but there was something odd about her being there now. Something was wrong. Her mother looked bewildered, in shock, her eyes large and fearful. And when she glanced at the girl, it was almost as if she didn't really recognise her at first. "Iris?" she said, snapping out of it. She grabbed hold of her daughter, seemingly as much for support as for the need to talk to her. She pulled her towards her. Margot knelt down, her voice deliberate, but brittle.

"I need you to do something. Can you do it for me, darling?" The words were tinged with desperation, making Iris realise that the only answer her mother wanted to hear was yes.

The girl nodded. But her mother still looked troubled, perhaps unconvinced. So she touched her mother lightly on the shoulder to reassure her. She had seen adults do that and it seemed to work. But here it was a silent promise. A child's promise.

And now, seven years later, 17-year-old Iris Dawson tried to put the memory to the back of her mind as she walked towards the church in the middle of Helmstead. She didn't realise that sometimes you get a second chance in life. Sometimes you get a chance to put things right.

It was a bright, sunny day when they buried Walter Storey.

The good and the great of Helmstead put on their finest clothes and trudged dutifully to the church to pay their respects to the young man. A man who had been taken too soon. Talking in hushed tones, they moved slowly down the paved pathway, their faces dappled with sun from above the oak trees lining the graveyard. The Reverend Henry Jameson, dressed in full ministerial regalia, was there to greet them and offer them comforting words as they filed into the church.

Iris Dawson stopped by the church gate. She was an eager-to-please and enthusiastic young woman with pale, flawless skin, large blue eyes and a shock of curly red hair that fell in natural ringlets. Currently her face was etched with a deep sense of foreboding, a chill spreading up her spine, as if it was being caressed by icy fingers. After everything that had happened she would rather be anywhere else in the world right now. She certainly didn't want to go inside. But she knew it would be frowned upon if she didn't show her face. She opened her small handbag and, being careful so that no one would see, removed a tiny rag doll. It was no more than two inches high, adorned in a battered red-checked dress, one of its eyes missing. A threadbare totem from childhood that had been there through everything. Iris gripped it tightly in her hand, knowing it wouldn't be visible. She took a deep breath and, without enthusiasm, walked slowly towards the church, offering a tight smile to the reverend as she passed. She hesitated on the threshold, took a deep breath, and stepped inside, her footsteps echoing on the stone floor. Beyond the rapidly filling pews, she could see the coffin, positioned in the central aisle. She edged away from it and found a seat, stoically looking at the stained-glass window ahead rather than the coffin. Thinking about the body would bring the traumatic events of the last few days flooding back into her mind, and she was struggling enough to hold things together without that. She had to focus on the window.

Walter had been Vernon Storey's eldest son. Vernon was not a well-liked man in the village. His grasping and suspicious demeanour might have made him unpleasant company, but it was his streak of callousness that really made people uneasy. There was something, a strange and intangible something, that festered in him. A dark heart. But most people had liked Walter. Displaying different traits to his father, he was a strong, principled boy, who seemed ready to blossom. Desperate to fight in the war, Walter felt constrained by his reserved-occupation status, which meant he had to stay on the home front. He wanted to 'do his bit' for king and country, but had to resign himself to running Shallow Brook Farm with his father. The two of them, with their personalities often at odds, found living and working together a stressful, combative experience. And frankly, given his parental influence, it was a surprise that Walter had turned out as decently as he had. Iris remembered that Walter felt conflicted and uneasy about helping Vernon do certain things that were not morally right; the petty scams and fiddles that he wanted him to take part in. But feeling duty-bound and with his father's taunts of 'blood being thicker than water' he would do them with gritted teeth. The ties of blood were important to Walter, innately enshrined in his conscience. Perhaps unable to see his father's faults, he strove for validation and praise from the older man. For his part, Vernon recognised this need in his son. But to Vernon it was just another weapon to use to get Walter to do what he wanted.

The crowd settled into the pews, every seat taken, much to the reverend's surprise. But then this wasn't quite an ordinary funeral. There were mourners present who hadn't just come to pay their respects. They knew that Walter had been murdered. They knew a man had been arrested for the crime and was locked up in the sole cell in the nearby police station. That added a frisson to the funeral service that that didn't usually happen when someone just died of old age. Iris calculated that half of the mourners were present for genuine reasons of sharing a loss, and half were present for the potential spectacle. Murder was unusual in such a small, sleepy village.

Iris sat in the church and listened to Vernon's tearful eulogy to his son. All the gathered people had their eyes opened to a level of paternal love that they had never suspected before. Apparently Walter had been the perfect son. A clever boy, who had worked hard to make Shallow Brook Farm a success. A friend who had kept Vernon company in the long days since his wife's passing. Many in the church had to stifle their surprise at hearing such warm words. During Walter's life,

Vernon had rarely offered so much as the smallest compliment, preferring to default to criticism and ridicule to get what he wanted from the boy. But in death, the eulogy of previously unspoken and unguessed words was fulsome. Frederick Finch threw Iris a subtle look of surprise. Were they hearing this right? They both knew that Vernon was the sort of man who would clip his son around the ear rather than say something nice.

But, perhaps predictably, Vernon couldn't maintain the kind words. The eulogy slowly turned from a glowing tribute to a desire for justice for the man who had killed his son. Iris shifted uneasily in her pew. For Iris, this was a great time of torment. Not because she was particularly close to Walter; in fact, if anything, she hadn't liked him for the way he would continually needle her and her friend Frank Tucker, the good-natured and kind handyman at Pasture Farm. No, Iris's torment stemmed from the fact that everyone thought Frank had been the man who'd killed him. It had been a war of words, and then fists, which had escalated between Tucker and the Storeys. Iris wondered if it stemmed from some historical rivalry between the two families, but the last few weeks had seen things get worse. Much worse. And Iris had been caught in the middle of things. She tried to talk reason into Walter. She tried to calm down Frank and stop him retaliating. But she hadn't been able to stop them. Things had spiralled out of control. Typical men!

On the fateful day that Walter Storey died, Iris had been working on a tractor in a nearby field. She was alarmed to see Frank moving away from the barn, staggering, with cuts and bruises around his face. She could see the state of him. She'd called his name and he'd given her the smallest of glances before hurrying away. Iris couldn't leave the tractor until she had finished operating the plough, but a few minutes later she'd noticed that Walter was staggering away from the barn. He'd looked battered and bloodied. There was no doubting that a vicious fight had taken place inside. Iris had known she had to check on Frank and see how he was.

Fearing the worst, Iris had finished her work and then ran to Frank's shed. His sanctuary. She'd been relieved to find Frank sitting down. His brow had been beaded with sweat and there was bruising on one of his cheeks, but apart from that he hadn't looked particularly injured. It had seemed that Walter had come out worse.

"Are you all right?" Iris had asked.

Frank nodded. "Hope that will be the end of it. That'll teach him never to creep up on a poacher." Whereas some men would be full of bravado at winning a fight, he looked ashamed that it had come to this. A quiet, kind man, Frank Tucker would only use violence as a final resort.

But Frank's hope that the spiral of events might have ended was quashed later that day, when Walter's body had been found in the barn. Vernon said that he had come searching for his son when he hadn't returned home and he had made the horrific discovery. He raised the alarm and soon everyone from Pasture Farm was gathered around the barn, trying to console the distraught man. Iris had been there with the other Land Girls, numb and confused. But she couldn't understand. Why was Walter here? Why was he dead? She'd seen him leave the barn. Maybe he had returned for a rematch and Frank had accidentally killed him. But that didn't make sense to her. So while the accusations started to fly and people started to wonder where Frank was, Iris knew, with total certainty, that she had seen Walter walk away from the fight. She tried to calm things down and said she'd ask Frank why another fight had taken place. She felt disappointed that Frank would have stooped to physical violence again. It didn't seem likely.

"Well, it looks as if he did," Esther said, sadly.

"Looks as though he couldn't stop himself this time," Joyce added.

But Iris felt that they were all wrong. Frank wasn't like that. But her protestations were ignored as rumblings of a mob mentality started to rise slowly within the large group. Finch thought they had to find Frank to get him to account for his actions. Esther thought they should call the police. Vernon urged them to do both things, a fury in his eyes. The man wanted justice for his son. When they finally found Frank Tucker, he seemed shocked by the news. Walter was dead? Frank seemed to crumple before their eyes, crushed by the intense regret that he felt. He must have hit the boy too hard. In the end, there was no need to call the police because Frank had turned himself in when Vernon had accused him of murdering Walter. If he was under suspicion, then he wasn't a man who would run away. And Iris guessed that Frank probably believed he was responsible. After all, he had given Walter a savage beating. Perhaps one of those blows had later proved fatal.

And now, as Iris stood by the grave, her attention wandered

as the Reverend Henry Jameson committed Walter's body to the ground. With the words washing over her, she found herself glancing slyly at the mourners. Mrs Gladys Gulliver, the town's busybody and self-appointed moral barometer, sniffing, in a mixture of indignation and judgement; Fred Finch, the ebullient farmer, nodding his head sagely at the words; Connie Carter, Iris's glamorous friend, smiling encouragingly as her husband, the vicar, delivered the words. And then there had been Vernon Storey, dressed in his best suit and looking suitably stern-faced. Something troubled Iris about this man. Something was wrong. It wasn't only the fact that when he had delivered an impassioned eulogy about how he had lost his boy, when the words seemed so out of kilter with their actual lives. Something also troubled Iris about when Vernon had scrunched his face up and cried; she'd noticed that no tears had come. She wondered if that was normal. Could you cry without tears?

Frank would know.

But unfortunately Frank had been arrested and was being kept in the village police station. Iris wanted to go to see him later, after the funeral. But first she needed to pay her respects to Vernon. That would be the decent thing to do. That's what a lady would do. Her mum might be proud of her doing that. She clutched her handbag, as if it was a protective talisman, and edged nearer, listening as Henry's words of comfort were carried by the gentle breeze.

When the service was over and the good and the great were dispersing, she approached a brooding Vernon. By this stage, her mind was so muddled. If Frank thought he'd done it and Vernon thought he'd done it, then surely that was the end of the matter. It might have been a tragic and regrettable accident, a fight gone too far, but Frank Tucker would hang for his crime. Iris felt bereft that her friend, Frank, had done this. Since she'd arrived at Pasture Farm, Frank had been like a surrogate father for her, guiding her and helping her as she navigated life as a Land Girl. He had been teaching her to read and write, painstakingly giving her lessons in the evenings. He was a good man. If he was guilty, then it was such a waste.

"Sorry about Walter," Iris stammered.

"Not your fault." Vernon scowled. "It was that flaming friend of yours. He battered my boy."

Iris was taken aback by his ferocity and found herself involuntarily taking a step away. The Reverend Henry Jameson tried to console Vernon with a warm smile. It wasn't the time or the place for such outbursts.

"Why did he have to go back to that barn?" Iris asked. It was a casual expression of regret that this was the one decision that had led to Walter's demise, nothing more. She hadn't intended it to be a searching question, but the answer surprised her.

"He didn't," Vernon said gruffly.

"Really?" Iris asked.

"He didn't go back, you silly girl."

"Are you sure?" Iris wanted to say she had definitely seen Walter walk away from the barn after the fight. He must have gone back. There must have been a rematch. But Vernon was obviously in no mood for splitting hairs. And the reverend was right; it wasn't the time or place. Vernon left her in the graveyard, her head swimming with a nagging feeling that something wasn't right.

As the last remaining mourners left, Iris kept her word to Frank Tucker and went to see him at the police station. The only policeman in the station was PC Thorne. On secondment from nearby Brinford, PC Thorne had found himself in the unenviable position of serving three villages and two towns as their sole source of law enforcement. All the other police officers had been conscripted into the armed forces. He didn't really have the time or inclination to help Iris, but he knew he was duty-bound to do so.

Iris was allowed to see Frank for five minutes and she was led into a cold room with a table and two chairs, walls decorated with half-green and half-cream walls. Frank was brought in. He was pleased to see her and tried to be pleasant and humorous towards her; as if they were just talking in his shed after dinner. But Iris could see the fear in his eyes; his shoulders stooped with defeat, his hair lank and unwashed. Had he already given up? She knew that he would be put on trial for this and, if found guilty, he would be hanged by the neck.

"How are you?" Iris said, somewhat redundantly.

"The food isn't as good as Esther's, but at least there's not so much yakking at meal times." Frank shrugged.

"You've come here just to get away from all us Land Girls, haven't you?" She smiled. Frank smiled too, warmth in his eyes. But the warmth bled away as an awkward silence filled the room. Then Frank sighed and told Iris what he wanted to happen. His words surprised her.

"I don't want you coming again," he said. "This isn't how I want you to remember me."

"Don't talk daft. You'll be back," Iris said bravely. "You've got to help me finish writing a letter home, haven't you?"

"Someone else will have to teach you." He nodded, closing the matter in his mind. Iris felt a little foolish for trying to lighten the mood at the wrong moment.

"I mean it, Iris. You forget about all this. Remember those evenings when you'd be chewing your pencil and I'd be helping you trace the alphabet. You remember those times, eh? Not these ones."

Iris knew better than to question such finality. His mind was made up and any entreaties she made would likely make his veneer of control snap. And she didn't want to show that lack of respect to a man she admired. So she decided it would be best to come straight to the point and tell him what had troubled her at the graveyard.

"There's just one thing I don't understand. Why did Walter come back for a rematch?" she asked.

Frank looked puzzled. She guessed that it all seemed a bit irrelevant to him now. What did it matter? As far as he was concerned, he'd killed a man and that was that.

"What do you mean?"

"I saw Walter Storey walk away from that fight a few minutes after you left."

"Yeah, but he died from what I did to him. The body is a strange old thing. Maybe it took time for the injury to kill him."

"What was he like after the fight?" Iris persisted.

Frank rubbed the bridge of his nose and thought about what had happened. "We'd had the fight. I'd given Storey a beating and left him in the barn. The boy wasn't unconscious or anything. There didn't seem to be any cause for concern."

"And what happened then?"

"What are you getting at?" But Iris's insistent look made Frank realise that she needed an answer. "I walked to my shed and got on with mending a couple of rakes. That's when you came to see me."

"But I saw Walter leave the barn."

"What are you saying?" Frank was clearly confused by what she was trying to tell him, so Iris decided she had to spell it out.

"You must have had another fight with him. A rematch?"

Frank shook his head. No, definitely not. "Maybe he came back to the barn looking for me and then collapsed?"

Now it was Iris's turn to sigh. She hadn't thought of that option. "Maybe," she whispered, deflated. The discussion seemed to make Frank withdraw into himself and a brooding silence filled the small room. There seemed to be nothing else to say.

As she wished Frank well and left the police station, Iris struggled not to show Frank that she was upset. Stiff upper lip and all that. It seemed to be how he wanted to play it too. There would be no big, tearful goodbye, just a matter-of-fact parting of the ways. The last moments of a friendship. She walked with unsteady legs down the steps of Helmstead Police Station, her mind more confused than ever. She decided that she had to see Vernon again.

"'Ere, I told you loads of times, I don't like pickle!" Connie protested, as she unwrapped her sandwich and realised that Esther had given her just that on her cheese. Esther shook her head and apologised. She rooted in her wicker trug for another sandwich wrapped in greaseproof paper. She found one with a 'C' written on the side.

"Here's yours, Little Miss Fusspot," Esther said.

"I can't help it." Connie handed back the offending sandwich in exchange. "Pickle's unnatural, innit?"

"I like it," Joyce commented.

"Well, you're unnatural." Connie smiled.

As the friends joked and started their lunches in the West Field, Iris took her greaseproof parcel with her and trotted across the yard. She could feel the other girls looking pityingly at her as she went.

"She's lost without that Frank, isn't she?" Connie said.

"Terrible business," Joyce replied.

When Iris was out of sight, she increased her speed, running in a jog all the way out of the gates of Pasture Farm. She ran down the lane, avoiding the pot holes as if she was playing hopscotch, and soon came to the neighbouring farm. Shallow Brook Farm. The Storeys' farm. Unlike Pasture Farm, this place looked deserted, a dark shell with decaying tractors and machines standing in a yard overgrown with weeds. Iris made her way towards the farmhouse. She rapped on the slatted wooden door, paint flakes peeling away on her knuckles. How many summers ago had this place been painted?

There was no answer. And yet, the door slowly creaked open. Vernon had left it unlocked.

Iris poked her head into the hallway, where a broken mahogany barometer pointed towards snow.

"Hello? Anyone here?" Iris shouted.

Nothing came back.

Iris's heart was pounding. She had come to see Vernon, but perhaps it was a good thing that he wasn't home. She could look inside and have a nose around. A regular Miss Marple. Should she do this? She didn't even know what she was looking for. Perhaps some sign that Walter had returned home before going back to the barn? What would that prove? Iris wasn't sure. All she knew was that a man's life was at stake here and if something was niggling her about the order of events, then she had to put her mind at rest. Something wasn't right. Iris wished for a moment that she had Miss Marple's abilities.

She moved cautiously from the hallway into the dining room. The fireplace smouldered with yesterday's fire. A garish red-patterned rug filled much of the floor space, held down by dark-wooden furniture dotted around the room. A bureau stacked with paperwork and bills. A telephone on a side table. An armchair with worn hand rests. She guessed this was Vernon's chair as his glasses rested on the edge next to a rolled-up newspaper. Iris tentatively moved across the room.

"Hello?" she shouted, feeling perhaps that she was covering herself from accusations of breaking and entering.

Again there was no reply. It was likely that Vernon Storey was holding some kind of wake in the Bottle and Glass, regaling people with tales of his son.

Iris moved towards the bureau.

Crack!

It barely made a sound, but something crunched under her foot. She looked down and peeled the edge of the rug back. A long sliver of glass from a bottle had broken in two. But as Iris examined it, she could see something sticky along one edge. A dark liquid. In sudden horror she realised that it was blood. Could it be Walter's blood? They said he had a wound on his head. Was this evidence? What would Miss Marple do? Her mind was racing. Thinking quickly, she plucked her handkerchief from her pocket and, as if it was a small, injured bird, carefully wrapped the glass up. Suddenly she knew she had to get out of there; show PC Thorne what she had found.

"Can I help you, Iris?" A soft voice, weary.

Iris span around to find Vernon in the doorway. He was blinking in the light, his face more crumpled than usual. Had he been drinking? Sleeping? It didn't matter. He was here and that was a problem. Iris hid the handkerchief behind her back.

"I came to ... pay my respects," she stammered.

"Again?" A note of suspicion in his voice, his shrewish eyes suddenly alert and scanning her face.

"Yes." Slowly, Iris slipped the handkerchief into her pocket.

"And that was all you came for?" Vernon took a step towards her. He was a short man, but his personality gave him a threatening demeanour. Iris struggled to stop herself taking a step backwards. She knew it wouldn't play well if she showed fear. If she was paying her respects, then she shouldn't show fear, should she?

"Anyway, I'd better get back. Esther will be wondering ..."

Iris smiled as winningly as she could manage. She took a step towards the door, aware that Vernon was still blocking any escape.

"Stay a little longer," he rasped, his words somewhere in that uncertain area between a threat and a pleasant invitation. "Have a drink to my Walter, eh? If you've come to pay your respects ..."

He crossed to the sideboard, where a motley and dusty collection of bottles formed a drinks 'cabinet'. Now the door was unblocked. There was a gap and Iris could make a run for it. But she didn't want Vernon to suspect that anything was wrong; she didn't want to alert his suspicions. After all, even if she got past him, she'd have to outrun him all the way back to Pasture Farm.

"I'd better ... you know." Iris glanced towards the door. To her surprise and relief, he nodded his consent. And as he busied himself pouring a drink at the sideboard, Iris started to walk towards the door, as slowly and as normally as she could manage. She thought she had got away with it, when, without turning his back, Vernon asked a soft and unnerving question.

"What's that in your pocket, Iris?"

She felt her mouth go instantly dry, her breathing becoming more rapid. She stopped in her tracks. He'd noticed what she was doing. How much had he seen?

"Nothing," she stammered.

Now he turned to her. A dark smile on his lips as he looked into her scared eyes. There was no hiding what she felt now.

"You put something in your pocket."

"No, I didn't."

Vernon put his drink down and edged towards her. "Have you been stealing from me, Iris?"

She shook her head. "No, Mr Storey. I wouldn't do that."

He glanced down towards her pocket, where the end of the handkerchief was poking out. "Show me, then." Carefully, Iris cupped her fingers around her handkerchief, hoping she could bring the bundle out without its contents falling onto the floor.

"It's just my handkerchief." The wrapped fabric was clasped tightly in her hand.

To her surprise, Vernon snatched it from her, grasping her wrist tightly with his other hand. As he took it, the handkerchief opened and the fragment of glass fell onto the rug, glinting in the light as it tumbled. They both knew the truth now.

"No one likes a liar, Iris."

"Let me go." She knew that she had to escape now. There was no point in pretending that she could talk her way out of this one. But Vernon wasn't about to let go of her wrist. She clawed at his fingers with her free hand, trying to release his grip. He kept a tight grip on her, staring impassively at her. They moved a few steps: a dark, silent dance as Iris tried to free herself, Vernon clasping tightly. Iris felt her head swimming. They were like a couple on the verge of a massive argument, trying to maintain some semblance of control and decency. But Iris realised she would have to do more to escape. She would have to make a scene. She was about to slap him, claw him, do something, when he moved with surprising speed and ferocity towards her.

Vernon grabbed Iris's neck and pushed her backwards until she felt the bureau hit the small of her back. She tried to lash out, but he grabbed her clawed hand and pushed her over the desk. On her back, Iris flailed and kicked, desperate to escape. She couldn't scream as Vernon had his fingers clasped around her throat. She tried to kick again, but only succeeded in upturning the nearby telephone table. The telephone clattered to the floor, the receiver coming away from its cradle.

"Please don't ..." she gasped.

"What?" he growled.

"Kill me."

Vernon let out a tight, unnerving laugh. "Why would I do that, you stupid girl?"

"I know what you did."

Vernon's brow furrowed. Still grasping her throat, tears came to his eyes. He seemed to sag, much like Frank had when he had heard the news about Walter. It was as if her words had ripped away his layers of desperate subterfuge, making it plain that this situation wasn't going to go away.

"That's a dangerous accusation."

"How could you kill your own son?" Iris said, emboldened by the reaction her words were having.

"Shut your mouth." A low rumble of anger, his fingers tightening around her windpipe. Iris felt her head swimming, as her lungs fought for air. "Do you think I wanted to do it?"

"You're hurting me ..." It was barely a squawk, as Iris couldn't gasp enough air to speak.

Vernon didn't seem to hear. He was lost in his own justifications for what had happened. "Walter made me lose my temper. I just lashed out. Didn't think. Didn't even know I had the bottle in my hand." Vernon's eyes were distant, lost in regret and torment. "As he fell, I knew what I'd done. Even before he hit the floor, Iris, I knew what I'd done. Don't you see?"

At last, he released his grip and Iris gasped for air. He was still looming over her as her back rested on the bureau. From the corner of her eye, she saw a tractor brochure offering a brand-new machine for rental. Iris wondered if it would be one of the last things she ever saw.

"What are you going to do with me?"

Vernon took a step back, releasing his weight from her. He clutched his forehead and shook his head in a violent, distressed manner, as if he didn't want to be here, in this situation, any more that Iris did.

"I can't let you leave, can I?" The words came out tinged with regret and sadness. She knew that he was right. His desperate attempts to cover his tracks had already seen the arrest of an innocent man. Vernon would eradicate any other potential threat that might cause his web of lies to unravel. He was already in too deep. There was no going back.

Still sprawled over the bureau, Iris knew she couldn't make it to the door without him dragging her back, and she knew that nothing she could say would alter what was about to happen. That didn't stop her mind racing, desperately trying to find a solution. The one thing that would stop him.

"Please," She gasped, a simple plea for mercy. As soon as she'd said it, she knew it would be ignored. Of course it would. With most of his body still blocking her escape, Vernon bent towards the fireplace and grabbed a poker. Either he hadn't heard her plea or was choosing to ignore it.

"You're a sweet girl, but I can't let you go."

"I won't tell," Iris pleaded again. But this time, she wasn't saying the words to try to change his mind. This time she was trying to buy herself time, as her eyes searched for something – anything – that could help her. There might have been a letter-opening knife on the bureau, but if there was, it was buried under all the paperwork behind her. On the armchair were Vernon's spectacles, the newspaper. Nothing to help her. The poker was the only 'weapon' by the fireplace and Vernon had that. There were bottles on the sideboard, but Iris couldn't make it to the drinks cabinet without Vernon getting in the first blow. He would beat her to the floor before she got there. What could she do? She had to do something. Vernon moved slowly forward, the poker in his hand.

Then she saw it; something that might just help her.

The telephone was upturned on the floor, the receiver knocked from its cradle. The fuzzy, muffled voice on the other end of the line: "Hello, what number do you require?"

Vernon saw it at the same time as Iris. The colour drained from his face. The operator might have heard everything: the confession, the threats. Vernon knew he was a doomed man. Iris used that moment of distraction to leap forward, pushing Vernon back against the fireplace. She sprinted for the door as Vernon collapsed into the dying fire, ash pluming into the air behind him. He struggled to get free, but then moved with surprising speed after the young girl, the poker in his hand.

Iris burst into the courtyard of Shallow Brook Farm and ran and ran. She could hear Vernon shouting behind her.

"I'll get you, Iris!"

And then, as she pressed ahead and he lagged behind, she heard his final words on the subject.

"I will come for you, Iris. Mark my words!"

She didn't look back. She didn't dare turn, in case Vernon's malevolent eyes were somehow right behind her, the poker raised in his hand. Iris never looked back. She kept running and running.

But after that dreadful day, everything seemed to slowly return to normal. A happy ending of sorts emerged from those awful events. With the operator corroborating Iris's account to the police, Frank Tucker was soon released from custody. Vernon's words had acted as a confession. As Iris collected Frank from the police station, she took him back to Pasture Farm, where the girls had made a garland and a rabbit stew to welcome him back. They all got tipsy on Finch's carrot whisky that night, with Frank more taciturn than usual as he listened to the celebrations and laughter around him. Several times, Iris asked if he was all right. Was he tired from his ordeal? But Frank just smiled and said he was fine. Iris suspected that secretly he was in shock, counting his blessings for a narrow escape from the gallows.

"Who's for another bottle?" Esther asked, her cheeks flushed red, as if a child had applied her blusher.

"Here, steady on," Finch grumbled. "There's a war on."

"Don't be such a tight wad," Connie shrieked, opening a

cupboard under the sink. She moved some pots and a metal funnel and produced a fresh bottle of carrot whisky.

"How did you know where I kept it?" Finch said, alarmed. Connie tapped the side of her nose.

The bottle was cracked open and the girls drank a new toast. Iris felt her own cheeks warming and then noticed that Martin was looking at her, holding his gaze just a moment too long. When she turned, he smiled with embarrassment. He was nearly 17, one year her junior, and filling out to be a fine young man, boyish freckles retreating on his face as he reached adulthood. Iris liked him. He was gentle and funny. He raised his glass in a silent toast to her across the table. Iris went to raise her glass of cordial, but the moment was broken when Esther turned and clipped him around the ear. He was her son, and as far as Esther was concerned, still her baby boy.

"How many of those have you had?"

"Four." Martin shrugged.

"Four?" Esther scowled. "Well, that's the last one."

"If I'd had four, I wouldn't be able to feel my legs." Joyce laughed.

The Land Girls raised their glasses again. Amid the warmth and laughter, the stone-cold-sober Iris found herself thinking about Vernon Storey. The man who had murdered his own son and who had tried to make another man hang for it. The man who had tried to kill her. How could people do such things?

By the time PC Thorne got to Shallow Brook Farm, he found Vernon Storey sitting in his armchair reading the newspaper, as if nothing had happened. He seemed surprised to see the policeman and, initially, Vernon tried to lie his way out of any accusations.

"No, I've not seen Iris Dawson. She's not been here. You must be mistaken."

"Come on, now, Vernon. We've got someone who heard everything. A young girl was in this room." PC Thorne noticed that the telephone had been righted on the table. He wondered whether Vernon would continue to brave-face the situation, but then Vernon's studied act broke down.

Vernon got up from his chair. "Why can't you all leave me alone?"

"Sorry, Vernon. You've got to come with me."

"I suppose."

Vernon stretched his arms in front of him, as if inviting PC Thorne to restrain his hands. It seemed as if he was seeing sense now. But as Thorne turned to apply the handcuffs, the farmer pushed him backwards as hard as he could. PC Thorne fell, hitting his head on the fireplace. And although he wasn't knocked out, by the time he got to his feet, Vernon already had a head start and was fleeing across the yard. PC Thorne yelled for him to stop, but by the time he reached the lane, it was empty. PC Thorne knew that Vernon must be hiding, but he didn't know in which direction. He tried to search as methodically and quickly as he could, peering over the hedgerows and looking over fences. But after about thirty minutes, he realised that Vernon had somehow managed to elude him. Defeated and worried, he trudged back to the police station.

Wanted posters were put up around Helmstead and neighbouring Brinford; PC Thorne checked outbuildings for weeks afterwards; and Reverend Henry Jameson made repeated entreaties to his flock to come forward with information, but Vernon Storey wasn't seen again. It was as if he had vanished off the face of the earth.

Chapter 1

Several weeks after Walter Storey's funeral, a dance hall reverberated with music and laughter. Times like these were precious, joyful releases after days spent under the spectre of war. The hall was hot and sticky, thanks to the combination of an uncharacteristically sultry evening and the gyrations of the many Land Girls and American soldiers crammed into the small space. But, despite the heat, everyone was determined to make the best of it; a few hours off the leash, dressed in their finery, flirting and having fun. A few hours to forget about the war and remember what it was like to be carefree, feeling the exhilaration of a warm body pressed against yours as you twirled and attempted to follow the steps of the dance.

Although she wasn't dancing, Iris Dawson was enjoying sitting on the edge of the action, her leg tapping in time to the beat. She had an awkwardness and lack of confidence that people either found frustrating or endearing. Iris felt she didn't quite fit in. She didn't know how to put on makeup, despite her mother's best efforts to teach her back at home, so she chose not to wear any most of the time. Tonight, though, she had experimented with some of Connie Carter's red lipstick, but with no guidance, she suspected she looked as though she had been messily eating cherries. Tonight was a blessed break from her troubles, and the two shillings admission price was well worth a night off from her thoughts. Iris was paid twenty-eight shillings a week and after bed and board she was left with half of that. She viewed it as her payment for the back-breaking work in the fields, payment for the aching legs, sunburned shoulders, blistered feet and sore hands. She would send as much of the money home as she could, but she knew her mother would be pleased if she spent some of it on herself for once.

Iris was laughing and joking with her fellow Land Girls, Joyce Fisher and Connie Carter, who were sitting next to her. A row of contented wallflowers. To Joyce's amusement, Connie was refusing a dance with another hopeful soldier. Sitting near the small, but loud, dance band, Connie would struggle to make herself heard. But a quick flash of her wedding ring, with a smile, usually deflected even the most persistent would-be suitor.

"Sorry, I'm spoken for."

The soldier smiled back and said something that Iris couldn't hear. She guessed by the shape of the words it was: "That's a real pity".

Like so many others before him that evening, he trudged the walk of shame back to his mates at the makeshift bar, where they perused the room for other prospective dance dates. If she'd felt so inclined, Connie could have marked her dance card with a long list of rejections as she was racking them up so fast. It was plain to see that Connie was breathtakingly beautiful, with long black hair styled into loose waves, unblemished skin and full, red lips. Iris couldn't blame the men for trying. She liked having Connie as her friend; a worldly young woman who had seen more of life than Iris could ever imagine. Connie was both fun to be with and a friendly source of advice. As Iris's mother would have said, Connie had an old head on young shoulders. For her part, Iris was far less experienced in dealing with life. She had no experience of men and had come from a sheltered upbringing in Northampton, living with her caring, but slightly distant, mother. So being in the big, wide world, billeted to Pasture Farm, had been a big shock to Iris. It was her first time living away from home; the first time she'd lived with a group of women thrown together from all corners of England, from all walks of life. And it was her first experience of back-breaking farm work.

Iris had been asked twice to dance, but she had demurely refused, knowing that across the room, Martin Reeves looked as though he was plucking up courage to ask her. She didn't want to quash his hopes or put him off by dancing with someone else. She liked Martin, but she wished he'd find the courage soon. He had always been slim, but the last few months had seen him bulk out slightly, the effect of constant manual labour on the farm. He'd gone from looking like a boy to a well-proportioned young man, a wave of sandy hair parted casually across his forehead, his brown eyes burning with life. Idly, she wondered if she could will him to ask her, as seeing his hopeful eyes and nervous face was making her feel uncomfortable. Maybe if she thought really hard and imagined him walking over, it would happen! She had tried offering an encouraging smile a few times, but it hadn't done the trick yet. Also across the room was Frederick Finch, the ebullient, portly, middle-aged tenant farmer who ran Pasture Farm. Looking as if he'd been tipped into his clothes, he was nursing two half-full pint glasses (for some unexplained reason) and talking to another middle-aged man about something that involved a lot of red-faced guffawing. Iris thought the conversation was probably revolving around some scam or dodgy deal. That's what Finch liked to do. His small victories in war time, as he called them. Finch was a good man at heart and Iris felt warmly towards him. In some ways he was a father-away-from home, someone who would look out for her, someone who would make sure she was all right.

The band started playing 'Chattanooga Choo Choo', a song that Iris loathed. She stopped tapping her leg in time; her own small, personal protest.

She noticed a tall, handsome soldier looking her way. Iris glanced around to her side, in puzzlement. Surely he must be eyeing someone behind her? Maybe he was looking at Connie and not at her? But no, his gaze was definitely fixed on her. And what a gaze it was – steely, intense eyes that somehow conveyed both intelligence and warmth were looking her way. Iris felt her cheeks flushing. He continued to look, flashing a confident smile. He was a tall, rangy young man with straight, straw-coloured hair and piercing green eyes; a catch by anyone's standards. Joyce noticed and nudged Iris, just in case she was somehow unaware of the young man's interest.

"I know," Iris whispered, feeling uncomfortable from the attention.

She risked a look up to meet the soldier's gaze, and to her surprise found that he was a few feet away, walking confidently towards her. Iris felt churned up; a mix of nervousness, excitement and confusion fighting for attention in the pit of her stomach. Her mouth felt very dry all of a sudden and she wondered if she would be able to talk.

"Hey? I'm Joe." The soldier smiled, extending his hand to shake hers. "Private First Class Joe Batch."

Iris was aware that Connie and Joyce were transfixed by this development and she struggled to shut them out of her peripheral vision and concentrate on Joe.

"Hello, Joe. I'm Iris. Iris Dawson," she stammered.

"Pleased to meet you."

"Yes." Iris felt awkward. She was dimly aware of Martin Reeves looking downcast across the room. Feeling a stab of pain, she noticed as he turned on his heels, pushing past some people and left the hall.

"Would you like to dance?" Joe Batch smiled, seemingly unaware of her nervousness.

"No," Iris replied. "I mean no, thank you. I don't like this song."

Joe laughed. Iris found herself smiling.

"Dance anyway," Joyce said under her breath, indicating with her eyes that Iris should just get up.

Iris nodded. "I suppose I can make an exception."

"Glad to hear it," Joe said, leading her onto the floor. "We can always pretend we're dancing to something else. What tunes do you like?"

"Anything." Iris smiled. "Apart from this."

They moved in time to the music, Joe holding her a respectful distance away. He seemed to behave like a gentleman. Not like some of the drunken soldiers in here, who were grabbing at women as if it was the last days of Rome. As they danced, Iris worried that her hands were clammy. She didn't want clammy hands, but she couldn't help feeling nervous. She wasn't used to dancing with men, feeling their proximity to her. Joe smiled at her. It was too noisy to talk, but when the dance had finished, he held her hands and looked at her.

"Thanks for that. You did pretty good considering you hate the song."

"Thanks. You were leading me, doing most of the work."

They walked to the bar and, without asking, Joe ordered two jugs of cider. He handed one to Iris and she looked into the cloudy, orange liquid, the smell of apples filling her nostrils. It wasn't the time to tell Joe Batch that she had never had a drink before, was it? Part of her was desperate to show that she was a grown up and that taking a drink with a gentleman suitor was par for the course. Before she had time to think too much, Joe clinked his glass to hers. She mirrored his actions as he put his glass to his lips and took a big gulp. Iris struggled not to pull a disparaging face when she tasted the liquid herself. It was warm and tasted of apple juice, but there was a kick to it. Joe gulped down his pint in a few seconds. Iris didn't think she could manage that, so she continued to sip at hers. She knew that was what a lady would do.

"I have to go. We're up early tomorrow."

"Sure," Iris said, feeling disappointment. Despite her nerves, she had enjoyed the experience and she was quite keen to dance some more with him.

"But would it be forward to ask if I could see you sometime?" Joe said.

Iris hadn't been expecting that. She felt flustered. "All right," she said. "I'm stationed at Pasture Farm."

"I'll swing by sometime. If that's okay?"

"That's okay," Iris said.

Joe Batch nodded and smiled, clearly pleased with the outcome. He tipped his head to her and made his way out from the hall. Feeling giddy, Iris returned to her seat with her half-finished drink, where her friends were keen for the gossip about what had happened. After Iris filled them in, Joyce and Connie were pleased for her. She found all the attention a bit bewildering and was grateful that no one else came over to ask her to dance. The experience had exhausted her. She contented herself with thinking about Joe Batch, finishing her cider and watching what else was going on in the room.

Near the door, enjoying the cooler air from outside, were a few people that Iris had never seen before. One of them was a glamorous but understated woman in her early fifties with blonde hair. When these people had arrived, Iris had asked the others who they were. But Connie and Joyce didn't know. Iris had pointed the glamorous woman out to Joyce, and Joyce, being a hair-dresser before the war, had commented that it was natural blonde hair. She was lucky. A lot of her clients would pay money to have their mousy hair turned that colour.

The woman sipped at a small glass of rhubarb wine and winced at the taste. Iris noticed that she was scanning the room, like the soldiers were. But unlike the soldiers, with their scattergun approach to seeing what available talent was out there, she seemed to be looking for one particular person. Searching, she would turn quickly away from unwanted faces before eye contact could be returned. From her vantage point across the room, Iris was mildly amused when the woman found herself staring directly at Mrs Gladys Gulliver. The sour face of the town busybody and self-appointed moral compass of Helmstead stopped the woman in her tracks. Mrs Gulliver frowned at the stranger in front of her. The fact was that Gladys Gulliver was perhaps only five years older than the blonde woman, but the choices they had made in life, not to mention differing approaches to fashion and makeup, showed that they were on very different paths. Mrs Gulliver had made a typical, snap judgement about the blonde woman before her. A judgement that, knowing Mrs Gulliver, probably involved an inner monologue including the words 'brassy' and 'tart'.

But then Iris noticed something unusual happen.

The stranger spoke to Mrs Gulliver and the busybody cracked a smile and actually laughed. The woman held Mrs Gulliver's arm as she added something to the joke and Mrs Gulliver laughed again. Iris was shocked that this had happened. She'd never seen Mrs Gulliver smile like that. She tended to smile only if it involved someone else's misfortune.

"Here look, Mrs Gulliver's made a friend!" Iris said to Joyce.

"It's her long-lost sister." Joyce looked over and smiled.

"Really?"

"No!" Joyce laughed. "You'll believe anything, you will. I've no idea who that woman is. But you know what?"

"What?"

"I'm sure Mrs Gulliver will tell us!" The girls laughed.

Iris couldn't hear what was being said between Mrs Gulliver and the other woman. She turned back to Joyce, who continued their conversation, forgetting about the momentary distraction. So Iris didn't notice the blonde woman again that night, and promptly forgot about her; just another face in the crowd. Iris found that her attention was taken by two American servicemen, who were engaged in a heated argument on the dance floor. A young woman, caught in the middle, looked sheepishly at the pair of them, wishing she was anywhere else.

At the bar, the blonde woman was busy charming her new friend, Mrs Gulliver. She had bought her a sherry and they were raising a glass together. And then the woman leaned in close.

"I suppose you know everyone here?"

"What do you mean?" Mrs Gulliver bristled a little, taking it as an insult. She was aware of her own reputation in the village, and whereas she liked to think of her inquisitive nature as a way of cementing community life through vigilance and sharing information, she knew that others viewed her as plain nosey.

"Oh, I didn't mean anything by that." The stranger smiled. "Just that you've been in the village a while and know these people."

"That's right." Mrs Gulliver smiled back, dropping her defensiveness. "That man over there –" She pointed to a dishevelled man in a badly fitting tweed suit. "He's the village doctor.

Dreadful drunk. I won't let him examine me. His hands are everywhere." And then she pointed out a thin, statuesque woman standing on the periphery, dressed more expensively than anyone else present. "And that's our ladyship. Lady Hoxley. This is her idea, this dance."

"To raise money for her Spitfire Fund?" The blonde woman asked, glancing at the refined beauty of Ellen Hoxley.

"That's right. She's a good woman. Lost her husband. Terrible business. It's too long a story to go into now, but suffice to say it involved another woman." Mrs Gulliver mouthed the words 'other woman' for reasons known only to herself. Then the older woman sipped her sherry and took a deep breath. She was about to embark on the details of that 'terrible business' anyway, but the stranger realised that the story might take some time. And time wasn't something she had.

"And who's that? Is that Freddie Finch?" The blonde woman said, pointing across the room.

"Yes. Do you know him?"

"No. I know of him." The woman laughed. "I've heard stories."

"Yes, well," Mrs Gulliver said, looking with disdain as Finch worked the two pints in his hands, alternating a sip from each as he lost himself in the music. "Everyone knows him. He's a disgrace, that one. Ran over my vegetable patch in his tractor, he did. He'd been sleeping in the pub. Blind drunk, he was. I made him repair the damage, mind."

But the blonde woman wasn't listening any more. She was already setting off across the room. "I've got to meet that man," she muttered under her breath, earning a baffled stare from Mrs Gulliver. But then Mrs Gulliver knew that people were strange.

The stranger straightened her blouse and gave her hair an imperceptible lift with her hand as she got nearer to Freddie Finch. He was watching the events on the dance floor, so he didn't notice her approaching. She was only two feet away from him, and about to speak, when the two soldiers who had been arguing flew in a messy heap of fighting limbs into a nearby table. Finch held his pint glasses high, out of harm's way, as other people scattered while the two men fought on the floor, knocking over chairs and tables. The girl who had been with them was screaming at them to stop. Connie and Joyce rolled their eyes. This was a fairly typical event thanks to the combination of alcohol and high spirits. Lady Hoxley ran across the room to the fracas, two military policemen in tow. She wasn't going to stand for it. The band stopped playing and the lights were turned up, the party over in an instant.

The blonde woman stood for a moment, contemplating the situation. Finch was edging away from the fracas, pints in hand, as if he was expecting to get the blame somehow.

It wasn't the right time to meet Frederick Finch. Not now.

No one noticed as the blonde woman turned on her heels and disappeared out of the door. By then Iris had returned to thinking about her own problems, as if the bubble of the dance had been burst by the fighting. The real world had come flooding back, bringing with it familiar feelings of unease and fear. Iris felt a chill, despite the warmth of the room and the contented giddiness in her head from the cider.

She'd half-hoped that the soldier might be waiting for her, but he wasn't.

Iris trudged back towards Pasture Farm. The other girls were singing and laughing, but she felt lost in her own thoughts. The shadows in the fields taunted her, while the girls seemed oblivious. Thoughts of Joe Batch had receded, to be replaced by her more usual preoccupations: thoughts of Vernon Storey and his promise to return for her. She wished with all her heart that she could put it out of her mind. When her head was woozy with cider, it all seemed a bit easier to cope with. Iris wondered whether she needed another drink when she got back to the farm. She decided that it probably wasn't a good idea. Instead she listened to the humourous conversation between Joyce and Connie behind her and tried her best to join in.

Chapter 2

The outbuilding stood alone in a corner of Pasture Farm; a crumbling rectangle of red bricks capped with a corrugated-iron roof and a green wooden door with more holes in it than one of Frederick Finch's moth-eaten old jumpers. It was one in a large number of dilapidated buildings, seemingly positioned at random positions around the nexus of the farm cottage, as if they were seeds from a wind-blown dandelion clock. But despite the building's basic construction, it looked welcoming, thanks to a soft-orange light emanating from within, visible through the single, tiny, grease-smeared window. In the daytime, it was a place where the Land Girls mended their tools. But in the evenings, it was a place of learning. Iris would go there to meet Frank and he would try to teach her. Their progress was slow and sometimes their nightly meetings would be mocked by the other girls with taunts about Iris meeting her fancy man. But she hoped that the dilapidated rectangular outbuilding would also be a place that would change her life.

"DeEr MUm"

The pencil scratched out the words with half a dozen

spidery lines. And then the letters started to form again, better this time.

"Dear MUm"

Iris was aware that her tongue was sticking out as she painstakingly scrawled the letters on the notepaper that Frank had given her. The large, flat carpenter's pencil seemed strange in her hand, hurting her fingers as she pressed it on the page. But then she wasn't used to writing and coordinating the pencil was hard work. It always looked easy when other people did it, but when she tried, she struggled to steer it across the paper. She didn't realise that she'd made a spelling mistake, but even she could see that the letters were an uneven bag of uppercase and lowercase, written in a size that bore no correlation to whether they were capitals or not, as if it was a ransom note made from glued newspaper letters. But she'd done it, and she felt a small sense of pride welling up in her heart.

And to cap it all, Frank seemed impressed with Iris's handwriting. "Not bad, Miss Dawson. Not bad at all."

"Did I spell it right?"

"Near enough." He cracked a smile, kindly fissures erupting around the corner of his mouth and his eyes. He didn't want to dampen the enthusiasm in his young trainee, but Iris was smart enough to know when she was being soft-soaped. Frank spotted the slight grimace on her face as she put the pencil down on his workbench.

"Hey, come on. You'll get there. That's two more words than you were writing before."

It was true. When she came to Pasture Farm as a member

of the Women's Land Army, Iris Dawson couldn't read or write a word. She had a sweet nature, which meant she always brought out the maternal and paternal instincts in older people. This was why she also had a good relationship with Freddie Finch, who seemed protective and kind.

Such was the case with friendly odd-job man, Frank Tucker, who worked on Pasture Farm doing many of the chores that the tenant farmer was too lazy to do. Their friendship had been cemented long before Iris had saved Frank from the gallows. They had struck up a relationship after Frank had spotted Iris's reading shortfall when she had failed to read a tractor manual. The contraption had very nearly ripped her arm off when she attempted to start the thing. He wasn't going to let her make such dangerous mistakes on account of the fact that she couldn't read instructions. So Frank had taken her under his wing, happy for the company, and he had started to teach her to read and write. They had begun with some of the children's picture books that had belonged to Martin, and now they had graduated onto books with fewer pictures. Iris was currently stumbling her way through Enid Blyton's *Five On A Treasure Island*, but it was hard going. She liked the fact that she was reading Martin's books; turning pages that he had turned, connecting with him, somehow, across time.

The writing was just as arduous as the reading.

"Why is it all so difficult?" Iris had complained.

"Nothing worth doing is easy." Frank smiled.

It was Iris's ambition to be able to write a letter home to her mother. Margot Dawson knew that Iris couldn't read or write, but she also knew that some kind soul would read out the letters that she sent to her daughter. So Frank had found himself providing a mouthpiece for the missives from home. He related to Iris about how her grandfather's leg was getting better ('It doesn't really play up much now. Mainly when he has to get coal in. Funny that!'). He told her about the gossip caused when a new racy neighbour moved in ('She only wears crimson. And I don't want to say she's fast, but the milkman spent a long time in her house the other day.') But as well as the light-hearted information, Frank had broken the sad news that her beloved dog, Neville, had died. He'd also told her about how her siblings were getting on, since they'd gone to stay with an aunt outside the city. And in return, Frank would dutifully write replies to Margot Dawson, dictated by Iris. She would search for a word and Frank would painstakingly suggest one. They had spent many an evening hour together with him reading and writing and her learning. Sometimes she would censor her thoughts when dictating. Certainly she wouldn't mention anything about how she felt about men, in particular Martin. So her letters home were mostly about the mundane matters of farm life; how hard she was working, the blisters she was collecting, the odd mention of a dance or a film she had seen in the village hall. She wouldn't dictate anything that gave away her troubled, inner thoughts either. They were best locked up until the time came when she could write them down herself. Or when she could go home and talk to her mum face to face.

She missed home. It was a comforting and familiar two-up, two-down on a terraced street in Northampton. With her dad gone, Iris felt guilty about having to leave her mother on her own while she was doing her duty in the war. But Margot Dawson understood. She was doing her own work towards the war effort too. And she was proud of what Iris was doing in the Women's Land Army. And if she needed proof, Iris remembered going to see her grandfather after she had enlisted. She would always relish his gappy, proud smile as she showed him her uniform. He reminisced about his own war, the one they called the Great War, and how his own mother had been just as proud when he first turned up in his uniform. Iris couldn't wait to wear her uniform, so she had put it on almost immediately. The shirt was too big, seemingly made for a woman with arms six feet long. And the trousers needed hemming. As she and her mother had set about pinning up and sewing at her grandfather's house, her grandfather remarked that there was no time to measure people. They had to just wear what they were given and get out there. But Iris had taken an instant dislike to one part of her uniform. The pullover was itchy and it smelled of mothballs, and despite her mother's best efforts with the scrubbing brush, the smell had prevailed. Even now, months later, it was Iris's least-favourite item of kit. When the alterations were finished, and Iris could walk around without treading on the hems of her trousers, the family had thrown a little going-away party for her. A few neighbours and the girl from down the road, whom Iris used to play with, were invited. Everyone drank tea from the best china and ate a sponge cake that her mother had made. And then, with many stoic faces holding back tears, Iris had taken her suitcase and headed off to catch a train to Helmstead, via Birmingham. That had been the last time that Iris had seen her mother and grandfather, and she couldn't wait until she was given some leave so she could go back home, see them and sleep in her own bed. But that wouldn't be for a while as she had to complete six months of service first.

Frank handed back her efforts at writing.

"It's a good start, Iris." Frank rubbed his eyelids down as if they were shutters on a shop front. "But I'm worn out. Would you mind if we picked it up tomorrow?"

Iris shook her head. It was fine. She would write some more tomorrow. She'd already decided it would be a short note home, but as it would be one she'd written entirely on her own, a short one would be a monumental achievement. She felt warm thoughts about her mum opening the letter and realising what she was looking at. A hand would go to her mouth; tears would probably well in her eyes. But Iris had had another idea. What if, instead of writing a letter full of everyday thoughts, she wrote the one letter she had always wanted to write? The one that spoke the words she couldn't say to her mother's face? She knew she would have to learn to write first so that she could write that one on her own, without Frank's watchful eye. She struggled not to cry at the thought. Those words she longed to say to her mother ...

No, that would have to wait. One day.

An image came without warning into Iris's mind.

Black patent shoes running over cobbles.

She shut the image out. It wasn't the time to think about that. Go away! She pulled herself together.

"You all right, Iris?" Frank asked, noticing something was wrong, spotting the look of concern on her face.

"I'm fine."

As Iris headed to the door, she hesitated. She hadn't realised that it would be nearly dark outside. How could she have been in the shed for so long?

"Hurry on up, then, Miss Dawson. You're letting a cracking draught in here." He was keen to get on and fix one of the rabbit traps that had seized up. But then he realised why she was hesitating, why she had changed. He recognised that she was afraid.

"It's all right. I'll see you over there, to the farmhouse," he said, warmly. And he rose from his chair, his thin gangly legs swamped by his ill-fitting, baggy grey trousers. "But there's no need to worry. You know that, don't you?"

"I know that, Mr Tucker. In my head, anyway. But in my heart it's a different matter." She squinted into the fading light as the familiar shapes of the hedges and outbuildings turned into sombre silhouettes. Each one could promise her overactive imagination some dreadful threat or surprise. "In my heart, I think Vernon's coming back for me."

But before Frank could offer further reassurances, Iris left his shed and crossed over the yard to the farmhouse. By the noise of her feet on the gravel, he could tell that she was running. Running fast.

Iris didn't have far to go. Within moments, she was in the warm kitchen of the farmhouse, sliding the bolt on the door behind her; aware of the heat and light from the kitchen stove even before she turned around. Nothing could prepare her for the sight that greeted her. Frederick Finch had his leg propped up on the kitchen table. Esther Reeves, the warden for the Women's Land Army, was wincing as she tried to cut his gnarled, yellowing toenails. It was clearly a job far beyond her comfort zone or job description.

She looked relieved at the sight of Iris. Iris knew what was coming and sought to wage a counter-attack before anything could be asked of her. "I'd love to help, but I've got an early start."

And Iris was bounding up the stairs before Esther could finish saying, "We've all got an early start."

Iris paused on the landing, listening to the sounds from the kitchen. A smile had returned to her face. Although it turned to a look of disgust as she heard Finch ask Esther, "Do you think that's a bunion or a big old splinter?"

It was time for bed.

Since Dolores O'Malley had moved rooms, Iris was temporarily on her own in the small bedroom at the front of the house. It used to belong to Finch's son, Billy, before he went away to fight for his country. A stack of beer mats on the bedside table and a brown suit hanging in the wardrobe were the only reminders that he'd ever been there. Iris wasn't allowed to decorate the room, but she felt at home in her little corner of Pasture Farm. Especially as the room had a lock on the door.

Iris closed the door and bolted it. She took off her thick jumper and unhooked her dungarees from her shoulders. She could feel the welt marks on her skin from where the straps had been digging in all day. Then she pulled off her blouse.

It was too small for her, so she felt like a snake shedding its skin as she pulled it free. Then, as was customary in a house without fireplaces in the bedrooms, Iris scurried into her nightgown as quickly as she could. In under a minute she had gone from a fully dressed member of the Woman's Land Army to a woman ready for bed.

She thought about the handsome soldier at the dance. The one who had asked her to dance to 'Chattanooga Choo Choo'. Several days had passed since then and he hadn't shown up at Pasture Farm. Iris had gone through every option in her head. Perhaps he had forgotten the name of her farm? Perhaps he had been called away on army business? Or perhaps he wasn't really interested in her. She tried not to feel depressed about it, trying to let it go. Her grandfather always said 'what will be, will be' and that's the philosophy she tried to adopt now. If the soldier showed up, that would be great. If he didn't, well, she would move on. Iris yawned.

But she knew she wouldn't be able to sleep.

She risked a look through the small window. It was frosted with condensation, so she wiped it clear with the cuff of her nightdress. The lights from downstairs illuminated the lawns at the front of the farmhouse. An old children's swing creaked in the night breeze. Iris hated that swing. It would keep her awake at night with its constant noises. And in her wilder flights of fancy, she sometimes dreaded looking out of the window in case she imagined someone sitting on it, staring balefully up at her. She wished that Finch would sell it as scrap for the war effort. But he was attached to the old relic.

Iris pulled her curtain across to block out the sight. The

unseen swing gave a final creak of defiance, as if it was determined to have the last word. She sat on her bed and flipped back the sheets, sighing as she felt the night closing in on her. A lonely room in a strange place. And here she was grabbing a few hours' sleep until Esther shouted up the stairs for them all to get up.

"Come on, you bunch of layabouts, let's have you down for breakfast!"

Iris closed her eyes and stretched her aching limbs. She could hear a muffled soundtrack from downstairs. Finch laughed at something. A cup or glass smashed on the floor.

She could hear Esther exclaim, "Oops, look what you've done."

"I didn't do it. It was me cardigan."

"And who's your cardigan attached to? Oh, mind your feet on the glass!"

Unable to sleep, Iris swung out of bed with a sigh. An owl hooted somewhere off in the fields, a late-night hunter ready to start its day. Iris's body felt exhausted, but her mind was racing.

The swing creaked outside.

It was as if it was taunting her through the thin curtain. Her fingers edged towards the fabric to pull it back, to look outside. But she was scared; her fingers touching the fabric but not having the courage to move it. The swing creaked again. Iris could hear her breathing, her heart pounding in her chest.

Then she remembered something else that Billy Finch had left in his room. Iris opened her wardrobe and moved a wicker box. It contained letters and photographs from back home and a couple of torn magazine pages from *Picturegoer magazine* showing hairstyles she'd one day like to try. Behind the wicker box was what she wanted: a clear, tall bottle, half full of a bright-orange liquid. Finch's carrot whisky. From the reactions of the others to the whisky, she knew it was a revolting drink that had the sole redeeming feature of being very strong. Should she do it?

Iris remembered the woozy feeling from the cider in the dance hall. It had helped things seem better when she was fretting about Vernon, hadn't it? So maybe a few swigs of Billy's stash could do the same. It would certainly get her off to sleep.

Iris took out the bottle, unscrewed the cap and took a swig. A stiff drink to help her shut out her fears was just what she needed. She winced at the taste, certain that her gums were retreating from the foul, strong liquid. She took another couple of big swigs, in quick succession, trying to swallow the liquid as quickly as possible. This wasn't one of those drinks that you swilled around your mouth, savouring the taste. It had one purpose and one purpose only. And for Iris, it worked reassuringly quickly.

She felt her head spinning, a reassuring warmth rising on her cheeks.

The swing creaked.

But this time, she didn't hear it. Or if she did, it didn't unnerve her like it had before. She took a final couple of swigs and replaced the bottle back in the recesses of the wardrobe. Her little secret. A useful stash to be eked out for as long as she could, whenever she needed it. She tried to focus her eyes, but her head was woozy. Her mouth had the remnants of the vile taste and she contemplated going to brush her teeth again, but fear of bumping into one of the other girls on the landing made her stay put. They might catch a whiff of her breath and know she'd been drinking. There would be questions: where did she get it? Why was she drinking alone? Could they have some?

Iris checked that her door was locked.

She turned off the light and curled up under the sheet. The room was spinning slightly and she felt surprise that such a seemingly small amount of drink could do this. But it was strong, dangerous stuff. Just the sort of sedative she needed. She thought of Joe Batch's smiling, rugged face and thanked him for introducing her to the delights of alcohol.

Sleep came quickly. But it wouldn't last for long.

Tap. Tap. Tap.

Was that the swing? Iris started to wake, her befuddled mind reaching and trying to place the noise. Dripping water? No, it was a more solid and insistent tapping than that. Not the swing, not water: then what?

Tap. Tap. Tap.

As Iris came round, she managed to piece it together and recognise the noise. Someone was tapping the wooden leg at the end of her bed. Tap. Tap.

She opened a bleary eye, half-wondering how someone had managed to get into her room. Then the horror hit her. The bedroom curtain was billowing and there was glass strewn like discarded diamonds across the floor. How had she not heard the glass breaking? Someone had climbed up and broken in. She wanted to scream, but she couldn't draw breath to make a sound; her lungs were like a wet tea towel that someone had scrunched up. With rising dread, she turned her head towards the source of the tapping. She knew she had to look, but she didn't want to. She knew what she would see.

It was no surprise who she saw standing there.

In the half-light, the glinting, malevolent eyes of a small, gnarled man. Vernon Storey. A man twisted by disappointment, cynicism and unrealised dreams.

Shaking with fear, Iris pulled herself up in her bed, the sweat of fear dripping down her temples. She stared at Vernon. He'd somehow climbed up and smashed the window. And now he was standing in front of her. He grinned and raised the poker in his hand. She was dimly aware of Finch and Esther downstairs, talking. She tried to scream for help, but all that escaped was a tiny, almost comical, squeak. Clutching the poker, Vernon's other hand drummed menacingly on the wooden leg of her bed.

Tap, Tap, Tap.

"Told you I'd come back for you, Iris Dawson," he said softly, his yellowing teeth bared like a shark.

"Please ..." Iris murmured, finding breath for a childlike whisper of desperation and hope.

He shook his head, unwilling to listen to any more entreaties. That's not why he'd come. There was no interest in discussing the right and wrongs of her betrayal, as he saw it. Or the rights and wrongs of his crime against his son.

"Time for talking is over, Iris," he said, moving closer, one step at a time. He knew that she had nowhere to go.

She could smell the stale sweat on his clothes, see the holes in his ragged pullover and his faded checked shirt as he got closer. His face looked almost apologetic. "Sorry it's come to this," he whispered. There seemed genuine regret in his voice, as if he knew he wasn't just ruining her life but his own too. Circumstances had brought him to this point; circumstances that had meant Iris had simply been in the wrong place at the wrong time.

Suddenly, his face changed to one of determination and anger as he knew what he had to do.

He raised the poker above his head and, in a savage, fluid arc, brought it crashing down towards her.

Chapter 3

Earlier that evening, Private First Class Joe Batch sauntered along the gravel driveway to Hoxley Manor. Stationed a few miles away in the nearby town of Brinford, Joe had never been here before. Wearing his summer fatigues uniform of khaki shirt, tie and trousers with a green belt, he glanced at fellow American soldiers dotted around the front of the house, not recognising any faces, but knowing they were comrades. He cleared his throat as he entered the cool interior of the building. He wasn't in a hurry to get inside, but he felt he couldn't delay it any longer. The place was just like they said it was, a slice of aristocratic history that was terribly British and terribly in need of repair. Instinctively, Joe folded his hat and tucked it into his belt as he made his way down the grand main hall towards the wards, his shoes clicking on the parquet flooring. A few months ago, the Manor had been seconded by the War Office and much of its living space converted into a makeshift medical hospital for treating men from the front lines. But it also treated men injured closer to home. Men like Private Chuck Wellings; the friend who Joe had come to see.

Asking directions from a passing nurse, Joe Batch made his way down a small side corridor. It smelt of damp, old wood and a dark stain had spread over much of the ceiling. Gee, he could renovate this place given half a chance. It would be an opportunity to use his talents as a builder and restore something to its previous splendour and beauty. But no one had time for such frivolities as renovation now. There was a war on. Joe knew that his job for the duration of the war was to serve his country in the army. Joe reached the end of a small side ward, three iron beds crammed into a glorified corridor. In the last bed was a figure wearing a bandage that covered most of his head and one eye. He was half-sitting and half-lying in bed, a newspaper in front of him, his head lolling. But Joe guessed he wasn't taking much notice of the text.

"Hey, how are you feeling?" Joe asked, flashing a warm smile with pearly white teeth.

It took a moment for Chuck to recognise his visitor. Perhaps it took a moment for his single eye to focus away from the newspaper and onto the man in front of his bed. "Joe?" Chuck cleared his throat, sounding surprised. His voice had the tell-tale catch of a man who hadn't spoken all day. "What are you doing here?"

"They've run out of surgeons so I said I'd have a go. I'm sure it's as easy as knocking up a dovetail joint."

Chuck laughed. He was a chubby, thickset man in his early twenties, with a red face. Most people would probably say he was 'jolly', but this was probably the first time there had been any hint of jollity since his accident four days ago. It had been a freak ricochet from another soldier's gun on the firing range, one second of miscalculation that had cost Chuck Wellings his eye.

Joe pulled up a chair. He twirled it around so that he could rest his arms on the frame, and sat down. In the other beds the occupants were asleep. Bandages obscured the head of one man and the other patient looked in good health until you looked down the length of his bed and realised that the shape of his body under the covers ended below the knees. Chuck was in the minority – a soldier injured on the home front. Most of the other patients at Hoxley Manor were shipped in from overseas battle fronts. Joe's smile faltered a little. War had always seemed scary to him, but the presence of his friends joining up at the same time as him made him feel they were an invincible little band, somehow immune to the cold, harsh realities around them. It was just as it had been when they had met on the first day of high school, just as it had been on the first day they had all got jobs in their home town. Chuck had been one such friend. They'd answered the call together, along with three other pals. They'd all gone to the recruiting office and enthusiastically signed their lives away together. They were determined to beat the Nazi menace in Europe, determined to help the allies that they had read about in the newspapers and seen on the newsreels. And now the invincible little band wasn't quite so invincible. One man down. But Joe was always the light-hearted joker of the pack, adept at being funny and charming. He knew it was his job to cheer up Chuck, even in such depressing surroundings as these. He said the first thing that came into his head, taking no time to filter his comment. But that was how the pals spoke to each other. If he pulled his punches now, Chuck would worry that things were even worse than he feared.

"Have they talked about you getting a discount at the flicks?" Joe said.

"What?"

"You're only seeing it with one eye, man. They've got to give you a discount!"

Luckily, Chuck was ready to laugh, even at such an off-colour joke. Joe knew it wasn't his best, but at least it was something. Chuck's laugh turned to a slight grimace as the reality of his situation hit him again. The friends chatted for a few minutes. Joe told him what was happening at their barracks. Chuck thought it was unlikely that he'd return to active service, but he hoped he could come back to perform some function or other. If not, his war would be over and he'd have to go home.

"You'll have to keep everything ticking over until the rest of us get back," Joe said.

"Yeah, I'll do that," Chuck replied.

Dr Richard Channing entered. A distinguished-looking, handsome man in his forties, he had been running the hospital since it opened. Joe knew there were rumours about him secretly courting the lady of the manor, but he didn't know if they were true or not. She was a good-looking broad. Probably rich too. Channing checked the clipboard of statistics at the end of the bandaged man's bed. He shot a quick, perfunctory smile over to Joe and Chuck, then busied himself as the men talked.

"When are you going back to Panmere Lake?" Chuck asked.

"Waiting for orders," Joe replied.

"But I thought they wanted to get the stuff moved as quickly as they can," Chuck said. "To somewhere more secure." The operation to move munitions from a temporary location near Panmere Lake to more permanent surroundings had been a mission that both Joe and Chuck had been lined up for.

"Well, if you need a pair of hands. I'm so bored sitting here all day. Not even smart enough to do the crossword." Chuck's fingers scrunched the newspaper on his lap.

"You've got to concentrate on getting better. Anyway, you wouldn't be here without a good reason."

Dr Channing walked back over from the other side of the room. "Quite right. As soon as you're able, we'll have you out of here faster than you can say good old Uncle Sam."

The soldiers smiled back. "Thanks, Doc," Joe offered. "Got to get this guy pulling his considerable weight."

Chuck cracked a grin and jokingly pushed his friend's arm.

Channing replaced the patient clipboard at the end of Chuck's bed and glided out of the room, his white coat billowing slightly behind him.

"So how's your love life?" Chuck asked.

"You must be bored if you're asking about that. I met a broad at a dance, a Land Girl ..."

"Another one?"

"This one's different," Joe said, a slight edge of annoyance to his voice.

"What? Different 'cos you haven't had your way with her yet?"

Joe afforded himself a smile. It was probably true. Chuck knew him well. Chuck had been on enough double dates with his good-looking friend to know how skilled Joe was at chatting up women. It was unlikely that he'd ever think about settling down, especially with the war. There was a need to let off steam after all they were dealing with, a need to have fun. And if that meant courting a lot of British women, then that was fine, in Joe's book. Chuck was different. He'd love to find the right woman and marry her straight away. But this was, Joe figured, because he didn't have the effortless charm and good looks. Chuck's lack of confidence meant that he would take love if it ever came his way, embracing it with grateful hands. Joe was happy to string women along, cheat and lie. It was all part of the game, as far as he was concerned. Chuck had heard Joe describe many women with the phrase 'this one's different'. It was baloney.

"I've not seen any other women since I met her at the dance, so that's something," Joe admitted.

"Losing your touch!" Chuck exclaimed.

"Been too busy, to be honest. But I might go and see her, get properly acquainted."

"Heaven help her." Although it was sometimes fun to watch Joe charm them, Chuck almost felt sorry for the women of Helmstead. They didn't seem worldly enough or skilled in the detection of charming lotharios such as Joe Batch. He preyed on them like a wolf in a sheep enclosure. And sometimes that made Chuck feel uneasy, especially when he knew he would treat any one of those women like a queen, with respect and admiration.

Joe leaned back in his seat. He eyed a nurse who passed down the corridor. Old habits died hard. Chuck smiled at his brazen nature. When they were alone again, he returned to the conversation about Panmere Lake. The Americans had used some covered buildings near to the lake, on the other side of Helmstead, as a temporary ammunition store. Joe, a skilled carpenter, and other men in his unit, were building a new, secure storage building near to their base in Brinford. It was imperative that they move the munitions as soon as possible. At the moment, they were vulnerable to enemy attack. Joe thought his friend should be grateful to miss the hard, exhausting work of lugging the ammunition onto the trucks for transporting.

After twenty minutes, Joe said his goodbyes and sauntered away from Chuck's ward. Reaching the main corridor, Joe unfurled his hat and positioned it back on his head. Silhouetted ahead, near the doorway, was the figure of Dr Richard Channing. He was talking to a beautiful and stately woman, a person whose aristocratic bearing was unmistakable. As Joe got closer, he could see her sandy hair neatly curled around her fine bone structure, the thin, porcelain-hued neck. He guessed she was Lady Ellen Hoxley. Channing moved aside to let Joe pass and they both glanced briefly at him. Joe knew enough about affairs and illicit looks to know that those two were seeing each other. The subtle hints in their body language, the angles they stood at in relation to each other, the imperceptible touches. He smirked, knowing their secret, as he walked down the gravel path, away from the big house.

He decided that he would visit that Land Girl tomorrow. Yes, that's what he'd do.

The next morning, shouts could be heard from the kitchen of Pasture Farm.

"Mind you get the collar! I need the collar doing." Finch poked a stubby finger at his best white shirt; a shirt that was currently stretched across the ironing board. He was leaning over Esther's shoulder as she ironed it for him, an unskilled manager of such things. Esther's patience was wearing thin at his interference.

"I have ironed a shirt before, you know," she snapped. She shot a long-suffering look at the Land Girls sitting around the farmhouse table near by. Joyce was eating a slice of toast as Finch busied himself around Esther like a bumble bee harassing a flower. Dolores O'Malley stared wistfully into her mug of tea, not quite awake, but lost in her own thoughts as usual.

"Where's Iris?" Joyce asked.

"Will you leave it!" Esther snapped at Finch, who was attempting to hold down part of the collar for her.

"Shouldn't she be up by now?" Joyce continued.

"Maybe she's having a lie-in until six o'clock," Dolores replied with a smirk.

Esther finished ironing the shirt and Finch plucked it off the board. "Very nice job, Esther." He giggled as he stretched it onto a wooden coat hanger. He glided over the floor with it, as if he had some ethereal dance partner, and hung it on the picture rail next to the larder. The shirt looked immaculate for about four seconds, until the hanger fell from the picture rail, crashing to the floor and leaving the shirt in a crumpled heap.

"Fred!" Esther scolded, going to retrieve it. Finch, for his part, looked genuinely aggrieved. Joyce hadn't seen him this agitated in ages. Usually he was a man who cared little for his appearance, but in the last week, she had witnessed Esther cutting Finch's hair and Finch wearing his best hat into Helmstead. Gone too were the trousers with holes in the pockets and his shabby cardigan. He'd even bought a brand-new leather belt from Mr Yardley in the town to replace the string that he had been using recently. Finch wouldn't win the *Picturegoer* magazine's Best-Dressed Man Award any time soon, but his appearance had definitely improved.

"Do you think it'll be all right?" Finch asked nervously.

"I'm sure you'll be fine." Esther smiled, finishing a brisk iron of the shirt. "Just relax and enjoy yourself."

Finch nodded. He'd try his best. Joyce thought it was sweet. She watched Finch amble out of the door into the yard outside.

"He's not meeting her now, is he?" Joyce asked.

"Not until this afternoon. He'll look a right state by then!" Esther laughed. Joyce and Esther were used to witnessing the love lives of the various girls on the farm and the estate, but both were surprised that they were now seeing Finch courting a woman. He'd shown little interest in women since his wife had passed away, but this lady had seemingly knocked him for six. Both women were surprised by the changes in him. But it was lovely to see him with a spring in his step, even if they feared for the inevitable disappointing end to the relationship. Could she be as keen as he was? Would his enthusiasm put her off? Esther feared that she would have to pick up the pieces when that happened. But for now, he was happy.

Joyce finished her last crust, wiped her hands on her overalls and asked Esther, "Do you want me to go up for Iris?"

Esther shook her head. "I'll do it in a minute, when I've got the ironing board put away."

The truth was she didn't know why Iris was always late down in the mornings. She wondered if the girl was staying up too late, talking to Frank in his shed. Maybe she should have a word with her and limit their late-night conversations to weekends? As the warden in charge of the Women's Land Army girls, Esther had the power to do that. It was her duty to ensure that the girls were fit for their work. The work was the priority. But she knew that Iris viewed Frank, and Fred, for that matter, as father figures, and she knew the girl was relieved that she'd managed to save him from the gallows after the murder of Walter Storey. Iris and Frank's relationship seemed to be something they both valued. However, these late starts couldn't continue. Esther glanced at the clock. It was five to six. Even for Iris, it was unlike her to be so late ...

Esther stowed the ironing board in the pantry, chivvied Dolores to follow Joyce into the fields and went through to the foot of the stairs. "Iris!" she called up. There was no reply. With a reluctant sigh, Esther trudged up the wooden stairs, muttering that she had better things to do than molly-coddling her girls. At the top of the stairs was the landing that split off into the various Land Girls' rooms. Esther knocked on one of the doors.

Nothing.

Esther tried the handle. It was locked. She sighed, cursing Iris under her breath. What had she told them about locking doors? If anything happened, there was no way to get inside to them. Esther rapped on the door.

"Come on, Iris! Move your bones!"

Joyce and Dolores were packing tools onto a wheelbarrow when they caught sight of a strange figure in the far corner of the yard. They nudged each other and stifled their urge to laugh. It was Finch, dressed in his best suit and wearing his freshly pressed shirt. He straightened his collar and pulled his jacket around his portly frame. He cleared his throat.

"May I have the pleasure?" he asked, offering his hands outstretched.

"What's he doing?" Dolores asked.

But Joyce couldn't see past Finch's ample body to see who he was talking to. Then Finch twirled around and Joyce had to stifle another giggle. The farmer had a broom in his arms and was dancing across the yard, eyes closed in solemn concentration. Joyce pressed a hand against Dolores, forcing them both out of view behind a tractor. She knew Finch would be embarrassed if he was caught practising his dance moves.

As Joyce and Dolores walked to the fields, Joyce commented that she thought it was sweet that Finch had found someone else. He'd been a widower for years and years, since his son, Billy, was born. Finally he had found a new person to share things with. Joyce wondered to herself whether she could ever love anyone besides her beloved John. It seemed unlikely. She and John had been childhood sweethearts, marrying before the war started. It had been their love that had saved them from dying, when the Coventry bombings occurred, Joyce had been with John in Birmingham. Joyce had lost her entire family that night as her family home had been levelled by German bombs. When she returned to the devastated streets of her home town, John had helped her sift through the wretched remains of her house, finding such grim artefacts as Joyce's sister's dress and the front of the radio that had been in the front parlour. John had been there to comfort her. Such was their bond that Joyce found it physically painful when John joined the RAF, flying dangerous bombing missions of his own.

But now John was back home. And closer than ever. John Fisher had been invalided out of service and was now doing his bit by trying to run the neighbouring Shallow Brook Farm. Vernon's old farm.

Esther rapped again on Iris's bedroom door. Where was that girl?

A few seconds' silence, but then the sound of the bolt being slipped back.

A sleepy Iris Dawson opened the door. Seeing Esther's face with its stern expression told her all she needed to know about what time it was. "You're late. Again," Esther said. Iris ran in a panic back into the room, hoisting her nightdress over her head as she went.

"Sorry, Esther. I really am," Iris said, her voice muffled by the garment covering her face. "I had a nightmare and then I couldn't get back to sleep."

"I don't want your excuses." Esther went to the chest of drawers and looked for a shirt for the girl. The drawers were empty. Esther glanced at the chair in the corner of the room, where a small pile of unwashed laundry formed a fabric hillock. Oblivious to this, Iris was fastening her bra.

"You don't have any clean shirts," Esther said, plucking her way through the clothes. It was the girls' responsibility to ensure that their clothing was put out for washing. Esther would clean their uniforms, but she wasn't going to go hunting for shirts and trousers around the house.

"This one will have to do," Iris replied, taking one at random.

"I want you to sort all of this out tonight, you hear?" Esther scolded. "Never mind seeing Frank Tucker tonight. This is more important."

Iris nodded meekly as she fastened a shirt that had a beetroot stain on the left breast pocket.

"And we need to talk about you and your attitude."

"I haven't got an attitude," Iris replied.

"You're a girl who wakes late every morning and whose mind isn't on the job. That's attitude, in my book." And Esther was gone. Her technique in these situations was to let the other person think about her words for most of the day. She was always letting people stew. Iris sighed, searching the pile for a pair of trousers that weren't too muddy. Her head was throbbing and her throat felt dry. She cursed herself for drinking. She guessed that Esther was right. She had been late most mornings. But she couldn't help it.

By lunchtime, her throbbing headache had blossomed into a bloom of pain in her temples and Iris was grateful to be asked to clear some fallen branches in the East Field, a location remote enough from the farmhouse to allow her a few minutes' breather. She picked up some sticks and started to assemble a pile that could be used as firewood. Some of the larger branches had to be stripped of leaves before they could be used. Iris used a small knife to cut them away. Finally by mid-afternoon, the relaxed pace of her own work and the silence of being alone had eased the pain in her head. Iris felt tired and decided she wouldn't drink tonight. That had been a mistake. But the drink had helped her get to sleep, shutting out the fears racing around her brain. She wouldn't drink again. But, of course, it was easy to keep such a promise in a sunny field in the afternoon. It was far more difficult to stick to promises at night, when every creak on the stairs or every shifting shadow could terrify her.

I will come for you, Iris. Mark my words.

And her nightmares and imagination were becoming more vivid and disturbing. Iris wished that she could stop thinking about him. But her mind just wouldn't stop. Each time she looked in the bathroom mirror, she would scare herself by imagining Vernon's face in the reflection. Iris tried to put the thoughts out of her mind. She continued her work, keen to fill her thoughts with the business of firewood collection and leaf stripping. Keep your mind on the things you can control. But things had been slowly getting out of control.

The nightmares were causing problems. Cracks were starting to show. Maybe a little drink to control things wasn't such a bad idea ...

Suddenly she heard a twig crack.

"Hello?" Iris shouted, fear taking hold of her. Had she seen a man walk behind a tree? Get a grip, Iris. She bent down and picked up a solid length of branch, brandishing it like a club. She edged towards where she thought she had seen a man hiding.

It must be a trick of the light. An overactive imagination, that's all. There wouldn't be anyone there, not this far out.

Could there?

Feeling the thump-thump of her heart in her chest, Iris reached the tree. She was just about to rush behind it when a man's hands thrust out at her. Iris cracked the tree branch across his knuckles.

"Youch!" Private First Class Joe Batch shouted.

Iris dropped the stick and rushed to help him. His fingers were red, but the skin was unbroken.

"So sorry!"

"What the hell are you –?"

"I might ask you the same thing!" Iris stormed, anger coming to the fore. "Why were you creeping up on me?"

"I was trying to surprise you," Joe admitted.

"I think I surprised you more." Iris smiled kindly, her fury subsiding. "Come over to the farmhouse and I'll get Esther to look at your fingers."

"They're okay, no real damage." Joe grinned. "This is all part of getting to know you. For instance, I know you ain't the type of girl who likes surprises. Logged and recorded."

"I don't mind surprises. Just don't like strange men creeping up on me."

"Strange?"

"You know what I mean."

Joe nodded, as if conceding it was a fair enough point. Then, seeing the Land Girls in the distance and knowing that Iris might have to get back to work, he decided that he'd better get to the matter in hand, the reason for his visit.

"I came to see if you fancied coming to the pictures on Friday night?"

"What's on?"

"Does it matter?" Joe said, amused.

"Yes," Iris said, confused. She felt out of her depth. Her experience of men could be written on a very small piece of card. Was this part of flirting? She had no real idea, but she decided that she kind of enjoyed it. It was fun when she'd referred to him as strange and she guessed that was flirting, wasn't it? "I mean, we should know what we're going to see."

"It's a Gary Cooper. Does that win your approval?"

"Possibly," Iris said, thinking fast as to what Connie might say in this situation. She decided a joke was in order. "Depends if there's a supporting feature."

"Newsreels?"

Iris pondered this with mock severity before agreeing, "Sold. It's a deal."

"It's a date." Joe Batch smiled and started to head off across the fields. Iris watched him go, proud that she had a date to look forward to, and proud that she had managed to flirt with him without becoming tongue-tied. Being around Connie must be rubbing off on her. It was reassuring that Joe was interested in her after all. Something to take her mind off Vernon, at least.

Later, as the rest of the girls stopped for a breather and mug of tea, Iris wandered away, not in the mood to talk. She looked at the folded-up letter that she had started to write with Frank. She felt joy in her heart that day for the image of her mother reading it. Iris sat by a tree, the sun dappling her face through the canopy of leaves. She was dimly aware of the chatter of the other girls by the tractor. They were discussing a trip to the flicks. It seemed that Joyce was keen to see the new Gary Cooper too. Dolores had more mundane concerns and was wondering why her tea tasted funny. Their voices became a low buzz of reassuring noise in Iris's ears, the warmth of the sun feeling good against her face. She felt herself relaxing, her eyes drooping shut. She didn't fight it. It would only be a little doze for a few minutes ...

Except it wasn't.

"Iris!" Connie shouted, "Wake up!"

Iris awoke with a start to see an angry-looking Connie looming over her. "It's nearly supper time."

Iris realised that the sky was a darker blue than it had been before. How long had she been asleep? Connie was already marching away, back towards the farmhouse, in no mood for a discussion. "I've got to meet Henry tonight. Got better things to do than search for you."

And Connie shouted back to an unseen group as loudly as she could. "Found her!"

With growing unease, Iris realised that other figures were dotted around the edges of the East Field. Joyce, Dolores and a thunder-faced Esther, who was making a beeline across to her. The last vestiges of sleepiness fell instantly away. Oh God.

"We need to talk, young lady. No excuses. We need to find out what's going on!"

As night descended, Esther, Frank and Joyce sat around the kitchen table. A subdued Iris sat at the end of the table, her throbbing headache having returned with a vengeance. She nursed a small glass of water as the stern faces around her tried to work out what to do. Esther had sent Martin off to find Finch, as everyone thought he should be here for this meeting. This examination. Iris knew that Finch would be annoyed to be pulled away from his afternoon date. This wasn't going to end well for her.

"You're our friend, Iris. Tell us what's on your mind?" Joyce implored.

"I don't know," Iris mumbled. Esther rolled her eyes. She wasn't in the mood for vague answers, or winkling the truth out of people. She wanted something concrete that she could work with. If it was a problem with being bullied or a problem caused by overwork, then Esther could sort that out and help fix it. But she needed something tangible to go on. Evasive answers were no use at all.

Esther pulled something from under the table and placed it for all to see. It was Billy Finch's bottle of carrot whisky.

"You've been drinking in your room!" Esther thundered.

"It's not mine."

"That's as maybe. But look –"

And Esther turned the bottle around. On the side was a black line near the neck of the bottle. The level of the orange liquid was a long way below it. "Billy marked this, so I know it's gone down since you've been in that room."

Iris slumped.

"Tell them what's troubling you, Iris," Frank said. He nodded his head and gave a half-smile by way of encouragement. He knew what it was, but he wanted Iris to tell it in her own words. To tell the others. "Tell them why you needed a drink. A problem shared and all that."

"Well?" Esther asked.

Iris took a deep breath. "I think Vernon's coming back for me."

She felt the mix of reactions in the room. Esther's slight snort that betrayed disbelief, Joyce's concerned face and Frank's impassive reaction. He'd heard Iris voice these worries before, during their writing lessons in the shed. Iris went on to say she felt ridiculous. She knew he was gone but it was just that each time she was alone, she'd think about him. And his final words.

"*I'll come back for you, Iris.*"

It was like a dark promise. And no matter how she tried to rationalise it, she couldn't make it fade from her mind. He promised to come back and it terrified her.

"He's not coming back. That's the end of it. Now pull yourself together," Esther said. "You've got to get a grip on your thoughts and stop them running away with you, young lady!"

"But what if he does come back?" Iris replied. She could feel rawness at the back of her throat. She was ready to cry. Why did she think they would understand when she knew herself it sounded ridiculous? "Part of me wants to do something and find him first, but I know I can't do that. And I know I'm being stupid, but I just can't stop it." And then the tears came, as if vocalising her fears had broken down any last control over her thoughts. The sobbing was loud, wretched. A shocked Joyce put a comforting hand on her friend's wrist, but still the tears came.

Esther turned to Frank and Joyce. "I'll see the doctor and find out if he can give her something to calm her down."

"I just need ..." But Iris trailed off. That was the problem. What did she need? The problem wouldn't be fixed by having a stronger lock on her bedroom door. It was something inside her head. The last words of a murderer. The promise. She knew the nightmares would continue, even though she desperately wanted them to end.

Eyes blurred with tears, Iris scraped her chair back on the tiled floor and went to her room. Ignoring Esther's calls to come back. Iris slammed the door behind her and felt torn that she wasn't allowed to lock it tonight. She slumped on the bed. And then she found her reddened eyes drawn towards the wardrobe. Logic told her that she shouldn't drink tonight. But she felt so wretched and desperate. And then she remembered that Esther had the bottle. Iris thought for a moment, and then, knowing that Finch kept more of his whisky under the stairs, Iris crept back down. She could hear the voices talking softly with concern beyond in the kitchen. Stealthily, she opened the cupboard under the stairs, reached in and took a full bottle of whisky. She scurried back to her room, closed the door and then opened the bottle, ready for its reassurance of numbing oblivion.

Finch placed his pint glass down, its sides etched with thin, cloud formations of beer foam. He was aware that he was drinking faster than his companion. Evelyn Gray had barely finished a quarter of her small glass of cider. Finch resolved to slow down. The problem was that his nerves meant he needed something to do with his hands, and that meant lifting the glass up and down to his lips and before he knew it, it was gone! Glancing around the room of the snug bar in the Bottle and Glass, he suddenly envied the men smoking cigarettes. They always had something to do with their hands, the performance of rolling a cigarette, lighting it, smoking it. Finch wished that he could smoke. But the truth was he had never got on with it, finding that the smallest puff would reduce him to a hacking, retching wreck. And that wasn't the ideal look he wanted to achieve on a night like this. An evening with his new lady friend, Evelyn.

Evelyn Gray was glamorous, but not in an over-the-top way. She was well turned-out in the latest fashions, but she wore them with a dignity that befitted a lady in her early fifties. Thick, naturally blonde hair was pinned into curls on her head, and her blue eyes stared at Finch with warmth and a hint of intriguing mystery. Finch wished he knew what women thought about. He knew he was thinking about whether to have another pint of beer: simple, straightforward thoughts for a simple man. But he guessed that a woman like Evelyn was thinking deeper thoughts than that. She was probably going over Churchill's latest address to the nation or thinking about the logistics of rationing.

"Would you like another drink, Evelyn?" Finch stammered.

"I've still got this one, Fred." She giggled.

Finch giggled too. He felt suddenly foolish, suddenly aware of his awkwardness and clumsy nature. His collar suddenly felt very warm and tight around his neck. The truth was, he felt out of his depth with this attractive, clever woman. Finch searched his brain for something to talk about. Something clever. Something that would impress her. Maybe he could tell her about the growing patterns of the turnip? He frowned inwardly at his own brain trying to make him look stupid. He was doing badly without further self-sabotage. But thankfully, Evelyn was quite capable of offering a conversational topic of her own.

"So tell me more about Pasture Farm. How long have you been there?"

"Came there after the war," Finch said, before needlessly correcting himself. "The last one, not this one."

"Of course." Evelyn smiled.

Finch was grateful that he could make her laugh. He continued his story, feeling suddenly wistful for those lost days. "After it was all over, I was looking for work. Ended up at the farm working as a labourer. The farmer in charge, a chap called Godfrey, taught me everything I know and most of what I've forgotten. When he died, Lady Hoxley asked if I wanted to try running the place on my own. And that's where I've been ever since. I've seen some times there, at Pasture Farm. Got married there. Saw my son being born there. My wife passing away. Watched my son go off to a war of his own. We had a big going-away party for that ..."

Finch's mind drifted off, as memories filled his head. He was so engrossed in his thoughts that he gasped when he felt Evelyn place a comforting hand on his across the table.

"It's good to remember the past, Fred," she said, kindly. "Don't ever forget the past."

"Yeah. I've got a grandson too, you know."

"You don't look old enough!" Evelyn smiled. Finch grinned, realising she was joking.

"Get away with you!"

They sipped their drinks at the same time. Finch was pleased that he had slowed down. But he was still thinking about his next one. Evelyn continued the conversation, "What is it like having all those Land Girls around the place?"

"It means I can be a bit more, erm, like a manager." He smiled. "It's really good because I don't have to get my hands dirty as much, with all of them doing it all. Truth is, I haven't planted a potato since this war started!"

They giggled together. "No, they're a good bunch of girls," Finch said.

"And there are two farms on the Hoxley estate, aren't there?" Evelyn sipped at her cider.

"Pasture Farm and Shallow Brook Farm," Finch confirmed. "My one is the better farm, if I do say so myself. Shallow Brook was run by the Storeys. Have you heard of Vernon Storey?"

Evelyn shook her head. She lived on the outskirts of Brinford, so there was no reason why she would know many people in Helmstead.

"Nasty piece of work." Finch scrunched his face as if he'd sucked on a lemon. "Wanted for murder, you know?"

"Oh gosh," Evelyn said. "What happened? Was it one of the Land Girls?"

Finch leaned in close to tell her. "No, his own son."

Evelyn wanted to know more, but Finch didn't want to spoil their evening with the whole sorry tale of Frank Tucker and Walter Storey, and how Iris had discovered the truth about Walter's murder. It would put a bit of a dampener on things. No, he wanted to make Evelyn laugh again. He liked it when she laughed because her eyes twinkled and she'd arch her head back. Suddenly Finch wondered if he was falling for Evelyn Gray.

"So I've taken over the other farm. Surprised meself, because I can barely manage one place let alone two!"

It had the desired effect. Evelyn's face broke into an amused grin and she arched her head slightly.

"Got some help, though. Martin, the warden's son, and John Fisher – he's married to one of my girls – are sorting the place out for me."

"Sounds like you're busy?" Evelyn smiled warmly.

"Which is exactly why I need relaxing nights out like this!" Finch got up. "I'll get us another round, shall I?"

"All right. But that will be enough for me."

"Me too," Finch said. As he carried the glasses to the bar, he glanced back to where Evelyn was checking her face in a powder compact. He had known her two weeks and they were getting on famously. Finch hadn't noticed her at the dance. As far as he was concerned, he'd clocked eyes on her for the first time at one of Lady Hoxley's agricultural shows. Finch had been showing his prize pig, Chamberlain, and was trying to get the pig into a gated enclosure. Evelyn and a group of women had been watching and Finch felt the weight of expectation upon him as he'd tried to manhandle the heavy animal.

"Come on, you blighter!"

But Chamberlain had turned quickly, taking Finch off balance, and the stout farmer had fallen face first into the mud. While some of the women couldn't help but laugh, Evelyn looked concerned and ran to his aid.

"Are you hurt?" she asked.

"No. Only me pride," Finch replied.

"Let me help you." And Finch had been surprised to see Evelyn outstretch her arms and try to corner Chamberlain in a bid to edge him closer to the paddock. She was gamely trying her best, but Chamberlain easily side-stepped her. Soon, Finch and Evelyn were working together in a pincer movement to cut off the pig's escape route. Finally, after several failed attempts and some swearing from Finch, they managed to get Chamberlain into the pen. Finch slid the bolt across with a triumphant smile and mopped his brow with the back of his hand.

"Thanks for your help, Mrs –?" Finch outstretched his hand to shake hers, but she scrunched up her nose instead. Finch looked down and realised his hand was covered in mud. "I'll wash it first."

"Then I'll shake it." Evelyn laughed.

And since then, they had seen each other three times. Two pub outings, including this one, and a trip to an entertainment show at the village hall. Finch was very happy with his new friend. Evelyn was happy too.

As Finch brought the drinks back to the table, he was surprised to see that a visitor had arrived by Evelyn's side. It was Martin Reeves, out of breath having run all the way from Pasture Farm.

"Mr Finch!" he gasped. "You have to come back. It's Iris!"

"What is it?"

"Mum is worried about her. She's gone to her room."

"Well, can't it wait?"

Martin shrugged. He wasn't sure. "She just told me to get you. She's worried that Iris has been drinking."

"You want me to come back just so I can discipline Iris?"

"Mum said it was important. Sorry."

Finch nodded, sighed and started to get his coat and hat. He said a hurried goodbye to the understanding Evelyn and made his way out of the pub to follow Martin back to the farmhouse.

When they got there, Finch placed his Homberg hat on the coat stand and started to take off his overcoat, with help from Martin. Finch's face was etched with concern as he glanced at Esther, thoughts of his romantic evening fading from his mind.

"How is Iris?" Finch asked.

"Asleep, I think," Esther replied. "Sorry to interrupt your night."

"No, this is more important." But Esther could see the hint of disappointment on Finch's face. She knew he'd been looking forward to it for some time. She couldn't help but notice that the shirt she had ironed was now looking creased and dirty, but she didn't say anything. As Martin made a cup of tea for everyone, Esther and Joyce told Finch what had been happening. They all agreed on what was the root of the problem. Iris was obsessed with the thought of Vernon coming back for her. She was imagining that she could see him and hear him, and she would have regular nightmares about him coming to kill her. And this was causing her to mess up at work, her mind too distracted to focus on the job in hand. They all wanted to sort this out.

"She's a bright girl, but she's obsessed about this. And nothing we can say seems to stop her thinking about it," Frank said.

"How about if we get Dr Channing up at Hoxley Manor to take a look at her?" Esther suggested. "If there is something wrong in Iris's mind, he might be able to treat it."

"She just needs a distraction. Something to take her mind off it," Joyce said.

"We've got to sort her out because she's pretty much good for nothing on the farm," Esther snapped.

"Yeah, we're all agreed we've got to do something. But what?" Finch said.

"I think we should vote on it," Esther announced. Joyce looked uncertain. She didn't like the thought of voting, somewhat arbitrarily, on someone else's future.

"All right." Frank nodded. "All those in favour of taking her mind off things?"

Joyce put her hand up. She was the only one. She put it down again, despondently. "So much for that, then."

"All those in favour of getting her seen by Dr Channing?" Esther said, raising her own hand.

Joyce shrugged and reluctantly stuck her hand in the air. It was probably the best thing. Channing might be able to cure the root of the problem, whereas something like going to a dance would only be a temporary sticking plaster. Frank added his own hand to the vote.

"Fred?" Esther said, turning to Finch.

"All right, then," he replied, adding himself to the vote. "Here, this is like one of those Women's Institute meetings, isn't it? All voting on what to do. Except we're not making loads of jam."

"I'll have you know we don't just make jam. Bloody cheek. Anyway, this is the closest you're going to get to one of those meetings." Esther smiled. "Motion carried. I'll talk to the doctor in the morning."

But as she and the others debated what to do, they didn't realise that Iris was sitting at the top of the stairs formulating her own plan of action. Her head felt pleasantly fuzzy from a few numbing slugs of carrot whisky and she had decided what to do. Holding the bottle in her hand, she felt her head swaying and her cheeks flushing. Suddenly it all seemed clear. The answer. And she had to do something fast as she didn't want to be seen by Dr Channing.

She decided she would go back to the place where Vernon Storey had made his promise.

I'll come back for you.

Tomorrow, she would return to Shallow Brook Farm and confront her demons head on.

Chapter 4

As the first rays of daylight started to beat away the shadows in the kitchen of Pasture Farm, Iris laced up her boots. She finished buttering a slice of bread and carefully lifted the latch on the door. It was four in the morning; perhaps an hour before Esther and the others would be awake. Iris thought she had time to walk the mile and a half to the neighbouring Shallow Brook Farm and get back before she was due to start work. She sneaked out the door, closing it behind her, the bread lodged in her mouth as if she was a bird about to feed its young. Then she set off down the path, crossing through the yard and finding herself on the single track that connected the two farms. The air was cold, not yet warmed by the rising sun, and Iris found herself gasping occasionally as she struggled to walk fast and finish the food in her mouth.

Eventually, she reached a blind corner and turned it to find herself facing a sign that read *Shallow Brook Farm*. Iris looked beyond the faded, painted sign, its black letters long since bleached grey by years of sunlight. There was the farmhouse itself, a small red-brick building with eves that hung low over the windows like drooping eyelids. And whereas this might give the appearance of a picture-book home, there was something foreboding and cold about it. The curtains were thin, plain white veils like cataracts behind dirty, darkened windows. Iris edged closer, past an ancient hay barrow. Something squealed from within and there was a flurry of movement as she moved alongside it. She didn't look, preferring not to know what was living in there. The stone cobbles of the yard were broken and smashed in places, and in one corner there was a bucket, trowel and a pile of cement under tarpaulin, where John and Martin had started to repair things. The work was progressing slowly as, with a whole farm to run, they couldn't focus all their time on the one job and much of the yard was still overgrown with weeds. She reached the front door. As she extended her hand towards the latch, she remembered the last time she entered this house. The time she had discovered the truth about poor Walter Storey. The time Vernon had made his dreadful promise.

This time, she knew that the house wouldn't be empty. John Fisher was staying here. She didn't want to wake him as she entered so, carefully she lifted the latch and crept inside. The broken barometer was still showing the prospect of snow. The side table in the hallway had a pile of unopened post and some bills that had been opened, presumably by John. Iris took a deep breath and moved towards the living room. She pushed open its door and felt her stomach lurch, as adrenaline and fear suddenly rose up in her body. It was just like it was before. There was the carpet, patterned, but predominantly red. The carpet where she had found the shard of broken bottle with Walter's blood on it. The mantelpiece that she had stood alongside when she made the discovery. And there was the small desk where Vernon had attacked her, forcing her onto it as he threatened her.

I'll come back for you, Iris ...

The words whispered around the ghostly room. Iris looked at the fire, where the poker was now cradled in the coal scuttle. The telephone had been put back in place on its small table near the desk. But apart from those two aspects, little had changed about the room since she had last been here.

Iris opened the drawer on the desk. It was full of papers, letters. She picked one up and could tell, by the way it was laid out, it was a bill for payment. But she couldn't read the words. She put it back and looked at the photographs on the mantelpiece. There he was. The small, dark figure of Vernon Storey, smiling as he posed with a gigantic pike he'd caught in the river. She wasn't sure which one had the worst teeth. Next to him was a small gate-fold photograph frame with Walter Storey in one half and his brother, Samuel, in the other. A hairbrush near the end of the mantelpiece caught her eye, the red-brown hair on it catching the early morning light that was peeking through the gap in the curtains. Vernon's hair. Iris found herself compelled to reach out for it, to touch it. As her fingers neared the hairbrush, suddenly a man's voice made her jump.

"What are you doing?"

She spun round. For a second, Vernon was standing there, his gimlet eyes squinting at her. But, of course, it wasn't Vernon Storey. It was John Fisher. He was good-looking, clean-cut with kind eyes. And at the moment, those eyes were trying to work out why he had an uninvited Land Girl in the house at this absurdly early hour of the morning.

"Sorry. I needed to have a look." Iris said apologetically.

John nodded. It was all right. He understood. He knew about what had happened here with Vernon and Iris. And he'd been through enough trauma of his own to know that she might need to come back. It would do her good to return to the scene of the event, knowing that this time it was safe.

"Want a cup of tea?" he asked kindly, turning to leave. Iris noticed that he was wearing his dressing gown. Now she knew for certain that she must have woken him up.

"Sorry, I thought I was being quiet."

"Stop saying sorry. I was getting up soon anyway. Farming keeps the same unsociable hours as the RAF. I'm used to it." His voice carried from the hallway. Iris went to follow, but was surprised to see another figure on the stairs, also in a dressing gown. It was a bleary-eyed Joyce Fisher, complete with a few curlers in her hair; one of which was dangling over her left ear. It looked as though she'd been dragged through a hedge.

"Iris?" she gasped.

"Joyce?" Iris was equally surprised.

Joyce pulled her dressing gown tight around her ample bosom. Iris couldn't help but smirk.

"Joyce stays here whenever she can," John explained. He revealed that they had a system. Joyce would wait for Esther to go to bed and then creep over in the middle of the night. Then, after spending the night together, they would get up early and Joyce would hurry back to Pasture Farm before everyone woke up. Even though they were married, they knew that Esther wouldn't condone Joyce spending anything other than Friday and Saturday nights at Shallow Brook Farm. It would be a distraction from her work and commitments as a Land Girl.

"But, why?" Iris asked. "Connie is allowed to live at the vicarage with Henry. Why can't you live here with John?"

"It's not fair, is it?" Joyce said, glancing at John, to perhaps indicate that they had discussed this same imbalance many times. "Truth is, Connie got permission from Lady Hoxley. And because she was married to a vicar, that was somehow all right. I asked and Lady Hoxley turned up her nose. It's simply one rule for the wife of a clergyman and another rule for the rest of us."

"She did agree to two nights a week, but wanted Joyce to spend most of her time at Pasture Farm," John said, trying to be diplomatic. The last thing he wanted was to upset Lady Hoxley and find himself turfed out on his ear.

"I'm the most senior, apart from Esther," Joyce said, refusing to let the matter go.

"You've been there longest, that's all." John laughed. He turned to Iris. "Truth is, we don't mind –"

"We do bloody mind," Joyce snapped. "I want to stay here all the time!"

"It's exciting this way. We feel it's dangerous,' John added. 'Which it is, if we get caught."

Joyce looked imploringly at Iris. Iris knew what she was about to say and got there first.

"Don't worry. I'm not going to say anything."

John smiled his thanks and went through to the kitchen to make a pot of tea. Joyce raised an eyebrow to Iris. "And I won't tell Esther about that new bottle of whisky you keep in your room." Iris wondered how Joyce knew, but Joyce explained, "I could smell it on your breath, so I put two and two together." The bottom line was that they understood each another. They walked through to join John in the kitchen. As he poured the tea, Joyce asked Iris what she thought about Finch being in love. Iris hadn't given it much thought. But she felt it was strange seeing Finch all dressed up and smart.

"I keep thinking he's off to see the bank manager." Iris laughed.

"Yes, he's certainly improved the way he's turned out," Joyce said. "I haven't seen her. Have you seen her?"

"I saw her briefly in the village, when I was delivering eggs." Iris nodded. "Seemed a very attractive older woman."

"He's done well for himself," John smiled, stirring the pot with a teaspoon. Joyce shot him a look, realising that he knew full well he was being playful with his comments about another woman's attractiveness. He knew it would get a rise out of his wife. Joyce bristled and tried to resist the urge to fall into his trap.

"Yeah, but what does she see in him?" Joyce asked. "I mean, he's funny and warm, but he's no oil painting."

"Isn't funny and warm enough?" John teased.

"Maybe." Joyce frowned. "I just worry she's after his money."

"What money?" Iris laughed. "Until two weeks ago, his trousers were held up with string!"

"But that's just it. He's got the money squirrelled away to buy himself a smart suit, a hat and a thick coat. He's been saving it up for years, all that money from his scams and wages. Think on, Iris. Men like that keep fortunes under their beds."

"Maybe we should keep an eye on things. See what she's after, then?" Iris asked. Something else was bothering her, but she couldn't put her finger on it. Before she could try to identify what it was, the conversation continued, further distracting her.

"Or we should just keep our noses out of it and let him get on with it. Now, drink your tea," John scolded. It was too early in the morning for all this gossip.

Joyce went to sip her cup, but John took it away. He smiled at her playfully. "Not you. You've got to get back to barracks."

"No!" Joyce said, realising the time. She said hasty goodbyes and kissed John, before hurrying out of the kitchen. They could hear Joyce's feet running up the stairs to go and get dressed.

As they waited for her to return, they sipped their tea and John outlined what he planned to do today. Martin was coming over at seven and they were going to start weeding the large field at the farm. The soil had been turned over and treated with manure before Vernon had left, but now nature had reclaimed it and it was a mass of horsetail and dandelions.

"You're welcome to stay and help," John suggested. "If Esther can spare you."

"I think she's got plans for me. As always."

Iris tipped the dregs of her tea down the butler's sink. She was about to leave when John spoke.

"Did you find what you wanted here? You know, to make you feel better."

"Not really," Iris admitted. "Don't really know what I was looking for."

John stared at her doleful expression. He could see she was scared and uncertain. "Come back any time, eh?" he said kindly as she nodded and left the room.

Dr Channing appeared to be picking at an invisible piece of lint on the knee of his trousers as he sat in the study at Hoxley Manor. Iris had glanced at his leg a number of times and now accepted that there was probably nothing there. It was just a nervous tic, like the way she'd clear her throat when it didn't need clearing.

Iris felt more intimidated than usual by the suave and charismatic doctor, as they sat looking at each other in the eerie quietness of the book-lined room. The meeting had been arranged by Esther. Iris was supposed to be here to talk about how she was feeling, about the problems she was having. But she never felt at ease with Dr Channing at the best of times. There was something cold about him. As her mum said, some people had a cold centre where their heart should be. She had wanted to bring her tiny rag doll with her, just to keep it in her hands for comfort. But she decided that Channing would spot it and read some mammoth psychological problem or other into it. So it was best it stayed back in her bedroom. The predominantly circular study was adorned with bookshelves arching around its walls, each filled with hardback books and encyclopaedias. Iris was sitting on a leather-backed green chair, ten feet away from Channing, who was seated in a similar chair. The grandmother clock near the door ticked in soporific calmness as they sat looking at each other.

"In your own time." Channing's words sounded encouraging, but they were said with the strained smile of a man who considered he'd wasted quite enough of his valuable time on this pointless activity. Iris noticed the irritability bubbling under the surface and realised she ought to say something. But, by the same token, it made her want to clam up.

"Just a bit scared at night, you know."

"You're worried that Mr Storey will come back?"

"Yeah. I know it's ridiculous." Iris struggled to put it across. "But it seems real enough at night."

"If he comes back, the police will charge him with the murder of his son." Dr Channing picked at the invisible lint again. "And it's highly likely that he'd be hanged by his neck for the crime. So it's not a probability that he'll come back just to scare you, Iris."

Suddenly Iris felt annoyed. It wasn't that she wanted to be at the centre of this situation, in fact she'd do anything to get away from it. She wasn't manufacturing this fear to receive attention. It was a real and palpable dread.

"It wasn't a probability that my mum would be kissed by Errol Flynn, but she was," Iris blustered.

"Sorry?"

For the first time during their meeting, Dr Channing looked

surprised. He gave a confused look and furrowed his brow at Iris.

"You're talking about probability, strange things happening and I'm saying that no one would have thought Errol Flynn would have kissed my mum, would they? But he did."

"Errol Flynn –"

"Kissed my mum, yes," Iris finished. She had been eight years old when her mother had been working as an assistant stage manager at Northampton Royal Theatre. The repertory company included a young actor named Errol Flynn. At the end of the final show, he had kissed Margot on the cheek and thanked her for her help. It was no big deal at the time – he hadn't made many films and wasn't famous. In recent years, though, it had become something of an interesting Dawson family anecdote. But Iris didn't see the point of explaining it to Dr Channing. She'd rather tease him and leave him wondering how it might have happened. Channing was writing something on the notepad on the nearby table.

"Esther Reeves said you had a ready imagination," he commented.

"I'm not making it up," Iris replied, alarmed that he seemed to be condemning her story as a fabrication.

But Dr Channing hastily changed the subject before she got a chance to explain. "I think it would be beneficial for you to go to Shallow Brook Farm and see that nothing can harm you there."

Iris nearly blurted out that she had already been there, but she guessed that she might get in trouble. So again, she stayed silent. Was this making things worse? Should she talk more and tell him more things? Should she explain about Errol Flynn? How should this work? Iris felt he wouldn't want to know, and besides, she didn't want to spend any more time here than she had to.

"And I'll give you some medicine that will help you to sleep."

This seemed as if the meeting was about to finish, and Iris felt relieved. She'd take any medicine just to get out of here.

Dr Channing scrawled something else on his notepad and got to his feet. Iris realised that the consultation had ended. She got up and stretched out her hand to thank him. But he was already on his way out of the room, his white coat billowing as he marched down the corridor.

"How rude ..." Iris mumbled to herself.

When Iris returned to Pasture Farm, the kitchen was already full of the steam and heat of the evening's stew. But a red-faced Esther still had time to ask Iris how things had gone with Dr Channing. "Has it made a difference talking to him?"

"Yeah. A lot." Iris smiled. She thought she might as well tell a fib. Esther and Finch had arranged the appointment for her, and the last thing they probably wanted to hear was that Iris hadn't appreciated it. No, it was fine. Case closed.

Thankfully, Esther didn't have the time or inclination for details. She needed the table to be laid and the plates to be put out before the rest of the girls returned hungry from the fields. So Iris busied herself. Just as she was laying the final place mat, the latch on the door opened and Shelley Conrad came in, wiping her brow. She was slightly older than Iris, with a mass of blonde curls and a rosy face. Prone to clumsiness, Shelley was the sort of person who could somehow manage to find a rake to step on in an empty yard.

"The others will be along in a minute." Shelley sat on one of the chairs and started to pull her boots off.

"Not in here, lady," Esther admonished, as she hauled the stew over to the serving plates.

"Sorry, forgot." But Shelley looked confused, as if she'd never been told this before in her life. Iris gave a warm smile. She liked Shelley and knew how distracted she was. Shelley rose from the seat and started hopping towards the back of the kitchen. Iris was just about to warn her about the dangers of trying to walk with a boot half on, when Shelley crashed out of view onto the floor. Thud. Iris ran to her side, but luckily Shelley was unhurt, just embarrassed by the awkwardness of her own body.

"How did that happen?" Shelley said, bemused.

Iris shrugged. She was used to hearing Shelley say that every time she fell over or hurt herself.

Iris helped her to her feet. "Are you all right?"

"Someone's put an extra step on this kitchen floor. That's what's done it." Shelley shook her head. Iris laughed, assuming that she was joking, but this earned her a confused look. Maybe Shelley was being serious? It was hard to tell sometimes.

"It'll be the stairs to the cellar, love," Esther chipped in, whilst she plopped generous amounts of potato stew onto each plate. "That cellar we haven't got." But Shelley had gone and didn't hear the joke. Iris returned to the table and greeted the rest of the Land Girls, who were pouring into the kitchen.

Joyce, Connie and Dolores entered, full of tales from the fields of exhaustion and sunburn. Martin came in, his cheeks flushing slightly at the sight of Iris. The girls talked about the drainage problems and the lack of manure. As Iris listened, she thought of the small bottle of pills in her pocket. She felt happy that they might allow her to sleep tonight. Maybe she wouldn't have to resort to getting drunk tonight. Maybe.

I will come for you, Iris. Mark my words.

The words didn't scare her. Not in the daylight. But Iris didn't have long to contemplate them because Shelley bounded back into the room. Taking a slice of bread and chewing it before she sat down, she turned to Iris. 'Are you going to the flicks tomorrow?'

"Yes, I am," Iris replied.

Martin struggled to hide his discomfort.

"Oooh!" Connie cooed. "Got yourself a date?"

"Well ..."

"'Ere, is it you, Martin? Are you stepping out with Iris?" Connie asked. Martin blushed and hurriedly shook his head. Iris felt her own cheeks redden. She didn't want to discuss this in front of Martin. She liked him and didn't want to hurt him. The fact was, if he'd got his act together and asked her first, Iris would have gone with him instead of Joe Batch.

To her surprise, Martin spoke. "Actually I'm going. But on my own."

Esther glanced from her plates. This was news to her. She didn't look entirely happy about the prospect of her son going out of an evening. But what could she do? He was growing up and getting more independent than ever. He spent a lot of time working with John at Shallow Brook. He wasn't her little boy any more. She was just relieved he hadn't set his cap at ditzy Shelley.

"You make sure you wear a clean shirt, that's all," Esther chided.

It was as near to an endorsement as he was likely to get. Martin nodded, taking it on the chin. John and Finch bustled into the room and sat at their places. Esther said grace and everyone tucked in. As usual, the room went silent apart from the sounds of contented eating, until everyone had finished what was on their plates.

After dinner, as Connie went home to the vicarage to Henry, Iris was about to walk the short distance from the farmhouse to Frank's outbuilding when Martin stopped her. He kept his voice low so that Esther couldn't hear him, but he indicated for Iris to go outside. Once in the yard, he produced something from behind his back. It was a small collection of hardback children's books, full of colourful pictures and big writing.

"Hope you won't mind, but I found these. Thought they might be useful."

"Thanks," Iris said, genuinely grateful. Martin knew that she was learning to read and write – he was one of the few who did. She flicked through the well-thumbed pages. A goose in a hat was falling into a puddle. A horse in a waistcoat was berating a cat.

"It's funny. I used to love it," Martin said.

"It'll really help me."

"How are you getting on?"

"Slowly. But Frank is very patient and he listens while I stumble over every word."

They smiled at each other. She got the impression that Martin wanted to say something, perhaps about who she was going to the film with, but he couldn't bring himself to do it. He nodded goodbye to her and, with the books tucked under her arm, she made her way to Frank's den. He was inside tinkering with a rusted metal trap. Its jaws were clenched shut and Frank was trying to prise them apart with an equally rusty chisel. He laid it aside and opened a drawer, taking out a pencil and a note pad, in readiness for their lesson. But Iris wanted to talk about her appointment earlier. She was worried about what Dr Channing had thought about her. Could he say she was mad? Get her locked up? And what would the pills do to her? After about twenty minutes of repeating the same things to her, Frank decided that they should call it a night.

"Come back tomorrow, when you've had a rest, eh?"

Iris nodded. She apologised for not being able to concentrate.

"Dr Channing thought I should go to Shallow Brook," she said. "I think I might ask Finch if I can work there for a bit. Just until it's not a scary place. That might help. Do you think?"

"I don't know, Iris. Might do." Frank picked up his trap and resumed trying to get its jaws open. He was no expert. Besides he dealt with problems by keeping them to himself and soldiering on. Iris picked up her books, left the outbuilding and walked back to the farmhouse. Back in her bedroom, she bolted the door and sat on her bed. She knew that Esther had forbade her from locking it, but she needed the security. She took out the small brown bottle of white pills. She put one in her mouth, but it was hard to swallow. Iris reached for the wardrobe, took the carrot whisky and downed a slug of the orange liquid to help the medicine down.

To her dismay, sleep didn't come any more easily that night. She was still haunted by every sound and creak in the yard outside, still wary of every long shadow in her room. After an hour of restlessness, Iris hauled herself out of bed and with a heavy heart went to the wardrobe. This time she drank until she passed out on the bed.

Scrish.

Scrish.

The sound of the homemade broom scraping its heavy twigs over the concrete was beginning to annoy Iris. She and Shelley Conrad had been working on the yard of Shallow Brook Farm for well over three hours, and both girls' backs were beginning to burn and throb with the exertion. At first it had been fun, a chance to chat and laugh about things with a girl she didn't see all the time. But now they worked in monosyllabic silence, willing John to come to the door of the farm and call them in for lunch. Surely it must be lunchtime soon? Had he forgotten about them?

Iris had been pleased that Esther had allowed her to work at Shallow Brook for the day. She'd looked surprised when Iris asked her, and glanced at Finch for approval. It made little odds to him. So Iris was seconded to the farm for a day, maybe more. If it helped get her back on track that was a good thing. She had overheard them talking this morning, not knowing she was awake and dressed.

"Dr Channing thinks she needs watching," Esther said.

"Watching, how? I can't watch her all day."

"He's worried that her imagination might not be all that healthy. About all this Vernon business."

From her sitting position on the stairs, Iris assumed that Finch had screwed up his face in a confused expression at this because Esther continued, "He said she comes out with things that clearly haven't happened. Her mum got kissed by Errol Flynn, apparently."

"Yeah, and I've got Betty Grable hiding in my shed!" Finch laughed. Iris felt a flash of anger, a moment of hot tears welling in her throat. She knew what was true and what was imaginary. Of course she did. She had half a mind to storm downstairs and put them right, but she felt too washed out. Having had about two hours' sleep, she didn't feel like fighting any battles. So she had taken a deep breath to force back any tears and when she was sure that the rawness in her throat had gone, Iris walked casually into the kitchen. Esther and Finch had stopped talking. And that's when Iris had asked about Shallow Brook Farm. She mentioned that Dr Channing thought it would be a good idea.

And nearly four hours later, Iris was regretting her decision.

"We've only cleared a quarter of this," Shelley said, arching backwards as far as she could to relieve the muscle strain. "I tell you, you'll be so tired, you'll fall asleep at the flicks."

"I'll try not to. It's exciting."

"Yes, I suppose. You are stepping out with a handsome GI."

"No, I meant the picture will be exciting," Iris said, hesitantly. "It's Gary Cooper."

Shelley laughed at her friend's naivety and both girls continued with their work.

Iris thought about her impending date. A proper date with a handsome GI. That was big news. She felt suddenly anxious. What should she do? What should she say? Would he know what to do? Would she? Maybe all this courtship business was innate and it just came to you when you needed it. It didn't even really help that Iris had once kissed a boy before. It had been a long time ago and it didn't really count. She had been 10 years old. Brian Marley had been 10 years old too and he had assured Iris that he knew all about kissing. Daring Iris to try it, they had gone to Brian's room. They sat on the floor, kneeling in front of each other and Brian moved forward. He smelt of toffees and he kissed her, chastely, on the lips. It was a second of contact. Iris had been confused that it hadn't resulted in some magical effect. Her ears didn't spin around, there were no fireworks or anything. She looked quizzically at Brian. He looked equally confused. But that was the end of it. In that scattergun children's way, they'd done that and then she raced downstairs to go back home.

A twinge of sadness filled her heart.

Black, patent-leather shoes running full pelt over the cobbles of a terraced street –

She had to shut that out. It wasn't the time to think about that. She had an outing to get ready for. She was stepping out with Joe Batch.

As Iris started to daydream, John called from the house to say that lunch was ready. Iris and Shelley didn't need asking twice. They dropped their rakes mid-sweep and were in the front door almost before the tools had landed on the concrete.

Finch was feeling more awkward than usual. He was usually slightly uncomfortable in his own skin, but walking along a riverbank with Evelyn Gray was making him feel particularly ungainly and out of his depth. He'd asked to see her, to make up for his early departure from the pub. And it had seemed a good idea to walk away from the bustling kitchen, where most of the Land Girls were having their lunch. It would be easier to talk. Besides, Finch wouldn't have to endure teasing looks from the girls if he didn't bring Evelyn in. But he hadn't thought things through, because the riverbank, with the sunlight dappling the trees and the bird song nearby was a romantic cliché that made him feel deeply uncomfortable. Yes, he knew he was courting Evelyn. And he wanted that. But did things have to be quite so explicit? The truth was that he had been on his own for so long. Agnes had been gone for twenty-one years now and he'd never really been interested in courting since. So hearts and flowers and sweet nothings were all alien to him. He didn't know what to do. And he didn't know when he was supposed to do it.

"You seem to have a lot on your mind, Fred," Evelyn ventured, breaking the uncomfortable silence.

"It's been, you know, a busy old day," he lied, knowing he wouldn't be able to explain the truth. How could he explain it when he didn't understand it? "I just wanted to say sorry for having to rush off the other night."

"You'll do anything to get out of buying a round." Evelyn smiled.

"Perhaps I could make it up to you? Would you like to have dinner? You know, a proper meal." Finch beamed, his large face open and nervous.

"Why don't we have dinner at the farm? I'd love to meet everyone."

"You would?" Finch looked baffled. "Why?"

"I can't just be your secret, can I? It would be nice to meet them all properly."

Her confidence, which bordered on brashness, surprised Finch. She was always forward. A woman without worry about what the gossips would say. Evelyn could never be accused of being a wallflower. No, she stood up and asked for what she wanted. And now it seemed Finch would have to arrange a dinner at Pasture Farm. Esther's face would be a picture. And not a good one. Finch knew that she'd find the extra burden of cooking something formal a pain in the neck. Which meant that he'd get a rocket from her. Still, that was a battle for another day. For now, Finch had made up with Evelyn, and he was going to see her again. That was all good.

"Is this all your farm, Fred?" she asked.

Finch shook his head. He pointed to the distant hawthorn hedges down the hill, where a country lane bisected the landscape, and then up to the manor house in the distance, looming over the fields like a crumbling guardian angel.

"That's the length of it, but we go off to the sides, three fields-worth that way, and four that."

"It's a huge estate to manage." Evelyn seemed impressed.

"You've got to have managerial skills." Finch gripped his lapels, trying to look the part.

"And what's to the left? I saw some other farm buildings."

"That's Shallow Brook Farm. The one I was telling you about. John Fisher manages that one at the moment, but he's not a farmer like me. Not born and bred."

"So you have to do a bit of managing there too, then?" She teased.

Finch liked this. This romantic-walk business was easier than he thought. The couple reached a small bridge that crossed the river. Finch indicated for Evelyn to go first.

"What a gentleman," she said.

"No, just want you to test that it won't break." He grinned. A stern, troubled look crossed her face and he realised that this romantic banter wasn't as easy as it looked. "Not saying you're fat ..." And then he was digging deeper into the dreadful hole. Becoming complacent had taken his eye off the ball and things were going downhill rapidly. But this time, Evelyn smiled and he felt a flood of relief. She was a woman of the world and she could recognise social awkwardness when she saw it.

"Don't worry, I know what you meant," she said, moving onto the bridge. "And look, my massive weight hasn't broken it into firewood!" Now it was Finch's turn to grimace as he puzzled whether she was offended or simply joking. But he soon realised that she was fine and relaxed with everything.

Evelyn asked about the vegetables they were growing and the types of bee that were hovering around the cabbages, and Finch knew that he could have a laugh and a joke with this woman. He'd been lucky to find someone so understanding and so easy-going. Lucky old Finch.

Chapter 5

Shiny, black patent-leather shoes. Small feet running full pelt down a cobbled street on a Sunday afternoon. A bloody, painful gash on the girl's right knee was hampering her progress, but she knew she had to block out the discomfort. She'd fallen over in her haste, but she knew she couldn't stop. She knew she had to keep running. Her small chest felt as if it would burst with the exertion as she ran over a wrought-iron bridge, slaloming around a mother who was pushing a large pram. The mother turned to scold the clumsy child with the mane of red hair. But the girl was already on the other side of the bridge, running, running, running. She had to keep running.

A brisk breeze rattled down the high street as Iris stood outside the village hall wearing a pretty floral dress. She had agonised over what to wear and this option was summery without being too revealing. She didn't want to appear fast. She had no experience of men, but she knew she didn't want to mess this up. Given the unexpected bite of the wind, Iris wished she had worn a pullover or a cardigan. The goosebumps on the top of her arms made the skin look like sandpaper. Added to this, she was still carrying around a pounding hangover that had refused to shift all day. Iris brushed her arms to keep warm as the hall began to fill up with expectant cinema-goers. There hadn't been a film shown on the makeshift screen for nearly two months, and with no other cinema facilities around for miles, this event looked as if it would be packed to the rafters.

She watched as the parade of villagers filed into the hall. She stared at a young man in a suit for a second or two before she realised it was Martin. He nodded nervously to her.

"How are you, Iris?" he asked.

"All right. Cold," Iris replied.

"I'd give you my jacket, but I don't think that would be a good idea." Martin looked up the street. "Where is he?"

Iris shrugged. The truth was she didn't know. And she was kicking herself for not having arranged things more explicitly. She didn't know whether Joe would meet her outside the hall or whether he'd be expecting to pick her up at the farm. She hoped she'd done the right thing.

Martin stood with her, watching the movie-goers.

"I hope you can get a seat."

"You should go in. Otherwise you won't get one either."

"I'm all right. I'll wait with you."

Iris smiled. That was kind of him. They glanced up the road, but there was no sign of Joe Batch.

"How are the books going?" Martin ventured.

"I haven't had a lot of time to read," Iris said.

"Do you mind me asking something?"

Iris nodded, wondering where this was going.

"It's just, if you ever need someone to practise with, I'm happy to listen."

Iris looked into his handsome, boyish face. She was about to say thank you, when a voice behind her made her turn.

"Hey! Iris!" It was Joe Batch, out of breath. "Your landlady said you'd be here, just caught you."

"Sorry, I didn't know what we'd arranged."

With a hint of a frown, Joe flashed a look at Martin. Who was this kid? Martin took the hint and edged away, joining the queue of people. Iris wanted to say something to him, but Joe blocked her view with his body.

"So? Ready?"

"Yes I am!" Iris said, finding a big smile.

Joe took her arm and ushered her into the hall. The hall was crammed with people, with row upon row of wooden chairs, tightly packed. They squeezed past a group of middle-aged men and women who were standing near the entrance. These people had been unable to get seats, but were intent on watching the new film, even if it was from the doorway. Iris couldn't see where Martin had gone. She peered into the gloom. Joe waved to someone and Iris noticed that another GI had saved two seats next to him. The soldier moved his hand to allow Joe to sit. Iris squeezed along the row and sat next to him. They were near the front, with an excellent view of the makeshift screen.

In front of the screen, a thin man wearing a bow tie and grey-checked trousers was urging for silence, his arms flapping as if he was a tweedy praying mantis. It was Eugene Dolland, the community-minded man and film buff who had organised the screening. He'd worked at Shepperton in the mid-thirties and somehow acquired a projector. And with that and his contacts he was able to find films to show to the locals.

He knew that they liked rousing action adventure films or romances, so he'd find whatever he could. Previously Lady Hoxley allowed him to show his features and associated news reels at the Manor House, but since it had been turned into a military hospital, that wasn't as easy as before. Even if the main room that he'd used wasn't now full of beds, the medical staff wouldn't have allowed a lot of unnecessary visitors to traipse through. But the village hall was a suitable alternative, even if it let in more light and draughts than he would have liked.

After a newsreel, the feature started and everyone in the hall sat transfixed. The sound was too loud and the screen was too small, but this was the only hope that the people of Helmstead had of seeing a film, of seeing Gary Cooper in action. This was their cinema and they loved it. The chance to escape into a fantasy of clean-cut heroes and beautiful women, a world largely unaffected by the war. And if the films did touch on the subject of the war, the audience could be certain that they would see the Nazis being beaten by British fair play and heroism. During the film, Iris was aware that Joe would periodically turn to look at her, watching the lights of the screen play over her face; the images reflecting in her eyes.

She felt his hand on the back of her chair, confidently snaking its way to her shoulder. She offered a little smile, happy to let it happen, and she felt the squeeze of his large hand on her shoulder. His fingers were warm and she liked the feeling. She turned to look at him and was surprised when he moved forward for a kiss. She nearly blurted out her alarm, but his face kept getting closer. She backed away as far as she could in her seat. This wasn't what she was expecting. She'd come to watch a film with him, not kiss him in public!

Because Joe was blocking their view, some people in the row behind started making disapproving noises and muttering comments. Joe scowled back at them. Then he took Iris's hand and tried to usher her to leave. But she pulled her hand back. "No," she whispered firmly.

Joe gave a little snort of derision and let go of her hand. He sat back in his seat and looked at the screen. Iris could see him drumming his fingers on his thighs, clearly irked by her rejection. She felt unsettled, her stomach churning like a mangle. Why had he tried to do that? They hardly knew each other and this was their first time out in public. Iris was aware that her cheeks felt hot. She struggled to concentrate on the screen as the black-and-white images played over their faces.

When the film finished, Eugene Dolland thanked everyone for coming. He urged the large crowd to take their time in leaving the hall. Iris felt the knot in her stomach tightening. Over the course of the picture, she had managed to relax slightly, knowing that Joe wouldn't try to kiss her again. But now she faced the inevitable prospect of having to talk to him about what happened. Joe was halfway out of his seat, waiting for the people ahead of him to leave. Iris stood and edged her way along the row. Suddenly she thought of her salvation. Martin. If she bumped into him, then she couldn't have any awkward conversation with Joe Batch, could she? But where was Martin? She scanned the rows, but there were so many people standing in the way that it was impossible to see.

When Iris and Joe got outside, they walked in silence for a few steps. He smiled at her. "Can we talk?"

Iris nodded. Joe took her hand and led her down an alley round the back of the village hall.

Now she realised that he was nodding as he looked her up and down. Small red marks on his cheeks showed that he was furious about what had happened.

"Look, Joe, I –" Iris began.

But Joe lunged at her, trying to pin his mouth against hers. Iris couldn't even scream. With all her strength, she pushed him away. She had to control the situation, and fast.

"Please don't –"

"You knew what this was about."

"What?"

"Coming out with me. You made me look stupid in there, just going for a little kiss."

"I didn't feel ready ..."

To her shock and amazement, he swung her round and forced her back against the wall. He started to kiss her. She felt a hand grabbing her right breast, which had the side effect of holding her even more firmly against the brickwork. She couldn't let this happen. She broke away and shoved the hand off. But Joe pressed his mouth against hers again. He wasn't giving up. Iris started to panic, desperately trying to force out words to stop him. But his tongue was pushing into her mouth, making even the act of breathing hard.

"Come on," he muttered.

Iris found sudden, unexpected strength and pushed him backwards. She moved to one side, moving away, as fast as she could.

"Get off me!" she panted. "Get off."

It was as if a switch had been turned off. As quickly as it had come, the fire faded and he suddenly shook his head, as if someone had thrown cold water in his face. "Sorry, I'm – I shouldn't have done that." Other people, passing the end of the alley, were looking now. Two old men, cigarettes in their hands, looked on with half-concerned eyes.

Iris took deep breaths, trying to stop her head from swimming. She felt woozy with fear and adrenaline. Was he just saying that because they had an audience? Or was it genuine regret?

"What got into you?" she said, her breathing almost returning to normal.

"We've got a dangerous thing on tomorrow. It's no excuse, I'm sorry." He was panting, and looking at the ground in shame. "But I'd been thinking about Chuck getting hurt and thinking how damn easy it is for any one of us to die. So I was seizing the moment." He sighed, looking disgusted with himself. Iris realised that he couldn't make eye contact.

"What's happening tomorrow?"

"There's a munitions dump near Panmere Lake. We've got to move it. That's all."

"I want to go now," Iris said.

She was confused, but she offered him a consoling look. She had been terrified, but she also knew about the uncertainty of survival, borne from the fact that no one was really safe during this war. It made everything seem more urgent. She'd heard many of the Land Girls talking about living for the moment because you might not have many days left.

"I'm just not ready, that's all," Iris said, taking another step back.

"No, it's me." Joe shook his head and started to walk away. "I understand if you don't want to see me."

She went to follow, to continue the conversation, but suddenly Frank appeared at the end of the alleyway. Stony-faced and ready for trouble, he glanced at Joe and Iris, before speaking to her.

"Are you all right, Iris?" It was obvious that he'd been watching at least some of what had played out and that he'd heard everything.

"Yes, I'm fine."

Joe was scowling at Frank, but the older man met his eyes and didn't look away.

"Maybe it's best if you get yourself back to barracks, eh son?"

Joe hesitated, a sour grin spreading on his face. He took a menacing step towards Frank, towering over the thin frame of the gamekeeper. Iris wondered whether this was going to end in violence. "If you say so, Pops," Joe said. Never had contrition sounded so much like a threat. Joe walked off up the high street. After he was sure Joe wasn't coming back, Frank turned to check on Iris.

"It was just a shock. I didn't think he'd force himself on me."

"You don't expect that in a public place," Frank offered. "Want me to walk you home?"

"I'll be all right."

Slowly she set off, reflecting on what had happened. All thoughts of the film had faded from her mind, replaced by trying to work out what had happened in the alley. As Iris walked over the bridge, past the offices of *The Helmstead Herald*, a voice shouted out to her.

"Iris?" It was Martin. Iris was relieved to see him as it was getting pretty dark and her bravado about walking home alone was fading. As they walked over the fields towards the distant lights of Pasture Farm, Iris was grateful that Martin seemed to have no knowledge of what had happened to her in the village hall. Instead, they talked about life on the farm, the war and their lives before. Such normality helped to settle the last of the butterflies fluttering around her stomach.

"So you live with your mum in Northampton?"

"Yes."

"What about your dad?" Martin asked.

"He died." Iris shrugged, as if it was just one of those things, like mislaying a book or being late to church. She didn't intend in any way for her words to belittle it, but the truth was she didn't really want to talk about it. She was sad that her father wasn't around, but most of her discomfort came from knowing how he'd died. It was a day that would haunt her forever.

It was very dark as they came to the fork in the path that

led to Shallow Brook Farm or Pasture Farm. Iris could see Martin's silhouette and sometimes catch a glimpse of the moistness of his eyes reflecting the moonlight, but most of the time it was too dark to make out much detail. He was talking about his own father, Stanley Reeves.

"I haven't seen him since he went to war." Martin brushed his hair from his face. "We know he's alive. Or we hope he still is. But he was captured by the Germans and put in a prisoner of war camp."

"Do you ever get letters?" Iris asked.

"No." Martin shook his head. Now it was his turn to not want to continue talking. They walked in amiable silence for a moment, until Iris saw a silhouette ahead of them. On the edge of the field, a black shape broke the line of neat hedge-shaped shadows. It was a man. The shadow of a short man. Iris didn't scream, but she felt a sharp exhalation of air leave her lungs. It was enough of a sound for Martin to glance in her direction. But Iris couldn't say anything. She was staring at the figure. He wore suit trousers and a pullover, a shirt underneath. She knew who wore clothes like those.

It was Vernon Storey.

Iris blinked and when she opened her eyes again, Vernon was gone. He'd never been there. A scarecrow stood wearing trousers, pullover and a shirt, its black button eyes sewn onto a hessian face.

"What's wrong?" Martin asked.

"I thought it was – a man," Iris said, pointing at the scarecrow.

"It's got some of Vernon's clothes on it." Martin walked up

to the blank-eyed figure and put his arm around it. Something ran out from one of the feet of the scarecrow and brushed against Iris's shoes. It was probably a rat.

"It made me jump, that's all."

They continued to walk to the farmhouse. Iris risked a final look back at the scarecrow.

I will come for you, Iris. Mark my words!

In her imagination, the words whispered through the night air, barely there. When they reached the house, Martin and Iris stopped. Martin smiled awkwardly.

"Thanks for walking me back, Martin," Iris said, opening the door.

"I'll see you tomorrow at Shallow Brook," he said, heading off with a spring in his step. Iris went inside the farmhouse, finding the kitchen deserted and lit just by a candle on the table. As she filled a mug with water from the tap, she was aware of Finch and Esther walking back into the kitchen. They were mid-conversation, although it sounded more like an argument. Esther gave the briefest of nods to acknowledge Iris, and then continued with what she was saying.

"As if I don't have enough to do," Esther said sulkily.

"Well, I'll help," Finch offered, eager to appease. "I can peel some spuds. Or wash the cabbage or something."

"I'm just not happy, Fred. I didn't plan on being housekeeper for you and your lady friend." And then Esther continued out into the yard, taking some rubbish with her. Finch rolled his eyes at Iris, as if bemoaning his lot and Esther's lack of understanding.

"What's this?" Iris asked, finishing her mug of water.

"Evelyn is coming for tea. Well, dinner. She thinks it'll be a dinner. And I want to make a good impression."

"You will."

"Not without any cooking on, I won't!" He slumped in one of the chairs at the table. "Oh, I wish I could cook, and I'd do it myself." Then his eyes started to gleam and he looked up at her. Iris knew exactly where this was leading, what idea he was about to suggest. "You couldn't have a word with Esther, could you?"

"I don't know." Iris winced at the prospect of that difficult conversation.

"Don't know what?" Esther said, returning from the yard.

"Don't know if –" Iris searched for a white lie, but found nothing. "Don't know if I wouldn't mind helping get things ready for Evelyn." And there it was, out in the open, an offer to help cater for the impending dinner. Esther shrugged, accepting this, and Finch looked pleased. This had worked out better than he'd hoped. Now he knew the meal would be a success.

The next day, at the Manor House, Joe sat at the end of Chuck Wellings' bed. Neither were in much of a mood for talking. Joe was still agonising about his behaviour the previous evening after the cinema and Chuck was nervously waiting for his bandage to be removed. A middle-aged nurse stood at the side of the bed, a metal kidney bowl in her hand. It contained gauze and scissors and some iodine in a small brown bottle. She kept offering muttered platitudes about how it would all be fine. Joe noticed that the nurse had a scar on her cheek; just a small one beneath the eye, like a crack in marble. Idly, he wondered what her story was. Then his thoughts turned back to his own problems. Why had he tried to force Iris? He felt so mad with himself. He knew he was a good-looking guy with an easy charm; and he knew he didn't have to behave like that. He didn't have to force women to do things against their will. More importantly, he didn't want to behave like that. Joe Batch was better than that.

His thoughts were interrupted by the sight of Chuck's knuckles whitening as he gripped the sheets. The nurse had cut away the bandage from around his head and she was carefully removing the gauze. More platitudes were emanating from her lips, a mantra to calm herself as much as her patient. Joe watched as the old dressing was placed in the kidney bowl. Nothing prepared him for the image that was in front of him. Chuck Wellings' right eye was just a socket of redness and congealed blood. And beneath that, his cheek was a mess of scarring. His good eye darted around, with a hint of panic. Joe had been unable to hide the shock on his face and Chuck had picked up on that.

"What's it like?" he stammered, keen for reassurance. "Is it all right?"

"You'll be fine," Joe said, managing a smile.

The nurse continued her job and went to place a clean gauze over the wound. But Chuck blocked her hand.

"No, I want to see."

"Are you sure?" the nurse asked. Chuck nodded and the nurse went off before returning with a shaving mirror. She angled it so that Chuck could see his face. Slowly he turned his head to see his wounded eye. Joe placed a supportive hand on his friend's arm. Chuck struggled to stop his tears as he looked at the horror in front of him. When the nurse asked if he was all right, Chuck nodded, but Joe could see that he was far from all right. He stayed by his bedside, waiting for him to talk about how he was feeling. After a few minutes' silence, Chuck eventually spoke.

"I thought it might be –" he searched for the words, "– there. You know, still there and that I might look normal."

"It's early days. I'm sure they'll fit you up with something."

"What? A glass eye?" Chuck slumped back in his bed, dabbing away a tear from his cheek. "Ain't no one going to give me a second look now, is there?"

"Hey, you don't know that."

"I do know that. It was hard enough before," Chuck snapped. His friend was in no mood to be appeased, angry at the injustice of his own circumstances. Dr Channing breezed into the ward. He glanced at the clipboard at the end of Chuck's bed and asked how he was feeling. Joe assumed that the nurse had told him about Chuck's reaction to seeing his injury. But Channing's officious manner made it readily apparent that he wasn't expecting Chuck to cry on him. Such behaviour wouldn't be welcomed. Chuck didn't repeat what he'd said moments earlier and just nodded that he was fine. Channing seemed willing to accept this comment at face value, relieved to be able to leave the room. Ten minutes later, Joe left the ward. He had considered dropping by the farm to apologise to Iris, but he wasn't ready to face her. Maybe tomorrow when the shame had had time to dissipate. He felt a prick of anger at himself. What had he been thinking? By the time he got to the main entrance of Hoxley Manor, he found himself nearly in tears. What was happening to him? Was this anguish brought on by his friend's injury? From what he'd tried to do to Iris? Or was one thing related to the other? Things were falling apart. Joe pushed his forehead against the brickwork of the doorway, letting the coolness soothe his temper. After a few minutes, he took a deep breath and set off back to the barracks, feeling he was in control again.

As the day turned to evening, no one had noticed that Chuck Wellings had sat in his bed, staring ahead blankly for hours on end. Nurses would come to check on him and he'd mumble that he was fine. When Joyce came to see if he wanted to get up for his evening meal in the Great Hall, Chuck refused. He wasn't hungry and wanted to stay in his bed.

"Well, at least let me get you a cup of tea." Joyce smiled.

When she returned with a green utility cup of lukewarm tea, she was surprised to see that the bed was empty; a heavy indent in the mattress where Chuck had been. Maybe he'd gone to have some dinner after all. Joyce left the tea and went about her business, soon forgetting about him.

Chuck Wellings was traipsing down the corridors. He spotted something that caught his eye in one of the wards. Checking no one was around, he walked towards the empty bed. On the bedside cabinet was a glass of water and a bottle of pills. Chuck picked up the pills and squinted at the label. They weren't what he was looking for. He put them down and looked around the empty room. By the other bed was another bottle of pills. This was what Chuck was looking for. He popped the small brown bottle of painkillers in his dressing-gown pocket and returned to his bed. There was a cup of tea next to it, steadily growing colder, the milk congealing a little around the rim as it cooled. He took a mouthful of tablets and a swig of tea. One of the other patients was looking in his direction and if the man had had the ability to speak, he might have asked what Chuck was doing or raised the alarm. Chuck took another few pills from the bottle, the bitter chalky taste in the cold tea filling his mouth as he tried to swallow them. And then he got back into bed. As he pulled the sheets up around him, Chuck thought about the times he'd run after his father's tractor on the family farm, with his beloved dog chasing behind them. He thought about the pals back home, the invincible gang. As the warm embrace of darkness enveloped him, the last thing he thought about was how the fields of corn looked as the sun was setting. Like yellow hands reaching up to heaven.

Iris had never seen the farmhouse table with a tablecloth on it. But then she also hadn't seen it with proper place settings either. Each place had a fine-china plate, white with a turquoise border, and a napkin folded on top, and the plate itself was flanked by two forks and two knives. In the centre of the table was a large, oblong plate with the same turquoise border. That was the serving plate for the fish that was currently cooking in the stove top. Martin had caught the trout himself the previous day and it had been in the larder room in a bucket of cold water ever since. Esther's face was red from the heat of the cooking. She wiped her hands on her apron and chivvied the girls to continue preparations. Dolores O'Malley was peeling potatoes, Shelley Conrad was cutting a cabbage on the chopping board while trying not to cut her fingers.

"Heh heh, how's that fish?" Finch wandered in, fiddling with a cravat. A cravat? Iris did a double-take. Finch's hair was slicked down with far too much Brylcreem and he was wearing a wing-collar shirt. He reminded her of Toad of Toad Hall from one of Martin's picture books.

"Hey! Who let Oscar Wilde in here?" Shelley laughed. Finch looked offended and mumbled that he was merely making an effort. Iris was grateful that she hadn't mentioned Toad.

"And I want you all to make an effort too. Make her feel really welcome!" he shouted. Iris took the tops off two bottles of homemade wine. Finch had been experimenting for the last six months, collecting dandelion heads and sloes to make wine. Iris hadn't tried any of it as Finch was saving it for a special occasion. And tonight was just such an occasion. Shelley put out some wine glasses. They weren't identical, unlike the rest of the place settings. Iris looked towards her own place setting and the glass in front of it. With some dandelion wine inside her, she hoped she would get straight to sleep tonight. She had stopped taking the pills that Channing had given her, feeling they weren't helping. As Iris and Shelley finished the preparations, Shelley asked about Joe Batch. Had he been back? Had Iris seen him?

"No, but I'm not sure I want to," she said. She didn't know how she would feel if she saw him again. Besides, maybe he'd be too embarrassed by his previous behaviour to show his face.

At eight o'clock the guest of honour arrived. Evelyn Gray was wearing a fur stole and a charcoal-coloured button-down dress. The Land Girls had lined up on one side of the kitchen, at Finch's request, as if they were about to meet the King. Evelyn was amused by this. She greeted each of the girls in turn, asking what they did, to much hilarity. Finch was perplexed by the laughter, not understanding why his idea of a formal greeting had failed. But he laughed along. All the time people were laughing, they were having a good time. And that made him happy and relaxed. He pulled out a chair for Evelyn and everyone sat around the table.

"There we are," Finch said nervously.

"Relax, Fred. I'm going to have a lovely time." Evelyn smiled.

Iris looked at Evelyn's face and her stylish blonde hair, thinking that she seemed familiar. She'd seen her from a distance in the town, while on the egg run, but now she was up close, Iris was sure that they'd met before. But where?

Esther brought the trout to the table and placed it in the centre. Dolores, Shelley and Iris sat one side of the table, with Finch and Evelyn at either end. Martin and John were having dinner at Shallow Brook Farm, but they said they might pop over for a late drink. As the sun started to set, everyone tucked into their food.

At first, Esther was a little wary of Evelyn. Iris had noticed that Esther had appraised Evelyn's outfit with an up-and-down look of barely disguised contempt. Iris supposed it was true that Evelyn looked flighty. But if you were feeling less judgemental, you could say her look was more worldly, cosmopolitan. Perhaps Esther felt threatened by her experience and was jealous of the opportunities that Evelyn had taken. The bottom line was that everyone around that table wanted to know more about Evelyn Gray.

"Where do you live?" Dolores asked.

"Other side of Stableforth. Near Brinford," Evelyn replied. She explained that she had a car.

"A car?" Shelley gasped.

Evelyn shrugged as if it was nothing. What else was she supposed to do? Iris went to the window to look out into the yard, where Evelyn's car was parked. It was a 1929 dark-green Riley Nine, a sporty model with four doors. After seeing this, Iris thought that Evelyn was a stylish, sophisticated woman and she hung on her every word, much to Dolores's amusement.

"I get a petrol ration because I'm a courier," Evelyn explained.

"Are you?" Finch looked surprised and Iris saw Esther shaking her head in disbelief that Finch didn't know what she did for a job.

"I told you that, the first time we went to the pub."

"I might have had a bit too much, you know."

Dolores poured some more dandelion wine. Iris eagerly put out her glass for a refill and Dolores obliged. Iris didn't really like the taste of the syrupy wine, but it was making her feel pleasantly woozy. It was strong and reminded her of whisky. She was aware of Evelyn watching her, an impassive expression playing on her face. Was she disapproving of Iris taking more wine? Didn't she like young girls drinking? Iris was starting not to care, the welcome side effect of drinking strong, homemade alcohol. But something was troubling her. Where had she seen this woman before?

After the meal, everyone adjourned to the parlour. This was the room at the back of the farmhouse where seats were adorned with antimacassars, a radio stood in pride of place and the carpet wasn't worn. The room wasn't used very often, so the girls trotted happily through with their drinks, savouring the opportunity. As they listened to Evelyn tell a story about her courier work – she had some amusing story about a mystery parcel that turned out to be a live rabbit – Iris sidled back to the empty kitchen. One of the bottles still held some dandelion wine, so she checked that the coast was clear and poured some into her glass. She gulped it down, the orange liquid burning her throat. She drank some more until the level in her glass was the same as when she had come out. Iris steadied herself on the back of one of the chairs. The skeleton of the trout in the centre of the table peered at her with a coal-black eye. Was it judging her? It reminded her of the eyes of the scarecrow that had been wearing Vernon's clothes. Iris shuddered. She poured a little more into her glass to calm her nerves. Her mind started to wander back to Northampton. She was thinking about her mum and how delighted she would be, one day, to read a letter that Iris had actually written, when she felt someone's presence in the kitchen. She spun round. Evelyn Gray was standing there. She was wearing the same strangely unreadable expression that she had earlier. She flicked open a silver cigarette case and proffered it to Iris.

"Cigarette?"

"No, thanks, I don't smoke."

"You should. Goes well with a drink." Evelyn lit a match and sparked her cigarette to life. "And it looks as though you like a drink."

Iris felt the other woman's eyes scanning for a reaction, so she stared resolutely at the floor. She looked up as she heard the familiar glug-glug-glug of more wine being poured. To her surprise, Evelyn was filling her glass.

"You need something. We all need something, whether it's drink, sex, gambling. Something to get us through the war. And you need to do whatever works for you." Evelyn smiled, the corners of her eyes wrinkling up. This was unexpected. Iris feared being judged for her drinking. Being encouraged was a strange new experience. Warily, Iris took the glass and put it to her lips. The rim was sticky from the liquid and it fixed itself momentarily to her lip. She felt the warm wine burning in her throat. This was a liberating experience, getting tipsy in someone else's presence, someone who seemed to approve. Or, at least, not to disapprove.

"Fred says you're over at Shallow Brook now?" Evelyn said.

Iris nodded. "Just for a week or so." She realised that she felt quite drunk. Her voice sounded far away and muffled. But there was no stopping her now. She put the glass to her lips and took a couple of sips. This was nice. In a weird way.

"Good to have a change of scene?"

"Not really."

"Is the work similar?" Evelyn exhaled on her cigarette.

"More clearing of weeds and things." Iris laughed, immediately feeling she had laughed too loudly. Evelyn took this in, contemplating it as if Iris had said something profound. This unnerved Iris a little, so she stopped laughing. She hadn't said anything deep or particularly intelligent. Why was Evelyn pondering it? Iris didn't know. It was as if Evelyn was thinking about something else entirely. Iris put the glass back to her lips. To her surprise, Evelyn was waiting with the bottle. She indicated for Iris to hold out her glass for another refill.

"No, I shouldn't," Iris said, aware that she was already slurring her words.

But Evelyn smiled, a big, warm, encouraging smile. "Go on! I won't say."

Iris watched as the amber wine filled her glass. She put it towards her mouth, but she was spilling some of it now, her actions jerky and haphazard. How had she got so drunk so quickly? Yes, the wine was strong, but she had been all right until a few minutes ago. Now, it felt as though someone else was steering her body and she wasn't doing a great job. What was happening? She knew that sometimes the drink would affect her more than others. Sometimes it depended on how much or how little she had eaten, or how tired she was. But she knew she had more tolerance to alcohol than this.

Iris struggled to focus. She staggered into a seat around the table, gripping the edge of the wood in case she might somehow fly away like an untethered balloon. Suddenly she felt ill and very inebriated. Through her hazy vision, Iris spotted something. Evelyn was putting a small bottle back in her bag. The bottle didn't have much left in it, but it contained a clear liquid.

"What's that?" Iris heard her voice sounding far away.

"Nothing."

"What have you done?" Iris slurred. "Have you done something to –"

"Helping you have a really good night, that's all." Evelyn smiled.

Something was wrong, but Iris didn't know what it was. But she knew she had to get help. Had Evelyn put something in her drink? Iris had heard about unscrupulous GIs doing this to girls they fancied. Iris didn't like feeling like this. She stood up from the table and staggered. Evelyn was quickly at her side, helping to hold her up.

"It's all right. I'm here."

Iris tried to bat her away. Everything Evelyn was doing seemed friendly, but Iris had a dreadful feeling that it was the total opposite of friendship.

"I'm sorry," Evelyn said, getting close enough that Iris could smell her perfume. "I really was just trying to help."

Iris fell forwards, crashing onto the table and sending the serving spoon from the trout flying into the air. The sound of the fall and the commotion meant that the kitchen quickly filled as Finch, Esther, Dolores and Shelley all came running to see what the problem was. Evelyn was holding Iris, helping her back to a sitting position.

"I caught her drinking. She's just had a bit much," Evelyn offered.

Esther shooed her out of the way so she could get to her young charge. Iris was unconscious, but roused when Esther gently slapped her cheek. "Let's get you to bed, young lady," Esther said with a frown. Shelley and Dolores helped get the slurring Iris to her feet and they carried her towards the back of the farm and the bedrooms. Finch stayed with Evelyn.

"She's been having problems," Finch said, by way of explanation.

"Poor thing," Evelyn replied.

Iris was dimly aware of being placed on her bed, with the looming faces of her friends swimming around her. They were concerned and anxious as they tried to get Iris into her pyjamas. But lifting a floppy dead weight didn't make changing clothes easy, so Dolores and Shelley gave up, leaving Iris on top of the sheets in her clothes. Iris felt the room spinning round. She struggled to remember what had happened in the kitchen. A small bottle being placed in a bag. The smiling older woman, who had encouraged her.

"She's just had a bit much."

Other thoughts, good and bad, jostled for attention as her head spun.

A young girl running over cobbles, her knee bloodied from having stumbled –

Vernon forcing Iris down onto the desk, his hand on her throat –

Martin walking back from the village with her –

A nagging, unformed thought about Evelyn Gray. Who was she? Where had they met before?

But before Iris could think any more, she felt as if she was going to be sick. She propped herself up in bed, but to her relief, nothing happened. She struggled to get under the covers, still in her clothes. The room was spinning and her cheeks felt impossibly hot. Thankfully she soon fell asleep and for once, by way of some small consolation, she didn't dream of Vernon.

Chapter 6

As dawn broke the next day, heavy boots ran in regimented formation along the muddy banks of Panmere Lake. The US military were conducting a night-time mission to move all the munitions from the temporary store by the lake to somewhere more secure. They had come without fanfare or announcement, eager to do the dangerous job as quickly and as quietly as possible. Even the local busybody, Mrs Gulliver, hadn't noticed any of the covert troop movements that had been happening during the previous day, as the army built up its manpower near the lake for the manoeuvre. Private First Class Joe Batch stood with twenty-five other men from his unit, awaiting more instructions. They had already worked for nearly two hours to load a truck with crates of bullets, and now there was a short break in proceedings while a new, empty truck was brought into position. Joe watched as the loaded truck made its slow and steady way from the banks of the lake to the country road that led to Helmstead. Some of the men were standing around, smoking cigarettes and chatting. Their sergeant had given them time to be at ease and grab a rest break while the trucks changed over. Idly he thought of Iris Dawson and their trip to the flicks. She was a nice girl. And he had the hots for her. But he knew he couldn't behave like he had outside the village hall. That felt like the actions of a ruffian, not him at all. Again, Joe wondered what had happened to him. He knew he wanted to make things up to Iris. If she wanted to see him again.

A sound caught his attention. Joe's first thought was that the truck engine sounded wrong, slightly different. Whining and higher-pitched than usual, as if the bearings in the engine had started to seize. But moments later, he realised it wasn't the truck making the noise, but a sound coming from further away.

Up in the sky. The realisation hit him as time seemed to slow down.

"Enemy planes!" he shouted, spotting three Messerschmitt 109 fighter planes coursing over the trees. They were banking lower over the pines, turning. They'd spotted the soldiers. Or they knew they'd be here. Either way, the planes were coming in for a surprise attack. Cigarettes were instantly discarded as soldiers scrambled for their weapons. Joe grabbed a machine gun and ran towards a raised bank by the lake, where four or five of his comrades had already taken up defensive positions. He could feel the wetness from the mud seeping through his shirt as he threw himself down. He watched as the planes banked around yet again. "They're scoping us!" the sergeant barked. "Let them have it when they've turned away from us!"

Joe squinted along the sights of his gun, aware that everyone was doing the same. He had one of the enemy planes in his sights and watched as it moved away, in formation with the others.

"Wait for it," ordered the sergeant, before shouting, "Fire!"

A barrage of gunfire broke the early morning silence, quelling the birdsong around the lake. Bullets whizzed through the air and the plane that Joe had been aiming at exploded into flames, hit by multiple guns at the same time. With black smoke pluming from the fuselage, the fighter careered out of control and dipped down below the trees in the distance. Joe didn't have time to listen for the explosion or celebrate his victory, as the remaining two fighters had now turned and were strafing the ground with machine-gun fire of their own. The mud along the banks was ripped up in a hellish inferno of fire, dirt and noise. Joe heard screams and thuds as two of his friends were shot, flying backwards with the impact onto the ground. The planes banked around again, but this time the soldiers weren't ready to take advantage. The sergeant's face was etched with worry. Joe didn't like the look of that. He wanted his commanding officers to be bastions of calm and capability. But the sergeant had already realised that the troops' current position offered very little in the form of protective cover. Joe didn't wait for any orders and just fired his gun, desperate to catch the planes while they were facing away. But this time, jittery with nerves and fear, he managed to shoot wide of his target.

The planes turned. Joe was dimly aware of one of his colleagues trying to make a run for it, perhaps for deeper cover, perhaps to get away. He would never know. The man was cut down, his body dancing like a grotesque puppet as the Messerschmitt's bullets tore up the ground again. Joe glanced to his sergeant for orders. The sergeant was looking at the surroundings, searching for somewhere where they could reach to be safe. Some other troops were firing back at the planes on their turn, but the resistance was diminishing as the casualties escalated.

Joe noticed that the planes were taking a wider angle on their turn this time. What were they doing? For a moment, he hoped that they had finished their attack, perhaps believing that most of the GIs were dead. But then, he realised the dreadful truth. They were arcing round so they could come back to attack a different target. The storage hut that contained the remaining boxes of munitions.

The sergeant realised the same thing. He ordered his men to stand up and indicated for them to make a beeline for the storage hut. Joe hesitated. What good would that do? It would only succeed in getting them all blown up. He watched as three of his friends followed the sergeant.

"We need to fire from that position to stop it hitting the hut!" the sergeant said.

Joe stayed by the bank, knowing that he was disobeying orders. He fooled himself into thinking he could provide some covering fire from here. Yes, that's what he could do. It seemed senseless to stand and fruitlessly defend a munitions dump that was about to be blown up.

"Joe! Get your ass –" The sergeant turned and shouted. But he never finished the sentence as machine-gun fire from the planes cut into him. The other men raised their weapons, but it was too late. The plane unloaded its cannons into the storage hut, causing a gigantic fireball to blow the roof and the walls off. Joe was thrown backwards several feet and felt his shoulder smash into a tree stump. Dazed and confused, he stared numbly at the sky, unable to move. It was as if it was raining, as he felt warm liquid splattering his face and clothes. He didn't have the energy to move, even when he realised it was blood from his fellow soldiers, the ones who had been standing near to the storage hut.

Joe squinted upwards, on his back. He watched the two Messerschmitts circle away through the thick plume of smoke coming from the ground. He didn't know where his gun was any more. He heard other, smaller, explosions, as more boxes of munitions were caught in the blaze. Fireworks, he thought numbly, and he remembered a Thanksgiving celebration in his parents' garden when he was 11. Ice cream and fireworks. And his neighbour, Mr Gressing, dressed up as a clown. A clown that scared him. Finally, as the explosions stopped and a long silence followed, Joe was aware of the tentative sound of birdsong resuming in the woods. It was as though nothing had ever happened.

Iris sat at the kitchen table feeling as if she'd died. Her head was pounding and she felt sick, a feeling that wasn't helped by the smell of the bacon that Esther was currently frying. If an aroma could taunt you, then the bacon was doing a great job. It was as if Esther was doing it on purpose because she was annoyed with her. Frank was putting on his boots. Finch was contemplating two slices of bread and butter in front of him that were ready for the arrival of the bacon.

"Don't think you'll be getting off work today, young lady." Esther pushed the bacon around the pan. "It's your own fault you showed yourself up."

"I told you," Iris protested. "She put something in my drink."

"Don't be ridiculous," Finch blustered. There was annoyance in his voice and because he didn't often show anger, it scared Iris a little. "Why would she do that?"

"Casting aspersions," Esther commented.

Iris looked to Frank for help and support. But his hands were tied. "I wasn't there, sorry."

"Where were you, anyway?" Esther asked, serving up the bacon. She put one rasher on Finch's plate and two on Frank's, to Finch's annoyance.

"I was trying to catch some rabbits over the Gorley woods. And I didn't have much luck." Frank looked consolingly at Iris. "Sounds like your evening was a similar affair."

"She's only got herself to blame," Esther said, returning the pan to the hob and peeling off some more rashers from some greaseproof wrapping for cooking. "Imagine blaming your guest for making you drunk! I mean, I'm not Evelyn Gray's biggest fan, but I don't see why she'd do that."

"She said she was trying to give me a good night," Iris said, trying to piece it together herself.

"Why would she be bothered about that?" Esther shook her head, not having any of it.

Finch picked up on something that Esther had said and suddenly interjected, his jaws chewing a chunk of sandwich like a rotivator churning soil, "Here, what do you mean, you're not her biggest fan?"

"I mean, I don't particularly like her," Esther stammered. "But I want you to like her!"

"What does it matter if I like her?"

"Why don't you like her?"

"I just don't. She probably feels the same about me."

Amid this exchange, Frank smiled at Iris and indicated that it might be prudent for them to make a hasty exit. Iris got shakily to her feet, eschewing the bacon sandwich in front of her. She made for the door, but both of them stopped in their tracks as they heard Finch say, "Because when I ask her to marry me, I want us to all get on!"

Iris's eyes widened in shock. Frank bustled her out of the door. The last thing Iris heard from inside was Esther's voice.

"Marry? What are you talking about, you daft fool?"

Frank walked with Iris to Shallow Brook Farm. The early morning air was fresh and bracing, but rather than clear Iris's head, it just made it thump harder. Frank was chuckling about Finch and Evelyn, saying he couldn't believe it. Finch had only known the woman a couple of weeks. Talk about fools rushing in! But Iris wasn't really listening. She was still working out what had happened last night. Was she misremembering things? Maybe she had just had too much to drink. But she remembered feeling uneasy around Evelyn, feeling perhaps that she'd met her somewhere before. She couldn't work it out as the details were frustratingly out of reach in the cold light of day. Maybe Evelyn had just wanted to give her a good evening, as she'd said. But why had she made that comment afterwards? Why had she said, "I caught her drinking. She's just had a bit much"? Had she felt guilty for having given Iris the alcohol? Maybe she wanted to distance herself from any blame. It all seemed very odd, though.

Frank was still talking about the marriage proposal as they branched off at the yard of Shallow Brook Farm. Iris made her way to the farmhouse. The front door suddenly opened and Joyce, with a hunk of bread between her teeth, bolted from the house.

"I overslept!" she shouted as she raced off, as Iris approached.

That morning, Iris worked in the yard. Martin and John had found a note on the mat asking them to secure the broken fence in the North Field. Apparently some sheep were getting into the field from a neighbouring farm. So the men had gone off to fix it. Iris was grateful that they weren't around. She didn't really want to talk to anyone when she felt so rough. The chill of the early morning hadn't lifted and now Iris could add feeling shivery and cold to having a headache. As she worked, she thought about the revelation in the kitchen. Finch was going to ask Evelyn to marry him! It was a major piece of gossip and she knew that the other girls would have a field day.

She wondered whether Evelyn Gray was a gold digger. If she was, it looked as if Finch was playing right into her hands. Should Iris say something? She decided that Finch probably wouldn't be in the mood to listen. Besides, after her accusations this morning, Finch already thought Iris had an axe to grind.

Every jolt of the tools was making Iris's head pound, as if there was a brass band in there. She decided to go to the kitchen to warm up with a cup of tea. She was sure that John and Martin wouldn't mind.

Iris walked into the house. It was strange being there alone, with everyone gone. Maybe this would be a good chance for her to conquer her fears. Iris tapped the faulty barometer in the hallway and took in the details of the house. The worn carpet near the front door. The grimy light bedecked with a cobweb. The ancient wooden carving of Jesus on the wall. Here was her chance to control the fear that always overcame her. On the hat stand was a flat cap. One of Vernon's hats. Iris took it in her hands, feeling the worn fabric, noticing the oil from his hair on the label inside. And there, tucked in the seam, was one of Vernon's hairs. Iris stared at it, took a deep breath. She told herself it was all right. Vernon was gone. She put it back on the hat stand and went to the stove to make a cup of tea.

The North Field was the largest field at Shallow Brook Farm. It was also the furthest field from the farmhouse. Martin and John walked along the perimeter of the fence, noting some small breaks in the wire. Although he wasn't an experienced farmer, John was baffled. There didn't seem to be any holes or gaps big enough to allow a sheep through.

"And where are the sheep that got in?" Martin asked.

John thought about what the note had said and sighed. "It just said sheep are getting in from the lane."

"But where from? There's no sheep around."

John shook his head. He didn't have any answers. "Maybe they got it wrong and it was someone else's field."

"Who wrote the note?"

"I don't know."

"Great! So we can't even tell them they got it wrong. What a flaming waste of time."

John decided that they should check the rest of the perimeter. This earned him a groan from Martin, who wasn't happy about walking all the way around. John thought they'd better be certain. But to Martin it seemed as if they had been led on a fool's errand. As they walked, John struck up a conversation, an amused grin on his face. "I hear you went to the pictures."

"Yes," Martin said, bracing himself for what he assumed would be inevitable friendly teasing.

"Was Iris there?" John said.

"Yes, but not with me. She was with a Yank."

"Sorry to hear that."

"Why should I care?" Martin said with enough anger to make John think he really did care, a lot. They walked on across the field for a few minutes and then Martin looked at John, with his confidence and easy charm. He wished he had more of that instead of feeling a bit awkward and tongue-tied all the time.

"How did you get Joyce to go out with you?" Martin asked as they trudged down the line of the fence. Maybe there was some secret about women to be learnt from this experienced man.

"Bribery, blackmail," John joked, before getting serious. "No, we'd been friends since we were kids. And it just sort of happened as we got older. Our parents thought we were too young, though."

"I think Iris thinks I'm too young."

"You're one year younger than her. That's all. And she likes you. Trust me."

Martin's face lit up. John realised that he would be deluged with questions now, all seeking reassurances and more details. It was plain to see that Martin viewed John as the Oracle on such matters as courting and talking to women. For his part, John was keen to close things down as quickly as possible.

"Joyce said she asked about you. I don't know any more. Now, come on, let's look for these gaps."

Iris woke herself with a snort, disorientated and dry-mouthed. Blimey! She'd been asleep and snoring on the back step of Shallow Brook Farm. With bleary eyes, she surveyed the empty back yard, a small concrete rectangle with various weeds striving for life through the cracks on the ground. An old metal incinerator stood in one corner, but apart from that, the yard was empty. Her cup of tea sat beside her, stone cold and untouched. She'd sat down and closed her eyes to try to relieve her headache and she'd gone clean off. As she got her bearings, Iris decided that she felt a little better. She picked up the tea cup and poured it over some wild flowers that were growing from between a crack in the concrete. Getting to her feet, she wondered what time it was. She hoped she hadn't been asleep for too long. In the kitchen, the clock was only at ten-thirty. That was good, she hadn't been asleep for too long. Something caught her eye as she washed up her teacup. A bottle of parsnip wine was on the draining board. Maybe a little sip might help her headache? After all, she'd heard Frank talk about the hair of the dog relieving a hangover. Iris decided it was worth a go. Anything to stop the thumping in her head. She uncorked the bottle and brought it up to her dry lips, the brown-coloured liquid burning her tongue as it went down. Iris coughed. It was strong stuff. She took another swig, longer this time, and felt the warmth of the alcohol down her throat. It was so comforting, the tender embrace that had helped her relax and forget about the horrors in her mind at night-time. It was helping with all her problems: Joe Batch, Esther and Evelyn. All of them were swimming away as she took more sips. Iris stopped herself, not wanting to get too tipsy. The last thing she wanted to do was fall asleep again. With conviction, she stoppered the bottle and put it back on the draining board. As the liquid settled, Iris realised that the level had fallen by an inch. She hoped that Martin and John wouldn't notice when they came to have their evening drink. She rinsed her mouth with water from the tap and straightened her uniform.

Deciding she felt better and more able to face her duties, Iris was about to go back to work when she heard a creak on the floorboard upstairs. What was that? Oh, it was an old house. It was probably just mice. But another creak sounded. That was bigger than a mouse.

"Hello?" she said, surprised that anyone was here. Surely Martin or John wouldn't be back yet? There was another creak from upstairs. Someone was definitely up there.

I will come for you, Iris. Mark my words!

The thought made Iris shiver. As she reached the foot of the stairs, she glanced at Vernon's old cap on the hat stand.

Could he be upstairs? What if he had come back for her? No, that was crazy. He'd risk being hanged if he came back, hanged for the murder of his son. Channing had pointed that out. But what if Vernon wasn't thinking rationally? What if he just wanted revenge on the girl who had alerted the police to the truth? If he'd gone mad, then there was no telling what he might risk. Iris listened for any noise, hoping against hope that there would be no more sounds. And then she could say that she imagined it. She could go off and forget all about this. But another creak sounded from upstairs. Someone was definitely up there. Someone was moving around on the old floorboards above her.

She felt her throat go dry, as if it had been lined with blotting paper. She wasn't sure what to do. Should she shout again? No, that would alert him. At the moment she might have the element of surprise. She knew he was here, but he might not know she was in the house. Iris felt ridiculous at this notion. What did she plan to do? Creep up on him? Iris edged back towards the front door. Her perspiring fingers struggled to turn the latch, but after a couple of fumbles, she managed to open it. She was prepared to run out into the yard, but then a new emotion entered her mind. She felt angry. Angry at running all the time, angry at jumping at shadows, angry at having to drink at night to shut out the fear. Iris would confront her demon. With conviction, she darted into the living room and emerged brandishing a blackened poker. It was the same one that had always been by the fireplace. Holding it like a sword, she carefully started to move up the stairs. Sticking to the walls, Iris thought the floorboards wouldn't creak as much. Three steps. Ahead of her, the gloomy top of the stairs. The landing curtains were still drawn, like milky cataracts, across the windows. Four steps. To her side were various small-framed photographs of solemn-looking people, presumably relatives of the Storey family. Iris was aware of her heart thumping in her chest, pumping blood around her temples. It made it hard to listen for any more sounds. She gripped the poker. Five steps. She stopped to listen. As far as she could tell, the creaks on the floorboard had stopped. Maybe he'd heard her coming. Maybe he was waiting behind the bedroom door. She looked over the banister towards the room that had been the source of the noises. It was Vernon's bedroom. She strained to make out different sounds that were now coming from inside. They were harder to define than a creaking floorboard. Perhaps something like a key turning in a lock. And a rustling noise. What was that? Papers being flicked through? Iris took heart that Vernon hadn't heard her. He was continuing to do what he was doing. Perhaps he was looking for something? Six steps. With confidence rising, Iris continued. She was nearly at the top when her foot hit the wrong part of the stair and a loud creak echoed out. The sounds from the bedroom ceased. This time he'd heard her. He'd definitely heard her. The element of surprise had just vanished.

Iris gripped the poker and waited. Waited for him to rush out and attack her. But nothing happened. There was just silence and the partially opened door, taunting her with its mystery. She moved to the very edge of the final step and then onto the landing. To her left was the bedroom door. Iris pushed herself flat against the wall and edged towards it. For a split second, she saw another door. It was her front door at home in Northampton, and it was closed.

Her mother had gone inside, leaving her numbly shocked outside. She stared, wishing that she could be allowed inside. Even if what was happening was bad, she wanted to see it. She wanted to be inside. But her mother had left her outside as if she didn't matter.

She shut out those thoughts. This was what she had to worry about. The bedroom door was in front of her, teasingly ajar. The mystery and horror of what was inside was compelling her forward. She had to face it. She had to be brave. Her face twisted in trepidation as she reached for the handle. The poker was gripped tightly as she moved to open the door and throw herself quickly over the threshold. Iris pushed the door and stumbled slightly as she entered, but she managed to keep the poker ahead of her like a weapon.

"I've got you!" she shouted as loudly and bravely as she could manage.

She gasped in utter shock at the sight that greeted her.

The screams were dying down as the doctors and nurses of Hoxley Manor treated the injured American soldiers. Eight men had died and seven were detained with varying degrees of injury. It was a brutal first taste of war for a lot of the young recruits, most of whom assumed they were fairly safe on British soil. Private First Class Joe Batch had been discharged fairly quickly after a nurse dressed the wound on his arm and put a plaster on the graze on his cheek. His shoulder was bruised but nothing was broken. He was currently standing in the main entrance of the Manor watching the comings and goings, trying to recognise the faces of his injured friends. He felt numb and distant. Knowing he was probably suffering from shock, Joe tried to collect his thoughts and take his time.

But then Dr Channing floated past and mentioned that a superior officer would be with Joe soon. The American military would want to ask Joe about his account of what happened.

"Sure." Joe nodded. But he had another thought as Dr Channing started to walk away. "Doc? Could I go see my friend while I'm waiting?"

"Who is your friend?"

"Chuck Wellings."

Dr Channing hesitated and Joe thought that he couldn't place the name, but then a familiar and dreadful look crossed the doctor's face. Joe had seen that look before. The bad news face. Suddenly he didn't want to hear what the doctor had to say, but he knew it was coming anyway. Channing fixed him with dark eyes tinged with regret.

"I'm deeply sorry, but your friend took his own life."

"What?" Joe wasn't going to accept this. "No, you must have that wrong. What are you talking about?"

"No mistake, I'm afraid."

"Come on! You're talking about Chuck Wellings? The same guy?"

"I'm sorry," Channing said with finality. "Now, if you'll excuse me?" And he moved away, collaring a nurse for a consultation about a patient as he went. Joe was reeling from this news. Not Chuck Wellings. Not his buddy from back home. With shaking legs, he sat back down.

He shook his head in disbelief. Four of his friends from back home, the original gang, had died in the last day. Joe couldn't help himself, and maybe it was delayed shock mixed with grief, but he started to cry.

All his buddies. They were joking this morning. Joking about the cold start and how they hated getting up early. And Chuck. He was talking to him yesterday. This couldn't be happening. This couldn't be right.

And then he saw something that didn't fit. Frank Tucker was in the doorway of Hoxley Manor, his cap in his hands, staring at the hustle and bustle. What was he doing here? Dimly, Joe saw one of the nurses thanking Frank, and beyond, on the driveway, Joe could make out Frank's pony and trap. On the back was a dead serviceman. Frank must have helped bring the bodies and the injured here. Yes, that was it.

Frank nodded his condolences to Joe.

"Sorry to hear about it all, son."

Something clicked in Joe's brain. A connection from the other night outside the village hall. Frank had been there. He'd heard about the Panmere plan. And here he was again, witnessing the aftermath. Joe looked up, his eyes suddenly quizzical, as if he couldn't understand the language that Frank was using. And then, suddenly, Joe leapt out of his seat and pinned Frank Tucker against the wall, his forearm pressing against his throat.

"It was you, wasn't it?"

"What are you talking about, man? Me what?" Frank was struggling to speak.

"You did it, didn't you?"

A nurse tried to prise Joe away, but he was too strong. Frank was gasping for air, his eyes darting questioningly around.

"You heard me talking about the Panmere mission. You got a message to the Germans!" Joe said angrily. "Outside the pictures, the other day. You heard me!"

And Joe took away his arm, letting Frank fall to the floor, clutching his throat. The nurse went to Frank's side and helped him up. Before she could admonish him, Joe scowled at the pair of them and marched away. The nurse checked that Frank was all right. He was coughing as he struggled to get his breath back. They watched Joe disappear across the driveway of Hoxley Manor. After a few minutes, Frank was adamant that he was all right and headed back to the pony and trap, setting off to Shallow Brook Farm. He didn't notice Joe standing under an oak tree at the end of the driveway. Joe stared intently at Frank Tucker as he passed. As far as he was concerned, this wasn't over, not by any stretch of the imagination. Maybe he'd found out who had betrayed them. He'd found out the identity of the collaborator who had tipped off the Nazis.

In Vernon's bedroom, Iris struggled to process what she was seeing. When she burst in, she had expected Vernon Storey to be ready to pounce on her. And she, by turn, had been ready to brain him with the poker. But Iris was completely thrown by the sight that greeted her.

Evelyn Gray.

For her part, Evelyn seemed equally shocked. Not least because she found herself at the sharp end of a poker, as Iris waved it in her face. It took Iris a moment or two to calibrate the situation and realise that Evelyn provided no immediate threat. It wasn't Vernon. She wasn't in danger from Vernon. She lowered the poker and was about to apologise for bursting into the room when she suddenly wondered what Evelyn was doing there. On Evelyn's lap was a small metal box, opened to reveal some papers – from their layout, they looked like letters – and a photograph of a man and a woman. Iris only had time to catch a glimpse of the contents before Evelyn snapped the metal box shut.

"What are you doing here?" Iris stammered.

Evelyn glanced around nervously. It was obvious she was searching for an answer. Iris had never seen anyone look so guilty. This was, she supposed, a perfect example of someone being 'caught in the act'. Iris was trying to piece together the jigsaw too, but she had even fewer pieces than Evelyn. Without answering, the older woman got to her feet and made for the door, the tin box gripped in her hands.

"I thought I'd come to help, that's all," she said, but Iris blocked the door. Something wasn't right, even though she had no idea what it was.

"But why are you here?" Iris couldn't work this out.

"I told you." And now, having had a few moments to think up something vaguely convincing, Evelyn continued, "Fred is snowed under with the other farm. He asked me if I'd come and sort some of the belongings in this one. Since the owner took off in such a hurried fashion. Is that all right with you, Iris?"

And now it was Iris's turn to have to find an answer. "It doesn't sound right, sorry."

"Don't be a stupid girl," Evelyn said. Any warmth in her eyes had gone. "Just mind out the way, and let me get on." It sounded like a threat.

"What's in that tin?" Iris said, refusing to be intimidated.

"Never you mind, it's –"

But Iris grabbed it out of Evelyn's hands. The older woman tried to keep hold of it, but that just resulted in the hinged lid flying open and raining the contents down like yellowing confetti onto the carpet. Evelyn bent down quickly to pick up the items, but Iris did too, resulting in a thud as their heads banged together. That was all Iris needed. She clasped her forehead in pain, her vision swimming. Evelyn was wincing from the impact and holding her right eye, the point at which they had clashed. In anger she pushed Iris backwards, sending her falling onto the carpet. Evelyn scrambled to get the pieces of paper back into the tin box. Iris felt herself breathing rapidly, shocked, not quite believing what had just happened. Has she really been pushed over by this woman? Iris blinked to try to clear her vision, regretting how woozy the parsnip wine was making her feel. She glanced over at the photograph on the floor. Dimly she noticed that it showed a middle-aged man and a middle-aged woman smiling awkwardly for the camera. They were outside a music hall somewhere, a bill-board showing the line-up of that night's show behind them. It took what seemed like a few seconds, but in reality was probably only the briefest moment for Iris to realise who she was looking at. Tiny cold claws of fear clambered up her neck.

Iris didn't have time to say anything about the photograph, even as a dozen questions burst into her mind. She didn't have to even mouth a single question because Evelyn punched her hard in the stomach. It was so unexpected, so shocking, that Iris felt all the air forced from her lungs, partly because of the physical impact but also because of the surprise. Already woozy, she saw stars and black spots appear in front of her eyes as she rolled on the carpet in pain. Examining her with a steely look, Evelyn collected up the last few yellowing pieces of paper and shoved them unceremoniously back into the tin. Clinically, she scanned the carpet for anything she might have missed and then, deciding that she'd got everything, she straightened her back, brushed down her dress and left the room. It was as if nothing had happened.

The last thing Iris thought about before she lost consciousness was the photograph that she had seen.

It was a photograph of Vernon and Evelyn.

Chapter 7

The cobbled streets were so familiar. The girl knew the way off by heart. And of course, she should know it off by heart as she'd gone there with her parents since she was old enough to remember. The kind man with the white hair would be there. Whatever problem they had, he would listen and then speak in a calming, warm voice that seemed to make any problem more manageable. She hoped that he'd be able to fix this problem. God, please let him be in! Please let him fix this.

She carried on running, running. Her black patent-leather shoes a blur as they ran along the streets.

When Iris came to, she was disorientated. Where was she? It was a place she didn't immediately recognise. A strange bedroom. And why was she on the floor?

Then it all came flooding back. Evelyn had knocked her out. Iris was aware that she was crying, but it was as if the noise wasn't coming from her own body. She was somehow disconnected, an onlooker of the experience. It wasn't a howl, just a soft sobbing, over which she didn't seem to have any control. She'd never seen that in any of the films she'd seen at the flicks. After a traumatic event, people just got on with whatever business they needed to do, stoically, with stiff upper lips. This wretched feeling of disbelief and dislocation wasn't something that ever troubled Vivien Leigh or Greer Garson. It was as if her body was letting some of the anguish out without her actually feeling upset. It was an odd and unsettling feeling. Slowly, she hauled herself up to a sitting position. She assumed that she had fainted after Evelyn had punched her. Standing unsteadily on foal's legs, Iris held onto the bedside cabinet for support. She sat on the bed, her brain trying to make sense of the bizarre and unexpected thing that had just happened. She wiped away the tears as questions whizzed around her head.

She'd found Evelyn Gray in the farm. Why?

What was Evelyn looking for in the tin box?

Why had Evelyn hit her?

So many questions and not a single answer. But it was that last one that was such a shock, so unexpected an occurrence. Iris had never experienced anything similar before. Not first-hand, anyway. She remembered when her mother had accidentally stepped in front of a car outside the Northampton Lyons Corner House and the driver got out from his vehicle and pushed her. That was shocking, a stranger assaulting someone she loved. The motorist had been shocked by nearly running her over and had taken out his confusion and stress by pushing the woman who had nearly dented his paintwork. Iris remembered her mother going ashen white. They walked home, briskly, in silence, her mother chewing her lip. And then Margot Dawson had downed a big glass of gin, her fingers shaking so much that it sloshed over the sides. And only then did she regain the power of speech.

So many questions swam to the surface, and each one made Iris's head spin a little more. She needed something tangible to think about, something solid to latch her thoughts onto. She needed to ground herself from this woozy nightmare. Then Iris remembered the photograph. That was solid. That was evidence. Evelyn had known Vernon. They were in a photograph together. How had she known him? When was it taken? Why were they together? With horror, Iris realised that maybe the pair had been courting. Evelyn had known Vernon before and they had been courting!

But then even the tangible fact of the photograph seemed to taunt her and Iris doubted what she had seen. Evelyn had pushed her backwards, so she had been in shock when she saw the photograph. And she'd caught no more than a glimpse of it. Could she really be so sure that it showed Evelyn and Vernon? What if she was wrong? But then why would Evelyn punch her to get the photograph otherwise? Iris decided she had to have the strength of her convictions. She had to believe in what she saw and not doubt her own mind.

The question now was what should she do?

She thought of good-natured Freddie Finch, the man who wanted to marry Evelyn Gray. He had been the happiest she had ever seen him. He'd had a spring in his step and been more jokey than usual. Sunshine beamed from his ruddy face and his kind eyes. He'd even started dressing smartly and bought a proper belt to hold up his trousers! If she told him what she had seen, would he still want to marry her? In her heart, Iris knew the answer. No, it would destroy him. Did she want to hurt Freddie Finch by telling him? He'd been like a surrogate father to her since she'd arrived.

And even if she decided to tell him, what would she say, exactly? What evidence did she actually have that any of this had happened? And Finch would want evidence if she was going to accuse Evelyn Gray of sneaking into Shallow Brook Farm.

As Iris wrestled with this dilemma, she got up from the bed and took a few steps towards the door. Something caught her eye. A glimmer of white amid the busy pattern of the carpet. There was a small, folded piece of paper. Evelyn had missed it when she had hurriedly collected up the contents of the tin. Maybe Iris had landed on top of it when she had raced to grab the tin. Whatever had happened, Iris had unintentionally obscured it with her body, so Evelyn had missed this one item. Iris plucked it from the floor and opened it. She knew she probably wouldn't be able to read it, but she might be able to tell what it was. She was expecting it to be a letter. But it wasn't. Instead she found herself holding a piece of paper with drawings over the surface of it. It was a map of some sort.

Quickly, Iris folded it and tucked it into her jumper. She ran out of the bedroom and down the stairs, two at a time. John and Martin were coming back from the fields and she nearly collided with Martin as she ran out of the house.

"Steady on, you nearly had the boy over!" John said.

"Sorry," Iris called, over her shoulder. "Got to go."

Martin looked concerned. He turned to John and asked in

a sheepish voice, "Is it normal to have women run away from you like that?"

By the time Iris got back to the yard of Pasture Farm, the blue sky was beginning to fade to grey. She could hear the other Land Girls inside, eating their evening meal. The chink of cutlery on plates, the pouring of water into glasses, the occasional laughter. Iris paced around the yard for a while, making grooves in the dirt with her boots. She couldn't say what she wanted to say in front of everyone. She had to compose herself and work out what to do. She decided that she would talk to Esther. A woman of wisdom and experience, she'd know what to do. And she was no fan of Evelyn Gray, so she might listen. Iris would tell her about what happened at Shallow Brook Farm. She'd tell Esther everything. Knowing she had to work out what was going on, Iris used the time pacing to try to piece things together. The trouble was that not much of it made sense. She went back to the events of the previous night. The dinner party for Evelyn. Why would Evelyn try to make her really drunk by slipping something her drink? Then the answer hit her like a bolt of lightning. Evelyn had been surprised to see Iris when she walked into the bedroom at Shallow Brook Farm. What if she had intended to make Iris too ill to work today so that she would have free and uninterrupted access without Iris being there? That could be it. That had to be it. Didn't it? She'd wanted Iris out of the way, so she'd fixed her drink.

Iris glanced across the yard to where Frank's shed was. The building was in darkness. How Iris wished it was bathed in light, like it was most evenings. Tonight that would have been a welcome sight. Talking to Frank about all this would have helped Iris get it all straight in her head. She caught a waft of the lamb stew that was being eaten in the farmhouse kitchen and realised that she was very hungry. But here she was, outside and alone, with her head pounding and her throat feeling dry. It took another forty-five minutes until Iris assumed the meal was over. The voices had faded from the kitchen and lights had appeared in the upstairs windows. She'd caught a glimpse of Shelley pulling the blinds. With trepidation, Iris took her boots off on the step, lining them up alongside Shelley, Joyce and Dolores's boots. She flipped the latch and entered the farmhouse kitchen. The heat from the stove wafted over her face as she pulled the door shut behind her. The plates and glasses were stacked on the dresser, washed and dried from dinner, and the table was laid with fresh knives and forks for tomorrow's breakfast. The room was empty. Iris heard Finch clearing his throat and the low tones of the *Light Programme*. He was in the parlour. Iris straightened her clothes, took a deep breath and went through. Sure enough, Esther and Finch were listening to the wireless. And it was a blessed relief that they were alone, with all the other Land Girls upstairs. On the wireless, two comedians were doing a cross-talk routine, but neither Finch nor Esther was giving it their full attention. Finch was reading the newspaper and Esther was wrestling with the first rows of a new knitting project. They glanced up at Iris as she appeared in the doorway. Finch turned down the wireless. Esther's face was stern, unsmiling.

"And where have you been, young lady?" she asked, raising

her eyebrows and looking down her nose, as if she was peering over half-moon spectacles. "You don't just not turn up for your tea without telling me."

"I've got something to tell you," Iris said. Despite having all the time outside, pacing and thinking, she had no real idea what she was going to say and when she opened her mouth, a torrent of words spewed out. "Evelyn hit me and stole some things from Vernon's farm. I don't know what she was doing there. But the only thing I managed to get was a map. And she obviously knew Vernon because they were in a photograph together and –"

Esther put up the flat of her hand for silence and shook her head vehemently. "Stop, Iris, stop. What are you prattling on about?" She looked confused, rightly so, Iris assumed, as her torrent of an explanation had made little sense.

Finch was frowning now. This wasn't going well, but Iris knew she had to soldier on.

"It's true. She was in a photograph with Vernon. And I think she put something in my drink hoping I wouldn't be at work today. That would have meant she wouldn't bump into me there!" Iris could tell that they didn't believe her – that was if they could even understand her garbled ramblings. Finch was rubbing the bridge of his nose, too confused or too angry to speak. He didn't want to hear these things about the woman he was courting.

"I thought better of you than this, Iris," Finch said, the words coming out softly, steeped in disappointment. "Maybe you should say this to Evelyn's face."

Before Iris could reply to this, she heard the flush of the

downstairs toilet. Suddenly she noticed that there was a glass of sherry on the armchair table next to Finch, and a black fur stole draped over the arm. She felt a sinking feeling in her stomach as she realised Evelyn was here.

Iris felt any resolve and fight fade away, her energy draining as if it was water from an unplugged bath. If Esther and Finch weren't going to entertain her story, what hope did she have when Evelyn was here. She heard the door creak as Evelyn left the bathroom and Iris glanced nervously round as Evelyn appeared in the narrow corridor leading from the parlour. Evelyn smiled, surprise on her face. But apart from that, there was no noticeable reaction playing on her features. Nothing to give herself away. She had expected this moment, perhaps.

"Hello. Iris?"

Evelyn looked confused by the tension in the room. She looked to Finch for some explanation.

"Oh, she's been telling us all sorts of rubbish," Finch said, shaking his head. Iris knew she had to persevere.

"You were in a photograph with Vernon. What were you doing in a photograph with –?"

"What are you talking about?" Evelyn said. "What photograph, dear? Who's Vernon?"

"He's that chap I told you about. A real wrong sort," Finch explained.

Even in the heat of the moment, Iris noticed how cool and calm Evelyn was. There was no need for her to vehemently defend herself and deny things. She simply had to play confused and let Iris appear to be the erratic, crazy one. "What is she talking about, Esther?"

"We've no idea," Esther said, putting down her knitting.

"She put something in my drink. Last night. And then she hoped I wouldn't be at Shallow Brook because I was ill today. But I was at Shallow Brook. And I saw her rifling through Vernon's things." Iris was aware that tears were welling in her eyes, the tears of impotent righteousness. She yearned for a glimpse of belief in their faces, or at least a sign that they were taking her seriously. But they were closed to her. Evelyn walked around Iris, surveying her like a curious artefact in a museum.

"How extraordinary," she mumbled, taking her seat next to Finch. "I really don't know what to say." Evelyn opened her cigarette case and lit up. Finch placed a conciliatory hand on hers. Esther was scowling.

"This is because she said you were drinking last night, isn't it?" Esther said.

"What? No."

"I did comment on the young girl drinking. But only in passing," Evelyn corroborated.

"Yes, you come in here with a load of lies to try to get back at her for making you feel bad. Well, I'm on to your game, young lady. I know what you're doing," Esther said.

"No, you're wrong."

"Go to your room!"

"No, you've got to listen to me. It's true. All of it. Ask her, ask her why she was in a photograph with Vernon!"

"I'm sorry, Fred, I don't know what the girl is babbling about," Evelyn said. "I don't know this Vernon person."

Iris knew she was losing, the situation tumbling out of her

control. She had to do something. She had to do something to make them believe her. She thought about Evelyn scooping up the things from the tin. Where had she put them after that? Suddenly it came to her and Iris thought she had the answer. She snatched Evelyn's handbag off her lap, the cigarette case and lighter tumbling out. For the first time, Evelyn lost her composure and shouted, "Hey, what do you think you're doing?"

"It'll be in here. The photograph!" And Iris tipped the contents of the handbag onto the floor. A small leather purse, a lipstick and a compact. A ration book, a library token and a cutting from a *Picturegoer* magazine. But there were no letters and there was no photograph. Iris could feel the cold eyes of everyone in the room boring into her. She'd taken a dreadful gamble and it had failed. Things would be even worse for her now.

"Pick all that up," Esther stormed. "And apologise to Mrs Gray this instant."

Iris bent down and scrambled to replace the items as quickly as she could, but each second seemed to stretch into ten as she fumbled to find everything. Finally she clipped the handbag shut and handed it to Evelyn.

"And?" Esther prompted.

But Iris couldn't apologise. Not when she knew the truth. She looked Evelyn in the eyes and said with defiance, "I'm going to bed. And this isn't over."

She didn't turn around as she walked from the parlour, ignoring the insistent shouts from Esther to come back and do as she was told. She had never heard Esther as angry as this. She knew that she had wrecked things for herself at Pasture Farm. Iris didn't stop walking until she reached her bedroom. She closed the door and ran straight to the wardrobe. She swigged hungrily at the bottle of carrot whisky until she stopped thinking about all the madness of the day. For a second night in a row, the ceiling light was spinning around as sleep claimed Iris. It was a fitful sleep, her body stretched at the wrong angle across the bed, her throat dry from drinking. But she wasn't asleep for more than an hour when she woke with a start. She realised that she was still dressed. As she straightened up and started to idly take her pullover off, the map fell out onto the bed.

The map!

It was evidence. Wasn't it? Should she rush back to the parlour with it? Iris listened for sounds from downstairs, but she couldn't hear anything. They had gone. Iris looked at the map, but although she could make out the drawings, she couldn't read the words. She glanced out of the window. The swing was creaking in the wind. If she craned her neck, she could see Frank's workshop. It was still in darkness. She had to show this to Frank. If he wasn't in the shed or the house, then it was likely that he'd only be in one other place. Iris slipped her pullover back on and crept out the door.

The beer tasted good. It was Frank's first drink all week and he raised his pint glass to the barman of the Bottle and Glass, grateful for the lock-in after hours. The pub had been closed for a couple of days because of problems getting deliveries of beer and spirits. Frank knew that things were getting scarcer as the war dragged on. It wasn't that beer was hard to make, and it wasn't rationed, it was just that there was less grain being grown to make it. Frank knew that as a regular customer of the Bottle and Glass he would usually be able to buy a couple of drinks. But he had seen strangers turned away after only one drink, the barman saving his wares for his favourites. Frank didn't mind, as long as he was on the right side of that grouping. A few regulars were dotted around, the lights kept low to avoid the attentions of anyone wandering by.

The talk in the pub was about the attack at Panmere. Frank kept himself to himself, but listened to snippets of conversation.

"They said it was an inside job. Someone tipped the Jerries off."

"All the armaments went up like a bonfire!"

"There's rumours that three Germans are on the loose. Shot down they were, but they parachuted out."

Frank didn't give much credence to such bar-room chatter. He was a quiet man, who didn't like to gossip. When he spoke it was because he had the facts to hand. He wasn't one for supposition. As the landlord urged them to go home, Frank finished the dregs of his pint, pulled his cap over his head and made for the door. He waved goodbye to the landlord and stepped out into the muggy night air. He felt guilty about not having another reading and writing lesson with Iris. He knew he had to keep up her regular sessions to ensure she kept learning to read and write. It was her ambition to write a letter home, and he knew she was a long way off that.

As Frank sauntered past the town square, he was aware of

the figure of an American soldier blocking his way. Frank smiled and took a step to the left to go round the person. But then he realised it was Joe Batch. The soldier looked earnestly at him, and Frank couldn't help but focus on the small but ridiculous detail that his eyes seemed oily around the lids.

"No one else heard what I said," Joe said, seemingly happy to start his conversation somewhere in the middle. Frank looked in baffled surprise and then he realised where this was going.

"I didn't tell anyone about it." He shrugged. "I'm no traitor." Frank went to pass by, but Joe caught his arm, gripping it tightly along the forearm. Frank spun around slowly, waiting to see what happened next, but not wanting to goad the younger man into a fight unless it was absolutely necessary.

"Hey, I shouldn't have said anything. I'm the one that ignored the posters. Loose lips lose lives and all that. I'm the bad one really, aren't I?" Joe smiled, seemingly filled with bonhomie. But his eyes told a different story, transfixing Frank with a steely, cruel gaze. "So you know, maybe I should be punished. But I think I've already had that punishment, don't you?"

"What are you talking about?"

"My friends have died. Boys I went to school with, good old boys I went to the dances with. We all joined this war thinking it would be something to look back on. To feel we'd done our bit. But they ain't going home to tell anyone, are they? And I'll go home, assuming I make it that far, and be alone, haunted by all those empty chairs at the bar."

"I'm sorry about your friends."

"Are you?" Joe's expression was cold and dark. It wasn't a look that inspired Frank to think there was any chance of a rational discussion. He feared that this conversation would only end one way. And he also feared that he wouldn't be able to defend himself against such a young, fit soldier.

"I had nothing to do with this," Frank said in as measured a tone as he could manage, as if trying to calm a vicious dog.

"Is that so?"

"Are you going to keep accusing me? Or can I go home?" Frank decided that he might as well risk breaking off from this unpleasant encounter. What did he have to lose? He made to walk off, but Joe continued to talk at his back.

"Brinford air base got bombed. A while back. I heard about that. Seems you were at Pasture Farm then. And then a month or so ago, a train was derailed on the way to Helmstead. People died. Again, you were at Pasture Farm."

Frank felt a flush of anger. He wasn't going to have this young kid accuse him in this manner. "So was a lot of people! You want someone to blame, fair enough. But it isn't me. Now don't be ridiculous and just get back to your barracks!"

As soon as the last word left Frank's mouth, he felt his jaw explode in pain as Joe punched him square in the face. Frank listed forwards and felt a hard right hook on the side of his head. Then another fist smashed against his nose. Frank started to fall, but not before Joe got in another punch, sending him crashing to the ground. Feeling disorientated, Frank started to drag himself up. Not to fight, but to talk, to try to stop this man's irrational and misdirected anger towards him. But as Frank reached a kneeling position, Joe kicked him hard in the ribs. Frank felt the woozy haze of unconsciousness falling over him. But he was dimly aware of Joe pulling back his foot for another kick. In cold certainty, Frank knew then that this man intended to kill him.

"Stop it! Bloody stop!" Iris hurled herself at Joe, knocking him over. They both fell in a heap. She scrambled to her feet, raising her hands in some kind of defence, unsure of what she would actually do. "Just leave him alone!"

"Stay out of this, Iris," Joe warned, hauling himself up.

"Or what? You'll beat me up too?" She watched Joe, but crouched down beside the broken body of Frank Tucker. A stream of blood was oozing down his chin and one of his eyes was closed and reddening. Joe hesitated, as if weighing up whether to continue the assault. Then he growled and walked away, tossing a cursory glance back at them. Iris cradled Frank to her bosom until she regained her breath. Then, mustering as much strength as she could, she helped him to his feet. "What a state," she said.

"I've had better nights," he gasped, earning a warm smile from her.

"Come on, let's get you back to the farm."

By the time they had staggered, with Iris supporting Frank, to the yard of Pasture Farm, it was nearly midnight. Frank had told Iris about how Joe Batch had been caught in a German raid at Panmere Lake and how he seemed to blame Frank for tipping off the Germans. She was shocked. She thought about Joe Batch and his behaviour outside the cinema. She didn't know him well, but he seemed hot-headed and prone to outbursts. Trying to be charitable, she assumed he was under a lot of pressure. After trying to force himself on her, he'd come to his senses and apologised. She told Frank that maybe he couldn't help himself when his feelings were all over the place. Frank thought she was being very sweet to offer this charitable view. As they surveyed the farmhouse, the building was in darkness. Iris went to open the latch on the kitchen door, but the bolt was slid home. No! They were locked out for the night. As Iris contemplated whether to call out or throw a stone at Esther's window, Frank turned away.

"No, I don't want them seeing me like this."

"What?"

"I'll sleep in the shed. You're welcome to join me." Frank took a step towards his shed and stumbled. Iris realised that she had no choice but to keep an eye on him tonight until she was sure he would be all right. Besides, the last thing she wanted to do was wake Esther and further blot her copy book. If that was possible.

The two friends forced open the rickety door of the shed and went inside. Warm, stifling air greeted them, the result of a hot day baking the air inside. Frank cleared a chair for Iris, removing some tractor parts that were wrapped in pages of *The Daily Mail*. It was the old armchair near the door, the most comfortable item of furniture in the place. Iris often sat in the chair while trying to read to Frank. Frank moved his wooden stool away from the bench and grasped the edge of the bench for support as he lowered himself down. His bottom landed with a soft thud on the dusty floor and he breathed out in relief.

"You can't sleep on the floor."

"I'm not on the floor. I'm propped up against the work bench."

"But with your injuries, you should have the comfy chair."

"You have it, Iris. I've slept in worse places." He shut his eyes to curtail the conversation. Iris pulled a hessian sack over herself and tried to get comfortable. The sack irritated her neck and the dust in the shed was making her cough. She watched Frank in the dim light, crumpled on the floor, his shoulders propped against the bottom of the bench. The tan clothes and cardigan that moved as he breathed. It reminded her of her father. How she wished he could be here. With numb disbelief at what had happened today, Iris was desperate for a paternal hug, something grounding to make her realise that she wasn't going mad. But her father wasn't here. And somehow the thought that he could never be here made her feel even more desperate and alone. Iris realised that no one would save her. She had to take care of this situation herself. Like the feeling she had experienced when she'd walked up the stairs of Shallow Brook Farm with a poker, it was time to fight back.

Four and a quarter hours later, the annoyingly incessant sounds of Finch's cockerel woke Iris. She spat out the hessian sack, which was gummed against her mouth and tried to straighten up. Her neck was a collection of spasmed muscles from sleeping in such a ridiculous chair and her body ached from the pulled muscles from helping Frank back to the farm. She watched Frank for a few moments. In a deeper sleep, it took the cockerel a few more goes of its dawn chorus before Frank roused. With one eye swollen shut, he opened his bleary good eye and took in the sight of Iris trying to massage her own neck.

"How are you feeling, Frank?" she asked.

"Bruised. But all right." He pulled himself up using the side of the bench and dusted down his clothes. "Let's go and see if Esther has made breakfast yet."

"I thought you didn't want her to see you."

"I can't avoid it, can I?"

"I need to tell you something first." Iris stopped him. He could tell by the tone of her voice that something was worrying her. Something bad. So he straightened up and arched his neck to relieve the knots as he listened as Iris told him everything that had happened, right up until the confrontation in Pasture Farm last night. Iris felt that it was all such a mess. What could she do?

Frank struggled to make sense of what she was saying. He put his hand under a pile of newspapers and produced a small tobacco tin. Inside were three rolled-up cigarettes. He lit one up and contemplated the problem. Iris carried on talking as she had thought of some other pieces that didn't fit the jigsaw.

"I can see how she hoped to get me out of the way, by giving me that strong drink, but John and Martin would still have been at Shallow Brook Farm. Wouldn't she need them out of the way too?"

"Well, they got a note saying that a fence had come down. John and Martin went off to fix it. They examined every foot of that blasted fence and there wasn't any damage."

"They got a note?"

"Yeah," Frank said. "Martin told me."

"So the men had been sent on a goose chase?"

"That's about the long and short of it." Frank exhaled into the crisp morning air. "So if she wanted you out the way, then she had a plan to get rid of you all."

Iris mulled it over. "But no one will believe me. Evelyn was so calm and cold about it all. It just seemed like I was being cruel, making things up to try to ruin things between her and Finch."

Frank nodded, but it seemed as if he wasn't really listening. Instead he offered his own question, "So did she want the photograph, do you think? If she wanted to marry Finch for his money, the last thing she'd want is him finding out that she knew Vernon, isn't it?"

"I don't know. Or it could be this." And Iris produced the folded piece of paper from her pullover. Frank took it, unclasped his wire-framed spectacles and stretched them across his face. He scanned the page's contents.

"It's a map."

"I thought it was. I couldn't read all the words. It says tree, though."

"Well done. It does, yes." Frank peered at the pencil lettering and drawing. It had faded but was still largely legible. "Tree. Brook. Fence. It's all very vague. This could be a dozen places on Shallow Brook Farm. If it is on Shallow Brook Farm at all."

"There's an X, though. That's where something is buried, isn't it?"

Frank nodded.

"Do you think it's treasure?" Iris asked.

"Or a body," Frank replied darkly.

"Would you look after it for me?" Iris asked. "It was the only thing that Evelyn didn't get. If she works out it's missing then she might come for me."

"I'm sure that won't happen."

"I'm not being crazy. You didn't see her attack me."

Reluctantly, Frank agreed to look after the map. He put it inside his tobacco tin and snapped the lid shut, before burying it back under the pile of papers.

"There. Safe and sound." He offered a smile, although it looked more like a grimace on account of his split lip and yellowing cheek. As they walked from the shed, Frank and Iris turned the conversation to different matters. He was interested to know who she thought was behind tipping off the Germans for Panmere Lake, the railway attack and the Brinford air base attack. Frank thought it might all be the same person. Iris didn't know. But she knew one thing, it wasn't Frank and it wasn't her. And she objected to having to distrust her friends and neighbours. But the uncomfortable and undeniable fact was that there was a collaborator in their midst. But who was it?

Someone else was thinking the same question.

Private First Class Joe Batch sat bolt upright on the hard wooden chair as his superior officer looked with weary eyes at him. Captain Harry Cosallo was a small crumpled man in his late thirties with deep-set brown eyes obscured in a doughy face. He was a kind man, experienced in the ways of war but with the heart to know the toll it had on young, fresh recruits. He recognised such a toll on the face of Private First Class Joe Batch, even though Joe was currently doing his best to effect a look of stony indifference.

"There was one witness who thinks it was you, Private," Harry Cosallo said in a soft voice. They were here to talk about the matter of the assault in the town square. The assault on a Frank Tucker.

"It was not me, sir," Joe stated, briskly.

"The witness," Harry consulted the clipboard in front of him for the name, "An old lady, called Mrs Fisk, says that she saw a frenzied attack." He scanned the face of the young soldier for any reaction and then proceeded. "Mrs Fisk said that the attack was only stopped by the arrival of a young woman."

"I wouldn't know, sir."

"Mrs Fisk did not know who the young woman was." Harry exhaled heavily. He didn't want to be doing this. He knew that morale was at rock bottom following the carnage at Panmere Lake. Even if Batch had been involved in the attack on Tucker, Harry had already decided that he would be as lenient as possible. But if Joe Batch wasn't going to admit it, did he really want to push this casual enquiry into an actual interrogation? Harry studied the young soldier, who was still motionless and steely eyed.

"I know what you've been through," Harry said softly. For the first time, there was a flicker of something on Joe's face. A flicker of emotion. "I lost some of my best buddies in Operation Torch in Morocco, watched as bits of them flew around me." Harry swallowed hard at his own horrifying memories, doing his best to shut it away and maintain his business-like demeanour. But he hoped making the point might get Joe to open up. "So I know, Private. I know how this can also hurt the men who are left behind."

Joe gave a tiny, almost imperceptible, nod. An acceptance of this fact. He had been feeling churned up and wretched since the events at Panmore Lake, bottling so many feelings inside. Rage and regret were just two of them. He didn't know how Iris would be towards him after his actions outside the cinema, but he guessed the assault on her friend wouldn't have improved her attitude.

"You feel guilty, you feel it should have been you. Those men died and yet you survived." Harry considered his young subordinate. "You wonder why you were the lucky one, even though sometimes it will feel like a curse to be left behind with the guilt. Hardly lucky then, eh?"

"No, sir," Joe said.

"I recommend you take some time to recuperate and to get yourself fighting fit." Harry wrote something on the clipboard. "I'm recommending two weeks" leave, to start immediately. You'll still be required to do basic drill training and chores, but you'll be exempt from military action. And you will not stray more than three miles from the barracks, is that clear? This isn't a vacation.'

"Yes, sir."

"Dismissed."

Private First Class Joe Batch rose quickly to his feet, offered a stiff salute and turned hard on his heel to leave the room.

Harry Cosallo watched him go, lent back in his seat and sighed.

Joe returned to the large dormitory that he shared with thirty-four other men. The hangar-like room was empty, rows of neatly made metal beds, flanked by identical wooden cabinets, awaiting the hustle and bustle of the men's return. Joe went to his bed, five along from the door, and opened his cabinet. He took out his cigarettes and matches and was about to pocket them, when the door opened and a tall, ginger-haired recruit entered. He was the same rank as Joe, but Joe hadn't seen him before. The man nodded a scant acknowledgement at Joe and moved down the line of beds, his lips moving as he counted them. When he reached the bed eighth from the door, the soldier stopped and produced a brown paper bag from his pocket. He straightened out the bag, opened the wooden cabinet and proceeded to empty the contents into the bag. The soldier stopped momentarily to examine a photograph of a girl before adding it to the bag. Joe's face was showing plenty of emotion now. He didn't like this one bit.

"Hey! That's Chuck's," he snapped.

The tall soldier turned, a perplexed look on his face. "Private Wellings?"

"Yeah, Chuck Wellings." Joe sauntered closer. "What are you doing?"

"I have been assigned to empty the lockers of the men we lost at Panmere and to ensure that they are sent to the relevant families."

"It's too soon for that." Joe scowled. "And besides, Chuck didn't die at Panmere."

"He didn't?"

"No, he damn well didn't." Joe was angry, feeling the same rage he'd felt at Tucker rising up inside. Even though this was probably only a clerical error, the impersonal treatment of his friend was riling him and pushing the wrong buttons. "Chuck was injured at the shooting range. He went to Hoxley Manor and then he took his own life. Got it?"

The ginger-haired soldier nodded, uncertain of where this left him regarding his instructions.

Joe snatched the bag from his hands, delved in and produced the small photograph. It showed a smiling young woman with an abundance of freckles and a big, kind face. "This is Lorraine. She's Chuck's sister. She's his reminder of home."

"I'm sorry, but I have been assigned to –"

"Empty the lockers of the men – I know." Joe held out the photograph for the soldier to take. "These possessions aren't just meaningless things; they mean something. They're important. And that means, you look after them, yeah?"

The soldier took the photograph nervously and placed it back in the bag, aware that Joe was watching him closely.

Joe turned quickly and stormed out of the dormitory, the fresh air hitting him like a welcome cold shower. He watched as soldiers trooped around the parade ground, following the barked orders of a drill sergeant. Joe lit up a cigarette, but it took him several attempts as his hands were shaking too much. He thought of Chuck Wellings. He thought of their laughter and adventures back home. He thought of long-suffering Lorraine, trying to keep her brother in check. How could Joe look Lorraine in the eyes again? He couldn't deal with seeing her kind face wracked with tears and heartache. She didn't deserve that. He didn't deserve that. He thought of his buddies who had died at Panmere. He saw himself walking down the main street when he got home, the relatives of the dead pointing at him. How did he survive? Why didn't he die with them? It wasn't fair.

If only he could make things right.

He knew that was impossible. He couldn't turn back the clock. And even if he could go back to the lake and follow his sergeant's orders, what then? He couldn't have made a difference to the outcome. He'd just be one more casualty having his locker cleared out.

There was nothing he could do, but live with what happened. It was then that a thought, big and bold, forced itself into his mind.

But what if he could find the man who'd tipped off the Germans?

Maybe then he could get some justice for the relatives, for his friends. A crazy thought tumbled into his mind. What if Captain Cosallo had known he had beaten up Frank Tucker, but he was letting him off the hook so he could finish the job? Two weeks' leave. Two weeks to get that son-of-a-bitch collaborator and make him pay. Maybe that was what Cosallo was up to. Although it was unofficially sanctioned army business, Cosallo was giving him time to finish the job. Could that be true?

Joe felt giddy. He knew he would be stepping over the line. He knew that it could be the end of his army career. But didn't he owe it to all his buddies? Cosallo would have done the same for his friends at Operation Torch, surely? That's why he mentioned it. That's what this whole thing was about, wasn't it? This was Joe's war. This was his destiny.

This was his chancc to put things right.

Chapter 8

The mid-morning sun played on the stream as Iris clattered the egg cart over the bridge into the village. She was grateful to be out and away from the farm, having endured a sullen silence in the kitchen before she left. The fact that Esther wasn't venting her emotions worried her. It felt like something had been irrevocably tainted and changed, and that the relationship between Iris and the rest of the inhabitants of Pasture Farm would never be the same again. If Finch's wedding went ahead, Iris knew already that she probably wouldn't be invited. But less trivially, she felt that something was being concocted; a punishment for her bad behaviour. It might very well have been paranoia, but there was a feeling of wheels being put in motion behind her back. She hated having to wait to find out what it would be. She hated the feeling of failure. She wished she could get a second chance.

Iris stopped the cart outside the butcher's shop, pushing the brake up with her foot. She took a tray of eggs inside and left them on the counter. Coming out again, she saw a familiar figure across the village square. Joe Batch was standing with two other soldiers smoking cigarettes. He spotted Iris at the same moment and the two of them looked uneasily at one another for a second. Then Iris decided to take charge. She left the egg cart and walked purposefully towards him. Joe indicated to his friends that he would be with them in a moment. He eyed the approaching Iris with caution. She stopped a couple of feet away from him and squinted against the sun.

"I didn't know," she said.

"Didn't know what?"

"About the attack at Panmere. I'm sorry. It explains why you were all riled up with Frank. But you still shouldn't have done it."

Joe nodded his gratitude at her understanding nature. "I guess."

"I could have reported it, but Frank didn't want to make a fuss. And sometimes we deserve a second chance, don't we?" She said, hoping that Esther might share the same sentiment.

"Thanks," Joe said. "And I'm sorry again. About what I tried to do with you. Outside the film."

Iris felt heat rising in her throat. Thinking about that upset Iris more than thinking about Joe's savage attack on Frank. That was personal to her, an assault that made her wary of Joe Batch, and perhaps of all men with their seemingly charming smiles. Iris had tried to process it and make allowances, and when she viewed it objectively she hoped it wouldn't colour her feelings towards other men in the future. She knew they weren't all like that. Even Joe Batch wasn't like that *most* of the time. But she wanted answers, or an apology at the very least.

"Why did you do that?" she asked.

They stood looking at each other for a moment, Joe shaking his head and looking at the ground. And then Joe broke the silence. "I'm a good guy. It's this war that's turned me upside down. First my pal, Chuck, and then the attack. It's all been too much. And if you never want to see me again, I'll respect that. I'm a bit messed up right now."

Iris nodded.

Joe's face fell.

"Oh, I didn't mean yes. No, that's not what I meant," Iris said quickly. "I meant I understood what you were saying, not that I didn't – stop talking, Iris."

"And?" he said, amused by her.

"Things have been horrible for me too. So maybe we could give it another go."

This time Joe's face broke into a grin, his white teeth gleaming. "We should go somewhere later. Just to talk."

"Let's talk now." Iris looked around to see if anyone was watching. She felt she had burnt all her bridges and she was going to be punished anyway. So why not go out in style? She felt butterflies filling her stomach. She had never misbehaved like this before. She walked with Joe back past the butcher's shop, ignoring the egg cart that had been left outside. Before she left she wanted to put Joe straight about Frank. They found themselves in a nearby field by the stream that ran along the edge of the town. They sat on the grass and looked at the water. Joe made no immediate attempt to get amorous with [illegible]r, to her relief. But that didn't stop her feeling as if she was [illegible]ving wildly just by being there; just by shirking her work.

"It looks so peaceful, doesn't it?" he said, pointing towards the slow-running water. "The fish in there, they don't know what we're going through, the awful stuff that's happening. That's why people behave oddly. They think they could be dead tomorrow."

"Frank Tucker isn't the traitor," Iris said.

Did she see a flash of anger momentarily filling Joe's eyes? If she did, he shrugged it away, covering his feelings. "Let's not talk about him. Not now." He stared back at the stream. "Let's not spoil it."

Iris wondered about her impending punishment and whether her days at Pasture Farm were numbered. She might never see Joe Batch again. Would she regret not having kissed him, not having put her hands on his muscular arms? Forty years from now, she might regret not being spontaneous, not taking a risk. As Connie often told her 'you want to regret the things you do, not the things you don't.' If these were her last few days at Pasture Farm, she wanted something good to remember.

Part of her wondered about kissing him, but had no idea how to do it. She was guessing that grown-ups didn't position themselves facing each other stiffly, like she and Brian Marley had when they were ten. But she dismissed the idle thought. She was attracted to Joe, but she didn't want to kiss him. Not after the way he'd behaved. If she wanted something good to remember, it wouldn't be kissing Joe.

But to her surprise, Joe seemed to have ideas of his own. He leaned forwards, slowly, tentatively, and his warm, full lips moved towards hers. For a moment, she thought how easy it would be to give in. But something snapped inside her, a sensible side that appeared just in time for her to take back control. She wasn't Connie and her life was already full of regrets, one more wouldn't matter.

"Sorry, I –" she said.

"What is it?" Joe replied, slight annoyance in his voice.

"This is what happens in films. It's not what happens in real life."

"Hey, it can be."

"Not in my life." Iris said. "I don't have long here. This may be the last time I see you. And I wanted to make sure that Frank will be all right when I'm gone." Yes, that would be the good thing she would remember. The time she protected Frank.

"Stop talking about that man!" Joe snapped. "Jeez. What have the two of you got going on?"

Iris felt her cheeks flush with anger. How dare he suggest that she and Frank were more than friends? "That's your trouble, Joe. You can't believe that two people can just be friends."

Before Joe could respond, a shrill voice screeched, "What on earth are you doing?"

Iris looked around to see a stony-faced Mrs Gulliver staring at them. She was standing on the path that lead from the village, open-mouthed in disbelief at what looked like a young couple canoodling on the river bank. Iris didn't have the inclination to point out that this wasn't what it seemed. Instead, she jumped to her feet, threw a final look of contempt at Joe and ran off across the field.

She made her way back towards Shallow Brook Farm, her mind buzzing with conflicting thoughts and emotions. The last few days had all been too much. She knew she was going to be punished. She knew that this might be the end of her days in Helmstead. But whatever was going to happen, Iris had put Joe straight. She had protected her friend. And whatever else happened now, Iris was going to face it head-on. That was all she could do.

A meeting was taking place around the kitchen table in Pasture Farm. A parade of grim faces, no one relishing the task at hand. Esther Reeves, Fred Finch, Joyce Fisher, John Fisher and Martin Reeves. Martin was allowed to be present against the wishes of his mother. Esther was concerned that he might tell Iris what they were doing, and she didn't want that particular cat let out of the bag just yet. Or worse still, he might just argue her corner without listening to the facts. Esther hoped they could be fair but thorough. And the emotional pleadings of a 16-year-old boy who was sweet on Iris Dawson would only hamper things. She went to take a sip of her tea and caught Finch switching his cup with hers.

"Fred!" she admonished.

"Yours was a better colour. Stronger," said Finch, batting away her concern. He didn't seem to know why anyone would have a problem with him switching mugs. It was a habit that annoyed Esther as he was always doing it. Changing a plate of food because another looked better, switching drinks because one might have more in it. She guessed that he only did it because it made her so mad.

After taking a slurp of the mug that was formerly Esther's, Finch cut to the chase. 'So what do we do?'

What could they do? Esther knew at least one option.

"We could drum her out," Esther said. "She gets disciplined and thrown out of the Women's Land Army."

"Mum!" Martin protested.

"Martin!" Esther snapped back. It had taken four minutes for him to stick up for Iris, and he hadn't even finished hearing them out yet. "I wasn't saying we would drum her out. Only that we could. It's one option."

"So she'd be disciplined for bad behaviour and sent home?" Finch said, mulling it over himself. He felt conflicted. He liked a happy home and he enjoyed having the Land Girls around the place, but he also wanted his courtship of Evelyn to go as smoothly as possible. If Iris had a grudge against her, it could be unpleasant for everyone. And it was unfortunate on another level as he liked Iris. She was a sweet girl, well, most of the time.

"What has she actually done?" Joyce asked, busy scraping a fingernail across the grain of the wood on the table. She seemed keen not to meet anyone's eye.

"She accused my fiancée of all sorts!" Finch stormed.

"Fiancée? You haven't asked her yet, have you?" Joyce said.

Esther didn't want the meeting derailed by discussing the minutiae of Finch's love life. She tried to keep things on track with a simple list of Iris Dawson's misbehaviour. "She's drinking. That's the main worry. Most nights, by the look of her in the morning. She's like a bear with a sore head. She falls asleep on the job and –"

"Mum!" Martin said. "She's not been like that when I've seen her."

"Well, maybe she's already had a crafty nap by the time she sees you!" Esther shook her head. "And besides all that, her mind is all over the shop. She sees Vernon in every shadow. She made up this stuff about Evelyn hitting her. She ripped Evelyn's handbag off her lap and threw all the things in it over the floor."

"Just because she doesn't want me to marry her," Finch grumbled.

"Why would she make that up, though?" Joyce asked. "She's a good girl, not one for flights of fancy."

"Sorry, love, but you might be wrong on that one," John interjected. "What was it she made up the other day?"

"That her mum had kissed Errol Flynn," Esther confirmed. "She told it to the doctor, as bold as brass."

Martin frowned at John for bringing this up, as if he'd personally been betrayed. He got up from the table and made his way to the kitchen door.

"Martin!" Esther said.

"Leave me alone." Martin left the room.

"Do you think he'll tell her?" Finch asked.

"Not if he knows what's good for him." Esther sighed. She opened her ledger, a large, heavy book with pastel-coloured lines decorating the width of the pages. This book contained all of her notes about the business of the Women's Land Army; everything from absences to dates of birth of the girls. Tucked inside was a small red book, printed by the Ministry for Agriculture and Fisheries, which contained the codes of conduct for the members of the Women's Land Army. Esther didn't really need to look at it as she was so well-versed in its contents, but she wanted to check it for peace of mind. To make absolutely certain.

"A lot of the poor girl's problems seem to stem from that business with Vernon," Esther stated. When she said the man's name there was a slight revulsion in her voice, but perhaps only Freddie Finch picked up on it. The truth was that Esther had her own history with Vernon Storey. It had been a dark point in her life, one that she didn't want to dwell on. Martin had had an accident that had affected his vision. Knowing he needed an operation to repair the damage, Esther set out to raise the necessary funds. But she found it practically impossible to raise all the money she needed. That's when Vernon had made his offer. He would give her the money for Martin's operation. Esther was overjoyed, until she realised this was no altruistic action. Vernon wanted to have sex with her in return. Esther had wrestled with this horrific dilemma, but with time running out for Martin, she agreed to the offer. For his part, Vernon had kept his word and paid up, but the incident had left Esther feeling bereft, and waves of revulsion would wash over her whenever she thought about that man. Finch had found out what had happened and consoled her as best as he could. But nothing could take away the shame of what she had done. So yes, Esther had her own history with Vernon Storey. But for now, she focused on the matter in hand.

"So maybe it would make sense to give Iris a fresh start. A change of scene."

John, Joyce and Finch mulled this over for a moment. John looked pained by the suggestion, whereas Finch was more sanguine.

"Dumping her somewhere new isn't the answer. She needs her friends around her," John said.

"She'll make new ones," Finch replied gruffly. Crossing Evelyn seemed to have evaporated any pity he might have felt for the young woman. "There's the fen work in East Anglia. They're crying out for girls."

Everyone around the table knew about the huge project to turn thousands of acres of fen land in East Anglia into suitable land for farming. A vast number of Land Girls from all over the country had been seconded for the job, operating heavy excavation machinery and tractors. Finch used to use the prospect of this work to tease Connie and Joyce. It had become a standing joke, the ultimate punishment. "If you don't behave, I'll send you to East Anglia". But now he was actually considering it for real.

"Wouldn't it be better to send her home? Back to her mother?" John asked.

"Not when there's a war on and we need people working," Finch replied.

"I think she should have one more chance to straighten herself out," Joyce offered. "This sounds like the only option that leaves her with her pride intact."

"I agree," Esther said, perhaps relieved that someone else had suggested this leniency first. "I will talk to her."

"How's that going to change things?" Finch blustered. "She tried to turn me against my fiancée –"

"She's not your fiancée!" Esther said.

"She will be." Finch wasn't happy about this turn of events. "I've put up with a lot of things in my own house, but having one of the girls making up lies about Evelyn." He shook his head to emphasise the seriousness of this offence. "I'll not stand for that."

With the meeting adjourned, Esther wrote up what had been discussed in her ledger. She hated this part of her job. It was fine being a maternal figure to the girls, laughing with them, helping them, but the disciplinary side of things brought her out in a cold sweat. With a heavy heart, Esther put on her hat and coat and walked over to Shallow Brook Farm to break the news to Iris that she would be leaving Pasture Farm.

Iris made her way slowly back along the lane. Her stomach was in knots but she felt pleased that she had talked to Joe about Frank. Since the riverbank, Iris felt different somehow. In a small way, she felt she had taken control of her destiny. So many people had, often unknowingly, controlled her life. Her mum had urged her to join the Women's Land Army; Esther controlled her time at the farm, dictating meal times and curfews; Finch ordered her around. And perhaps an insidious feeling of failure – from all those years ago – predisposed her to taking such orders. It was easier to do as you were told. It was easier to let others shape your destiny. Because taking control meant that you could fail again –

– Black, patent-leather shoes were running as fast as the young girl could go as she raced over the cobbles to –

And Iris didn't want to fail again.

But she had made a small breakthrough in standing up to Joe Batch. No one had ordered her to do that. Iris rounded a bend and saw the familiar, brooding spectre of Shallow Brook Farm. The skeletal scarecrow of her broom stood in the yard. It was back to reality.

Martin was in the lane, idly kicking stones with his shoe. He smiled awkwardly as Iris approached.

"What's the matter?" Iris asked.

Martin shrugged. "They're not happy with you."

"I didn't think they would be."

"I tried to stick up for you. But maybe if you could stop with the drinking, it would help."

"I don't drink all the time." Iris bridled.

"It's all that idiot soldier's fault. He was the one that got you into alcohol." Yes, Joe had given her the first drink at the dance, but it had been her decision to drink more to blot out the terror she felt at night. She was to blame for that.

"Well, I've put him straight about a few things." Iris said, attempting to close down the conversation.

"You have?"

Iris felt touched that he was so concerned, but she wished it was for something else. The thought of being judged for drinking sent a chill of embarrassment through her bones.

"I can stop drinking." Iris looked Martin in the eyes. He smiled back, but something about his expression already told her it was too late.

A pair of heavy boots scuffed their way across the overgrown grass as Frederick Finch shambled across the graveyard. Some crows cawed in the distance as Finch reached a small headstone. The stone had turned green with a thin layer of moss. Finch had tried scrubbing it some fifteen years ago, but the incumbent vicar at the time had told him it was a fault in the stone, a porosity that meant moss would grow and change its colour even after you scrubbed the moss away. And the moss would always return, a life after life. Finch could still read the inscription: Agnes Finch, Beloved Wife of Frederick, Mother of William, 1892-1920. She had died while giving birth to their only son, Billy. So as he grew up, each birthday was a celebration tinged with the sadness of marking a loss. Finch had loved her and he would always raise a glass of whisky to Agnes, finding a quiet corner to shed a silent tear. And then he would go back to play with his son, kicking a ball or playing chase as if nothing was wrong. Over the years, it had got easier, Finch learning that time really does heal, the raw anguish of loss fading to a resigned but controllable sadness. Eventually. But this steady lessening of grief meant that Finch felt guilty sometimes. Shouldn't he feel worse about Agnes being gone? There were days, weeks when he wouldn't think about her. He guessed that the passage of over twenty years had enabled him to come to terms with his loss.

And now he was about to change that status quo by asking Evelyn Gray to become his new wife.

Finch looked at Agnes's name on the headstone. What would she think? Would she feel betrayed or satisfied in some small way that he was moving on and finding happiness again? She might think he had grieved enough perhaps, having allowed a respectable passage of time to pass before embarking on another relationship. Finch felt he was ready. To him, it was a sign that he had fallen so heavily for Evelyn, when usually he didn't really register women around him. Perhaps now it was time to feel the warmth of a woman next to him again. Finch spoke to Agnes, staring down at the grave. He told her about Evelyn and about his desire to marry her. He asked Agnes if he was being a stupid old fool. He wished she could answer. The truth was that Finch hadn't really been interested in finding someone to love. He had steady companionship with Esther Reeves at the farm, and most new arrivals would assume that they were married – much to Esther's chagrin. Finch had become used to his bachelor ways, finding enjoyment in small money-making ventures or games of cards with his friends. The farm was never quiet these days, with its walls full of Land Girls and their problems, so that meant he rarely had to feel the loneliness of a quiet room. Evelyn was the first woman who had been interested in him romantically. And yes, he knew what the naysayers thought.

What if she's only after your money?

What if she wants to get her hands on the farm?

But Finch didn't think she needed his money. She had her own cottage on the edge of Brinford. He hadn't seen it yet, but he hoped that he would soon. As well as owning a car, she seemed to have her own means of support thanks to her job as a wartime courier. So Finch's concerns weren't the whispered suspicions of the women at the farm, rather his own insecurity about rushing into something. He'd barely known Evelyn for three weeks, and here he was standing by his wife's grave, a small engagement ring burning a hole in his pocket and a plan forming in his head.

"Hello, Fred?"

Finch turned to see the boyish face of the Reverend Henry Jameson, who had noticed him and stopped on his way back to the vicarage. "I thought it was you."

"I'd just come to see the wife, you know." Finch nodded towards the grave. From the serious look on Finch's face, Henry guessed that he was wrestling with some problem. He cocked a concerned eyebrow and went to join Finch at the grave. "Wanted to know if I was doing the right thing and not just being a stupid old fool. See, I've met someone."

"Connie mentioned something. I'm sure you aren't being foolish," Henry said. He hesitated in case Finch wanted to say any more, but the farmer just stared intently at the green headstone. "And what have you decided?"

"I think that life has to move on, doesn't it?"

Henry smiled at Finch, the nature of his dilemma becoming clearer in the reverend's mind. "You'll never forget Agnes, whatever you do. And she'll be waiting in heaven for you with understanding and love."

Finch nodded, comforted by the younger man's words. "Thanks, Reverend."

Henry patted Finch on the shoulder and walked slowly off towards the vicarage and his own wife. Finch smiled warmly at the grave and turned to walk away, his hand holding the ring in his pocket. His mind was made up. Foolish or not, he would ask Evelyn to marry him. As he reached the main road outside the graveyard, Finch noticed the battered figure of Frank Tucker waiting for him. The thin man had his cap in his hands, which somehow accentuated the dark bruising on his cheek. One eye was bruised shut, a macabre, perpetual purple and red wink.

"Fred?" Frank said.

"Blimey, what happened to you?"

"A Yank. But it doesn't matter. The boy needed to get it out of his system," Frank stated.

"Hope you're not looking for time off!" Finch half-joked.

"No," Frank said. "I was looking to have a word about Iris. I just heard that you want to send her away."

"That's right, and save your breath. She needs a new start away from Shallow Brook. Daft idea to be so close to that place after what happened to her there." Finch focused on Frank's good eye to see if the message was getting home. It seemed it was. Frank nodded with a resigned air. He started to walk away. Finch followed.

"You know, Fred. What if you let her stay?"

"No, out of the question. Not after what she did."

"I'll be responsible for her. Keep her in line."

"She made up all sorts of stories. You didn't see her. She was mad at Evelyn for catching her out about her drinking."

"I believe her," Frank stated, simply, waiting to gauge Finch's reaction. The farmer glowered angrily, small beads of sweat forming on his brow. "No, hear me out. Iris showed me a map."

"What map? What are you talking about?"

"It was the only thing she said Evelyn didn't get from Shallow Brook." Frank smiled, trying to make Finch relax and see that he was overreacting. "It's evidence that something happened, isn't it?"

"It's evidence that Iris drew a map!" Finch snapped angrily. He started to storm off up the high street, but Frank managed to stop him in his tracks.

"Iris can't write, though, Fred."

Finch stopped as he took this in, wondering if it was important or whether it was irrelevant. What did the map prove either way? If it existed, so what? There was nothing linking it to Evelyn or to Shallow Brook Farm, was there? No proof that it meant that Evelyn was in the farm as Iris claimed. After a couple of moments, Finch shook his head in frustration. He'd had enough. Frank could side with Iris if he liked, but Finch was going to send Iris away. It was the best thing for everyone. He stomped away, leaving a defeated Frank staring after him.

The clatter of cutlery on metal plates and the loud, excitable conversation made the mess hall a noisy place. The sound would amplify thanks to the cavernous acoustics of the metal hall. Joe finished his lunch. It still riled him thinking about what Iris had said by the stream. He'd thought she was going to rekindle their relationship, but instead she had the front to tell him what he should do about Frank Tucker. She wasn't going to change his mind. Besides, it was his patriotic duty. He lent back from the table, watching his fellow soldiers talking and eating. He felt removed, distant from them. How could they be smiling and laughing when he'd lost so many friends? Sure, they felt the loss too, but the men who died weren't friends they'd grown up with. To them, it was a case of thanking God that it wasn't them this time, and moving on, nothing more. As they laughed, Joe guessed that they were letting off steam, showing relief that they had survived this time.

How should he deal with Frank?

Joe knew that he needed a weapon. That way he could deal with Frank Tucker quickly and efficiently. But getting a gun would be hard since he'd been taken off active duty. Now he couldn't just obtain a gun from the armoury without authorisation. Joe had tried to wing it with some good ol' boy charm, but for once charm wouldn't cut it.

"Why don't you get lost and stop wasting my time?" The armoury officer scowled at him.

"Sure, I can do that," Joe said, conceding defeat. The last thing he wanted was to escalate the situation so that he was put on a charge, with questions being asked. As it stood, the armoury officer probably assumed he was a green private who didn't know the rules. Joe was happy to get lost, for now. But he still needed a gun. And perhaps it would be better if it wasn't one from the armoury, so it couldn't be traced so easily.

In the mess hall, he glanced to his right, towards the entrance and saw a sombre-faced Captain Harry Cosallo enter the room, scanning the tables. Was he looking for someone? He had a face that meant that bad news was on the way for someone. In the captain's hand was a folded piece of paper. Probably a telegram, Joe thought. Definitely bad news. So it surprised him when the Captain locked eyes with him and smiled.

"Private Joe Batch? Come with me," Cosallo didn't wait for any reaction, as he turned on his heels and left the room as abruptly as he had come. Joe was aware of the intrigued faces of his fellow soldiers as he got up and followed, but soon the men busied themselves with the rest of their lunch, his fate forgotten.

When Joe got outside, he found Cosallo waiting for him.

"Sir?" Joe asked, fearing more bad news. Who had died now?

But Cosallo cracked a warm smile, his face relaxed. This made Joe relax too.

"I know you're off active duty, but I need you to run an errand," Cosallo said. "We use a variety of couriers to ferry stuff around between bases, but the one we scheduled for today, well, she didn't show up. I need you to drive a box of steak to Vasham Fields."

"Steak?"

"Steak. Meat. You know?"

"Sir," Joe replied, acknowledging the order. He knew that the base at Vasham Fields was nearly thirty miles away. He would be gone most of the day, driving a truck across the countryside.

"And as you're going, I thought I'd kill two birds with one stone."

"Sir?"

"I wouldn't trust it to a courier, but you can take two crates of munitions and weapons in the same transit."

"Yes, sir." Joe saluted. Suddenly, he saw a way of perhaps getting a gun. "May I ask if I could be armed for this mission, sir?" Joe was aware that carrying armaments was a high-risk activity. There were many people who would like to get their hands on such weapons.

"Yes, of course." Cosallo nodded. "I'll authorise a pistol and twenty rounds of ammunition. But no one knows about this mission other than the two of us and the receiving officer at Vasham, so I don't expect any trouble."

Cosallo handed the folded piece of paper to Joe. On it were the specific details of the cargo and the journey, along with a requisition order for an army truck with petrol allowance for seventy miles. Joe Batch watched his superior officer walk off. He lent against the corrugated metal wall of the mess hall and smiled. Cosallo was so smart, wasn't he? It may have looked like a happy coincidence but that was because Cosallo knew what he was doing. This was further proof that Cosallo was sanctioning a revenge mission. Why else would he have picked Joe? Here he was giving Joe access to a hand gun. He might not have said so, but if you read between the lines, Cosallo was ordering Joe to get a confession from Frank Tucker. Joe knew that the captain couldn't say it, this was a strictly off-the-radar mission. Now, finally, a plan was forming in Joe's head. He set off to get the truck and the crates for the delivery.

Iris was busying herself with clearing the yard at Shallow Brook Farm when she heard the trundling wheels of the egg cart coming down over the concrete. Shelley Conrad had gone back to Helmstead for her to retrieve the cart. Iris nodded her thanks.

"One tray had been stolen, but that's all," Shelley puffed as she applied the brake to the cart. "Not bad."

"Thanks so much," Iris said. "I forgot all about it after I ran off."

"At least Esther might not find out about it now."

"Yes. That would only have made it all worse." Iris smiled, "Mind you, Esther's not talking to me, and the mood in the kitchen this morning was awful. It was as if someone had died. So I don't think it could be worse."

"It'll pass," Shelley said. "They'll soon have something else to worry about."

"Have they said anything to you? About me?" Iris was worried.

"Not really. I heard Dolores saying that you'd had a set-to with Evelyn in the parlour. She didn't know why, though."

Iris explained the background and that it stemmed from her finding Evelyn rifling through things at Shallow Brook Farm. "She was so keen to get away that time – she hit me."

"She hit you?"

Iris nodded. "It made me pass out."

"Blimey. And she'd taken a bit of a risk going there, hadn't she?" Shelley mused.

"Evelyn had tried to make me ill so I wouldn't be at work. The men were away fixing the fence in the North Field. So it wasn't a massive risk."

"But she wouldn't have known they'd be away, would she?"

Suddenly another thought formed in Iris's head. It was crazy, but then so were some of the things that had happened over the last few days. "What if she left the note?" Iris said.

"The note?"

"Who left the note for John and Martin? The note telling them to go to the North Field. The note about the sheep?"

Shelley shrugged, looking slightly unnerved. Iris guessed she was coming across like some sort of mad woman, but she couldn't stop now, not while the train of thought was gripping her. She had to work it out as it came into her mind.

"And when they got there, there was no damage to the fence, was there?" Iris's eyes lit up with a fervour and she didn't wait for an answer. "So whoever sent that note knew it would be a wild goose chase that would get them out of the way! I need to speak to John or Martin. I need to find that note to see if the handwriting matched Evelyn's!"

Perhaps that would be the proof that she needed for Finch to believe her. Perhaps that would stop whatever was going on. Perhaps that would stop Finch marrying the wretched woman.

The cascade of tumbling thoughts was abruptly curtailed by a voice calling from across the yard.

"Iris, love? I need to have a word." It was Esther, dressed in a smart coat and hat. She was also wearing a smile that told Iris that something unpleasant was about to happen. She was here on business. And Iris knew that it would involve being reprimanded for her behaviour last night. Iris walked warily over to Esther as Shelley busied herself with clearing the yard.

"I'm really sorry, but things aren't going well for you here," Esther said. "We've discussed everything. The drinking, this business you've got into your head about Evelyn."

"I can stop the drinking, Esther. I promise."

"No, it's too late," Esther said, sympathetic to the desperate plea. "It's affecting your mind. All these lies."

"They're not lies. Ask Martin about the note –"

"What note?" A hint of anger bristled in Esther's voice, the softly spoken compassion suddenly evaporating like dew on a warm morning. She didn't want to hear any more of these tall stories. First a map and then a note. She didn't want any more lies. Shelley looked over, intrigued as to what was happening. Esther flashed her a cold look that said to mind her own business and get on with her work. Shelley took the hint and moved away to sweep elsewhere.

"Evelyn left the note. The note that got them to go away. She must have done." Iris soldiered on, pleading. She was aware that her words weren't making much sense, but her mind was too muddled and tired and stressed to focus.

Esther moved her round to face her, holding her gently by the elbows. She looked tenderly into Iris's eyes. "This has all come about because of Vernon. You're worried that he's somehow going to come back. But he's not, love. He's gone. And, believe me, I'm just as relieved as you are."

"You?" Iris asked.

Esther smiled a small, unreadable smile, a forlorn pain in her eyes. Iris assumed that she wasn't about to explain what she meant. The memories were obviously too painful, too unpleasant. "Let's just say, I know what it's like to be haunted by the memory of someone. Of him." She kept hold of Iris's elbows, gently holding her as if to ensure that she had her full attention. "We think it's best if you start again. Somewhere else. Somewhere new. Somewhere without all this –"

She indicated the bleak, foreboding building of Shallow Brook Farm. A place of harrowing memories and darkness for both of them.

"I don't want to go away!"

"It's been decided, love."

"No!"

"It's what the Women's Land Army wants for you." And there it was, suddenly an official-sounding edict from above. The die had been cast and Iris's future had been changed without her having any say in the matter. The courage she felt about taking charge of her destiny at the stream fizzled away as she realised nothing would change Esther's mind, no matter how empowered Iris felt.

Iris was aghast. "Please, I can stop the drinking," she pleaded.

"You need a fresh start. Away from all the memories of Vernon Storey and Frank Tucker."

"Frank is my friend!" Iris said. "I thought Finch was too. They've both been –" She wanted to say the words 'like fathers' but they snagged in her throat. Just as Finch had felt guilt about asking a new woman to marry him, Iris felt guilt about somehow besmirching her father's memory. No one could replace him, but the truth was that Frank and Fred had come close.

"I know, love." Esther smiled. "And who knows, you might only be gone a few months. Just time to clear your head and put all this Vernon business into perspective."

"I'm not making it up. Evelyn was in that photograph with Vernon."

"There is no photograph."

"There is! And Finch is going to get hurt by her." Iris broke down. It was all too much. The continued refusal of Esther and Finch to listen to her warnings was exhausting her. "Please, she is up to something."

"What? Give me something solid. Some proof?"

"I don't know."

Esther's face hardened. She took her hands away from Iris's elbows and took a step away. "There we are, then. Just rumours and gossip. I've said what I had to. I'd like you to pack and be ready to leave by the end of the week. You're going to East Anglia to work on the fens."

Esther walked away. Iris watched forlornly as she went back to the dirt track that connected the two farms. Out of the corner of her eye, she saw Shelley run to her side, her face full of concern. "What did she say, Iris?"

Iris didn't really hear the question. Everything seemed as if it was in a fog. Her own mind was racing with thoughts as her survival instinct kicked in. "I've got to put an end to this," Iris said. "And I've got to do it now."

Joe Batch was driving a large green US Army truck across the country lanes of Helmstead. His head was buzzing with ideas and schemes. The bottom line was that he needed to keep the gun that was currently holstered on his belt. But the more he thought about it, the harder he knew that would be. He would have to hand the gun and the bullets back by the end of the day, and yet he wasn't ready to confront Frank Tucker yet. He needed the gun for longer. Or he needed a gun. So he needed to hand his gun back unused in order to not arouse suspicions. What were the other options?

Joe wondered if he could steal one from the munitions crates, just a single gun. But he realised that wouldn't be a good plan. There would be questions about the missing weapon. The guns would have been accounted for when they were packaged by keen-eyed soldiers back at the barracks, so the receiving officer at Vasham would realise it had gone missing on the way. And the finger would point at Joe. He could try to brave-face studied ignorance, but he wasn't sure he could carry that off.

The logistics of obtaining and keeping a gun whirled around Joe's head. What would Cosallo want him to do? How should he show his ingenuity? Then he remembered what Cosallo had casually said outside the mess hall. Cosallo had already given him the answer. Good old Caption Cosallo.

He heard the Captain's words in his head, 'But no one knows about this mission, other than the two of us and the receiving officer at Vasham, so I don't expect any trouble.'

There it was. The loophole. *I don't expect any trouble*. That was very different from saying that there definitely wouldn't be any trouble. What if someone else knew about Joe's mission? Someone who Joe could invent in his head? Saboteurs!

He drove the truck to three miles outside of Helmstead and parked on the side of the lane.

Joe had been over things in his head a dozen times, checking for loopholes. He went to the back of the truck, opened the doors and slid out one of the metal munitions boxes. It was heavy as it was usually a job for two soldiers and it took a lot of effort for him to haul it out. He staggered with it over to a hedge and pushed it against the foliage. Then using as much leverage as he could muster, he slowly raised his arms, tipping the box up the side of the hedge until it reached the top. With one big final push he managed to tip it over the hedge. Clunk. It fell heavily onto the earth on the other side. Joe struggled to regain his breath and braced himself to repeat the process with the second munitions box. When he had managed to tip that one over the hedge, he felt like collapsing in a heap. But he knew he had more to do.

The meat box was much easier, much lighter. He tipped it over the hedge and then checked that the road was still clear. Joe went back to the truck and went to the toolkit in the back. He pulled the drawstrings and unfurled a pickaxe, a shovel and an axe. Selecting the shovel, he fastened the tools up again, and wandered over to the hedge. He pulled himself up until he had reached the peak and he was able to look around. There were fields for as far as he could see. No farmhouses within easy reach. That was good. Joe dropped down in the field and began to dig with the shovel. Digging three smaller holes was easier and faster than digging one big hole. After a while, he had managed to bury the three crates, but not before removing one hand gun with thirty rounds of ammunition. This gun could be used as it couldn't be traced back to Joe. Instead, it looked as if someone had stolen both crates of munitions and the meat, and vanished off the face of the earth with them. He stashed the stolen gun in his rucksack back in the truck. He still had the gun in his belt, the one he would have to hand back. The first part of his plan had gone smoothly.

He got back in the truck and drove on about a mile. When he was sure there were no witnesses, he grabbed the steering wheel, wrenched it hard to the right and skidded onto a large verge, braking as hard as he could. Joe got out and inspected the tyre tracks, satisfyingly deep furrows across the grass. It looked as if he had been forced off the road. This was where he would say the ambush had happened. It was far enough from where he had buried the munitions and the meat so that they wouldn't be found by any army investigators. The second part of his hastily thought-out plan had worked.

He took his rucksack, moved to the front of the truck, took out the stolen hand gun and fired it twice into the wind shield. The powerful hand gun kicked back hard as the bullets exploded from its nozzle. A portion of the glass shattered over the steering wheel and the seats, but some of the glass stayed intact. He put the stolen gun back in his rucksack. That would be useful later for when it came to tracking down Frank Tucker. He calmly walked to the middle of the road where a storm drain was positioned at the intersection. Using the axe from the back of the truck, he prised up the manhole cover, put his rucksack on the small ledge inside and closed the cover again. Putting the axe away in the back of the truck, Joe realised that he had to execute the hardest part of his plan so far. He had to injure himself to make it look as though he had been ambushed and that he had tried to defend the truck.

Joe braced himself as he put his forehead against one of the metal frames in the back of the truck. They were rigid structures that kept the tarpaulin covering taut and in position. He felt the coolness of the metal against his throbbing temple. There was no going back now.

Joe closed his eyes, pulled back his head and smashed it as hard as he could into the frame. It was surprisingly effective as it knocked him out cold.

Chapter 9

In the North Field, Martin was raking the earth, a faraway look in his eyes. The clouds were forming shapes above him, and he imagined he was piloting a Spitfire through the blueness. Fantasy Martin was dressed in flying goggles and he sported a body, caged within an RAF shirt, which was notably more muscular than Real-life Martin. Fantasy Martin had just shot down fourteen Germans and was coming home to see his girl. He snapped out of his daydreams as he saw Iris approaching. She had a determined look on her face, as if she was on a mission. What did she want? Was she angry?

"Martin! I need you to do something," she said, stomping towards him.

"Sure?" Martin replied, nonplussed.

"Do you remember the note that told you to come here yesterday?"

"The one saying the sheep were getting in?"

He nodded.

"What happened to it?"

"The note?" Martin scrunched up his eyes as he sought to remember. Iris tried to mask her impatience. She knew that obtaining the note would be proof. She was certain that the handwriting would match Evelyn's. She needed the note. And the longer Martin took to remember what happened to it, the more uneasy she felt.

"I think John put it in his pocket," Martin said finally. Iris asked him if he was sure and when he nodded, he was dismayed to see Iris instantly turn on her heels and stomp off back the way she had come. "I might be wrong!" he added. Iris didn't turn back. "Iris?" He watched her diminish into the distance.

Fantasy Martin wouldn't have lost the girl.

The penlight flickered brightly across the young man's bruised face as Dr Channing peered into the eyes of Joe Batch. Satisfied that there was no ocular damage, Channing then encouraged Joe to follow the path of the torch as he moved it from side to side. Nearby, a concerned Captain Cosallo and a sergeant watched the examination. They were in the medical hut of the American barracks. Harry knew that Dr Channing would have preferred to have treated Joe at Hoxley Manor, where he had all of his equipment, but Harry had insisted that he wanted Joe at the base. He was worried that one of the bandits might try to finish Joe off to keep him quiet, so keeping Joe secure in the base seemed the safest option.

Joe had been found by a passerby on a bicycle. He had raised the alarm and Harry had scrambled some troops to go to the scene of the crime. Harry had been shocked by what he'd seen. Joe had been recovering in the back of the truck, his head bloodied, the doors wide open and the front window smashed. It had seemed like a clinical and clean operation. Someone must have known about the transfer taking place. But Harry didn't know how.

"Did the guy see anything?" Harry whispered to his sergeant. He was referring to the passerby who'd found Joe.

"I don't think so, sir," the sergeant said, "He's in the office if you would like to question him?"

Harry nodded and started to leave. "Let me know when the doc has finished."

Channing watched as Harry left and then returned to his patient.

"You were very lucky, weren't you?"

"How do you mean, Doc? I got my head busted open."

"Bandits don't usually leave survivors. It minimises the chances of them being caught." Channing seemed as if he was being warm, friendly and conversational, but there was an intensity in his eyes that unnerved Joe. He felt as if the doctor was seeing through his whole charade. But how could that be possible? It was probably Joe's own guilt feeling that people knew what he'd done. He had to shrug it off. Anyway, it made no sense that this medic would be interrogating him.

But before Joe could say anything, Channing turned with a pair of tongs and a wet lump of cotton wool and started to dab at the wound on his head, the liquid stinging into the cut. Joe winced.

"Awfully sorry." Channing smiled.

John Fisher made a pot of tea. Joyce stood behind him in the kitchen of Shallow Brook Farm. She had sneaked away from working in the fields to have a quick cup of tea with him. John stirred the pot, before brandishing the hot spoon playfully in Joyce's direction, determined to put it on her nose. Joyce squealed with laughter and fought his hand to get the spoon away from her face.

"You rotter!" she laughed.

"Hold still, I'm sure it won't hurt! Much."

"You hold still." Joyce grabbed the teaspoon from his hand and quickly cupped the end of his nose with it.

"Ow!" John said in mock anger. "You're right, that does hurt."

He poured the tea into the green utility cups and then pulled out chairs from the kitchen table. Joyce and John were about to drink the tea when a breathless Iris ran into the room. She took a moment to catch her breath. John went to her side.

"Are you all right?" He flashed a look to his wife. Was the girl all right? Joyce joined them, but Iris indicated that she just needed a moment to get control of her breathing. A moment to calm down.

"Ran all the way," she gasped. "I need that note."

"That what?"

"She said note, I think," Joyce clarified. John looked blank. "What note?"

"The note that told you," Iris panted, "to go to the North Field."

John nodded his understanding. He moved quickly over to the safe: a small, mesh-fronted cabinet that sat on the kitchen work surface. He unlatched the safe door and took out a small bundle of papers. Joyce gave him a withering look as she noticed what they were.

"I put the bills there, that's all," he protested.

"That's just what you used to do at home." she said, "Put the bills and letters somewhere safe and forget all about them."

"Please, I need the – note," Iris gasped.

"I've not forgotten, though, have I?" John replied to Joyce. "I put the note here while we went off to the field." He thumbed his way through the letters as Iris waited expectantly. "Everything is here, kept in perfect order so that I can ..." He trailed off, a worried look appearing on his face. "That's odd."

"Lost it, have you?" Joyce smiled. "There's a surprise."

"No, it was definitely here," John said, looking again. "I remember shoving it in there as Martin and me left."

"You're sure?" Iris asked.

"You're welcome to check," John handed her the bundle of letters and paperwork. She quickly scanned through it, looking for anything that could be a note.

"So you haven't got it?" Iris said, a note of panic in her voice. John shrugged. That looked to be the case.

"Why did you want it, anyway?" Joyce questioned.

"It doesn't matter," Iris said, running out of the door. John and Joyce shared a baffled look, before sitting back down to finish their tea.

Iris ran across the yard of Shallow Brook Farm. She stopped, suddenly aware that she had nowhere to run to. The note was gone. Her only piece of proof had gone. So what had happened? Maybe Evelyn had searched the house before she left. Maybe she had found the note and taken it with her.

Iris slumped over, exhausted. A bad night's sleep in an armchair in a stifling hot shed and the emotional drain of her current predicament were taking their toll. She clasped her knees as she fought to control her breathing. There didn't seem to be any solution. No options were left. It looked as if she was going to the fens and the joys of East Anglia. But still, she couldn't give up. Not without a fight.

Iris knew there was only one thing left that she could try. She had to confront Evelyn. And this time, Iris would be ready for her. She set off, determined.

The girl stumbled, catching her knee on the cobbles. It stung and even before she looked, she knew she'd ruined her Sunday-best long-socks and cut her knee open. She didn't have time to look. Bravely she hauled herself to her feet and carried on running.

Harry Cosallo moved through to the office. In reality, it was simply a partitioned area within the metal hangar that housed the medical unit. Waiting at the desk was Henry Jameson, a tweedy young man with a panama hat. As Harry sat opposite, he noticed for the first time that the man was wearing a white band around his neck. A dog collar. So he was a vicar.

"Hey, padre," Harry said, offering his hand.

"I'm a vicar, a reverend, actually," Henry Jameson stammered. "Is there any reason you needed me to stay, Captain?"

"I just wondered if you saw anything at all. You might not have seen the actual hold-up, but maybe you saw some men hanging around earlier?"

Henry shook his head, frowning slightly at the thought.

"Anything you can tell us would help," Harry pleaded.

"I really didn't see anything. I was on my way back from visiting a sick parishioner and just saw the truck on the verge."

"And it was stationary?"

"Yes, pitched round at a crazy sort of angle."

"As if it had been stopped in a hurry?"

The reverend pondered for the briefest moment before nodding.

"So the attack had happened before you got there?"

"Yes," Henry said, a little annoyance in his voice. Harry knew he'd been over all of this with the sergeant, but it always paid to check every detail.

"How long ago do you think it happened?"

"How would I know?"

"Was there any smoke from car engines? The smell of gunpowder in the air to indicate a handgun had recently been fired? Was the engine of the army truck warm?"

"I really didn't think to touch it," Henry said, shaking his head.

"Well, okay, but if you think of anything, Reverend –" Harry enjoyed trying the word out for size, "– You be sure to let me know. We need to catch these crooks."

Henry stood up, tipped his hat and left the room. Harry followed him out, pointing out the way to leave the building. When the young reverend had gone, Harry returned to the treatment room, where Channing was putting the finishing touches to the plaster on Joe's head.

"How is he, Doc?" Harry asked.

"He'll live," Channing said, putting the tape and bandages back into his medical bag. Harry turned to Joe and smiled.

"Will you go back to your dormitory, Private? I'll finish up here and come see you."

Joe hoisted himself off the medical bed, offered a stiff salute and left the room. Harry waited for a moment and then turned to Channing, who was checking his pen torch as he put it away.

"How is his mental state?"

Channing didn't miss a beat before replying, "Hard to say. He seems upbeat and pretty positive."

"It's just he lost a lot of buddies the other day, another buddy topped himself and now he's been held up and beaten," Harry said, shaking his head at all the kid had had to bear. "It's got to take its toll, right?"

"You know as well as I do that trauma affects people in different ways. For now, he's coping. I'd take things easy with him and see what happens. If he has any issues in the next few weeks, let me know. I can recommend some people he could talk to."

"Thanks, Doc."

Channing clipped his medical bag shut, slipped on his greatcoat and trilby hat and went to leave. But he paused at the door and turned to Harry. "I'd just say one thing."

"What?"

"That the attack seems unusual. We haven't had any terrorist activity since the bomb that derailed the train on the way from Brinford. So this lot might be novices. They might make a mistake."

"Thank you, Doctor," Harry said. "I'll bear that in mind."

Channing tipped his hat and left the medical room. Harry pondered the details of what had happened. Maybe he should increase the number of patrols his men did of the local area? Maybe they should hunt these men down? The trouble was that Joe hadn't seen their faces. He just described three men of average height, dressed in balaclavas. Harry thought about what Channing had said. He wondered if they were novices. These people might make a mistake. But it worried him that two boxes of US munitions were out there somewhere, and that they were potentially in enemy hands.

Where was Evelyn?

That was the question that filled Iris's thoughts as she marched from Shallow Brook Farm to Helmstead, the skies starting to darken overhead. She knew that Evelyn would be working and that her job involved being a courier. Esther had commented once that Evelyn would drive around, sometimes taking parcels, sometimes people, from place to place. Employed by the War Office, she had a petrol ration for her work. But Iris needed to know her schedule. She needed to know where to find her. Iris knew she would be in even more trouble for marching off from work, but she hoped that Shelley would cover for her, at least for an hour or so. And anyway, what did she really have to lose?

Near the vicarage, Reverend Henry Jameson was talking to a gaggle of old women. They were fawning over the young man, hanging on his every word as if he was Gary Cooper. She recognised Mrs Gulliver in the group, but not the others.

Iris moved towards them and could hear Henry quoting something from the Bible. She decided that she didn't have time to worry about being polite. Time was against her. She had to prove to Finch and Esther what was going on before tomorrow afternoon. Before she got sent away.

"Excuse me, Reverend?" Iris piped up.

The coterie of old woman turned their heads as one to see who this interloper was. Several of them poked their noses up into the air, perhaps worried that Iris would snatch Henry's attention away from them.

"I need to find Evelyn Gray," Iris said. "Would you know where she is?"

"I'm sorry, Iris, no." The reverend shook his head.

Iris was about to walk away when a voice stopped her. It was Mrs Gulliver. "Well, I know where she will be."

"Really?"

"I knows her schedule, see."

The other old women looked impressed with this bit of news. Henry shrugged in a well-there-you-go kind of way. Mrs Gulliver knew so much about the comings and goings in the town. She really was like the local oracle.

Something about what Mrs Gulliver had just said was troubling, but Iris didn't have time to make the connection. Feeling exhausted and stressed meant that she wasn't thinking straight. Wasn't seeing the thing that was in plain sight.

"Yesterday she did runs from different villages around the area. Today she usually does runs between Brinford and Helmstead. But sometimes she mixes the routes and the timings so that no one can predict where she'll be exactly."

"So where is she today?" Iris insisted.

"Why do you want her?"

Iris should have known that she'd have to trade information to get anything back from Mrs Gulliver. Her mother had always told her to tell the truth. But Mrs Gulliver would probably explode if Iris started babbling about photographs and notes and being attacked by Evelyn, so she decided to lie. "Finch has a message for her."

"What's the message?" Mrs Gulliver asked, with no hint of embarrassment.

"It's rather personal," Iris said, wondering how long this stand-off would last and who would break first. Luckily help was on hand and stacked in her favour.

"With all due respect, I don't think the contents of the message is our concern, Mrs Gulliver," Henry interjected. Mrs Gulliver pulled a face. Iris assumed she thought it was a matter of opinion and in the public interest to know, but Mrs Gulliver backed down. Henry's words carried some sway.

Iris was wondering how Mrs Gulliver had got so close to Evelyn as to know some of her schedule. Then the answer hit her, almost taking her breath away. If you wanted to learn about Finch or anyone else in the town, who better to befriend than the town busybody? But of course, to learn from such a person, you would have to trade some information, as Iris had just discovered. So Evelyn must have used Mrs Gulliver to find out all the information she needed, cosying up to her by pretending to be her friend.

Mrs Gulliver accepted Henry's comment, but still milked the moment before revealing what Evelyn was doing. Iris guessed she saw it as privileged information that stood Mrs Gulliver head and shoulders above the other gossips in Helmstead, so she was going to play to the gallery. When she was sure that all the old women in the group were hanging on her next words, Mrs Gulliver decided to speak.

"All right," she said. "In about ten minutes, she will be picking up some parts for a printing press from the office of *The Helmstead Herald* and delivering them to –"

But Iris was already running off. She raced across the town square and past the Bottle and Glass. In the distance she could see a small car parked by the bridge where the newspaper office was. A woman dressed in an expensive dark-blue coat and hat was peeling off her driving gloves and making her way into the building. It was Evelyn. Iris ran over and crouched down on the other side of the car so that she couldn't be seen. In the newspaper office, Evelyn was talking to the rotund figure of Roger Curran, Editor in Chief, photographer and the only reporter on the local newspaper. It was his job to cover everything that was newsworthy in the town of Helmstead and the surrounding areas. Iris watched as he packaged up a round cylinder into some sheets of newspaper. She guessed that the cylinder was a part of the printing press. She wondered how best to confront Evelyn. She wanted her to give her the note that had told John and Martin to go to the North Field. Iris didn't have any real idea how she was going to make that happen. But she knew her chances of convincing Evelyn were even slimmer when Evelyn had the easy means of escaping in a car. Inside the office, Roger Curran packaged up a few more items and smiled at Evelyn Gray.

Then with three metal cylinders and some cogs safely wrapped in newspaper, Evelyn put them in her wicker basket, bid him good day and left the shop.

Evelyn got into the Riley Nine and placed the basket on the passenger seat. She unclipped some reading spectacles and checked where she had to go. Satisfied, she put them away and started the engine. As Evelyn went to put the car into gear, Iris reached from the back seat, where she'd been hiding, and clamped her hand over Evelyn's. Evelyn gasped, but didn't scream. She turned slowly to see Iris crouched in the foot well of the back seat.

"Just drive off, normally," Iris whispered. Evelyn wasn't going to be intimidated. She gave a wry smile, as if to say she was merely indulging the whims of this foolish girl and drove off over the bridge. Iris shifted uncomfortably in the foot well of Evelyn's car. The seats were cream-coloured leather and the steering wheel was unusually large. The vehicle smelled of damp and mould, as if it had been stored in a wet garage for some years. When they had driven out of sight of the newspaper offices, Evelyn glanced round.

"Are you kidnapping me?"

"Drive around the corner and stop."

"Very dramatic. If you insist," Evelyn replied. She drove another twenty yards and pulled over. Iris glanced over her shoulder. She could see the edge of the small parade of shops in which the newspaper office sat, but there were no windows from this side, so they couldn't be seen. And the angle of the road meant that they were probably out of range of the eagle eyes of Mrs Gulliver and the gossips by the church too.

Iris plucked the keys out of the ignition, opened the door and ran round to the passenger side of the car. She squeezed in alongside Evelyn, putting the basket on the back seat. She turned to face Evelyn, giving her the keys back.

Evelyn calmly started the car.

"Why are you here? I thought you should be in East Anglia by now."

"I've got until tomorrow. But you're going to come clean and tell everyone you were in Shallow Brook Farm and that you hit me and that you're up to something!"

"I don't know what you're talking about." Evelyn smiled coldly.

"I thought you were just after Finch's money. But it's something else, isn't it? Something to do with Vernon."

"Is it really?"

"You latched onto Finch so he could get you close to Shallow Brook Farm. You befriended Mrs Gulliver so you could learn all about him and the farm, didn't you?"

"You really do have the most overactive imagination."

"You set all this up, didn't you?"

"I met Fred by accident, don't be silly. We met at Lady Hoxley's Agricultural Show. Fred was wrestling with a large pig."

Iris struggled to process these facts. She knew that that was what had happened. But if it was a coincidental meeting, how could it have been planned?

Then, Iris started to see clearly what had been nudging at her mind when she had been talking to Mrs Gulliver. The old woman had known Evelyn's schedule; she was a sort-of-friend of Evelyn. Yes, but she'd worked that out already. Think, Iris! There was something else. The friendship. When did it start? Yes, that was it! Of course!

The friendship had started on the night of that dance in aid of the Spitfire Fund, weeks ago! The dance where the fight between the GIs broke out and Iris had first met Joe Batch.

'Chattanooga Choo Choo' had been playing.

And Evelyn had made a beeline for Frederick Finch, who was holding two pints. She had pulled herself up to her full height and plumped her hair. Iris had seen her move across the dance floor. But when she was a mere foot away from Finch, the fight broke out and the moment was lost. Evelyn had turned away and walked off.

"You didn't meet by accident," Iris insisted. "You planned to meet him at the dance a couple of weeks before, but it didn't happen. So later, when you saw him at the Agricultural Show, you already knew who he was from Mrs Gulliver. So then it seemed like a coincidence."

"Impressive theory." Evelyn bristled and Iris wondered if she'd hit the nail on the head.

"It's right, though, isn't it?"

"Yes, it is." Evelyn stated flatly. "Happy now?"

Happiness wasn't the first emotion that came to Iris's mind. Instead she felt a cold tingle of fear playing on the back of her neck. Her mother said that this was what it felt like when someone walked over your grave. She had never really appreciated what it felt like until now.

"Look, I don't know what your plan is. You used Finch to

get close to Shallow Brook Farm, so you could get those papers and the photograph from the tin under the bed."

"Yes. Go on. And what then?"

"But why?"

"I'm not going to tell you." Evelyn laughed. "A clever girl like you should be able to work it out. And I think if you had more time you probably would. So it's such a shame you won't be here after tomorrow, isn't it?"

That was true. She was getting nowhere fast, so Iris decided that it was time to talk bluntly. There was only really one thing Iris was interested in.

"I want that note. The one you wrote to John and Martin. You've got what you came for, haven't you?"

"The tin of old documents and letters?" Evelyn snorted. "I suppose I have."

"Just give me the note and I don't have to go away. Then we'd both have what we want."

"So I go off and you live happily ever after? Well, it's a nice idea but it rarely works in practice." Evelyn looked troubled, but Iris had no idea what she was thinking. "If I gave you the note, I'd incriminate myself, wouldn't I? And why would I do that?"

"Because you've got the tin, you've got what you came for. Let me have the note, so then I can stay in Helmstead. Please."

Iris looked with pleading eyes. Suddenly her bravado had vanished and she was a nervous, awkward 17-year-old again. A young woman scared of being sent away. Evelyn exhaled heavily, looking straight ahead. Her breath steamed up the windscreen. Then, she turned to Iris. "If I give you the note, it'll break Fred's heart because he'll know what you said was true. And yet, as you say, I got what I came for, so there's little need to maintain the charade. However, I really need to have easy access to Shallow Brook Farm for a bit longer, so I'm loath to burn all my bridges. Sorry."

A thought burst into Iris's head. Why would Evelyn still need easy access to the farm? She'd got the tin. She'd got what she came for, hadn't she? No, it was because she didn't have everything that she had come for. The map! The map had been left behind.

"You need the map," Iris stated.

"You've got that?" Evelyn seemed visibly relieved. "I wondered ..."

"I'll give it to you, if you give me the note."

There it was – an easy and straightforward deal to give them both what they wanted.

For the first time, Evelyn's composure faded and she looked angrily at the young woman next to her. Iris enjoyed this shift in the power dynamic between them. She had something to bargain with, something that Evelyn desperately wanted. The big question was whether Evelyn wanted the map as much as Iris wanted to stay in Helmstead. Evelyn mulled over this proposal. There was no easy answer and it took nearly a minute before she spoke again.

"Prove that you've got the map", She said.

"No," Iris replied. "Otherwise you'll take it off me."

Evelyn nodded slowly. "The thing is, I don't really want to hurt Fred. Not yet. Not until I'm farther away. There are too many loose ends at the moment. And if I give you the note, then I'd have to move really fast."

"But you'd have the map," Iris countered, knowing that her offer was intriguing the older woman.

"Tempting," Evelyn said, before smiling again. The cracks in her composure were covered up again by an icy veneer as she came up with an alternative proposal. "Here's an idea. You give me the map, and I talk to Fred and get him to send you somewhere nearer. There is a farm some eight miles from here."

Iris went to protest, but Evelyn continued, "I talk to Fred and say that I think you should just go away for a few weeks and then you can come back and resume your life on the farm. By the time you're back, I'll have gone. And perhaps that will be the happy ending."

Now it was Iris's turn to mull things over. She guessed that Evelyn would have that sort of sway over Finch. She could get him to do whatever he wanted. But this new deal made her uneasy. Irrespective of the fact that she felt she couldn't trust Evelyn, Iris didn't like the idea of not being able to prove her innocence. Yes, she may be shipped to a nearby farm for a few weeks, but everyone would still think she had imagined all the things with Evelyn. She couldn't live with that hanging over her.

"No deal," Iris said. She fumbled for the door handle as she added, "The note for the map. You've got until the end of the week, otherwise I'll take it with me." Iris got out of the car and walked back towards Helmstead. She was confident that Evelyn would cave in and accept the offer, half-hoping that Evelyn would call her back right now. But she didn't.

Evelyn watched her go, gripping the steering wheel in frustration.

Later that evening as the sky darkened from grey to black, a smart black car pulled up on the other side of the lane where Joe had been found in his truck. Dr Richard Channing got out, pulled his trilby down tightly on his head and walked purposefully across to the verge. He gave a cursory glance at the deep tyre tracks in the grass and mud, and then moved to where the back of the truck would have been. He looked closely at the grassy area between the twin tyre furrows. He moved the grass with his fingers. It wasn't worn down or trampled, at least not in the way he'd have expected if the truck had been emptied of its contents. With men jumping out of the back of the truck with heavy boxes, he thought he'd see scuff marks, churned earth, flattened grass. But it was pristine. Almost as if the attackers had emptied it without going over the grass.

"Walking on air," Channing mused, with a smile. He wondered why the army investigators hadn't spotted it. But then he guessed they would have been more interested in the damage to the truck and the search for the missing armaments.

He glanced around for any other clues, but returned his gaze to the grass between the tracks. No footprints, no crushed blades of grass.

"How could they have unloaded it?" Channing muttered to himself. He'd hoped that if he was right about them being amateurs, then maybe there might be signs of their haul, perhaps a discarded ammunition box or a dropped packet of rounds. Anything that he might be able to examine to get information on the perpetrators. But the untrampled grass was confusing things. Maybe they weren't amateurs? Maybe they had lifting equipment that they kept on the road?

Channing shook his head. Any lifting equipment wouldn't reach that far. And besides, it would attract attention in getting it here or in setting it up.

Aware that he couldn't stay for too long without attracting attention himself, he walked to the hedgerow and peered over. There wasn't any sign of the discarded boxes. He walked back towards his car, walking over the storm drain in the road, little realising that Joe Batch's rucksack was hidden a few feet beneath with a stolen hand gun inside. Dr Channing got back into his car and looked at the patch of earth where the truck had been. He wasn't going to solve this puzzle tonight. He put his car into gear and set off down the country lane, back towards Helmstead and Hoxley Manor.

Chapter 10

The next day, Private First Class Joe Batch woke early. He was still under observation in the medical wing of the barracks. The first face he saw was that of Captain Harry Cosallo sitting by his bedside and reading some reports.

"How you doing?"

"Okay, thank you, sir." Joe sat up in bed. The cut on his forehead felt taut and itchy under its dressing. It must be healing, Joe thought, idly.

"I need to know everything about the men who ambushed you." Harry said.

"Okay," Joe said, pushing himself up to a sitting position.

"What accents did they have? Did you recognise their accents? I mean they must have spoken, right?"

Was Harry suspicious? Did he not believe the story? Joe knew he had to tread carefully. He had to close down any possible suspicions. But then, part of him thought the officer might just be 'box ticking': asking questions so he could fill the report, when they both knew the truth. After all, Harry had sanctioned what he'd done, right? But until he knew that for certain, he had to play safe; he had to walk the line and say what was expected. Say what they both wanted to hear.

"They didn't speak much." Joe spoke slowly, wondering if he'd mentioned if the men had spoken or been silent before. He couldn't remember, so he hoped that saying this covered him both ways. "Irish accents!" he exclaimed, as if remembering this key fact.

"Irish?" Harry leaned forward on his seat. Some Irish nationals, keen to unify their country, had been involved in Hitler's war. But ambushing an American Army truck seemed a bold and risky move, beyond what they had previously attempted. "I'll have to inform the British War Office. They might have more questions."

Joe nodded, inwardly pleased that doubt seemed to have been replaced by enthusiasm on Harry Cosallo's part. But then he guessed that any bone he threw would be caught by the Captain. Joe suspected that Harry wanted him to complete his mission in getting a confession from Tucker about the Panmere Lake attack. They both knew that, even if Cosallo wasn't saying it. The captain rose from his chair with Joe guessing that he was going off to make a phone call to the War Office.

"Sir?"

Harry turned at the door.

"Permission to go off base and see my girl, sir?"

"Granted," Harry replied, leaving the room. Joe swung his legs off the bed. But he had no intention of seeing Iris. She wasn't even his girl, but Cosallo didn't know that. He was going to see Frank Tucker. Cosallo had probably guessed, but like everything he was doing, he seemed to sanction it even if he didn't say it outright.

Joe stopped by the mechanic's shop and lifted a small crowbar from one of the soldier's toolkits. He'd need that to lift the manhole cover to retrieve his hidden rucksack containing the gun. He left the base and walked the same route he had driven in the truck. When he reached the cross-roads with the tyre tracks in the grass, he checked that the coast was clear. Then he crossed to the manhole cover in the middle of the road and lifted it with the crowbar. He removed his rucksack from inside, briefly checked that the handgun and ammunition were still there and slipped it onto his back. As he went to replace the manhole cover, he contemplated throwing the crowbar into the sewer, but then realised that it might be a valuable additional weapon. He slid it into his rucksack, kicked the manhole cover shut with his foot and set off back to Helmstead, a man on a mission.

Iris ducked under a branch and looked into the trees. She could make out Frank in the distance. He'd finished fixing the feeding trough in the fields and was checking traps in the forest that bordered Hoxley Manor. She crouched down and squeezed through the foliage. It didn't take long for Frank to look up and spot her crashing through the undergrowth towards him.

"Blimey, it's a good job I'm not trying to catch a rabbit." Frank laughed.

"Sorry, Frank." Iris batted a bramble away from her face as she emerged into the clearing.

"What are you doing out here?"

"We've got a problem with the tractor."

"That old relic," Frank said, sighing in frustration. "Come on, then, let's finish here and then go and take a look. Help me with these, could you?"

He handed Iris a couple of empty, closed traps. She collected them up and started to follow him towards a small outbuilding located in the trees. The red-brick structure was the size of a small bedroom, complete with a pointed roof. From a distance, Iris always thought it looked like a cottage in the forest. In reality it was used for storage. Frank opened the door and took the traps from Iris, placing them inside. He noticed that she had a small smile playing on her face.

"Why are you smiling? Has Esther changed her mind about sending you away?"

"No," Iris said. "But she will."

"You sound very confident, Miss Dawson."

"I am."

"Do you want to tell me why?" Frank hung the traps on hooks along the inside wall. "I mean, I hope you do stay. In fact, I even tried to talk Fred round, but he wasn't having it."

"No, I'm confident because Evelyn is going to come to her senses."

Frank went to argue, so Iris revealed the reason she believed everything would be all right.

"She needs the map. So to get it, she'll give me the note that sent John and Martin on a wild goose chase. And with that note, it proves that she wanted to get them away so she could get into Shallow Brook Farm." It all seemed straightforward when she said it like that.

Frank locked the door of the outbuilding and pocketed the key. "I hope you're right. But I can't see her messing things up with Fred on your account."

"Don't you see? Marrying Finch isn't her goal. Her goal was getting the map."

Frank winced as he contemplated Iris's words and worked out the logic of what she was saying. "I suppose it could work and you could stay and –"

He trailed off, the words unfinished. Iris noticed that he was looking past her, his mouth agape. Slowly, Iris turned around to see what had stopped him in his tracks.

Joe stood a few feet away, dressed in his uniform with a bandage on his head and his rucksack on his back. He was staring intently at Frank Tucker as if Iris didn't exist. In his hand was a gun. He had it pointed straight at the gamekeeper, sunlight bouncing off its barrel.

"Joe?" she said, confused. "What are you doing?"

Joe ignored her.

"It's time to confess," Joe growled.

A crow cawed loudly in a nearby tree as the gamekeeper raised his hands in the air. Iris noticed that he was watching Joe keenly, perhaps trying to pre-empt his every movement and the likelihood of him shooting the gun. Joe glanced towards Iris, seeming to notice her for the first time. His nose wrinkled in irritation as if to say, what was she doing here? Iris noticed that Frank was motionless, biding his time, knowing it was safer to let Joe make the next move.

"What are you doing here, Iris?" Joe barked, his voice sounded wounded and upset, as if her presence had personally betrayed him. "You shouldn't be here!"

"Nor should you, son," Frank ventured, testing the water.

Joe flashed an angry look, turning his full attention back to Frank. Joe slid the rucksack off his shoulder to free up his shooting arm. Iris watched as the rucksack fell to near Joe's feet. It made a dull metallic thud as it hit the forest floor. Whatever was inside, it was heavy. Knowing she had to help Frank, Iris wondered if it held something that might be useful as a potential weapon.

"Why are you here, son?" Frank continued.

"Shut up, traitor!" Joe shouted.

He indicated for Frank to get down on his knees. Frank stayed where he was, his hands raised in surrender.

"Think about what you're doing," Iris shouted.

"I am thinking!" Joe said. "Get down on the ground. Now!"

"We can talk about this. Rationally, like adults," Frank said.

"Down. Now. Or I'll blow your head off where you stand!"

Frank glanced with concern at Iris, and slowly did as he was instructed. He went down on his knees and Iris could hear his joints click. Then, she glimpsed the water on the ground as it blotted into the knees of his trousers. Was this how it would end for him? She couldn't let that happen.

"You were in the square," Joe growled. "You heard me talk about Panmere!"

"Yes."

"You admit it?"

"But I can't have been the only one who heard you!"

Iris piped up. "You were telling me! Why couldn't I be the spy, eh? I heard it too. That could make me the spy, couldn't it?"

Joe looked confused. For the first time, he trained the gun on Iris.

"No, Iris, don't," Frank warned.

Joe winced as he took this in. She realised that he was struggling to process the possibility. Yes, she had been the one he'd told, but he'd been so convinced that Frank was the traitor, he'd glossed over that. Was he now really thinking she could be the traitor? Could Iris be a spy?

But Iris watched as the gun went back to Frank.

She guessed it suited him to focus on Frank. Frank had been lurking in the shadows when he was speaking. Frank could have all sorts of unpatriotic political views. Even if they weren't outright fascists, there were British people who saw merit in the Nazi ideas of improving the economy through employing business leaders to government. What if Frank yearned for a different type of control for Britain, a way of making it prosperous again?

"You were there, man! I saw you there," Joe said, seemingly convinced.

"But you might have mentioned it another time. To someone else." Frank was losing his cool, losing his control. Iris knew that there was no denying that he was feeling slightly worried now. If he couldn't talk his way out of this, was he convinced that Joe would kill him? Iris knew that they were too far from the farm for anyone to come to their rescue, too far for them to run for help, even if they could get away. Iris wished that

Frank had been out vermin-hunting because at least he would have had his shotgun nearby. And that would have given him a fighting chance. But as it was there was nothing that she could think of to end this dreadful confrontation. As she tried to clear her head, she listened as Frank tried to reason with Joe, stalling for time.

"You're upset, son. Upset because of how many of your men were killed."

"Don't tell me how I feel. You hear me?"

"I'm not. Just saying I can appreciate what you're going through. We've all lost people in this war."

"Yes, we're all on the same side!" Iris shouted, her throat feeling raw.

"Admit what you did," Joe said, lowering his voice. Now he wasn't shouting, it felt less of a threat and more of a confessional. It felt worse. Iris knew that things would end soon, unless she thought of something. But what could she do? She took a step forward, her face showing panic and anxiety, tears keen to well up in her eyes.

"Please, Joe ..."

"Stay back," Joe said, waving the gun in her direction. Iris took a hasty step backwards. Satisfied that she was no threat, Joe brought the gun round again to train on Frank, who was looking up at him, one eye still swollen from their fight the other night. Frank shrugged and sighed, and Iris saw him wilt as if something had died inside him. It was the dreadful acceptance that this was the day he would be killed, after all the battles he'd endured, all the times he'd lived through. So many lives. Iris saw him dropping his hands to the ground, where his hands scrunched a handful of leaves up in frustration. Joe pressed the barrel of the gun against Frank's forehead.

"Frank is a good man," Iris stammered, her voice higher than usual, tremulous and scared. "He's a good man. Please, he's a good man."

As arguments went, it wasn't the most persuasive, but Frank smiled his appreciation at her. Thanks for trying. She'd given him a nice send-off if nothing else. "If you do this, you let her go. You hear? She had nothing to do with this."

"It's you I want."

Frank nodded, with grim finality. He turned back to his executioner and looked him in the eye. Joe looked calm, controlled and confident. She thought that Frank would have had more hope of escaping with his life if Joe had been nervous, or angry. But Joe had obviously thought about this a great deal. Iris assumed he thought he was doing the right thing and that there was no doubt in his mind.

She had to say something else. She had to try.

"Shooting him will make you feel better, about those men who died. Your mates." She spoke slowly, deliberately, but in barely more than a hushed whisper. "It'll help you get over that. But it won't last long, because the real collaborator, the real person who told the Germans, he's still out there, isn't he? And sooner or later, he'll betray you again. Because someone else must have known." Iris paused, trying to think of how to sum up her thoughts. And then it came to her. "When that happens, you'll realise that what you did today didn't need to be done. That gamekeeper didn't need to die." Her voice cracked with the last few words.

Joe didn't acknowledge the words with anything more than a single blink of his eyes. He unlocked the safety catch on the gun and pushed the barrel harder against Frank's head.

"Thanks for trying," Frank whispered to Iris, his eyes wet with tears.

"Confess," Joe hissed.

"I can't."

"Okay ..." Joe straightened his arm and his finger went to press down on the trigger. Iris knew that words had had no effect, so she did the one thing she could do under the circumstances. She launched herself at him. Seeing her coming, instinctively, Joe took a step away, pushing himself off balance as the gun fired. The flash of flame and the bullet flew inches past Frank's ear, the bang deafening him. Joe arched his body back as Iris threw herself towards him, knocking her around the face with the gun barrel. She crashed to the forest floor, but not before she'd managed to grab the rucksack.

Joe arched his body back towards Frank, but he was hopelessly off balance. Frank saw him coming, even though he couldn't really hear him. Iris fumbled inside the rucksack, hoping that it would be some kind of weapon. To her bemused delight, she found the crowbar.

Joe's back was facing her as he levelled the gun at Frank. From the ground behind him, Iris gripped the crowbar and brought it up as hard as she could into Joe's groin. Crump! The American doubled over in pain and fell into a gasping heap. He retched on the ground, twisting in agony, spittle falling from his gaping mouth.

Frank staggered over to Iris. His world was a fuzzy, distorted haze as a monotonous high-pitched whine filled his ears. He couldn't hear himself ask Iris if she all right. It sounded like a muffled, distant radio, but he hoped the words sounded like he intended. He could hear the noise as he tried to shake her awake. He couldn't hear the noise of Joe slowly recovering. Iris looked alarmed and Frank realised that she was looking behind him. Frank turned round and punched Joe as hard as he could in the face. Joe's nose shattered and blood sprayed across his face as he went down again.

Frank took Iris's hand and told her to run. She bolted from the clearing. Frank checked that Joe wouldn't immediately follow. The American was clutching his nose and whimpering on the ground so Frank staggered off after Iris.

"We've got to get out of here!" he shouted.

The two of them ran breathlessly through the trees, with Frank glancing back from time to time to see if they were being followed. After a few minutes, he couldn't see anyone, so they kept on running, crashing through branches and thorns in a desperate attempt to get away. Fragments of sound started to return to Frank's ears. He could hear the muffled sound of the undergrowth being trampled, the distorted sound of his breathing, all through thick cotton wool. As he passed a large silver birch, Frank stopped behind it, swinging Iris round so that both of them were obscured by its thick trunk.

"Is he following?" Iris asked. By the way he screwed up his face to concentrate on her words, she assumed his hearing had been affected by the gunshot. After a moment's delay, Frank shrugged. "I don't think so," he said.

"We must have lost him," she panted. "If he was even following."

"You gave him quite a whack in the crown jewels!" Frank laughed, his voice sounding nearly normal again.

"We have to get to the police. They'll know what to do."

"Yeah, but there are a good few miles of fields and forest between us and the police station." Frank said.

"Not to mention a soldier with a gun," Iris added. "I guess we have to keep going."

"Come on, then." Frank said, moving away.

But suddenly, a bullet smashed into the trunk, sending some of the silver bark flying away in the explosion. Frank and Iris darted off deeper into the trees as another shot rang past them. Joe must be close! They knew that they had to keep running, running for their lives. They burst through some undergrowth, the brambles trying to snag them, and tumbled down an incline in a clearing. Iris scrambled to her feet and helped Frank to his, then they ran across the mud to reach the next clump of tree cover.

They raced along a ridge and Iris glanced to her left. She could see a building in the far distance. "Hoxley Manor is across the road up ahead. If we can get there ..." Frank said.

"The soldiers will help us?" Iris said, not quite believing that finding more soldiers was the answer to their prayers. What if they all wanted to kill Frank? But Frank seemed to think it was a good idea and he was already thundering on through the trees. And as she didn't have a better idea, Iris decided to keep following. The two of them raced into a dip in the forest as the trees began to thin, the canopies of leaves allowing more sun to reach the heathers on the ground. In the distance, Frank could see the driveway of Hoxley Manor. There was a US Army truck parked up, with some soldiers smoking around it. They were too far away to help. Iris knew they had to get out of the woods and cross the road before the soldiers had a hope of hearing their shouts for help.

Frank stumbled on a tree root and Iris hauled him to his feet. He winced as she continued running, but Iris smiled encouragingly. It was only a little further. Come on. They could do this.

Another shot zinged out, hitting a tree to her right. She risked a look behind him, but she couldn't see their pursuer. Quickly Iris tried to calculate where Joe must be, but she couldn't. She urged Frank to cut to his left, aware that it might be a quicker route through the foliage. They couldn't afford to attempt a route that was blocked with too many trees and bushes. It would slow them down and allow Joe to gain on them. Iris crashed through the bushes and heathers, taking a route that would get them to the road quicker than if they had stayed on their original course. Frank was struggling, so she slowed down to help him.

"Put your arm around my shoulder," Iris shouted. Frank hesitated, unsure as to whether she could shoulder his weight, but Iris just scooped her hand under one of his arms and heaved him along. Flashing a grateful smile, Frank placed his arm over her shoulder so that Iris could help him take the weight off his ankle. They struggled down the embankment, slightly heartened that they hadn't been shot at for a couple of minutes. Frank could see the road ahead, just another few yards to go. Iris was very tired, but this sight spurred her on. The section of road ahead was near a blind bend, but she knew that around it was the sanctuary of Hoxley Manor. Their salvation.

Iris adjusted her grip on Frank's arm to get a better purchase. The incline was steeper than before, so the problem now was not to lose control and tumble down the hillside. They passed the last two silver birch trees lining the descent and reached the edge of the road. Iris was almost giddy with relief. The concrete of the road was mere feet away.

But then the figure of Joe Batch stepped out from behind the last tree, standing on the road and blocking their path. His nose was a bloodied mess, his hair was slick with sweat and dirt, and his uniform was torn at the lapel. He was breathing heavily, but a smile of satisfaction filled his face. Iris realised with grim finality that this was what he was trained for. He raised his gun.

"Wait, Joe," Iris pleaded, putting her body in front of Frank's.

"Get out of the way!" Joe shouted.

Iris stayed still, blocking Joe's aim. She wasn't going to let this happen. If Joe wanted to kill Frank, he'd have to have her blood on his hands too. She stared into Joe's deranged eyes and wondered how he could be so damaged and deluded. He looked back with glassy eyes, his feet moving rhythmically up and down on the tarmac of the road, agitated. It was a stand-off.

But then Frank hobbled to the side, sighing. He glanced at Iris and shook his head.

"What are you doing?"

"I can't let you take a bullet for me." Frank said, his voice trembling. "Go on then, son."

Iris was distraught. She watched as Joe clicked back the safety catch on his gun.

Frank closed his eyes.

Joe took a step back onto the road to get a straighter aim at Frank. He levelled the gun at Frank's face.

"Say goodbye, you Nazi trait–"

The words were curtailed with a loud bang, too loud to be a gun, as time slowed down. Iris knew something else had happened, but her mind struggled to process what she was seeing. She saw a lorry, laden with munitions skidding across the road. She realised it had just turned the blind bend from Hoxley Manor and smashed into Joe Batch, sweeping him aside as if he was a rag doll. Even as it braked sharply and careered across the road, Iris knew that Joe Batch must have been killed instantly. Her senses came rushing back to her as she heard the noise of the squealing brakes, the tyres ripping into the tarmac, the rumble as its engine stalled mid-skid.

Was Joe dead? He must be, surely.

But she had to check, so she ran to the road, her senses assailed by the smell of petrol, tyre rubber and smoke from the road surface. The lorry had jack-knifed across the narrow road and the dazed driver and his wingman were clambering out of the cab. Iris couldn't see the front of the cab, but she could see that the windscreen was smeared with blood. As she reached the passenger door, she could see a hand poking around from the front of the lorry, laid across the tarmac. She walked slowly, numbly, round. The hand was still gripping the gun and Joe was twitching on the ground. He clenched his teeth and grimaced, his face a bloodied mask. There was one more spasm and then he was still.

The driver and his wingman bent down to their fallen comrade, as Iris shuffled slowly back to Frank.

"Hey, miss!" the driver shouted, but Iris was dazed and ignored him.

She had to check on Frank. His face was ashen and his fingers were shaking. They looked at one another, amazed at what had just happened and shocked to their cores. Slowly it dawned on them that the ordeal was over.

Shish, shish, shish.

It sounded like the rhythmic beat of a drum brush, relaxing and hypnotic in its own strange way. As she sat in her chair, Iris rested her head against the thin wall so she could hear the steady marching of the American soldiers on the parade ground outside. The sound of a multitude of boots stepping in unison had calmed her. And while she had hoped the ordeal was finally over, she knew that it wasn't quite finished. She was waiting in a corridor at the American barracks, while Frank was being questioned in another room. She had already been interviewed by Captain Cosallo and Major Warrender, a special investigator for the US military. They wanted to know everything that had happened and Iris knew that they would question her again after Frank, as he'd already been in twice. They'd told her that Frank had recounted his list of confrontations with Joe, from the earliest one outside the village hall to the fracas at Hoxley Manor to the beating outside the pub to the desperate chase through the woods. Iris recounted her times with Joe and how he had turned on her outside the film screening. Harry Cosallo had commented that Joe certainly seemed prone to changeable and dangerous behaviour.

"Did Frank have a beef with Joe?" Harry asked, his crumpled face looking weary.

"No," Iris replied. "If anything, it was the other way round. Joe got all sort of fixated on Frank. See, he was sure Frank was the one who betrayed you lot to the Germans at Panmere."

Cosallo and Warrender shared a look. The Major made a note in his folder. Iris couldn't see what it said.

Later, Cosallo and Warrender questioned Frank for a third time. He was getting tired and irritable with all this rigmarole, but the Americans seemed to prefer it when he was off-guard and tetchy. He guessed they hoped he'd make a mistake that way.

"Surely it's obvious that your chap was after us? We did nothing to provoke him," Frank said, wearily.

"We'll find out in good time, Mr Tucker," Cosallo said. "At the moment, Joe isn't able to speak."

Frank looked surprised and shocked. "You mean, he's not dead?"

"Did you hope he would be?" Cosallo jumped on the comment.

Warrender touched his arm lightly, taking a more measured and reasoned approach. "He's in a very bad way, he might not make it," he said, his voice an unexpected laconic drawl. Frank was still reeling. Like Iris, he was certain that the impact had killed Joe. He assumed that it must be touch and go with his odds of surviving being very slim. "But if he regains consciousness, we'll be able to ask him for his version of events. And, while you and the girl have a plausible story, you can appreciate why we need to hear his side."

"Sure." Frank shrugged, not really appreciating that point at all. As far as he was concerned, it was obvious what had happened. A soldier, reeling with grief and loss, had gone spectacularly off the rails and had engaged in a one-man vendetta. "Can we go now?"

Harry stared hard at Frank. It was Major Warrender who broke the silence. He nodded his consent and as Frank rose from the chair, added, "But stay at the farm. We may need to speak to you again."

Frank went outside. He waited for Iris to be released, and then, as darkness fell, the two of them trudged wearily back to Pasture Farm. It wasn't until they had nearly reached the door to the farmhouse that Frank told Iris the news that Joe Batch was still alive ...

Chapter 11

A few days later, the dawn sunlight fumbled through the windows and roused Iris from her slumber. Despite being exhausted from her recent ordeal and from the last week's events, it was some small relief that this time the pain in her head came from a stress headache rather than a hangover. The temptation to dive into the orange liquid in the wardrobe had been strong, almost overwhelmingly so. But Iris had fought the urge, knowing that she would need a clear head for today. Her final day at Pasture Farm.

After the showdown in the woods, the girls and Esther had rallied around Iris, making sure she was all right, offering comforting words, warm drinks and smiles. It was like old times. Iris had wondered whether the benevolence would stretch to letting her stay at Pasture Farm. She hoped that Esther would give her a reprieve, but the reality was that nothing was going to change. In fact, the ordeal in the woods seemed to give Esther further proof that it would be best for Iris to make a new start. She needed to get away from this place. Iris hadn't been that surprised. She guessed that Esther and Finch wouldn't budge. So last night, her last night at

Pasture Farm, sleep had taken a long time coming, kept at bay by wondering whether Evelyn would show up today to trade the note for the map. She knew that Esther and Finch wouldn't change her destiny. But would Evelyn make everything right?

Until then, Iris knew she had to go through the motions. She hauled out her battered brown-leather suitcase from the top of the wardrobe. It had been her mother's old case for her stage management work and a playbill for Northampton Theatre was still pasted to the side. And although some of it had been torn away over time, Iris could still make out the names of some of the acts. Belview and Morris, The Wild Bunch, Sparrow Soprano. Names forgotten in the mists of time. Iris flipped open the case and began to fold her clothes. She placed her small rag doll into a pocket on the case. As she packed her few possessions, she thought about her meeting with Evelyn in the car. She regretted leaving things in Evelyn's court. It meant that every minute today would be spent wondering if she would appear. Her gut feeling told her it was a simple deal that would benefit both of them. Iris would get proof to show that she hadn't been lying. And Evelyn would get the map.

The map!

Iris thought that she must remember to get it from Frank's shed before she left. She must take it with her. At least that way, she would have it if Evelyn later changed her mind and wanted to trade.

There was a rap at the door, followed by Esther's voice. "Breakfast is ready." Esther went to the next door along the landing – Joyce's room – and repeated the phrase, although Iris doubted that Joyce would be inside. At this very moment, she would be racing back from Shallow Brook Farm after a night with John.

When she was dressed in her uniform, Iris went to the kitchen and joined Shelley and Dolores for breakfast. Esther had made porridge and tea, a meal that would leave them all feeling uncomfortably hot on such a warm day. Frank was already finishing his. He had recovered well from the run through the forest and the bruises on his face from his beating in the village square were beginning to fade as well.

Joyce bustled in from outside, her hair dishevelled.

"Where have you been?" Esther asked, suspiciously.

"Checking on the cockerel," Joyce said with a straight face. Iris smiled at her, knowing the truth. Joyce sat at the table and Esther slopped some porridge into a bowl for her. The mood around the table was more subdued than usual but it didn't have the sombre, funereal feeling of the last few days. Having a meal at five in the morning would never result in sparkling conversation, but there was a downbeat feel as they all knew that Iris was leaving. Esther brought her mug of tea and sat down at the table.

"Now then," she said emphatically. "Fred said he'd drive you at two o'clock to the station. He'll sort you out a ticket to East Anglia. I'm not sure if you'll have to get two trains or three, but don't worry, he'll arrange all that. We can get the funds back from the Women's Land Army."

Iris nodded, feeling that she would still be saved from this by some magical last-minute reprieve.

Joyce smiled warmly at her. "You'll be fine and you'll have to come back and see us, won't you?"

"Yeah," Iris said brightly.

"You keep practising the writing and you can write letters to us," Frank offered. Bless him, trying to keep things positive. But Iris doubted that she could continue to learn to read and write without him. She'd miss their lessons in the shed. She saw her dream of writing a letter home to her mother slipping away.

Esther gave Iris a curious look, perhaps uncertain as to whether Iris was brave-facing her situation or whether she had merely accepted it with remarkably good grace.

After breakfast, Iris went back upstairs and closed her case. She checked the drawers by the bed for any forgotten items and then put the case on the landing to take downstairs. Finally she went to the wardrobe. It was empty apart from Billy Finch's suit, the coat hangers swinging like wooden skeletons. She pulled the bottle of carrot whisky from the bottom; her reassuring companion for those bleak, terrifying nights. The bottle was nearly empty, but Iris didn't want anyone to find it. She walked across the landing to the bathroom and tipped the contents down the sink. Then she tucked the empty bottle under her arm, picked up her suitcase and went downstairs, giving her old room the briefest of glances. She found Finch's stash of brewing paraphernalia under the stairs, in the cupboard. She added the empty bottle to the collection and closed the door. She left the suitcase in the kitchen and went off to work a final shift at the military hospital at Hoxley Manor before finishing off at Shallow Brook Farm.

But on her way, she noticed Joyce collecting some tools from the shed in the yard. Checking that no one was around, Iris approached her. She'd decided that she needed a back-up plan in case Evelyn didn't show up.

"Joyce?"

"You all right? Well, as much as you can be?"

"Do you remember that dance a few weeks back? The one that was really hot and sticky. When the fight broke out?"

"Oh yes. Those GIs taking lumps out of each other! Way to break up a party, wasn't it?" Joyce smiled at the memory of that strange evening. But Iris wasn't here to just reminisce.

"Do you remember Evelyn there?"

"What?"

"She came in and she was looking for someone. You said about her hair – it being a natural blonde colour."

Joyce narrowed her eyes, obviously trying to recall the details. "Yes, you're right. She was there, yes."

"It was the first time we saw her."

Joyce stared at the bundle of rakes and forks in her hand. Iris assumed they were getting heavy so she cut to the chase.

"The thing is, she was looking for Finch that night. And it's only because the fight broke out that she didn't meet him. It stopped her. And then, later, she bumped into him at the agricultural show, seemingly by accident."

"What, so you're saying she set out to meet him?"

"Yes. She planned it right from the start. And it always involved that tin at Shallow Brook Farm and Vernon. She never just bumped into Finch by accident. It was planned."

Joyce nodded. "I believe you. I've always believed you. But what can we do? Finch has got his heart set on her."

"This shows she's up to something. Maybe we should both have a go at convincing him? If we go together, he might listen, don't you think?"

"It's not going to do any good." Joyce looked uncomfortable.

"Why?"

"Finch is in love. He won't listen to this story. He won't think that Evelyn set out to snare him, will he?"

"But I've got to try. If Evelyn doesn't show up to trade for the map, I'm finished here."

There was a long, awkward silence, then Joyce put her hand on Iris's shoulder, looked her in the eyes and said sadly, "Sorry, love."

Iris watched as Joyce collected the tools up in her arms and made her way across the yard.

What could Iris do now?

Iris hated making the beds. But it was an inescapable part of the job at the military hospital, so she and Shelley Conrad were busy stripping a bed of its covers and preparing new linen to replace it. In truth, Iris didn't have to work many shifts at the hospital. She wondered if this was because of her age and Esther not wanting her to see too much blood and guts. Shelley had been watching her with a concerned expression for the last ten minutes, as if she wanted to say something but didn't know how. Iris was deep in thought. For once, she wasn't thinking about whether or not Evelyn would show up to save the day. No, this time, she was thinking of Joe Batch, knowing he was somewhere in this building, in one of the rooms. After they had finished the bed, Iris asked if she could have a few minutes' break before they did the next one. Shelley smiled and nodded her head.

Iris walked from the ward to the main corridor. She caught a passing nurse.

"Excuse me? Do you know where I could find Joe Batch?"

"Third door," the nurse said, pointing up the corridor, before heading off. Iris walked slowly towards the door. She hesitated, not certain that she wanted to see him ever again. But a grim fascination meant that she wanted to see his face one last time, to look into his eyes and see how he could have become so twisted.

As she waited at the door, Iris was startled by the arrival of Dr Channing behind her.

"Hello?" he said, concern in his voice. "Did you want to see him?"

"I'm not sure."

"He was trying to shoot you, by all accounts, wasn't he?" Channing said, obviously trying to steer her away from such a meeting.

"He was after Frank. I was just in the way."

"Because he thought Frank had tipped off the Germans about Panmere Lake?"

Iris nodded. "Frank overheard him talking about it. But I'm sure Joe told other people. It's just he probably couldn't remember it. So he concentrated on taking it out on Frank. Look, maybe I should see him, just to see if I can put him straight?"

Channing's face changed from pleasant and warm to distant and concerned.

"What is it, Doctor?"

"Nothing," Channing said, finding a warm smile to cover whatever he was thinking. Iris couldn't know that he was worrying whether Joe could remember talking about Panmere to his friend Chuck Wellings in the hospital. Channing was worried that he might remember. And if he did, then he might remember who else was in the room too ...

"How is he?" Iris asked. Part of her had to know.

"What? Oh, he's unconscious. It's touch and go. He's got a huge amount of injuries." And then the professional mode kicked in. "I'm very sorry."

Iris nodded her understanding and walked off, back to Shelley and the waiting beds. She had two more to do before she could leave this place. Dr Channing watched her go, deep in thought. He was wondering whether Joe would remember ...

At lunchtime, with barely two hours before she was due to leave, Iris sat on the back step of Shallow Brook Farm. Although the hope that Evelyn would show up was fading, Iris was still banking on it happening. The woman would probably leave it to the last minute, to make Iris sweat as much as she could. But yes, it was going to be all right. Hang in there.

Martin appeared with a sandwich, a mug of tea and an awkward smile. "I thought I'd make you lunch on your last day. You were always doing it for me," he said.

"I never made you lunch!" Iris laughed, realising that Martin was joking. He had a dry sense of humour, but didn't often use it, probably because of a fear of appearing foolish. It was moments like these that made her realise how little time they spent alone. There were always other people at the farmhouse at meal times, always other people in the fields. She was grateful for this moment, even if it looked like being the last one. She budged up on the step, making room for him to sit beside her. He was wearing a pullover, shirt and corduroy trousers – the uniform of a child – but with his slim, muscular arms and legs he looked older than his sixteen years.

"It's a shame you're going," he said, resolutely not making eye contact. And then, taking the plunge added, "Can I write to you?"

Iris nodded. "I hope to be able to continue reading the books. I'm taking yours with me."

"It won't take you long to learn."

"It would be lovely to hear from you. Thanks," she said. "I'm just going to miss this place, that's all."

She picked up her sandwich. It was a doorstop with lettuce and cheese wedged between two gigantic slices of potato bread. Iris wasn't sure she could get the thing in her mouth and as she was nervous enough eating in front of Martin anyway, she didn't want to try. So she picked a crust off and started to eat that, hoping it would look more ladylike than tackling the monster in one go. They sat in silence for a few long moments, the only sound the engine of a tractor in the next field.

"Will you come back?" Martin looked at her, genuine sadness in his eyes.

"Maybe one day. But probably not until the war's over," she said, sighing. "Can you imagine when this is over?"

"It will end." Martin stared into the distance. "It will be over, and things will go back to normal."

"And on the day it ends, I hope they end rationing."

"And farm work," he added with a grin.

"Yes, I never want to see another spade or a rake afterwards. When I get a house of my own, I'm not even going to have a garden."

They laughed together.

Iris looked at Martin. This time he held her gaze. She stared into his warm eyes. Slowly he extended his fingers across the step until the tips were touching Iris's fingers. She felt a frisson of excitement and smiled encouragingly at him. He took the hint and moved his head forwards to meet hers, his sandy hair glinting in the sunlight. Iris closed her eyes, waiting for his lips to touch hers ...

But suddenly Joyce Fisher cleared her throat noisily, breaking the moment. Iris and Martin jumped in surprise. They had been inches away from kissing when they noticed their friend standing behind them, in the doorway to the kitchen. Martin stood up, brushing his backside from the step. "I'd better be off, then," he said.

"Oh, you don't have to go," Joyce said, unintentionally making both of them squirm a little. She realised that she had broken up something.

"See you, Martin," Iris said, sadly.

Martin walked across the yard, and Joyce took his place on the stoop.

"Sorry if I scared him off," Joyce said.

"It's all right."

"Are you all set for the off?"

"I'd give anything not to go. And I've still got a bit of time before I'm due."

"You'll make new friends. And we won't forget you, you know?" Joyce put a sisterly arm around Iris's shoulders, before getting to her feet. "I'd better take John his tea. And I'm sorry I couldn't help you with Finch."

Iris watched Joyce march off with a mug of tea to the next field. She listened to the sounds of the farm, the rustle and clucking of the chickens, the bleat of the sheep in the lower field. The tractor noises stopped in the next field and Iris assumed that Joyce had reached John and he'd turned off the engine to have his tea. Life went on. Life would always go on. It's just that Iris's life would go on somewhere else.

Over the course of the next hour, Iris had a steady parade of visitors coming to say their goodbyes. She tried to remain stoic for each visitor, still believing, hope against hope, that Evelyn would appear.

Connie and Henry popped by to wish her farewell. As a parting gift, Connie gave Iris one of her red lipsticks and winked at her.

"Wear this and you'll be fighting them off you!"

"Hang on, you still wear that colour!" Henry realised.

"I know." Connie giggled. "Got to keep you on your toes."

After they had left, Frank sauntered by, his injured ankle giving him a slight limp. Iris mentioned that she'd seen Evelyn and given her an ultimatum. Frank was disappointed, thinking she shouldn't have kicked that particular hornet's nest. Maybe he could have talked Finch round if she hadn't kept on digging. Iris dismissed his comment. It didn't matter because she still hoped that Evelyn would show up. But there was one more thing she wanted to say to Frank before she went.

"Thank you for trying to teach me to read and write."

"That's all right," he said. "You make sure you keep it up, eh?"

And he handed her a copy of a *Rupert Bear Annual*. "It's called – can you read the title?"

"More ..." Iris struggled. Frank gave an encouraging look.

"*More Adventures ...*"

"*More Adventures of ... Rupert?*" Iris looked pleased with herself.

"There you go," Frank said. "Hope you enjoy it. And I hope you write me a letter sometime."

"I will. It might have the words 'more' and 'adventures' in it, though."

"That's good. That's what life is all about, isn't it?" Frank patted her on the shoulder and ambled off.

Later on, at ten to two, Iris said goodbye to Shelley Conrad and she walked slowly back to Pasture Farm, where Esther was waiting for her. Finch was tying the laces of his boots at the kitchen table. He didn't look up, busying himself with the task at hand.

"You all set?" Esther said, matter-of-factly.

With minutes until her deadline, Iris knew for the first time that Evelyn wasn't going to show up. She surveyed the kitchen. This place had been the centre of her life since she'd arrived. The oven and range, the wooden work surfaces, the large farmhouse table, the pot plants of herbs on the windowsills, the big brass kettle, the teapot with a floral cosy that rode up, too small, like one of Finch's jumpers. She could hear the laughter from the girls, the stories and anecdotes; Connie Carter dumping her bare feet on the table and telling everyone they were ruined; Finch gagging as he realised Joyce had forgotten to cook his fish; the girls getting merry on potato wine as the sunset created a strange red colour in the sky outside. And the sad times, the tears. Joyce telling her about how she'd lost her parents and sister in the Coventry bombings; Esther worrying about whether Martin would regain his sight after he'd had an accident; and Iris herself worried about the death of the little lamb she had been nursing. This place had seen it all. If a room could talk ...

Esther broke the moment by shouting at Finch. "What have I told you about switching drinks?"

Finch looked embarrassed, caught red-handed switching his tea for Esther's.

"It was a stronger-looking cup."

"I'll give you stronger-looking! You'll be the death of me!" Esther admonished.

Iris took one final look around the room. "I'm ready." she said, blankly, her heart sinking.

Esther shook her by the hand. "I'll inform your mother about your change of address, so she can send letters to the new place."

"Thank you." Iris went to get her suitcase, but Finch already had it. For the first time he looked at her. He nodded perfunctorily in a disengaged well-this-is-happening kind of way and motioned for her to lead the way. As Iris got outside, she was expecting to see Finch's tractor with its trailer attached as their means of transport to the station. But instead, another vehicle stood waiting.

A 1929 dark-green Riley Nine Kestrel. Evelyn's car.

Iris felt a twinge of hope. Was Evelyn here? Was she going to do the deal at the last moment?

"Evelyn's let me borrow it," Finch said, opening the passenger door for Iris. With fading hope, she got inside, checking quickly to see if Evelyn was sitting in the back. She wasn't. Finch opened the boot and placed Iris's suitcase inside. He came around the car and sat got in beside her, his bulky frame struggling to fit in the small space. He pushed the seat back, but he still looked as if the car had been moulded around him, like Mr Toad. Finch broke her from her reverie with the random comment, "I remember Sparrow Soprano."

"Sorry?"

"Your suitcase. The playbill on it." Finch started the car. "I saw her play at Birmingham, I think. Dreadful voice."

Iris couldn't resist smiling at this remark. Why was it people remembered bad nights at the theatre?

Gingerly, Finch steered the car slowly out of the yard, its tyres crunching on the gravel. When they reached the single track outside Pasture Farm, Iris could see seven or eight Land Girls busy at work in a field of golden corn, dotted around as if they were raisins in a sponge cake. She fought the sadness in her heart, knowing that she would probably never come back here. This would be a footnote in her life, a place of ghosts and long-gone days.

When they reached the end of the lane, Finch turned right onto a country road. He still maintained a careful, steady speed. Iris thought he was probably worried about causing an accident in Evelyn's car. They drove in silence. Iris wound down the window. She noticed the hedgerows moving by, an undulating green wave. And she remembered that she hadn't taken the map back from Frank. Oh, well, it didn't matter now. It was probably safe in his shed. The motion of the car and the rhythm of the engine washed over her, calming her, as the hedges blurred alongside the car.

But after about ten minutes, she realised they were going the wrong way.

"This isn't the way to the station," Iris said.

"I know," Finch said, staring resolutely at the road, his large hands gripping the wheel in a five-to-one position. "That's because we're not going to the station. You're not being sent to the Fens."

That was an unexpected surprise, and perhaps not a welcome one.

"Where are we going, then?" Iris felt her hope returning. Was he taking her to see Evelyn?

"There's a farm about eighteen miles away," Finch said, still not turning. "It's called Jordan Gate. Strange name for a farm, don't know how that came about."

"Why am I going there?"

"You just are. I had a change of heart."

"Did you? Why?"

Finch shook his head in annoyance, obviously hoping she would drop the matter. But Iris kept staring, waiting for an answer and he realised he couldn't avoid it.

"All right! Evelyn talked me round," Finch said. And now, he glanced at Iris, as if stressing the point that she had Evelyn to thank for this. "She thought I was being harsh sending you to do Fen work. This way, perhaps you can come back in six months or so, providing you've straightened yourself out."

Iris's mind was reeling. She supposed that this was good news. It literally wasn't a million miles away and Finch was talking about it being a temporary measure. That was great, surely? And yet, something was nagging at her. She had to ask the question. Even if it risked upsetting him.

"Why did Evelyn want to help me?" After all, she had been content to drug her, punch her and get her sent away. This wasn't a woman who seemed inclined to do good deeds for Iris Dawson.

Finch shrugged, his large lips forming into a fleshy overhang on his face. "I don't pretend to understand you women. But just be grateful that she's been kind to you. She didn't have to be nice, not after how you carried on!"

Iris nodded. She had no choice in the matter and could tell that Finch didn't really want to talk about it. Besides, she had a new set of worries to think about. Evelyn hadn't done the deal she was anticipating and yet she had seemed to help her.

"What's this Jordan place like, then?"

"I've no idea. Never heard of it," Finch said. "Still, I'm sure you'll settle in."

"I wasn't making trouble, you know." Iris said. Finch put his hand up to cut her off. He didn't want to hear any more.

"I understand some of it. Don't pretend to understand it all. Fact is, you've got to sort yourself out. Stop spreading lies about people. Let people do what they want."

"I didn't want you to get hurt," Iris said. And it was true. She didn't want to see Finch destroyed by Evelyn Gray. And she knew, with cold certainty, that he would be, sooner or later. Evelyn had admitted that to her herself. But to her surprise, she didn't have to explain what she was thinking because Finch got there first.

"I had suspicions, like you. Suspicions she was using me."

"You did?"

"Yes. See, my boy, Billy, was getting married. To a Land Girl."

"Really?" Iris wondered where this was going. What relevance did this have to Evelyn and him?

"Before your time, by about six months. Anyway, she was pregnant. Not by him." Iris looked at Finch, wide-eyed. This was quite a revelation! "I'm telling you this to make you see. I don't want it spreading about."

"It won't be," Iris said. "So he was marrying her, but the baby wasn't his?"

"And this is where I didn't believe why she was doing it, see. I accused her of not loving my Billy, that she were just using him for decency's sake. She was using him to get a roof for her baby's head, a father's name on its birth certificate." Finch glanced at Iris, again, for emphasis. "Just like you thinking Evelyn was trying to get me for my money."

"That wasn't why I thought –"

But Finch cut her off. Hearing anything different would conflict with his theory, which he was obviously happy with. "But I saw that she really did love him. This Land Girl. It was me who was wrong, see?"

Iris nodded. There was no point arguing. She didn't want to upset him, especially as he had mentioned her coming back after a few months.

They came to a fork in the road and Finch took the right-hand fork. She watched the scenery as Finch talked some more, about what had happened to Bea Finch and his grandson, William, but the words washed over Iris as she tried to process the last few days. They passed a windmill on her left, one of its sails battered and in disrepair. She knew she had to focus on her new beginning. Without the note that Evelyn had written to John and Martin, she would never have the proof needed to convince Finch that his fiancée – soon-to-be fiancée – was a bad lot. And until she got that note, she knew Finch wouldn't see any wrong in her. But maybe she should just walk away now. Maybe it wasn't Iris's concern any more.

As the miles ticked by, Iris looked sadly at the big figure next to her. A kind, ebullient man, often armed with a ready quip and a warm heart. She would miss him. She cared for him and hoped that he would survive the inevitable heartache to come.

Then she saw her own father at the wheel, a thinner man in a smart three-piece suit with a pencil moustache and waves of sandy hair. He was looking down at her, a smaller Iris in the passenger seat. She was a child. The sun was behind him, almost silhouetting his face. But she knew he was smiling. Her father was always smiling.

Finch took a wrong turning and he cursed the lack of signposts. "It's not just the Germans that get lost here," he mumbled, reaching for a map and spreading it out over the steering wheel. When he was satisfied that he knew where he was going, he gave Iris the map to fold and set off again. She had barely folded it the correct way, when he got lost again and demanded another look. By late afternoon and many blind alleys, they reached a hill. A single track weaved its way up to a white-walled, double-storey farmhouse perched on the top. This was Jordan Gate. It had none of the homely charm of Pasture Farm, none of the welcoming atmosphere. Around the farm building were some outbuildings in a semi-circle, including a barn and four grain silos. Two tractors stood near one of the silos, and a mangy black dog skulked around the yard looking for rats.

Welcome to your new home.

Finch brought the car to a standstill and turned off the engine. He squeezed his large frame out of the vehicle and crossed to the passenger side, where Iris was already getting out. They collected her case from the back. Iris eyed the dog warily as she slowly followed Finch to the front door. He rapped on the wood and offered an awkward smile to Iris. This was it. The final moment was coming. The moment when they would say goodbye.

"I hope it goes well for you, like," Finch offered.

"I hope you don't get hurt," Iris replied, having decided

that it was her last chance to warn him about Evelyn. Finch frowned. He opened his mouth, no doubt to give Iris a piece of his mind, when the door opened and a Land Girl stood looking with curiosity at them both. A sallow-cheeked woman, perhaps thirty years old, with large brown eyes and mousy hair flattened against her head with clips, she made no attempt to smile or welcome them in. Instead she looked past the visitors to the car that had brought them here.

"Hello, I'm Fred. This is Iris, your new girl," Finch said. "Do you like the car?"

"Sorry?" the woman said, seemingly lost in a world of her own.

Suddenly a tall man wearing a long brown overall coat bustled the woman out of the way and opened the door wide to allow Finch and Iris inside. "I'm Horace, the warden," he said. He was about fifty and as skinny as a rake. A ring of long white hair traversed the perimeter of his skull from ear to ear, but apart from that, he was totally bald. He moved his head back slightly, as if adjusting the focus of his eyes, so he could take in Iris. He looked her up and down as if appraising a horse.

"Looks a strong one," Horace said. "Is she a good worker?"

"Yes, she's good," Finch replied, feeling nearly as uneasy as Iris did. Why didn't he address Iris directly? Should he say something?

"Well, leave her with me," Horace held out his hand to shake Finch's, all the while keeping his eyes on Iris. She smiled awkwardly. "When I get the transfer paperwork from your warden –"

"Esther."

"Esther, that's it. When I get the paperwork, I'll file it with the ministry." And then Horace turned to Iris and smiled a toothy grin. She wasn't sure if Horace had more teeth than a normal person or just that it looked that way on account of them being like large yellow tombstones, ridiculously confined in his thin face. "Welcome to Jordan Gate."

Finch nodded his goodbye to Iris and with a palpable air of relief left the farmhouse. Iris offered a friendly smile at the sallow-faced Land Girl, but all she got back was a blank stare. Horace produced a small leather pocket book and feverishly flicked through the pages, squinting at the text. The room was furnished with a long wooden table with benches either side. There was a butler's sink on one wall and a Welsh dresser with a lurid collection of blue utility plates and bowls. It lacked the comfortable touches of Pasture Farm. The crockery was all utilitarian and that was the feel of the whole place, a functional place designed for work.

Horace motioned for the sallow-faced Land Girl to join him. "Go and get Clarence. He'll want to welcome this one."

The girl obediently went off through a door that led to the rest of the house.

"She's Vanessa, she'll show you the ropes here."

"Thanks," Iris said, her feeling of disquiet growing. "Shall I put my suitcase upstairs?"

"You won't be sleeping in the house. I've got a room and Clarence has got a room, but there isn't space for you lot." He motioned to the barn outside the kitchen window. "That's where you all sleep. There's four of you out there, and it's pretty warm most of the time."

"It's a barn," Iris heard herself voicing her thoughts aloud.

"Just be grateful you lot have a roof over your head."

Iris saw red. "Us lot? We're doing you farmers a favour. Without us, you wouldn't be able to cope."

"That's a matter of opinion." A resonant, rich, upper-class voice stated softly. Iris whirled around to find herself facing an imposing figure, dressed in riding britches, a red waistcoat and a checked white shirt. His hair was jet black and combed meticulously back in glistening parallel tracks. "I'm Clarence Trubb, the owner of this farm."

"Pleased to meet you," Iris said, apprehensively. Clarence almost snorted in derision. She had heard stories about farmers who were less than friendly to Land Girls. She guessed she might have been lucky with Finch. Obviously not all farmers were as welcoming and tolerant to female workers as he was. So Clarence Trubb and his warden, Horace, seemed to fit the rumours she'd heard of farmers who didn't appreciate the girls that were sent to them.

"You've got a bit of fire, haven't you?" Clarence said, appraising Iris. She stood her ground, staring straight back at him. "And not just in the colour of your hair." He moved his hand towards her hair and allowed the tips of her ringlets to cascade over his knuckles, seeming to enjoy the sensation. Feeling queasy from the contact, Iris pulled away and brushed her hair back with her hands, out of his reach.

"If I was you, Iris Dawson, I'd get an early night," Clarence said. "Tomorrow we'll see if you're cut out for life at Jordan Gate." He threw an amused look to Horace, who looked equally amused at whatever private joke they were enjoying. Iris decided to let it wash over her. Stuff their games.

Vanessa, the sallow-faced girl, entered the room. Finally she spoke to Iris, but it wasn't a message tinged with any warmth or hints of friendship, rather an instruction. "I've run you a bath."

Iris thanked her, picked up her case and went upstairs, Vanessa following. Clarence and Horace watched her go. Iris went in the direction of the sound of running water and finally reached a bathroom, where the tub was glistening with a generous three inches of water at the bottom.

She put her case next to the bath and started to unbutton her coat. Vanessa went to the bath and turned off the taps. Iris managed to reach the edge of the door with her elbow and pushed it shut. Now they were alone, she wondered if Vanessa might be a bit more approachable, a bit more forthcoming. She remembered that strange woman that Connie Carter had brought back to Pasture Farm, Glory Wayland. It took a while before Glory had felt comfortable enough to communicate with the rest of them. Perhaps Vanessa was shy or reserved like Glory had been.

"What's it like here?" Iris asked, expecting perhaps a playful rolling of eyes and a dismissive comment. Nothing prepared her for the reality.

Vanessa glanced nervously at the door, her large brown eyes full of terror, and then whispered, fearfully, "It's horrible. It's hell." She checked again for the sound of anyone on the stairs and when she felt confident that they weren't being spied on added, "When you have a bath, wedge a towel over the sink. There's a gap in the wood by the mirror and Clarence watches."

"Watches? What?"

But Vanessa scurried out of the room. And with that deeply unsettling comment hanging in the air, Iris went to lock the door behind her, but realised there was no lock. Of course. What could she do to get some privacy? Suddenly she had an idea. She took one of the towels from the storage table, unfolded it and did her best to wedge it over the mirror so that it covered the crack in the wood. Then, with her back to that part of the room, she hurriedly pulled off her jumper and blouse. After discarding her trousers and socks, she stepped into the bath. It was lukewarm. Iris leaned back, partly to obscure her body from view in case she hadn't managed to fully block the gap, and partly to try to relax. She looked idly up, where small star-shaped cracks seemed to cover the ceiling. But as she peered more closely, she realised that it was dozens of daddy long legs, their spiny black legs looking like hairline fissures in the plaster, sprawled across the ceiling.

Iris decided that she would keep her head down and make the best of this awful place. She might only have six months here and she would be ticking off each and every day. And then maybe, just maybe, she could go back to her old life at Pasture Farm.

Chapter 12

It had been one of those nights when Iris had been certain that she hadn't had a wink of sleep. And yet the hours had somehow passed more quickly than if she had really been awake the whole time. But whether she had snatched any sleep or not didn't matter, the outcome was that she felt threadbare and shattered. The barn was cold and draughty, and the continual padding of the black dog around the perimeter meant that it was one of the most uncomfortable places Iris had ever been in. It made Frank's shed seem like the Ritz. The beds in the barn were makeshift camp beds, with the four Land Girls grouped at one end, and the other end of the barn was full of straw. As Iris tried to go to sleep, even if the dog wasn't walking around, she would hear the rustle of some unseen creatures in the hay, gnawing or moving. And above her head, there was a gap in one of the roof joists, so she could see the night sky. Luckily it had been a warm night, but Iris dreaded to think what would happen on a cold one or if it was raining. A pile of folded blankets on a table near the bathroom gave her the answer. Last night, Vanessa Collins had been asleep – or pretending to be asleep – by the time

Iris had finished her bath and trotted warily over to the barn. The other two girls were just as taciturn to Iris. She decided that all three of them shared the same haunted look, as if they all felt they were in hell. Iris pulled her old rag doll from a pocket inside her suitcase and squeezed it tightly. It had helped her through some awful times and she hoped that it would make her feel better now. The threadbare face, with its single eye, stared at her. Iris collected herself and dredged up some courage to face the day. It was a new place, a new environment. It wasn't as homely as Pasture Farm, but she would survive it, albeit by counting down the days until she could leave. Yes, she would survive it.

She sighed and placed the rag doll back in the pocket of the case.

When they were dressed for work, Iris followed Vanessa and the other two girls over to the farmhouse. Horace was reading a book at the table, sitting near four bowls of rapidly cooling porridge. The other girls ate the gloop hungrily and in silence. Iris felt that she had better follow suit. When they had finished, each girl picked up her bowl and spoon and washed it in the butler's sink, before drying it and putting it back in the Welsh dresser. Again Iris followed suit. Horace feigned disinterest, but she caught him casting a crafty eye over the thoroughness of their washing and drying. With all the plates and spoons put away, the girls went outside and put their boots on. Iris noticed that a pair of bicycle clips stood by each pair of boots – including her own.

"What are these for?" she asked.

"Just put them on," Vanessa said, walking off.

Iris was about to query whether they were going to ride bicycles, when a familiar voice called her name.

"Iris?" She turned to see Clarence Trubb. He was sporting a different-coloured waistcoat today, but the same riding britches. In the cold light of day, she realised he was quite an attractive man, in a saturnine kind of way. Physically he was dark and rugged, with piercing eyes. It was just a shame that any attractiveness was undone by the sour personality and creepiness inside. "You're not going to work with the others. Not yet," he growled.

"What do you want me to do, then?"

"I said last night that we need to check you are suited for life here." He eyed her up and down. Iris felt a desperate need to fold her arms tightly across her breasts to obscure her body, but part of her didn't want to give him the satisfaction in knowing she was unnerved. "In that silo, is a bag of corn." He pointed to the silo behind her. "And a bag of wheat. All you have to do is bring me the corn."

Iris mulled over this challenge for a moment. She glanced at the silo. It seemed simple enough. What was the catch?

"Will I be able to lift it on my own?" she asked.

"Yes, it's not heavy."

"Right," Iris said, taking this in. "You just want me to get the corn?"

"That's it. Just bring me the bag of corn."

"So you want to check I can recognise corn?"

"Just get it."

Iris stepped inside the gloomy silo, her eyes squinting to make out anything in the dark. It was a large and circular space, with a pointed roof that was nearly three storeys high. It could house a lot of bags of grain. But at this moment, she could just about make out the shape of two small hessian sacks that sat in the centre of the cavernous space. Iris guessed that these silos usually had clear ceilings so you could see inside, but this one had some sort of dark covering over the pointed roof, making the gloom quite impenetrable. She moved across the room, her footfalls echoing around the chamber, her hands outstretched to guide her. All she had was the light from the opened door to make out what was inside, and that didn't penetrate much of the darkness. It was about to get worse. She heard a loud clunking noise and turned to see that the door had been slammed shut. The silo was suddenly pitch black. She stopped in her tracks.

"Hello?" Iris called. There was no answer. "Is this part of the test? Doing it in the dark?"

There was no answer.

She turned back to the bags of grain and walked nearer to them, hands outstretched. So this was the test, identifying corn in the dark and not getting spooked by Clarence's sick games. She would show him! She was confident that she could work out which grain was which from touch. Iris fumbled for the sacks, kneeling down on the cold stone floor. The edge of one of the sacks brushed her knee. She found the opening and put her fingers inside. From the texture, it felt like wheat. She moved her hand away and went to find the opening of the second bag. That must contain the corn. The edge of the bag somehow managed to touch her knee again. That was odd. She soldiered on and pushed her hands into the open bag, but her fingers didn't find corn. Instantly, she recoiled as she found something warm and furry. And moving. But it wasn't just one thing, it was dozens, the whole sack was full of squirming, warm, hairy bodies thrashing around, each animal possessing a scaly, segmented tail. They were rats! As she instinctively pulled back in revulsion, Iris lost her balance. They were spilling over the floor, squawking and chirruping as they poured over her knees and ankles. Iris snapped her hand back from the sack, but only succeeded in upending it, causing more rats to pour out. Desperately she tried to stand, but found herself pressing on furry bodies to find purchase, the rats squealing beneath her. Finally she rose to her feet, aware that her jumper was pulling at her, with the unnatural adornment of two huge rats hanging from the front. She batted them off and ran towards the door, the squawking of excited vermin filling the cavernous space. But she couldn't find the door as the walls of the silo all looked and felt the same in the dark.

"Let me out!" Iris shouted. "Let me out!"

The sound of scurrying rats filled the silo. Iris banged on the wall so hard it hurt her hand.

Finally, seven or eight feet away, the door clunked open and a sliver of light pierced the gloom. Iris ran to it, squashing some rats that had the same idea. She burst through the door, the morning sun stinging her eyes. She slammed it behind her, but not before two rats got through. They stopped to get their bearings in their new surroundings.

Clarence Trubb was smiling at her.

Iris frowned at him, furious, trying to control her breathing.

"The test isn't over," he said. He handed Iris a thin steel machete. "You've got to show me you can kill 'em."

Iris held the knife in her hands. At that moment, she would have liked to have used it on Clarence Trubb. She looked at the huge brown rats on the ground, starting to explore the outside world. Could she do this?

"Big part of your job here is going to be vermin control," Clarence said. Iris knew that some Land Girls had been formed into dedicated anti-vermin squads. And she'd seen various posters imploring people to 'Kill the rat – it's doing Hitler's work'. Finch had told her that there were over fifty million of the blighters in England and Wales. He thought they would seriously harm the crops if they weren't kept in check The War Office obviously shared that view, so as well as the anti-vermin squads, volunteers were encouraged to catch rats, with children given a penny for each rat tail they could bring to the farmers.

"You'll be using poison, mostly, but I need to know you can do this. Need to know you aren't squeamish."

Iris looked at the rat before her. It was a big one, brown-furred with a long, cartilaginous pink tail. She felt the weight of the knife in her hands, the blade was criss-crossed and shiny at the sharpest edge where it had been repeatedly sharpened over the years. She wondered how many rats it had killed. Clarence watched her as she got closer to the rat. She raised the machete back and brought it down hard. But Iris didn't kill the rat. Instead, she embedded the blade into the soil inches from its body. The rat, feeling the force of the blade in the earth, scurried away, hiding under the nearest tractor.

Clarence scowled at Iris. He retrieved his machete, wiping the soil off on his britches. Then he inspected the blade to check it hadn't been damaged.

"Maybe I'm not cut out for this," Iris said, defiantly. "Maybe you'd better send me back to Pasture Farm."

The truth was that she wasn't particularly squeamish. In fact, she had helped Frank set traps for predators like foxes at Pasture Farm. But in this situation, not killing the rat made a statement. It said that Iris wasn't going to play Clarence's twisted games. She wasn't going to be subjected to his controlling nature. She wasn't going to become a broken spirit like those other dead-eyed girls.

"You'll learn," Clarence sneered. He pocketed the knife and walked away. With no instruction, Iris headed off in the direction that she assumed the other girls had taken. She had been at Jordan Gate for barely twelve hours and, like the rats in the silo, she already wanted to escape.

Mist had collected in the valley and Iris could barely make out the stone farmhouse in the distance.

"We need this barn for storage," Vanessa Collins announced, showing Iris and the other Land Girls a barn in the forest on the next farm along from Jordan Gate. The holes in the ancient dark-green planking had been haphazardly repaired with newer wooden panels, giving the barn a patchwork appearance. Vanessa insisted that it was pretty much watertight, thanks to their efforts over the last couple of weeks in mending the carpentry. The problem was the rats. The whole underside of the barn was infested with rats' nests and despite laying bait for the last two weeks, the problem persisted. Vanessa explained that they had to get rid of the rats before the crops were brought in for storage, otherwise the harvest would be ruined. By this stage of her first day, Iris had barely exchanged a dozen words with the girls; all of them lost in their own worlds of isolation and loneliness. It seemed that none of them wanted to be here. It also seemed that Iris had found herself, without any consultation, in an anti-vermin squad. Iris was relieved that she didn't have to do any digging, but she feared that rat-catching would prove to be an even worse occupation. Vanessa went over the basics of what they would be doing. They would block all the visible holes in the underside of the barn with old fertiliser sacks, shovelling soil on top to ensure a good seal. Then Iris would use the foot pump to pump deadly gas into the one remaining hole. Vanessa told Iris to wear a wet scarf tightly wound around her mouth and nose to stop her breathing in the gas. She warned that as Iris started pumping, the rats would try to escape. They would flee from the underside of the barn and it was up to all the other girls to stop them. Iris noticed that the girls were going to a nearby wagon and fetching two-pronged pitchforks. This was going to be a gruesome and unpleasant massacre.

Vanessa helped her to position the nozzle from the foot pump into the one remaining hole, as the others finished filling as many gaps as they could with fertiliser sacks and earth. Everyone secured their bicycle clips onto their ankles to stop desperate rats from going up their trousers. Then Vanessa gave the order to start pumping. Iris pressed her foot on the pump again and again, but realised she wasn't doing it fast enough to generate any gas. Vanessa ordered her to go faster. Iris increased the pace. Finally, she could hear the thrusting hiss of the deadly gas as it went from the canister into the area under the barn.

Pssst, pssst, pssst.

The Land Girls waited, pitchforks and axes at the ready, a grim tableau on a fine day.

Pssst, pssst, pssst.

Iris felt her head swimming slightly. Thinking it was probably the effort of pumping the pedal so fast, she tried to take deeper breaths. But the scarf was wedged tightly against her nose and mouth, making breathing difficult. She gasped, trying to not succumb to the dizziness, all the time aware that Vanessa was urging her to pump faster.

Psst, psst.

Pin-pricks of brilliant light played over Iris's eyes and she blinked madly to try to clear her vision. Out of the corner of her eye, she was aware that the forest floor was moving, a flow of black leaves moving like an oil spill from the barn. Dimly she realised that they weren't leaves, but rats. She heard the muffled shouts of the other girls as they tried to impale as many of the creatures as they could. There were screams from the women and squawks from the rats, but the sound was fuzzy and somehow distant, as if she was dreaming it. Iris felt her foot slipping off the pedal. Vanessa was shouting at her, but she couldn't hear the words. They were just muffled noises from another room.

Pssst.

Iris tumbled in what seemed like slow-motion off the pump,

falling backwards on the forest floor. Some of it moved beneath her and she dimly realised that she had landed on some fleeing rats. The blue sky was exploding in tiny white fireworks as consciousness slipped away and Iris Dawson passed out.

She expected to see the forest and the sky, but when Iris blearily opened her eyes, she was sitting in an armchair. And yet she was sure she could see the sun, burning brightly. Near. Too near. As she regained her wits, she realised it was a large globe gas lamp that stood burning in front of her. She was in the parlour of the Jordan Gate farmhouse. Whereas the parlour at Pasture Farm was decorated in tasteful wallpaper, the walls here were bare brick. It didn't even have the decency of a skirting board. Beyond the lamp, Iris could make out a clock on the simple wooden mantelpiece. She squinted to read the time.

It was eight o'clock.

Daytime? The next day?

Iris looked towards the bare window. The sky was greying but not dark. She guessed it was evening time.

Suddenly a face loomed into view. The smiling, pink face of Clarence Trubb. He spoke softly, in what he supposed was a calming voice, but which Iris found creepy.

"How are you feeling?" he asked. "You took a tumble in the woods. The gas."

"Am I all right?" Iris stammered. She felt quite sick and her head was pounding.

"You didn't die, so I think you'll be all right."

For a moment, Iris wondered if this was an example of his

black humour, but then she realised that he wasn't joking. Had he fetched her any medical attention? At Pasture Farm, Esther would have called Dr Wally Morgan, even if he was as useless as a Spitfire without wings. But had Clarence really done nothing but sit and watch her?

"Have I been checked?" Iris said, nervously. "What is that gas? If it kills rats ..."

"Relax." Clarence smiled. "I've checked you over."

Feeling a wave of panic, Iris glanced down at herself, fearing that her blouse might be undone, or worse. To her relief, she was still wearing her pullover and clothes. But her alarm amused Clarence. "Don't flatter yourself." He moved away, padding across the bare wood floor and exited the room. Iris realised that she was holding her breath until he'd gone. She loathed the man and didn't trust him as far as she could throw him. When she'd woken this morning, she thought she could bide her time and count down the days, but now she knew she had to get away from this place. Hurriedly, she tried to get to her feet, but her head still felt woozy and she faltered. Gripping the arms of the chair, Iris tried again, more slowly this time. She edged towards the door, using the scant pieces of furniture for support. Finally, she reached the entrance and left the room. She didn't know where Clarence had gone as the kitchen was empty. That made this easier.

Iris went outside, the early evening air making her feel dizzy all over again. She had to get herself checked over by Dr Channing or someone. What if she was dying? That stuff was poisonous!

Iris staggered towards the barn where she had been billeted.

She crept inside and scrambled to her camp bed. Pulling out the suitcase from underneath, she gripped the handle and was about to turn when a figure blocked her path.

It was Vanessa Collins, harbouring the same impassive look as she had when Iris had arrived.

"Where are you going?"

"I've got to get away," Iris stammered. "I've been poisoned and no one cares. And Clarence is really creepy and I don't trust him."

"Don't worry about him."

"But you said he watches us have a bath and –"

"I know." Vanessa lowered her voice. "But he's busy with Maureen. As long as he's got her, he'll leave the rest of us alone like that. Please, trust me. Don't make a fuss and it'll all be all right."

"And does this Maureen want to be with him?" Iris protested.

"Just be grateful she is," Vanessa snapped.

The idea of Maureen being some kind of sacrifice to keep Clarence away from the rest of them made Iris's skin crawl. She didn't even want to ask what Maureen's 'arrangement' was with Clarence. They couldn't be courting, could they? No one would want to be with that unpleasant man, surely? Who was Maureen, anyway? Perhaps she was one of the other Land Girls that Iris hadn't met yet. Feeling overwhelmed, she slumped down onto her bed, the case falling limply from her hand. The room was spinning.

"You need to rest. Let the gas wear off."

"I don't – I need to get a doctor."

"Clarence won't allow it," Vanessa said, cracking a strangely unnerving and unexpected smile. "We'll look after you. And you'll get used to life here. You'll be all right. I promise. We've all taken in lungfuls of that stuff."

"But –"

Without waiting for her consent, Vanessa swung Iris's legs onto the bed and started to take off her boots. As Iris went to protest, Vanessa indicated for her to lie back. "Just relax. You need to sleep." But Iris found that she was thinking of a hundred different things, each swimming into focus in her mind. The glimmer of hope when she found out she wasn't going to be draining marsh land in East Anglia. Finch had made that sound like an act of benevolence from Evelyn Gray. But now she was beginning to think that Evelyn knew what a hellish place this was. This was her punishment for not handing over the map, wasn't it?

"I thought she was being kind," Iris said, feeling desperately tired, her words hardly more than a slur.

"What? Who?" Vanessa asked. But Iris was fast asleep.

The next few days passed like a blur for Iris, as she got used to the systems and routines of Jordan Gate. She didn't like it, but she knew what was expected of her, and she knew how to keep her head down to get through each day with the minimum of incident. The sickness from the gas had passed by the afternoon of the next day. So she assumed she wasn't going to die of Cyamag gas poisoning. And luckily she hadn't seen much of Clarence Trubb since she'd woken up in the chair in the parlour. That was a blessed relief.

The days were long and hard, and Iris found herself working until nearly ten o'clock at night before rising again for a six o'clock start. Working with Vanessa and some other girls from another farm, Iris would travel short distances away from Jordan Gate to tackle vermin problems wherever they were found. Over time, she had learnt how to avoid inhaling the gas quite so much by tightening the scarf around her mouth and nose and breathing away from the pump. She would still feel light-headed and sometimes a little sick, but she hadn't blacked out since that first time. She had also discovered that Horace's repertoire of meals was severely limited, with porridge being served for breakfast, cheese and potato bread for lunch, and some gloopy vegetable stew appearing most evenings. Iris had queried how a man was allowed to be a warden in the Women's Land Army and Vanessa, who had slowly become more talkative, thought he was a temporary, unofficial replacement for the woman who had left before.

"Why did she leave?"

"Why do you think?" Vanessa mimed a pair of groping hands. Clarence.

Iris liked Vanessa now, and for her own part, she seemed to have brought Vanessa out of her shell. She didn't say as much as Joyce and she wasn't as much fun as Shelley, but at least a few jokes and a bit of conversation would pass the time more quickly for the pair of them. From time to time, Iris wondered what Martin was doing. Would he be thinking of her? She wished she'd spent more time trying to get to know him rather than wasting her time with Joe Batch.

The fragments of conversation with the girls was the closest that Iris had to a social life since moving to Jordan Gate. Being on top of a hill, several miles from the nearest village meant, according to the girls, that pub visits and dances were exceptionally rare. Vanessa had revealed that the nearest pub was a village haunt called The Flag, some three miles away. Pasture Farm had also been a couple of miles away from the village, but at least the way over the fields and the country roads were fairly easy to navigate, lit most evenings by moonlight and aided by wide country lanes. But to get to the pub from Jordan Gate you had to make your way through a dense forest on the side of a steep hill. Vanessa cited a story, probably apocryphal, about a girl who had broken her ankle when she got her high heel caught on a branch root. Since that event, they had rarely ventured out.

"If I'm still here on Friday, we should go to the Flag," Iris announced.

Vanessa pulled a doubtful face. "I'm not sure."

"Go on. What's the point of working all the time? We need an hour or two off. Get away for a bit."

Reluctantly, Vanessa nodded.

If Iris was still there on Friday, they would go to the pub ...

Chapter 13

As the week edged towards Friday and the tantalising prospect of escaping for a few hours, Iris had an accident. She cut her hand on the gas pump. It was only a minor cut, but Vanessa told her to go back to the farmhouse to wash and dress it. The last thing she wanted was gas getting into an open wound. So Iris ran back to Jordan Gate and went inside the farmhouse. Bracing herself to see Clarence Trubb, she was instead surprised to find someone else in the kitchen. A girl of about the same age as herself, wearing the uniform of the Women's Land Army. The girl was thin, pretty with long blonde hair. She reminded Iris of Shelley from Pasture Farm, albeit a Shelley who had had all the life sucked out of her.

"Hello?" Iris ventured, wondering who she was.

The girl didn't answer at first, but then turned and offered a thin smile.

"I'm Iris Dawson. I'm new. Are you new too?" Iris laughed as she said the words, realising that they rhymed. But the girl didn't laugh. She had the same troubled look that Vanessa had had when Iris first saw her.

"I'm Maureen Hinks," the girl said, her voice thick with a Birmingham accent.

Maureen? The name sounded familiar. Then Iris remembered where she'd heard it. This was the woman who Vanessa had mentioned, the sacrificial lamb that was keeping Clarence occupied. Iris felt a wave of unease. This girl seemed so unhappy, a shadowy figure lost and alone. Iris didn't quite know what to say. She thought of Clarence making her do things against her will and remembered the panic and fear she'd felt when Joe Batch had tried to assault her outside the village hall. She was grateful that she had managed to stop him. But to ask Maureen about her relationship with Clarence seemed presumptuous and rather forward, especially as they'd only just met. Instead, she steered a safer path to the comforting reassurances of small talk.

"I haven't seen you before," Iris said.

"I work on a neighbouring farm. I come here every now and then," Maureen said. "When Clarence needs me."

Iris felt her skin crawl, but once again, avoiding asking about that side of Maureen's life and what she'd heard.

"Well, we're having a drink at the Flag on Friday. You're more than welcome."

Maureen nodded, but even her acknowledgement was non-committal. Iris knew that she wouldn't be raising a glass with this girl in the pub any time soon.

"You're hurt?" Maureen noticed. She pulled a first-aid tin from under the sink and started to open a bandage. "Run it under the tap."

Iris put her hand under the tap. Then Maureen helped her

dry her hand before applying the dressing. Iris watched her working. Although they were both the same age, thereabouts, Iris felt a protective streak. Maureen looked so fragile and vulnerable, like those porcelain figurines that Iris's mother kept on the bookshelf. But despite her feelings, Iris knew she had to return to the rat-catching.

"Thank you."

"Pleasure."

"See you around, then," Iris offered as she left the kitchen. She didn't get a reply.

Iris walked back over the fields. In the distance, she could see a gang of Italian prisoners of war working, under the watchful eye of Horace. The warden had a Lee Enfield rifle slung over his shoulder, but she knew that it was just for show and that he wouldn't need to use it. These prisoners were classed as low-risk and were likely just biding their time until the war was over. They were counting the days until they could go home. Just like Iris was.

On the edge of the field some British men were toiling, in shirtsleeves and flat caps. They were middle-aged, too old for service. These were the itinerant workers, perhaps displaced because of having their homes bombed, who needed to earn a living. These wanderers relied on people helping them, people such as Clarence Trubb. Iris headed into the trees, where she knew her gang of vermin-hunters were having lunch. She joined them, sat on a tree stump and took a sandwich that was offered to her. As they ate the lumpy slices of bread, she decided to broach the subject of the girl in the farmhouse.

"I saw Maureen. The girl you told me about," she said to Vanessa. There must have been something about Iris's tone of voice that made Vanessa wary, since immediately she seemed keen to close down any thoughts Iris was having about intervening.

"You don't want to rock the boat."

"But she's obviously really sad."

"If it's not her, it would be one of us," Vanessa whispered under her breath. "Is that what you want?"

"No," Iris conceded, before adding, "What I want is for him to stop what he's doing. To any of us."

"Well, there's as much chance of that as Hitler just giving up," Vanessa said.

She tipped the remains of her mug of tea away and chivvied the girls to get back to work. Reluctantly, Iris wolfed down the rest of her sandwich and joined them. Maybe it was none of her business. Maybe she shouldn't get involved. She thought of Esther telling her to sort herself out and focus on her own lot. Getting involved in a crusade to save a young woman wasn't going to help Iris sort herself out, was it? Maybe she should just turn a blind eye, like Vanessa and the others. But that course of action didn't sit well with her. Evelyn had manipulated Finch to dump her in this ghastly place, but Iris was determined not to be dragged down by it. She glanced back towards the farmhouse and started to work out how she could help Maureen Hinks.

When Friday came, Iris managed to chivvy the girls along so that they had finished work by seven o'clock in the evening.

Horace wasn't happy about them finishing early, but Iris promised him that they would make it up on Saturday. He wasn't happy about them going to the pub, but he knew they were entitled to some time off. The girls didn't have time to change or freshen up, so they went as they were, dressed in their jumpers, heavy dungarees and long coats, to the village pub down the hill.

"We're so glamorous!" Iris laughed.

"This isn't going to help me find a man," Vanessa replied.

Gingerly, they navigated the steep incline, the hazards of tree roots snaking across their path. At this time in the evening it was relatively easy, but on the way home, this would become a relentless series of ankle-breaking traps to weave around in the near-dark. But Iris was hoping that alcohol would help the return journey. The thought of alcohol made her think of Vernon Storey. She hadn't thought about him since she'd been here. Maybe Esther had been right, being away from Shallow Brook Farm might have been the best thing for her. It was just a shame that her new environment wasn't a rose garden.

The Flag was a small, white-walled village pub with a thatched roof. Its tiny beer garden was overlooked by the ominous hills on which stood Jordan Gate, so even while they tried to relax, and even as the light faded, the girls had a constant visual reminder of what was waiting for them. Vanessa and Iris sat at a table in the garden, sipping ciders, while the other two Land Girls played darts inside. The pub was busy, full of farmers and trekkers spending their hard-earned pay on a few hours of relaxation at the end of the week. Vanessa smoked a roll-up as they talked about life on the farm. She revealed that she had been there for two months and she had been applying for a transfer for nearly as long. She was desperate to leave.

"There's no reason to move me if rats still need killing," Vanessa said, licking down another roll-up.

"I don't know if I can stand it for six months," Iris grumbled.

"And that's if your farmer back there keeps his word," Vanessa said.

"Finch will keep his word. I hope so anyway." Iris felt a sudden doubt. What if he didn't? She was gone, out of the way. Finch could resume his courting of Evelyn without anyone ruining the party. There was no one to sour his romance now. Why would he want to bring troublesome Iris back now he was shot of her?

"Just be aware that you might be here longer than you think, that's all." Vanessa sipped from her cider and then took a drag on her cigarette. She was trying to fit as much in as she could, all too aware that they had been given a curfew of nine-thirty to be back at Jordan Gate.

Iris went to the bar and got two more ciders. As she waited, she asked the bar man for a gin to keep her going. She downed it in one, feeling it burning her throat. Could she survive here for the rest of the war? And it wasn't just her own survival that was troubling her. Part of her felt that she shouldn't give up on Finch. Despite his faults, she cared for him. Surely she should go back, damn the consequences, and make him realise that Evelyn was a bad lot? There she was again, trying to fight everyone's battles. But she couldn't help it. Iris felt a desperate need to put peoples' lives back together, a desperate desire to save people. It wasn't just that she was a kind person. No, she knew the real reason for it.

– black patent-leather shoes running, running, running –

No, shut that away, shut it out. She winced as she tried to stop the painful thoughts coming back. She knew what would help shut them out. She asked for another gin. The barman gave her a wary look.

"It's my birthday," Iris lied.

He nodded and poured her another measure. Iris tipped it into her cider and took the drinks towards the garden, sipping hers as she went. It tasted disgusting, but Iris was determined not to waste it. A group of middle-aged itinerant workers – trekkers – were blocking the door to the garden, laughing and joking. Not really looking, Iris went to weave around them. Suddenly one of their hands grabbed her shoulder, gently pulling her back.

"Here, leave off, what are you doing –?"

Time stopped still as she turned to find herself looking into the small, wrinkled face of a middle-aged man.

The face of Vernon Storey.

Her legs turned to jelly and her mouth went dry with fear, opening and closing without any words. Sporting a beard and an exhausted look, he went to speak. This couldn't be really happening. It was impossible. Iris tried to say something, but nothing would come out. She took a step backwards, away, dropping the drinks. The glasses smashed to the floor, explosions of golden liquid and glass silencing the room. Everyone looked around, but Iris was transfixed on the thin, gnarled figure in front of her.

It wasn't possible. He couldn't be here. How could he be here?

No, no, this wasn't possible.

"Iris?" he said, softly and imploringly. Was he surprised too? His silky, sinister tones were the same, etched into her brain from before. His small brown eyes burning fiercely as they had in every nightmare she'd had since that ordeal in his living room.

Finally, Iris managed to shrug off her paralysis. She found the strength in her legs to run. She bolted for the door and tumbled out into the back garden. But Vanessa wasn't there! Maybe she had gone to the toilet. She wasn't there to help. Iris scrambled to her feet, as Vernon moved slowly towards her, coming out into the garden, where darkness had nearly fallen.

"Stay away from me!" she screamed.

Iris ran for the back gate, jumping over the low fence, as Vernon gave chase.

"Wait, Iris!"

Iris ran down the small high street, desperately looking for a house with its lights on, desperately looking for some sort of sanctuary. But the row of terraced cottages stood in darkness, the owners probably in the pub. Iris scrambled up a hill at the end of the street and bolted past a wishing well.

"I will come for you, Iris. Mark my words!"

The phrase echoed around in Iris's head as she ran full pelt up the hill, tripping and stumbling on roots as she went. How could Vernon have been here? What was going on? She knew that she had to get away. The forest was nearly dark now and Iris crashed through foliage and past branches, twigs gouging at her face as she went. She jumped over tree roots and stumbled up the hillside. Finally she got to the top of the hill and threw herself against the trunk of a large oak tree. Then she risked a glance behind her, back down the hill. It was hard to see in the gloom, and the trees cast disturbing shadows that moved in the breeze. But after a few moments, Iris became reassured that Vernon wasn't down there. She turned and went to continue running, when a man grabbed her mouth.

Iris went to scream, but she couldn't make more than a muffled noise of protest.

She struggled violently, lashing out with her hands and kicking with her legs. It took a few seconds for her to realise that she wasn't fighting Vernon. It wasn't him. Her brain finally believed her eyes. It was Clarence, and not Vernon, who had grabbed her.

"What are you doing running out here?" he barked.

"Please. You've got to let me ... me ..."

"What?"

"We've got to go to the farmhouse and lock it! We're not safe!"

"Why?"

"He's here," Iris said, pulling away from Clarence and running hysterically towards Jordan Gate. She couldn't afford to wait to convince him. Clarence threw a final look down the hill and ran to follow her. He couldn't see anyone. By the time he reached the farmhouse, Iris was already inside and clutching a large bread knife.

"Put that down and tell me what the hell's going on?" Clarence slammed the door behind him. Horace entered from upstairs, wearing an apron and a curious look. Agitated, Iris paced the kitchen as if she was a wasp confined in a jar. There were two men here, they might offer some protection. What if they knew Vernon? What if they were in on it?

But as she spoke, she breathed deeply to try to calm herself, to try to make sense of the madness. She had gone for a drink in a village pub and Vernon Storey had been there. How could that have happened?

"It's Vernon. His name is Vernon."

"Who?"

"The man I was running from." Iris looked Clarence in the eyes. He didn't look particularly sympathetic, but at least he was listening. "Back in Helmstead, he tried to kill me and he said that one day he'd come back for me." Iris clasped her hands to her temples, trying to fathom what had happened. "He's one of your workers. One of the trekkers."

"Vernon?" Clarence flashed a look to Horace, who shrugged. "There's no one called Vernon."

"But there must be. He was with some of the others I've seen around here." The farmhouse door opened and a concerned Vanessa Collins ran inside.

"They said she'd run off in a panic," she said. But Clarence ignored her. "We have to have all their names. And I'm telling you, there's no Vernon." He looked at Horace for clarification.

Horace nodded and Clarence returned his gaze to Iris. "Have you been drinking, girl?"

Iris felt a flash of anger. How dare he pin this on drinking?

She hadn't imagined it. He had been there as plain as day. Her worst nightmare had returned. He had kept his promise to come back for her.

"Has she been drinking?" And now he turned to Vanessa, keen to hear what she had to say.

With some reluctance, Vanessa nodded.

"And did you see this Vernon man?"

"No."

"She wasn't there!" Iris shouted. "And the other girls were playing darts. But they might have seen me drop the drinks."

"And what would that prove?" Clarence sighed and mulled this over. "Knew it was a mistake to allow you to take them off drinking. You have a few drinks and spook yourself out in the forest –"

"I saw him! He spoke to me!"

"There's no Vernon," Clarence shouted, his voice so loud that both Vanessa and Iris flinched.

"He might be here under a different name." She looked imploringly at Horace, but he stared impassively back. "Surely he could be under a different name?"

Clarence had had enough. He turned to Vanessa and lowered his voice to a whisper, the sort of whisper that a doctor would use when expressing concern about a patient's mental health. "Take her back to the barn and see she gets some rest. And keep an eye on her."

Iris started to complain, but she found that Horace was steering her towards the door. "You heard what he said."

Vanessa opened the door and led the way. Iris followed her to the barn, looking nervously at every shadow around the silos. Was Vernon out here? Hiding like one of the rats? By the time they got to their beds, Vanessa gave Iris a chunk of bread to eat 'to soak up the drink'. Iris waited for her back to turn and she pocketed it in her coat. She knew she might need it later. But for now, a plan was forming in her head. Vanessa had shut herself off again and she was the uncommunicative soul that she had been when Iris had arrived. Iris supposed she had ruined things for them all. They would never be given permission to go to the pub again, thanks to this seemingly hysterical display. Iris didn't have the energy to talk. She knew she would have to leave this place. Otherwise Vernon would wait until the barn was in darkness and he would creep in and throttle her. She had no choice but to escape. She would go back to Pasture Farm. She would convince Fred Finch that Evelyn was using him and then everything would be all right. Yes, that's what she would do.

She waited for Vanessa to go to get changed, and then Iris slid out of bed. She put her jumper over her nightie and stashed the rest of her Women's Land Army uniform in her suitcase. Slipping on her boots, Iris crept as quietly as she could from the barn. Once outside, she pushed the door until it was nearly closed. The moon was high in the sky, illuminating the silos and the ground like the slightly unreal lighting of a movie set. Iris crept past the farmhouse and reached the first silo. To get out of the main gate without being seen from the farmhouse, the easiest route away from this place, she had to move in a loop around the silos.

As Iris emerged from one side of the silo, she nearly cried out in shock.

Maureen was standing in front of her, on her way to the farmhouse. She eyed Iris and spotted the suitcase, knowing immediately what Iris was doing. Maureen looked towards the farm. Would she raise the alarm? Iris realised that she was in two minds.

"Listen, you can come too."

"What?" Maureen looked surprised by the notion.

"He's using you and you don't seem happy. Come with me. Go your own way. But you have to leave right now!" Iris hissed as loudly as she dared. The mangy black dog padded its way around the silo to see what they were doing. Iris chose to ignore it.

"I am leaving. But I have to do it my way," Maureen protested.

"Why wait?"

"If I go now, I'll be a deserter, won't I? But if I stay they will send me home and I'll be free."

"What are you talking about?"

"You don't have to run away to finish serving as a Land Girl ..." Maureen said.

Suddenly the penny dropped and the awful realisation of Maureen's desperate plan hit home. "You think that if you get pregnant, you'll get sent home?"

"I know it," Maureen muttered. "Paragraph 11 of the rules says they have to send you home. I hate it here, so I thought that my best bet was to seduce him."

"Please don't," Iris protested. "Come with me and you can serve at Pasture Farm. It's nice there and you won't be a deserter. And you won't be having that man's child!"

Maureen looked towards the farmhouse. "You should go. I have to go inside. I won't tell him I saw you."

"At least tell me you won't do it. Get pregnant."

"I don't know."

"Leave here and head to Helmstead. You'll find Pasture Farm a couple of miles from the town. Ask for Esther. She'll take you."

"You should go."

Iris realised that arguing would be futile. And she had to leave right now. She picked up her suitcase, the cold night air biting at her uncovered calves, and walked off as quickly as she could. She moved around another of the silos and could see the gate of the farm up ahead. She would be unlucky if she was spotted now, as it would mean that Horace or Clarence were in the parlour looking out along the driveway. Iris had no choice but to chance it. She set off as quietly and as quickly as she could, swinging her case. She had reached the end of the drive and the salvation of the gate, when a new threat appeared. The mangy black dog was at her heels. It looked excitable, jumping up at her, as if it might bark at any time. Iris willed it not to make a sound.

"Please be quiet," she hissed.

The dog started to jump even more and it started to whine. Iris grimaced. No, please no.

How could she stop it?

Then she remembered the bread in her pocket. She pulled it out and threw it on the ground. The dog hungrily wolfed it down and Iris used the distraction to lift the latch on the gate and head off. She picked up her pace, knowing that although she was free of the farmhouse, she had about eighteen miles or so to walk before she got to Pasture Farm.

Iris walked and walked. She had the vaguest idea of the direction but whenever she reached a junction or crossroads there was no helpful signpost. Her big fear was that she would end up back where she started. She followed the quiet country roads, keeping near to the hedgerow. It was all so desolate and sparse, and she didn't pass another person. Owls hooted and rats scurried. The squall of foxes mating would startle her, their screams like howling babies, but still she kept doggedly on. She had contemplated opening her suitcase at the side of the road and putting on her full outfit for warmth, but decided instead to keep going. Keeping moving would keep her warm. The night sky started to shift from a velvety black to a bruised purple and Iris knew that she was heading towards dawn. How far had she gone? She had no idea. The roads stretched on and on, miles of identical hedgerow. Her feet and legs were aching and her hand held onto the suitcase with all feeling gone from her fingers. She longed to see the welcoming, warm lights of Pasture Farm each time she reached a bend in the road. Maybe the next bend would have a familiar sight around the corner.

Iris reached a crossroads. It looked familiar. She was certain that she had seen it with Finch in the car. Or was it her imagination? A mind playing desperate tricks on her to convince her she was going the right way. Suddenly a noise broke the serenity of the night, a strange and at first unfamiliar noise. But then Iris recognised it. A car engine. Some way down one of the lanes forking from the crossroads, a car was ambling its way along, faint yellow beams emanating from the slits of the blackout tape on the headlights. Iris had a few moments to decide what to do. She could push herself back against the hedgerow and hide, waiting for it to pass. Or she could flag it down and ask for a lift. Seeing as she had been walking for hours, she decided to risk it and flag down the car. As it got nearer, Iris put down her case and stepped into the road. Even though the lights were dim they meant that she couldn't see beyond them. She couldn't see what type of car it was. She waved her arms and, to her relief, the car slowed to a halt in front of her. Because of the lights she couldn't see it was a dark green Riley Nine.

As the driver's door opened, Iris moved around the car towards her benefactor.

"Thanks so much, I was –"

And then she recognised the familiar, tight grin and the dark little eyes amid a sea of wrinkles. Vernon Storey.

Iris backed away, stumbling over her feet.

"I need to talk to you, you stupid girl!" Vernon shouted, running towards her. But Iris batted him off and ran hell for leather back the way she had come, her case forgotten and abandoned. She had never been so desperate to escape something, so aware of her body's limitations when it came to running for an extended time. Why hadn't she got better at it? Why hadn't she practised?

A warm summer's day and a ten-year-old girl was running as fast as she could.

She blotted it out. She didn't have time for that now.

Black patent-leather shoes running fast down a cobbled street –

No, not now.

She just needed to escape from Vernon. That had to be her sole focus. She felt her lungs bursting as she powered down the lane, her nightdress billowing as she went.

Vernon ran back to the car, got in and turned it in the road. And then, with a squeal of tyres, the car ate up the gap between them. Iris realised that she needed to get off the road. She ran onto the verge, jumped the ditch and launched herself at the hedge. Behind her, she could hear the car braking and Vernon getting out to pursue her. The hawthorn hedge was eight feet tall and she had to scramble up, against the spikes that were intent on bringing her down. A thorn ripped open her forearm, but Iris didn't have time to scream. She hauled her legs up, finding some sort of purchase point, and then pushed up again to find somewhere to grip.

Iris dragged herself over the last few feet of hedging, hardly aware that it was ripping her hands and legs to shreds. She pushed herself over the top and tumbled down the other side. Expecting to find herself in a field, it was a stomach-churning shock to find herself falling into nothingness. She was cartwheeling out of control down the sheer side of a quarry, despite her hands trying to claw onto the chalky outcrops. Her stomach lurched as gravity took hold, and she swung round, banging her head on the rocks on the way down. She tumbled hard, out of control, the air smashed from her body. All she could do was hope as she fell like a rag doll.

By the time Vernon got to the top of the hedge, he looked down to see the still figure of Iris Dawson lying in a bloodied heap at the bottom of the quarry.

Chapter 14

This was how Joyce thought she would always remember the place. The warm glow of orange lights through the curtains of the farmhouse kitchen, the smell of baking enveloping your nostrils as you neared the back door. And inside, the warm smiles and laughter around the long, wooden table, as everyone made the best of their lot. She neared the farmhouse with John, having gone to collect him from Shallow Brook Farm. He squeezed her hand and they gazed lovingly at one another. They had endured so many dark days apart when John was in the RAF, with Joyce frequently out of her mind with worry. Would he make it back safely from each bombing raid? When his letters were delayed, she would be frantic. All the girls who had husbands and loved ones in the forces feared the arrival of the awful telegram. The one that said it was deeply sorry for their loss. But now Joyce had him back and he was a civilian again, signed off from military action and doing his best to run a farm. And the icing on the cake was that she was right next door. It had worked out beautifully. It was what they deserved after so much pain and loss.

And tonight, they were here to let their hair down for a few hours. Esther smiled at the two new arrivals as they stepped through the door into the kitchen. It had been her idea to play cards tonight. Not for money, but just as a fun way of spending a Friday night at the farm. She had prepared a pot of tea and some beetroot buns. Already sitting around the farmhouse table, Finch and Frank were preparing to play Pontoon. Finch wasn't keen, partly because Esther wouldn't allow him to play for money, and partly because he would rather be seeing Evelyn. But Esther had pointed out that he'd soon be able to spend all his time with her when they were married. This would be one of the last times they might all do this together. They should make the most of it before he was tied to the apron strings of his new wife.

"Has she said yes, then?" Joyce asked, a cheeky smile on her face. They all knew the answer. Frank and John grinned in amusement.

"Oh, will everyone stop going on about it?" Finch grumbled. "I'll ask her in my own good time."

"He's waiting for the right time," Frank said. "When she's lost her marbles!"

Everyone laughed. Finch scraped his chair back and rose in anger, throwing the pack of cards down on the table. "Stop it!" The laughter died down as they realised they had gone too far. Esther knew that this outburst didn't just come from Finch's sensitivity about asking Evelyn to marry him, but from his guilt over his treatment of Iris. Since Iris had gone, Esther had had several conversations with Finch about it. He would clam up and become uncomfortable, knowing that he had done a selfish thing in shipping her off. But he couldn't bring himself to talk about it, hoping instead that the awkward feeling would just fade away. Sometimes the hardest truths to confront were the ones that made you uncomfortable.

"She treated you a bit like a father," Esther had pointed out.

"That's probably true, but I couldn't have her spreading lies about Evelyn," Finch muttered, before adding a heartfelt and honest explanation. "Do you know how long I've been on my own, Esther?"

Esther felt some sympathy for him. He had a lot of love to give, but had simply never looked at another woman in a romantic way. And in Esther's mind, with her knowledge of some of the lecherous farmers out there, that was a Godsend. She would hear tales of other farmers leching over girls, perhaps even assaulting them. But Finch got on with running the farm, helping the girls, amusing himself by taking his little victories where he could. Life had simply passed by, the years tumbling slowly away, until he'd found himself in his current situation. Alone but with a second chance at love. She knew he was conflicted, feeling all sorts of guilt towards his wife, towards Iris, so Esther had reassured him that it was probably time to move on. No one could accuse him of rushing into a new relationship. She had only said one further thing on the subject of Iris and Evelyn. A simple, but searching question.

"Why would Iris have lied?"

The words hung in the air as Finch sighed, shook his head. Esther knew that he didn't have a cast-iron answer but he had a theory, and it seemed that sticking to a shaky theory made him feel better, made him feel justified. "Evelyn picked Iris up on her drinking. She made us all know what Iris was doing. So Iris wanted to get back at her."

"That doesn't seem like Iris. She's a sweet –"

"She's not been the same since that Vernon business."

"But I don't think she would –"

"Let's not talk about it, I'm not in the mood," he snapped. And to definitively close the subject, Finch had stomped out to check on his pigs. Esther hadn't tried to broach the subject again. For her part, she was grateful that somehow Iris had ended up at Jordan Gate. She didn't know how Finch had wangled that, but at least it was closer than East Anglia.

So now, sitting round the table, about to play cards, everyone realised that Finch had probably endured all the joking and ridicule that he was prepared to on the matter. Esther knew it was time to leave it. But as they sat in an awkward silence, she knew that everyone probably had a lot more to say on the matter, even if Finch didn't. She hoped they wouldn't try tonight. It might be best to leave their grievances and opinions until Finch wasn't quite so raw about his own guilt.

"Who's going to be the bank?" she asked, bringing things back on track.

"I'd better do that," Finch said, a sly smile returning to his lips, even if the humour didn't quite reach his eyes.

"You're going to cheat, aren't you?" John laughed.

"That's a serious accusation!" Finch grumbled in mock outrage. "How did you know?" Everyone laughed and the atmosphere of awkwardness lifted for the moment. Finch dealt out the cards to each player, one card face down in front of each of them. Tentatively and secretively everyone checked their card. Joyce was first to place a bet. Two matchsticks. Finch grumbled that it would be more interesting with real money.

"Don't you mean, more expensive?" Esther laughed.

They played the game and after four hands, Finch had a large pile of matchsticks in front of him. He chuckled with the same joy that he would have done if it had been real money.

"Soon have enough for a whole tree, Fred," Frank smiled.

By the time it reached eleven o'clock, everyone's interest in the game had petered out and Joyce and John left the farmhouse. Esther was happy to allow Joyce to stay at Shallow Brook Farm with her husband tonight as it was the weekend. Frank was about to attend to some business in his shed, when he turned to Finch.

"I wanted to go to see Iris, take her more reading books."

"All right," Finch said. Esther could see mild discomfort playing on his face. He'd obviously thought he'd buried the subject for the evening, but it wasn't to be. "You can go over on your day off. Sunday."

"Can I borrow Evelyn's car?" Frank asked hopefully.

"No, you'll have to take the pony or walk," Finch grumbled. "It's not a blooming taxi."

Frank nodded and left the house. Esther cleared away the cups and the empty pot of tea, while Finch put the cards away. Esther desperately wanted to talk about Iris again, to see if there wasn't some way of bringing her back, but she knew Finch wouldn't be receptive. She would have to bide her time, work on him. She was hopeful that she could change his mind and perhaps broker some sort of peace deal between Iris, Finch and Evelyn. But that wouldn't be on the cards tonight.

As Frank approached his shed, he was surprised to see golden light pouring from inside. He was certain that he had turned off the light earlier, so he tensed his body in readiness. Wary that someone had crept inside, Frank moved quietly towards the door, his fists ready to batter any intruder. Silently, he counted to three before flinging the door back hard and rushing inside. To his surprise, a startled Martin got up from the workbench, banging his head on the shelf.

"Ouch!"

"Sorry!" Frank fussed around the boy. "I thought you might be a German or a vagrant or a –"

"I'm not." Martin winced in pain. "Jesus."

"Are you all right?"

"No!" Martin rubbed the top of his head.

"What are you doing here?"

Then Frank spied that Martin was holding an old sheet of paper in his hands. The map that Iris had found. "I found it in your tin, sorry."

"You shouldn't have been looking." Frank snatched the map back. "That's Iris's map."

"I was looking for a smoke."

"Since when did you smoke?"

"Since never. But I wanted to try it."

"Best leave it alone, son," Frank chided.

"What's it for? The map. Pirate treasure?"

"Grow up."

"Yeah, well tell me who else has maps with mysterious crosses on them?"

"It might not be treasure. It's something. I don't know what it is. We've not had time to look." Frank examined the page again. Simple sketches of a tree and a road and a compass with map points on it, and a big X near a big tree. What was buried there? He'd never had time to ask Iris what she thought, and they'd never had time to look. Then Frank came up with one of those plans that seem like a good idea at midnight on a Friday. "You know, we should find out what it is."

"What, now?" Martin asked, confused. It was pitch black outside and they had little chance of finding the stables in the dark, let alone treasure under a big tree, somewhere on Shallow Brook Farm.

"No, we'd better do it in the light," Frank decided, feeling foolish that a 16-year-old boy was being the sensible one. "Do you want to help? It'll have to be our secret, though, eh?"

"Why?" Martin asked.

"She wanted me to look after it, keep it out of view. Iris was certain that Evelyn wanted to get her hands on it," Frank said. Martin nodded, accepting that and trotted off, closing the shed door behind him. "See you tomorrow, then."

Frank unclipped his reading spectacles and had another look at the map. It was extremely vague, almost just an *aide-memoire* to someone who already knew where to look. Frank squinted at the map for any clues. Was it even drawn to scale? He guessed they would find out. Placing the map back in the small tobacco tin, Frank caught sight of the battered children's books that were tucked on one corner of the workbench; some of Iris's reading books. Frank smiled, happy to think he could see her on Sunday, check that she was fitting in to her new surroundings. On the front of one book was a drawing of Rupert Bear running a race.

At ten o'clock the next morning, Martin asked John if he could help Frank for an hour and hurried off to meet him in the big North Field of Shallow Brook Farm. Frank was waiting, sitting on the pony and trap, looking intently at the map. In the back of the wagon were two spades. "I've copied the map onto squared paper. Just in case there's any scale to the whole thing."

"Clever. Where do you think we should start?"

"It's one square south-west from a big tree eight squares from the farmhouse. That's all I know."

Martin glanced around the field. It was used for grazing, not growing, so there were several large trees dotted around. Martin counted four that could be the right one. Frank smiled, noticing the overwhelmed expression on Martin's face. "We'd better get digging," Frank said.

The two of them walked to the first tree. Frank checked his compass and pointed to an area to the south-west of the tree. He leaned against the trunk and then took an exaggerated single step in the correct direction. "Here," he announced, plunging the tip of his spade into the grass.

"How do you know the scale's right, Mr Tucker?"

"I haven't a clue, son. But we've got to start somewhere. Come on." They started to dig, quickly finding a rhythm, where as one person removed a spade of soil, the other started to dig the next one. Soon they had dug down three feet. Frank indicated for Martin to stop. He checked the hole, removing some stones and a broken length of root with his hands. There was no treasure chest. But then, they didn't know they were looking for a treasure chest. It might be an envelope or a box or an old watering can. And not only was the map frustratingly vague, they didn't know how wide to make each hole. What if the treasure was inches away to the left or right from where they had dug? What if it was another six inches deeper down? Frank realised that they would have to be very lucky to find the buried item.

Frank took another spadeful before deciding that they weren't going to find anything here. Martin started to fill in the hole as Frank tried to dig another a foot away. They might as well be thorough, even though that would take a lot longer. As they worked, Frank could tell that Martin was keen to speak about something, plucking up the courage to get the conversation rolling. Frank guessed what it was about.

"You thinking about Iris?"

"Yeah," Martin sighed. "It wasn't right my mum sending her away like that. She didn't do anything wrong."

"You don't have to tell me, son," Frank replied. "But it wasn't your mum's fault. Finch wanted rid of her. He'd do anything to keep Evelyn Gray sweet."

Martin scowled. "What if we show Finch the map? Then it's proof that Iris found some papers at Shallow Brook."

"Yes," Frank said, mulling it over. "But it doesn't prove Evelyn was there, does it?"

"But Iris finding the map ..."

"It's not proof. Not enough, anyway." Frank rested on the end of his spade. "We should keep the map to ourselves because sooner or later, Evelyn is going to realise it's missing. And then she might come for it. And who knows, maybe that will give us some better proof, eh?"

Martin nodded obediently as he started on another hole. By the time an hour had passed, the base of the tree looked as if it had been subjected to a mole invasion, even with their best efforts to fill each hole afterwards. They started on what Frank had decided would be the last hole for this tree, some three feet further out from the trunk, just in case they'd got the scale wrong from the map. Martin crunched his spade through the grass to take the first load, when a familiar voice called out from across the field.

"What's going on here, then, eh?" It was Fred Finch, wearing his usual scruffy farming clothes but adorned incongruously with a smart, yellow-checked waistcoat.

"Drainage," Frank replied as quick as a flash.

"How's that helping drainage?" Finch raised a questioning eyebrow.

"It's holes, isn't it?" Martin chipped in.

Finch wasn't stupid, even if sometimes he liked to act as if he was. He jabbed his finger in the air at the two men and laughed, assuming he had caught them out. "You know what that reminds me of, Martin? That time we thought we'd found gold coins on Mrs Gulliver's land."

Martin nodded and winced, keen that Finch wouldn't make a similar 'treasure connection' here.

"Oh, you should have seen us, Frank. We dug up half her plot!"

"Don't you mean I dug up half her plot?" Martin protested.

"I wasn't a well man!" Finch snorted.

As the farmer's attention was taken with Martin, Frank used the opportunity to tuck the map into his jacket pocket. He needed to distract Finch from what was happening here, and he needed to do it quickly.

"That's an interesting waistcoat you've got there, Fred," he said, stifling a laugh. Finch glanced down at himself, as if he'd forgotten what he was wearing. "Did you steal it from a dandy?"

Martin burst out laughing. Finch glowered. "It's not that loud, is it? I don't think it's that loud."

"It's very bright!" Martin howled.

"Don't be daft!"

"It might have looked darker in the shop," Frank said, laughing.

Taking umbrage, Finch turned and started to stomp away. Martin and Frank smiled at each other, mission accomplished. They waited until they were certain he wasn't going to turn back and then they resumed their work. But after two hours of fruitless digging, their hands and backs sore, Frank conceded defeat. As they walked away, waiting crows swooped down and patrolled the recently disturbed earth for worms. Frank and Martin both had legitimate chores to attend to, so they put the spades back in the trap and rode the pony back to their respective farms. They agreed to meet up in a few days' time to make another attempt. As Martin got off the trap, he grinned to Frank.

"Can I come with you tomorrow? To deliver the books."

"Why not? I could do with the company." Frank got the pony to move forwards and Martin watched as they clip-clopped out of the yard.

Chapter 15

Shiny, black patent-leather shoes. Small feet running full pelt down a cobbled street on a Sunday afternoon. A bloody, painful gash on the girl's right knee was nearly hampering her progress, but she blocked out the discomfort. She'd fallen over in her haste to run, but she knew she couldn't stop. She knew she had to keep running. Her small chest felt as if it would burst with the exertion as she ran over a wrought-iron bridge, slaloming around a mother with a large pram. The mother turned to scold the clumsy child with the mane of red hair. But Iris Dawson was already on the other side of the bridge, running, running, running.

Iris opened her eyes, her vision murky and hazy, the light was too bright. A ceiling with a spider's web of small cracks emanating from a light bulb covered in a floral shade. She could feel bedclothes around her.

She blinked, trying to focus, aware that she could hear a low moaning noise. And then she realised it was her. Something hurt, but she wasn't sure what it was. She tried to haul herself up slightly, trying for a sitting position but failing. She fell back weakly on the pillow. A smell of sandalwood filled her nostrils as she started to black out again –

The patent-leather shoes squeaked with each footfall as she ran. Before Iris had found this feature of her shoes amusing, happy to demonstrate it to any relative who would indulge her. But now the noise didn't matter. All that mattered was getting there –

Squeak, squeak, squeak.

With great effort, Iris opened her eyes. Was she hearing the shoes? No, it had become something else, not a memory, but something real. Something that was here now. Out of the corner of her eye, she could see a small metallic tea trolley being wheeled nearer to her.

Squeak, squeak.

Its wheels were making a noise on the wooden floorboards. On it was a bowl of water, its contents catching the light as small waves formed because of the movement. Iris glanced around, aware that she was somewhere strange, somewhere unknown. Was she back at Jordan Gate? A wooden wardrobe stood near the door. On top of it was resting the one familiar item in the room, her suitcase. But then her vision blurred again and she could only see the vague shapes.

Where was she? What had happened?

She felt something warm and wet as a cloth was dunked in the bowl and wiped around her face. Iris tried to focus, but her vision was coming and going. She could see the shape of someone in front of her, wearing something dark. As she squinted to focus, she saw it was a woman. Water got into Iris's eyes. She realised the woman was washing her face. She stopped and put the cloth back in the water. Then Iris was aware of a hand grabbing her behind the head, moving her forwards, as a second hand brought a glass of water up to her lips. She couldn't coordinate her drinking, so water spilt down her chin onto her nightie –

Her nightie?

Iris remembered running in her nightie, the pullover on top, running as the car chased her along the lane –

And she remembered running before, ten years old in squeaky patent-leather shoes.

Both times desperately trying to get somewhere. Recently it had been to escape Vernon Storey. When she was ten, it was –

Why wasn't she a better runner? Why hadn't she got better?

The woman's hand let her head drop back onto the pillow and Iris felt tiredness wash over her again. She wanted to ask questions, she wanted to get up, but she felt disconnected, damaged and not really present.

Where was she?

She tried to focus as the trolley was wheeled from the room, but all she could see were vague shapes. A woman in black or at least a dark dress, the glint of the water in the bowl on the trolley, the wardrobe standing like a fuzzy monolith.

Iris let her eyes close and sleep quickly took her.

Sometime later – was it hours, days or weeks? – Iris opened her eyes again. One of her senses had roused her. She could smell something cooking. Baking. An apple crumble. Was she back home? Her mother was very good at making crumble.

In the last letter that Frank had read to her, Margot Dawson had promised her daughter an apple crumble when she came home on leave. Maybe she was at home somehow. But, no, Iris hadn't accrued enough service to warrant a weekend off yet. In a few weeks, she would be able to go home for a long weekend, the train fare paid for by the Women's Land Army, but for now she had to keep working.

Unless she had somehow been sent home early because she was hurt.

Where was she?

The quarry. Suddenly memories rushed back. Vernon! Iris remembered Vernon chasing her. What was he doing chasing her? She remembered tumbling like a rag doll down the side of the chalky cliff. But what had happened after? Maybe someone in the quarry had found her and sent her home? But even with poor vision, Iris didn't recognise this room. It wasn't one of the bedrooms at home. And it didn't look like a hospital room. She wasn't at the Manor House, nor in a room at Pasture Farm. She craned her neck, feeling it twinge with pain, to see the doorway. The wooden door with its glinting bronze handle was shut tight.

"Hello?" Iris called, surprised at the weakness of her voice. It was barely a croaky whisper. She tried to moisten her lips for another go, but they felt cracked and sore. "Hello? Where am I? Please?"

The sound didn't carry. She spotted the alarm clock on the bedside table and a plan formed in her fuzzy brain. With great effort, Iris lifted her right arm, shocked to see that her fingers were bandaged with a splint. Had she hurt them in the fall? Her hand fumbled towards the bedside table and she managed to hook her fingers behind the clock and knock it off, its ringers clattering on the wooden floor. Iris listened, tensing every muscle, as she heard footsteps on the stairs. Someone was coming.

Iris was running along the country lane, with Vernon at the wheel of the car, chasing –

The door handle turned and a woman dressed in dark green entered. Slightly clearer now. She wore a hat and gloves, her coat complemented with a fur stole. It was Evelyn Gray.

"Hello, Iris. You took quite a tumble."

Iris tried to move back, to somehow snake herself out of the bed and away onto the floor, but her legs hurt too much. She winced as she leaned on the mattress, pressing against her bruised elbows.

"I wouldn't try to get up. Nothing broken, as far as I can tell. But you might have concussion. Is your vision a bit blurry?"

"What am I –?" Iris struggled to say the words, her throat dry with fear.

"What are you doing here? I'm making you better. If I'd have left you at that quarry, you'd probably have died of exposure. Mind you, when Vernon ran to your side, he thought you were dead. So that's a blessing, isn't it?"

Iris flashed a terrified look. Vernon rescued her? Where was he? How had he brought her here? How could that have happened? It was all too much to think about. She felt her head spinning with confusion and pain. She tried one last time to haul herself up in bed, but felt dizziness consuming her. She slumped back on the pillow, unconscious. Evelyn Gray looked coldly at her. She picked up the alarm clock, replaced it on the bedside table and left the room.

Iris tumbled into a fitful sleep, fragments of memories competing to attract attention, as if they were a roomful of excited children.

Iris is in Brian Marley's room. They sit on the floor kneeling in front of each other and Brian moves forward. He smells of toffees and he kisses her, chastely, on the lips. After they are done they both race downstairs to go outside and play football. Brian lives two doors down from Iris and she has known him most of her young life.

As she bursts out of his front door, she sees her mother, Margot Dawson. Her eyes are large and fearful. Something is wrong. "Iris?" she says, grabbing her daughter and pulling her towards her. Margot kneels down, her voice deliberate and brittle. "I need you to do something. Can you do it for me, darling?" –

Grown-up Iris swigging from the bottle of carrot whisky in her room at Pasture Farm. She hears the wind outside blowing the tree branches against the side of the house.

"I will come for you, Iris. Mark my words."

She tries to shut out the awful words, the awful thought of Vernon looming over her as he tried to throttle her –

Iris pushing at Joe's hands as he struggled with her in the alleyway. Get away, no, get away –

At Shallow Brook Farm, Evelyn pushing Iris on the floor, knocking the wind out of her. Iris hearing her scrabbling around for the pieces of paper and the photograph from the box as darkness –

Running through the forest, with her arm around Frank, as a bullet smashes into a nearby tree –

Patent-leather shoes, a 10-year-old girl, running, running –

Sometime later, Iris awoke with a sheen of sweat on her forehead. She guessed it was night-time as there was no light coming in through the curtains. The whole house seemed still and dark, an eerie quietness hanging over the place. She tried to move herself up in the bed, and this time she managed to sit up a little, blocking out the discomfort from her bruised arms. Her head didn't feel quite as fuzzy but her legs were sore and bruised. She looked at her injured right hand, splinted with a bandage wrapped around it. She tentatively lifted the sheets to see what damage had been done to her legs. A motley patchwork of purple, brown and black bruises covered the skin. There was a bandage around her right thigh, so she assumed she must have cut the skin in her fall. Flexing her splinted fingers, Iris wondered if she had enough strength to get out of bed. She knew she had to escape. The photo had shown that Vernon and Evelyn knew each other. And now Vernon had brought her here, to Evelyn's place. So it made sense to think that Vernon might be here too. Yes, she had to get out.

She pulled at the bedclothes, which had been tucked in such a way as to form a restrictive harness over her body. With effort, she managed to pluck the sheets free. Then, slowly, she was able to slide her bottom around and bring her feet so that they hovered just above the floor. Her feet were dirty, chalky and bruised. When she had been brought here, Evelyn obviously only had the time or inclination to tend to her most immediate problems, patching her up with bandages but not washing her. Iris flexed her toes and brought them softly down on the wood. It felt cool beneath her feet and she paused for a moment, to catch her breath. She was surprised how the exertion of getting up was tiring her. Gingerly she pushed herself up from the bed, a bolt of pain coursing through her hand. But she was upright, even though her legs wobbled slightly under her weight. Iris took a tentative step forward, mindful of being as quiet as possible.

Creak.

The floorboard protested as she stepped on it and Iris muttered a silent curse. It had sounded loud to her, in the still of the night, but was it enough to bring Evelyn running? She stood motionless, listening for any movement outside the room, watching the door handle. After a few seconds, she was satisfied that the noise hadn't woken anyone, so she took another tentative step. To her relief, the second floorboard didn't make a sound. She was three steps from the door now. Iris glanced back at the wardrobe with her suitcase on the top. She didn't have the strength to lift it down or the time to get it. She would leave it for now and just worry about getting herself out of this place. She took another step forward and the next floorboard creaked slightly, although not as noisily as the first one had. Iris was aware that her breathing was speeding up and perspiration was beading on her forehead; an intense weariness trying to take over her body. She took another step and she was now close enough to open the door.

Iris swallowed hard, bracing herself for what she might find on the other side.

"I will come for you, Iris. Mark my words!"

She gripped the handle, wincing as she forgot about her splinted right hand. Maybe the fingers were broken. She wasn't sure. She gripped the handle with her left hand and pulled it quietly down. The door didn't open. She tried it again, mindful of making too much noise. But then she realised that the door was locked. Of course it was!

Disappointed, Iris felt as though she wanted to scream. Could she scream? Maybe there were other houses nearby and someone would hear her scream. Yes, maybe. But if this place was a cottage or a house on its own, she could be in trouble. It could be a big gamble to take. Iris bent down to look through the keyhole, in the hope of seeing some more of the house. Perhaps she could see where the stairs were or the other rooms. But she couldn't see anything. The key was in the lock on the other side.

Feeling crestfallen, Iris carefully retraced her steps to the bed, avoiding the creaky floorboards. She scooped herself back into bed and pulled the covers over her legs. Sleep didn't come. Instead, she sat in bed, in the semi-darkness, wondering how she would escape this place and what would happen to her if she didn't.

After Sunday service, Martin and Frank returned to Pasture Farm and set off on his pony and trap to see Iris. It was a hot, sunny morning, but with enough breeze to make it a pleasant ride. Nevertheless, by the time they had got near Jordan Gate, Martin felt his shoulders burning and he noticed that Frank's face was reddened by the sun. Frank asked Martin to open the gate at the farm, so he hopped down from his seat. A mangy black dog was circling around on the other side, so Martin flashed a questioning look back at Frank. What should he do? Frank tethered the reins and got down. He neared the gate, reached into his pocket and showed something to the dog. It sniffed with wary interest and then bolted off as Frank threw it as far as he could.

"What was that?" Martin asked, as they unhinged the gate and ran back to their ride.

"Toffee," Frank replied. "Should keep him busy." And he mimed a dog laboriously chewing a sweet. Getting back into the driving seat, he clicked the reins, moving the horse forward. As they neared the farm building, a tall, saturnine figure with a shock of black, slicked-back hair came out and eyed them suspiciously.

"I've got all the trekkers I need," Clarence Trubb growled. After a moment, he was joined by a thin young woman with blonde hair. Dressed in Land Girl clothes, she stood nervously at his side, looking haunted.

"We're not trekkers," Frank said.

"We're from Pasture Farm. Came to see Iris," Martin offered.

Clarence continued to eye them with contempt. Martin and Frank exchanged a look. This was going well.

"She's not here," Clarence said, spitting a glob of phlegm onto the path.

"She's working in the fields?" Frank asked.

"No, she's bleeding well run off, hasn't she?"

"Yes, she ran off on Friday night," Maureen offered, following it with an obedient look towards Clarence, who indicated for her to go inside. He'd take care of this.

"I thought she'd be back with you lot by now, run back with her tail between her legs." Clarence scowled.

"We've not seen her. Friday, you say?" Frank asked, starting to worry.

Clarence spied the storybooks in Martin's hand. "So you might as well take your children's books with you."

"Did she say anything? I mean, why did she run off?"

"Some girls aren't cut out for life here. We don't run a cosy little setup like you've got at your farm. My girls are here to get their bloody hands dirty." Clarence turned to go, "Now, piss off. I can't waste any more time on her. I've got to replace her as quickly as possible."

Frank bridled, but contained his anger. "You'd better hope we find her."

"Or what?" Clarence said, relishing the idea of a confrontation.

Frank stood his ground for a moment, staring into the wide face of his overfed opponent. "Or we'll be back."

Martin was already back on the trap and turning the horse around, ready to leave. Frank didn't take his eyes off Clarence as he hauled himself up onto the seat. Martin shook the reins and the horse started to trot away from Jordan Gate, passing a dog struggling to chew a toffee. As they got a mile along the country lane, Martin had to steer his way around a large group of men and women who were emerging from a small church. In the vain hope of seeing Iris, he glanced at some of the girls, obviously Land Girls stationed at Jordan Gate. He didn't pay any attention to the men, the itinerant workers from the farm. If he had, he might have noticed Vernon Storey in amongst the crowd.

As the sky started to turn purple, Esther poured more tea for the people gathered around the table at Pasture Farm. It wasn't the happy and fun atmosphere of a few nights before when they had played Pontoon. Now, Frank, Martin, Finch and Esther were concerned about what had happened to Iris, their faces etched with worry.

"I mean, what are the options?" Esther asked, pushing a cup and saucer towards Frank. "She's run away from Jordan Gate?"

"Or they're covering up the fact she's gone?" Frank offered.

"What do you mean?" Martin asked, already looking nervous of the answer.

"Girls have accidents on the farms. I've seen a Land Girl lose her arm in a threshing machine back on one farm. Some farmers might try to cover up things like that." Frank sighed. "I'm not saying she's had an accident, but it's a place she's not used to, equipment she's not used to ..."

"Why didn't you say this to me on the way home?" Martin blustered, alarmed by the prospect that Iris might have died.

"Didn't want to worry you."

"Well, I'm worried now! We should go back!"

"We're just discussing all the options, son," Finch offered, trying to calm the situation. "So she's either run away under her own steam, or she's had an accident and they're saying she ran away so they can cover it up. What else?"

"I think she ran away," Martin said. "The man who owns that farm is a real bastard."

"Martin!" Esther scolded.

"Well, he is," Martin said, sheepishly.

Esther turned to Finch and Frank for confirmation. They'd both met Clarence Trubb, she hadn't. Both men shrugged and nodded their heads. "He's right. He is a bit of a bastard."

Esther took up the reins. "So the question is, where has she gone?"

"She'd be back here by now, if she was coming. She's had two days," Finch said.

"She wouldn't come back here, not with your fancy woman," Martin said, emboldened by being included in the discussion.

"Here, you mind your lip!" Finch replied. Martin looked at the floor.

"Would she go back to Northampton?" Frank asked, tired of the bickering and looking directly at Esther. The warden winced, knowing that it would open up a huge can of worms if she had to telephone Iris's mother to find out. Especially if there was the chance that Iris might not even be there. And yet, the rules of the Women's Land Army meant that any unexplained absence had to be treated as desertion. Esther had a duty to discover if Iris was hiding out at her family home. And if she wasn't, well, then they would cross that bridge when they came to it.

"I'll telephone her mother tomorrow," Esther said.

"Why not do it now?" Finch said. "At least then we'd know where she was."

"I'll call Mrs Dawson tomorrow. Give Iris one more night to show up."

Birds were fluttering in the trees outside the window. It was the only sound that Iris had heard for the last few hours. No one had come to her room all morning and she was beginning to wonder what was happening. The room contained very little in the way of amenities. There was a bedpan under the bed and a jug of water and a glass. Iris had finished the water in the jug.

By what she assumed was the middle of the day, for the first time since contemplating her escape she felt hungry. She wondered whether she might have been abandoned. What if Evelyn had suffered a car accident? She was a courier, after all, and that increased the likelihood of her having a crash. Or what if she had fallen unconscious downstairs? Iris could die of starvation before anyone realised she was locked in this room in this house. She jiggled the handle of the door, not caring if she attracted attention, shouting for someone to come. She followed a pattern of shouting and then pausing to listen for any sounds of a response, the cycles getting shorter and more desperate. Eventually she stopped because her throat was sore and she was close to tears.

She stretched the calf muscles in her legs, pressing against the door to get purchase. She was aware of the stiffness in her legs from the tumble and she was trying to get her legs working well enough to escape.

Iris slumped on the bed. Her bruised legs were still aching and tender, and she hadn't dared to take off her finger bandages to see what damage lay beneath. She looked up at the ceiling, feeling her eyelids getting heavy from exhaustion and hunger. A fitful sleep washed over her. Images of the past flashed into her mind.

Looking up, as a young girl, as her mother smiled and brushed her hair.

And then – running for the train with her mum and dad. Even as a child, Iris knew that Ivor and Margot Dawson were a stylish couple. He would wear an immaculate three-piece suit, complete with pocket watch and chain; she would wear a tailored orange woollen coat and gloves. They were running as a family to get the train to see her grandfather. She remembered that the train started to pull out of the station as they reached the platform, and her father doubled over with the exertion of the failed run. Iris and her mother went to tend to him, but he said he was fine. And as he regained his breath, instead of cursing their luck, her father laughed and smiled. It was one of those things, not worth getting upset about. He ruffled Iris's hair and suggested that they use the time while they waited for the next train to get a cake and some tea. It sounded a splendid idea.

Cake and tea.

Iris felt something push against her arm. She opened her eyes, not entirely sure if she was still dreaming or not. Evelyn was looking down at her, narrowed eyes searching her face. Suddenly, Iris felt fully awake, and pushed herself back, recoiling from Evelyn's touch as if she'd been scalded.

"It's all right," Evelyn said without emotion. "I brought you some food."

Iris glanced at the bowl of green soup that was steaming on the bedside cabinet, a chunk of potato bread next to it.

"Where have you been?"

"I had to take a package somewhere. Part of my job."

"Let me go." Iris scowled.

"I need something from you first."

"What?"

"As soon as I have the map, I'll let you go. Now, eat."

"What's the map for?"

"You don't need to worry about that. Just tell me where it is." Evelyn's eyes darted to the top of the wardrobe. "I looked through your case and couldn't find it."

"Let me go!"

"I need the map first. We can take as long as we need," Evelyn said, coldly. "Now eat. You must be starving."

Evelyn didn't wait for a reply. She turned away from the bed and started to walk back towards the door. The open door. Starving or not, Iris knew this was her chance. Perhaps her only chance!

She lunged forward from the bed, grabbing Evelyn round the neck with both arms, her momentum and weight sending Evelyn crashing forward onto the wooden floor. Evelyn's leg flew up as she fell, knocking the bowl of soup into the air. Iris landed hard on her injured fingers, bending them up against the splint with the force of the impact. Evelyn's body was underneath hers, and it had cushioned some of her fall. But then, further pain came as gravity caught up with the bowl of soup. It fell on her back and shoulders, scalding her. The bowl shattered as it bounced off, but Iris didn't notice. She was fighting through the pain and trying to pin Evelyn's thrashing limbs to the floor. Evelyn managed to kick out, knocking Iris off balance, but Iris fought to subdue her opponent. Evelyn rolled onto her back so she could face her attacker and the two women tumbled over each other, a messy collection of flailing limbs as they both scrambled for the upper hand. They clattered into the bedside table, the alarm clock falling onto Iris's head. She batted it away and tried to land a punch in Evelyn's face. But Evelyn wedged her knee under Iris's ribcage, using the leverage to send her smashing back against the wardrobe. Iris winced as a burst of pain exploded in her head as she hit the wardrobe door. She tried to get up, but Evelyn was already on her feet and running for the open door.

Iris had almost got back on her feet by the time the door slammed. She heard the key being turned in the lock, followed by Evelyn's laboured breathing as she ran downstairs. Iris felt despair seeping back into her bones. She looked at the carnage in the room, smears of green, gloopy liquid had somehow managed to cover most of the bed and the floor, as well as the back of Iris's nightie, which was stuck to her skin. She picked herself up and looked at the shattered bowl. It had broken into three jagged pieces of pottery. Iris picked up the longest and sharpest one. She staggered, still winded, over to the bed. She opened the drawer of the bedside cabinet and placed the jagged shard inside. The thought of using it filled her with horror, but she might need it to fight for her life. At least she had a weapon now. Something to threaten Evelyn with.

Iris leaned forward and picked the chunk of potato bread off the floor. This was what she was reduced to, scavenging off the floor like that mangy dog at Jordan Gate. She ate the bread and then watched the door, fixing it with all her attention. She guessed that, elsewhere in the house, Evelyn was recovering from their fight. But she knew she'd be back sometime. And Iris knew she had to be ready. Would she be punished for what she had done? Her splinted fingers were throbbing from being bent back during the scuffle. Iris tried to block out the pain. She closed her eyes and tried to think of something good. She thought about her father.

She saw the Lyons Corner House that they had gone to when they missed the train. Ivor Dawson was smiling at the waitress, as he ordered a fabulous selection of cakes. It was 1934 and, with no rationing, and the rest of the kids staying with grandfather, they could have ordered as many as they wanted, but her father reined in his family's desire to try all the menu. Time was against them, with her father checking his pocket watch at regular intervals. They had one hour until the next train, and they couldn't afford to miss that one. So her father ordered a chocolate eclair for Iris and a slice of Victoria sponge for himself and Margot. Iris was amused by the antics of her father as he joked at the table, carefree and happy. When Margot poured the tea, Ivor liked the look of her cup more than his own. He distracted his wife by pointing at something and then switched the cups. But the action was clumsy and he spilt some tea, giving himself away. Margot played at being indignant, but she found it funny. Why did he do that? All he had to do was ask.

Iris realised something. Finch did the same thing. The switch trick. She'd never made the connection before. Maybe it was a 'man thing', but she'd never seen anyone else do it. Only her dad and Finch. Daft buggers.

But thinking about Finch brought her back to the present, happy thoughts of laughter and eclairs dissipating like morning dew on warm grass. Iris pulled her wet, soup-stained nightie away from her back and shoulders. Her stomach was still rumbling, and she guessed that Evelyn wouldn't risk bringing her any more food for a while. But she had her crockery dagger and she would be ready.

Martin sat in Frank's shed, watching as Frank tried to oil an old rabbit trap and get the mechanism to work. Esther knocked on the door jamb and entered. "Hello, love," Esther said.

"Hello. Any news about Iris?"

Esther shook her head. "I was going to telephone her mother today, but the records show she doesn't have a telephone," Esther explained. "I might have to go to Northampton."

"You're too busy to go to Northampton, aren't you?" Frank asked.

"Yes, but what choice do I have?"

"I could go," Martin piped up.

"You?"

"Yes, me," Martin stated, a little hurt. "I can do it, Mum. I am old enough."

Esther mulled this over for a moment. "If you find Iris there, you tell her to get herself back here as quickly as possible, yes?"

"Of course!" Martin said, excited by his mission and by the chance of getting away from farm work for a while.

"I don't want to have to report her as missing until she has a chance to come back. She may be worried about showing her face," Esther said. "But if you go, you have to think about the other option."

"What other option?"

"If Iris isn't there, then we don't know where she is. And that means her mother is likely to take the news badly." Esther frowned. "Oh, I'd better go. If that happens, you won't know how to handle it."

"I can do it, Mum. I can be caring and sensitive and all those things you say I'm not."

Esther looked at her son, a proud smile coming over her face. She nodded her consent. "I'll arrange a train ticket with the Women's Land Army."

Now it was Martin's turn to beam.

Chapter 16

"Iris?"

A soft but masculine voice, a cautious enquiry, whispered. She opened her bleary eyes and struggled to focus on the shapes in the room. A small, weasel-like man was crouched on her bed, looking over her. "Iris?" His brow was furrowed with lines and his eyes shone like shimmering dark coals in his weathered face. She knew immediately who it was.

I will come for you, Iris. Mark my words.

The words reverberated in her head, never far away in the recesses of her memory. And here he was, in front of her. Vernon Storey. Her nightmare made flesh. She had tried to convince herself that the man she saw in the Flag, the man who had chased her down a country lane in the middle of the night, was a mirage. Some illusion dredged up in her terrified brain. But here he was, a reality, so close that she could smell his stale sweat and see the stitches on his pullover. Iris did her best to back away, but she realised that Evelyn Gray was standing on the other side of her bed.

"Get away from me!" Iris hissed.

She fumbled for the drawer by the bed, pulling it open to

get the sharp pottery dagger. But the drawer was empty.

"I don't want to hurt you, Iris. I wasn't trying to hurt you when I chased you from the pub. I just wanted to talk." Again, his voice was soft, kind even. It had none of the anger she expected, none of the anger she remembered. He held up the jagged, dangerous shard of crockery. "This wasn't very nice, was it?" He threw it towards the door, safely out of reach.

"I want to help you. But to help you, you've got to help me. Help us."

Iris glanced between the two of them. What was going on? Vernon looked at Evelyn, seemingly for consent. Then he took a deep breath and said, "Evelyn had to find Finch and get him interested. I needed her to do that so she could get my tin of things. That's because I couldn't very well wander back to Shallow Brook Farm, could I?"

"But you used Finch!" Iris spat. "You're still using him!"

"I didn't want to hurt him," Evelyn said, looking sheepish.

"Enough people have got hurt already, Iris. But I need that map so that I can get away. You'll never see me again. You'll never see either of us again," Vernon said gruffly, as if he found this difficult to say. As far as Iris could tell, he was opening his heart to her. This wasn't what she expected at all. She suspected that he would change quickly enough into the Vernon she despised if she refused to help, so for now she stayed silent, wanting to hear him out. "We thought we had it all worked out, you see? Evelyn just had to get the box and that was that. I'd have the map. But the map is the one thing missing. With it, I can start again. Otherwise, I have to skulk around, earning money on farms like Jordan Gate, like the other drifters, the other dead-beats."

"You killed your son! You deserve everything you get," Iris said, unable to stop herself.

Evelyn started to reply, to silence Iris with a sharp word, but Vernon raised his hand, urging her to not get involved. He looked down at Iris and smiled a bitter smile. "I know. Part of me thinks I should turn myself in. Hang by my neck for what I've done. But I can't do that. I owe it to Evelyn to survive. See, I'm doing this for her."

"How long have you been together?" Iris's eyes darted between them. Evelyn and Vernon shared a look. It was time to come clean.

"All our lives," Evelyn replied. For a moment, Iris struggled to process this, until Vernon finished the explanation.

"She's my sister."

Suddenly and with blinding clarity, Iris could see some slight family resemblance between Vernon and Evelyn. She was lucky not to have been burdened with his small eyes and uneven skin, but, if you looked for it, there was something about their eyebrows and the shapes of their faces that marked them as being related.

"You tell us where the map is and you'll never see me or her again," Vernon said, his voice low and calm as if explaining a simple fact to a young child. "You can go back to Pasture Farm and your old life. Now, where is the map?"

Iris looked fearful. Did she want to give that information?

"And please don't say you've destroyed it," he said. His eyes flashed with malevolence. The cold look that Walter had probably seen when his father was about to strike him –

With grim certainty, Iris had no doubt that if she couldn't produce the map, Vernon and Evelyn would kill her.

"I haven't destroyed it, it's safe."

"Where?"

"It's not here, so you'll have to let me go," Iris replied. "It's at the farm."

Vernon nodded, already having worked out that fact. "That's the problem, Iris," he stated. "If I let you go back to Pasture Farm, then you'll just go to the police, won't you? Pull together a lynch mob."

"I won't. You have my word."

"Oh, that's all right, then," he said, smiling coldly. "If you give your word, then I don't mind trusting my freedom, my life to you, Iris. Yes, that'll be fine. What do you think I am? Some kind of damn fool?"

"I mean it," Iris said, feeling the hope drain out of her.

"You'll say anything to get out of here," Vernon said, a hint of weary annoyance cutting through his voice. "I'm not going to the gallows and that means I can't trust anyone."

"Please, no, I just want this to end." Iris found herself suddenly tearful. All those nights terrified and drinking while she worried about this monster coming back, and everything that had happened since. She struggled to stop the tears. She had to be strong and her mind had to be clear to work out how to get out of this situation. Vernon flashed a look at Evelyn. Iris suspected that they would have liked nothing more than to be able to take her at her word. But the stakes were too high for all of them.

"We want it to end too. Where is the map?"

"At the farm. Pasture Farm."

"You said that. I meant, whereabouts?"

Iris had a sudden dark thought. "If I tell you, how do I know you'll let me go?"

Vernon grinned, a shark's grin of yellowing teeth. "You have my word."

It hung in the air. The fact was that Iris couldn't trust this man any more than he could trust her. It was a stalemate situation. Desperately Iris tried to think of another solution.

"I daresay I could find it, eventually. The problem is," Evelyn said, "Even with Finch around my little finger, I can't go rooting through the rooms at Pasture Farm. For one thing that old bag, Esther, would stop me."

"So that leaves us with a problem, doesn't it?" Vernon smiled. Iris hated it when he smiled, as his eyes remained as cold as unlit coal. "We can't get the map from the farm. But you know where it is. You could get it."

"Yes?" Iris said, wondering where this was going.

"But I don't trust you to do that without going to the police." Vernon nodded his head slowly, seeming to relish this dilemma. A logic puzzle to be solved, like Iris's father used to enjoy wrestling with the crossword in *The Northampton Echo*.

"But here's the thing. You could go and get it if we knew that you would come straight back," Vernon announced. "That way we'd all be happy. I could trust you then."

"All right." Iris sat up in the bed, her head woozy with confronting her demon in the flesh. She realised that she wasn't fully recovered from her fall in the quarry, feeling exhausted, with a headache throbbing in her temples.

"But for this to work, we need some insurance, Iris," Vernon stated, again using his talking-to-a-child voice. "I need to know you'll come back to this cottage with the map, without telling anyone."

"I will."

"It's not enough, Iris," Evelyn said with annoyance.

"But we thought of a good idea earlier." Vernon smiled.

"That's why I plan to ask Finch to come here tomorrow night. I'm sure I can get him to come for dinner."

"What? Why?"

"If he arrives at seven o'clock. You can leave just before then and run to Pasture Farm, get the map and come back," Vernon said.

Iris struggled to process all this. "Finch is the insurance that I'll come back? But how?"

"Because if you're not back by nine o'clock, I'll poison him," Evelyn stated, her eyes staring with contempt at Iris. It was such a matter-of-fact statement that Iris was chilled by its ruthlessness. She realised how little Fred Finch meant to Evelyn, to either of them. They had come so far, done so many bad things that they viewed him as being totally expendable. Nothing was going to get in their way.

Iris couldn't help but utter a nervous laugh. How would they get away with it? But then she remembered how ruthless Evelyn had already been, getting her thrown out of Pasture Farm to save her own neck, punching her to stop her. And that was without thinking about the dark depths into which Vernon had sunk. He had already murdered his own son, albeit in a moment of immediately regretted anger, and pinned the murder on another man. Iris realised, in horror, that this pair really would carry out their threat. They were dangerous and she couldn't underestimate them.

Two hours to run from here to Pasture Farm and back again? Could she even do that?

"We don't want to have to do that, Iris, but we will if we have to," Vernon said.

"We're desperate," Evelyn added. "All you have to do is get the map and Finch will be fine. But if you double-cross us, I will kill him."

Vernon nodded at Iris for added emphasis. Then his arms moved quickly and he clutched Iris's chin tightly in his hand, his fingers pressing hard into her cheeks. She yelped in surprise and pain. "Do you understand, Iris?"

Iris nodded, terrified.

"Good girl," Vernon stated. He released his grip and got up from the edge of the bed. Evelyn walked around towards him and they moved towards the door. Vernon stooped to pick up the shard dagger of soup bowl on his way. He offered a cheery smile to Iris, the sort of smile that you'd give when it had been nice to see someone again. It felt hugely inappropriate under the circumstances and only served to chill Iris even more. She watched as they left and was, for once, mildly relieved when she heard them lock the door behind them. At least it was a barrier, of sorts, even if they controlled it. Iris slumped back into the bed, her mind spinning with what had happened.

Vernon had kept his promise to come back for her.

And now she had to keep her promise and get the map. Finch's life depended on it.

"How about that one?" Esther pulled out a maroon-coloured tie with a tasteful pattern of tiny silver rectangles and showed it to Martin, who was standing in his only suit in front of the dressing-table mirror. "It's one of Fred's, but I'm sure he won't mind." Martin shook his head. On his bed was a selection of ties, from the garish to the conservative, and he liked none of them.

"You're going to have to wear a tie, meeting Iris's mother!" Esther said firmly.

"I know. I just don't like any of them. They all make me look like I'm a bank manager or I'm going to a funeral." He tugged at the shoulder of his suit. It was a light grey two-piece that was too big for him, the shoulders swamping him like something Boris Karloff would have worn in *Frankenstein*.

Martin felt uncomfortable, and at first Esther assumed it was just his reluctance to wear a suit. But fairly quickly another thought had crossed her mind. He was nervous about going to meet Margot Dawson in Northampton. As he tutted and debated which tie was the least dreadful option, Esther decided to tackle the elephant in the room.

"You'll be fine tomorrow. She's a nice woman, by all accounts."

"It feels odd."

"In what way?"

"Dunno." Martin shrugged, accidentally accentuating his large padded shoulders. "I'm not sure I know what to say to her."

Esther sat on the bed and took a deep breath, seeing the insecurity in his eyes. It was at times like these that he seemed like a young 16-year-old rather than the man he aspired to be the rest of the time. She saw the years melt away and she wanted to hug him like she'd done when he was six. But realising that he might reject such contact now, Esther merely patted the space next to her on the bed. Martin moved towards her and sat down.

"It's difficult. She might be there at the house, in which case you have to encourage her to come back here. Continue her service in the Women's Land Army. But if she's not there, you're going to have to deal with Margot Dawson being upset. She won't know where her daughter is and she'll be worried."

"That's what I'm worried about," Martin said. "If Iris is there, it'll be easy."

"I know."

"It's just, I want to do it. I know I could do it. But –"

"But what?"

"But if Iris and I ever get serious, I don't want this to be the way I meet her family. Coming to say she's deserted."

Esther nodded, her eyes full of understanding. She started to fold up the ties that were on the bed.

"What are you doing?"

"Putting them away, because I can go, if you want me to."

Martin gritted his teeth and shook his head, annoyance at himself for not being able to do this. Part of him really wanted to go, to prove himself. After a moment, he looked at Esther and smiled in relief. For the first time since they had come to his bedroom to choose his outfit, she saw his face relax. This was what he had secretly wanted. The one thing he couldn't ask for outright.

"Would you mind?" Martin asked.

"Not at all, love." Esther ruffled his hair, and to her surprise, he let her do it without complaint. She looked proudly at her boy. "You wanted to do it, and I'm proud of you. And you're right, it's no way to meet her family for the first time." She rose to her feet and placed the folded ties in the wardrobe. "Especially if you ever start courting her!"

As night time came, Iris couldn't sleep. She stared through the small window of her prison, her breath condensing on the glass, contemplating what would happen. The garden was small, but most of its space had been turned over to growing vegetables, in line with the Government's instructions to 'Dig for Victory'. She couldn't see much beyond the tall hedges of the garden, but she supposed it was a remote and isolated cottage as she couldn't see any other people walking past, and no other buildings were dotted on the horizon.

She thought about what she would have to do tomorrow. She heard Vernon's words in her head:

"If he arrives at seven o'clock, you can leave just before then and run to Pasture Farm, get the map and come back."

Her legs were bruised and painful and she wondered if she would be able to run fast enough on them to get back in time to save Finch. Even if she was fully fit and healthy – could she do that?

The black patent-leather shoes of a 10-year-old girl, running full pelt along a cobbled street –

Iris had to focus. It couldn't become clouded by the emotions of the past; the time she'd tried to shut away forever. Instead she thought about Finch and the dreadful fate that was in her hands. Iris felt despair in the pit of her stomach that they could view Finch as their insurance. He was expendable. Iris had to save him.

Suddenly she spotted a figure down below, in the garden, walking down the rows of potato plants. It was Evelyn Gray, dressed in a long, blue casual dress. She had thick gardening gloves, secateurs and a small wooden trug. Was she gardening at this time of night? Evelyn passed the rows of potatoes and bent down to a green plant growing nearby. Carefully, she held the top of it while she snipped at the base. Then she used the secateurs to edge it onto the trug, trying to touch it as little as possible. Iris could see it wasn't a potato plant, and as she focused her eyes, she recognised its distinctive spade-shaped green leaves. A plant that would grow happily near to potatoes. Deadly Nightshade. It was appropriately named as even getting the juice onto your skin could make you quite sick, and ingesting it would result in an agonising death. Iris had often dealt with it in the fields.

As Evelyn started back towards the house, with her toxic cutting, she glanced up and smiled at Iris.

Iris felt her stomach knot inside, sick with the knowledge that Evelyn was really going to do this.

Iris stayed at the window, staring numbly at the garden, a place now illuminated in monochrome solely by the moonlight above. In her head all she could hear was the desperate breathing of a 10-year-old girl –

– running, running.

Chapter 17

Amongst the crowd of passengers disembarking from the afternoon train at Northampton Castle, was a middle-aged woman with an address on a piece of paper and a troubled expression. Esther Reeves stood in the middle of the concourse as soldiers and workers walked around her. She was dressed in her best coat and gloves, but she had decided not to wear a hat, fearing it might appear slightly too much; too formal. She imagined it would be tough enough for Margot Dawson opening the door to her without it seeming too official a visit. Esther hoped everything could be solved amicably, over a cup of tea, without recourse to having to officially report Iris for desertion. And desertion would be what it was, since conscription had come in. Esther walked out of the station, surprised to see that the streets were shiny and black with recent rain. Martin had made her a sandwich that she had eaten on the train, but that didn't stop her feeling tempted as she passed a street vendor selling hot sweetcorn cobs. Esther felt tired, in need of a pick-me-up. But she eschewed the idea of a cob, fearing she would get butter on her coat, and set off for Stanley Street and the Dawson family home. She hadn't had time to inform Margot that she was coming, as the Dawsons didn't own a telephone, and there was no time to write. So she knew the visit would be a surprise. Esther hoped that Margot would be at home.

It wasn't a long walk from the station, but Esther found herself trudging down streets, each less busy than the last, until she reached Stanley Street, a cobbled street full of near-identical terraced houses stretching into the distance. She looked for the right house as she walked along, passing a group of dirty-faced children playing happily with a football. An old woman was sitting on her front step, watching the world go by, so Esther nodded hello as she passed. The woman looked her up and down, perhaps wondering what her business would be. Finally Esther reached the Dawson house, aware that the old woman from along the street was still watching her, with no hint of shame at staring for so long. Esther realised that, like it or not, she would have to do this with an audience. The Dawson house had a single front window downstairs and two upstairs, bedecked with net curtains. A light-blue front door had a heavy brass knocker and was in a better state of repair than the houses on either side. Esther gave the knocker a short rap with her gloved hand. She waited for a moment and then stepped back onto the cobbles to look up at the top windows. Was anyone home? She couldn't see any sign of movement. She knocked again and waited.

Finally Esther thought she might as well use the nosey neighbour to her advantage, so she walked back to the old woman on the step.

"Excuse me, I'm looking for Margot Dawson. Do you know where she might be, please?"

"She's working. Working at the munitions factory," the old woman said, eyeing Esther with interest.

"And where is that?" Esther asked.

"It's down the end, right, then second left. You can't miss the building. Big old bugger."

Esther nodded her thanks and started off down the road, aware of net curtains twitching in her wake.

Soon she reached the factory. It was a large converted sawmill that had been turned over to war use. Workers were heading back to work through the wooden gates after having a break for lunch, desperately finishing their cigarettes. The metal gates had long since gone to help the war effort and the wooden ones were temporary, hurriedly erected affairs. Esther scanned the faces of the workers, women like herself, mostly wearing headscarves and overalls; men with flat caps and trilby hats. There were dozens of women who could have been Margot Dawson. Esther had no description of the woman, so she knew she would have to go in to talk to a manager and ask to see her.

Esther waited until no more workers returned, assuming that everyone would be inside now. Then she headed into the factory and found the foreman's office. To the sides of the office, workers busied themselves assembling bullets and bombs. The factory was noisy so Esther had to raise her voice to make the foreman understand her. When she explained who she was and that it was official war business on behalf of the Women's Land Army, he agreed to fetch Margot Dawson.

Esther waited, glancing at the posters on the wall. Among them, cartoon drawings urged women to make do and mend, a woman in a headscarf held a drill and urged people to work for the war. Esther thought how lucky she was to be spending her war on a farm and not in a dangerous munitions factory. Both were equally hard work, but the surroundings of idyllic countryside made it more bearable for her. She had become so distracted that at first she didn't notice the slightly built woman with red hair tied up under a scarf. Margot Dawson stood with folded arms and a worried expression on her pale face. She looked so similar to Iris it was uncanny.

After Esther introduced herself, she steered Margot towards the exit.

"Can we talk in private? Somewhere we can hear each other?"

They went outside into the courtyard of the factory. Esther outlined what had happened, that Iris had run away from her current placement. Margot took this in, her face etched with concern.

"Has she come home to you?" Esther asked.

"No, I've not seen her," Margot said anxiously. Her voice had no trace of an accent, and was instead like the presenters on the radio. She sounded more like a lady than a factory worker, but fear was rising in her voice. "Where can she be?"

Esther sighed. She wished that Iris was with her mother. It would have been so much easier. Now she didn't really know what to do or say to help the situation, and ease this anxious woman's concerns about her eldest daughter. They were both now looking for a missing person. Where was Iris Dawson?

Iris had woken early, after only a few hours' sleep. Her head was throbbing and her right hand was hurting like hell. She was desperate to take the finger splints off and see what the damage was, but part of her thought she'd wait until this whole episode was over. At least her hand was bandaged and secure for now. Evelyn brought in breakfast. A cheese omelette.

"You should eat. Get your strength up for later."

"What have you put in it?" Iris scowled.

Evelyn smiled, amused. "Nothing. I need you fit and well. But I'm glad you saw me fetching the nightshade. It always strikes me as incredible that something so deadly grows so freely in the countryside."

"It's something we're always finding," Iris replied grimly.

Iris looked at the congealed egg on her plate. It wasn't an appetising omelette, but she was starving so she wolfed it down in a few big, messy mouthfuls. Evelyn watched, impressed at her appetite.

"That will help you with the running. I've invited Fred to dinner. He's very excited, as you can imagine."

Evelyn went to take the plate, but Iris grabbed her arm. Evelyn readied herself for another fight, but Iris just wanted to ask her a question, something that had been troubling her. "Why do I have to run there? Why can't Vernon drive me to Pasture Farm to get the map?"

"It's simply that he can't drive. Oh, he can chug about on a tractor, but driving a car badly might attract unwanted attention to himself. So that's why." Evelyn smiled. "Anything else?"

"No." Iris sighed. "It's just I don't know if I can run."

"Well, let's hope you can," Evelyn replied, her eyes icy and blank. Iris felt a chill of horror; the hairs standing up on her neck.

"Where will you go? When you have the map?" she asked.

"That's something I'm hardly going to tell you, is it?" Evelyn raised an eyebrow.

"There's one more thing," Iris said, holding out her bandaged hand. "It hurts. I need it looking at."

Evelyn sighed in frustration. She didn't reply as she left the room with the plate and cutlery, so Iris didn't know whether her request would be ignored or not. But about a half an hour later, Evelyn bustled back in with a metallic kidney dish, a dressing, a bottle of iodine and some scissors. She cut off the old bandage and both she and Iris recoiled at what they saw. Iris's fingers were swollen and badly bruised, looking like glistening purple sausages against the splint.

"I was worried about this," Evelyn said, setting to work with the iodine.

"What is it?"

"They might be broken. But I don't think they're infected."

"You don't think? I need them looked at, by someone who knows what they're doing," Iris snapped.

"I'm not fetching anyone to look at them," Evelyn replied, coldly. "You'll be gone tonight and you can sort it out after that."

"I need them sorting out now. I can't run with them throbbing like this."

"You're going to have to."

"But they really hurt."

"Then you'd better be a brave girl, hadn't you?" Evelyn looked distressed, as if this was all getting too much for her. Iris wondered if she was being coerced by Vernon. Why was she doing this for him? She watched as Evelyn wound a new bandage around her fingers, pushing them tight against the splint.

"You don't have to go along with this," Iris said, keeping her voice low.

Evelyn busied herself with the bandage, not making eye contact.

"Please. You could let me go or leave me here and I promise not to call for help until you've had time to get away. Then you get away, Vernon gets away and no one gets hurt."

"No one will get hurt if you're back at nine o'clock." Evelyn fastened it together with a pin and then started to collect her dish and accoutrements. Iris tried to flex her hand, but it was bound too tightly to move the fingers. As Evelyn went to leave, Iris caught her arm with her good hand to stop her.

"Why?" Iris asked.

"He's my brother." Evelyn shook her head, as if that was enough of a reason, before continuing falteringly, "Truth is, he helped me. When I was younger. Our father was –" She shook her head again, tears in her eyes. She wasn't willing or able to finish what she was saying, but Iris got a sense that another dark shadow was hiding in the Storey family history.

And this was payment of a sibling debt. Evelyn shook away her hand and left the room. Iris leaned back on the bed and tried to sleep, despite the insistent throbbing in her fingers. She knew she should rest as much as possible, conserve energy, if she wanted to save Finch.

By late afternoon, Frederick Finch had turned the air of the kitchen at Pasture Farm blue. He had tried to iron his own shirt, but the sleeves were still creased. He didn't know how Esther did it. But because she wasn't here, he was forced to tackle it himself, although he had tried to collar Joyce, who flatly refused. She said it was enough that she had to iron her own clothes, without doing his as well. Finch finished fastening his shirt and gave the sleeves several tugs, in the hope that it would straighten out the creases. He decided that he would keep his jacket on. That would be easiest and it would avoid having to wrestle with the iron again. A thin sheen of perspiration had formed on Finch's forehead. It wasn't just the exertion. He was nervous as so much was resting on tonight.

Going to Evelyn's house for dinner. The perfect time to take charge of his future by asking for her hand in marriage.

Finch checked that he had the ring in his pocket, wrapped in a clean handkerchief. It was the eighth or ninth time he'd checked and to his relief it was still safe.

He stomped his way to the bathroom and checked his appearance in the mirror. Suddenly seeing a foolish middle-aged man looking back at him, his shoulders slumped. Was he doing the right thing? If only Esther was here, he could ask her advice. She'd be against him marrying Evelyn, but she might give him some encouragement, knowing it was what he really wanted. But Esther wasn't here and the house was empty as Joyce, Dolores and Shelley were working at the hospital at Hoxley Manor tonight. Finch walked to his room and found an old photograph of Billy, his son, holding his grandson, William. He looked at his son's young face.

"You took a risk marrying that Bea," Finch said softly to himself. "Lots of folk said you were mad and that it wouldn't last. Including your old dad. But that worked out fine, didn't it?"

Finch sighed, putting the photograph back in his drawer. That worked out fine. He glanced at the bed, kindly made up by Esther before she left for Northampton. It was a double bed and Finch remembered his wife lying on her side of the bed, gazing at him as the morning sun came through the windows. The excitement of living on the farm as a young couple, the idyllic walks to the pub in the evening, running through the fields in the summer. Even after all these years, Finch still mainly slept on the other side of the bed. His side. He noticed the broken catch on the window frame; something he had promised Agnes that he would fix. It was a job that had never been done and probably never would be. Instead life had moved relentlessly along as the days were eaten by months and the months were eaten by years. And here he was, about to take a terrifyingly uncertain gamble. Would Evelyn say yes? And if she did say yes, what would their life be like together? What would happen next? Finch couldn't handle thinking about all that at once. He had to get through the proposal first. And if she said yes, then he could worry about the next steps. Well, they could worry about it together, that's what couples did.

Finch was about to leave the room when he realised he needed a tie. Even though he hated the things – feeling they were like patterned nooses – he recognised that they finished off a suit, added a level of respectability. And he wanted Evelyn to think he was respectable when he asked her to marry him. As he went to the wardrobe for a tie, he was surprised to see one on his wife's bedside table. It was a maroon-coloured tie with a tasteful pattern of tiny silver rectangles. He wasn't to know that it had been left there after Martin rejected it and Esther forgot to put it away as she hastily made the bed before she went out. To Finch, it was a sign from Agnes.

"You want me to do it?" Finch said, deeply shocked by this apparently unexplainable sign, his eyes filling with tears. "Thank you." The wave of relief was palpable. Agnes consented to him moving on with his life. She was happy to encourage him to marry Evelyn. Finch fumbled the tie around his neck and after several attempts pulled it into a ramshackle Windsor knot.

Taking one final look at himself in the bathroom mirror, Finch pulled a wry smile. He radiated respectability and his eyes were shining with purpose. Filled with renewed confidence, he knew he was going to ask her. Tonight would change his life.

Iris had no way of knowing the time. She didn't wear a wrist-watch and although the room had an alarm clock, it hadn't been wound up. So she had to make vague guesses based on the amount of light outside, the positions of the shadows and the position of the sun. The guesswork was made harder because, with nothing to do, each minute stretched into what seemed like ten. But she thought that it was late afternoon. She stood by the window, watching the wild birds as they flew into or past the garden, as it was the only thing to do. She envied them their freedom, but each time she thought of her own freedom, a queasy feeling of unease washed over her, filling her stomach with huge butterflies. Time was ticking down to her release, but it might result in the death of a man she liked. Iris had spent a lot of time thinking about what Vernon and Evelyn wanted her to do, wondering if there was any other option, any wrinkle in their plan that she could exploit. They wanted her to run to Pasture Farm, find the map, and run back to the cottage. It seemed simple, but she had no idea where she was, or how far it was from Pasture Farm. How far would she have to run? And what if Frank didn't have the map any more?

Oh, why didn't she bring it with her like she planned?

Then Vernon could have found it in the suitcase, taken it and he and Evelyn could have left her alone.

She continued to stretch the muscles in her legs, trying to get herself into some state to run.

Suddenly, she heard the scuffing of feet on the stairs and the metallic click of the key in the lock. She tensed as the door opened and Vernon stood there, his face dark and brooding. In his hands, he held a tray with a plate and a fork on it. It was another appallingly made omelette.

"You'll need to eat this, to give you strength," he said, placing it on the bed, keeping his eyes on her the whole time.

"What time is it?" Iris asked. Vernon was about to question

why she needed to know, so she explained. "If you want me to run there and back, I need to know what time it is. I need a watch."

Vernon mulled this over, as if she was trying to trick him. Then he unfastened the old wristwatch that was on his arm and handed it to her. She recoiled, as if it was an engagement ring. "It's the only watch you're getting. Take it and don't be stupid."

"Thanks. And it keeps good time?"

Vernon nodded with a shrug.

Reluctantly, Iris took the watch and fastened it on her wrist. Even on the smallest setting, it didn't fit tightly, and the watch face hung loosely on her wrist. But at least she knew the time. Frank had taught her to read numbers fairly early on, so she knew it was five o'clock in the evening. They said Finch would arrive at seven. And just before then she would set off. Iris moved to sit on the bed to eat her food. She eyed Vernon with contempt, not wanting him present to watch her eat. Why couldn't he leave?

"I wish I'd killed you, Iris," he said softly. Instantly, Iris lost her appetite, feeling panic rise in her throat. "Back at my house. Would have made everything easier. No one would know what I did to my poor boy, I wouldn't have to skulk around as a travelling labourer and I'd still be at Shallow Brook Farm."

"You didn't kill me, though, did you? You messed it up," Iris said, defiantly.

"If I could turn the clock back ..." Vernon glared at her.

Iris felt angry. She wanted to shout that even when this was over, when Finch was safe, she would ensure he was hunted down and made to pay for his crimes. But something inside, some self-preservation, stopped her from voicing her feelings. He had killed his own son and was prepared to kill Finch. Her life would mean nothing to him if she provoked him. So Iris stayed silent, in the hope that Vernon would just leave. But he wasn't finished yet. Vernon moved towards her.

"If I get a chance to, I will. Deal or not. I don't care," he hissed.

Iris couldn't disguise the shock and fear on her face. She backed away, but before she could reply in any way, Evelyn appeared in the doorway, appraising the situation. By the heavy atmosphere, she knew that something unpleasant was happening, and she knew that her brother was probably orchestrating it.

"Vernon, don't upset the girl," Evelyn said. "We need her to get the map and come back, that's all."

"Even if you have the map, how will you get whatever is buried? You won't be able to go back to Shallow Brook after tonight." Iris immediately wished she hadn't voiced her question, as Vernon's face darkened further.

"Never you mind about that, girl."

"If you get back in time, Finch won't know anything has ever happened, will he? So I can bide my time, carry on courting him, carry on going to Pasture Farm and I can use the map when I get a chance," Evelyn said, seemingly the calming presence in the Storey family.

"But I'll know. What, do you expect me to be silent?" Iris noticed that Evelyn momentarily broke her gaze, unable to look at her. That tiny action unnerved her more than Vernon saying he wished he'd killed her. Evelyn couldn't look her in the eye! She couldn't lie to her face. What were they planning? How would they ensure that Iris didn't spill the beans at a later date?

A dreadful thought tried to gain a foothold in her mind. They would kill her anyway. She couldn't ignore it and her pulse started to race, her heart thumping with adrenaline in her chest. She couldn't breathe fast enough, aware that she had started to make desperate sounds, like a dog panting on a hot day. Iris couldn't get enough air, she started to feel faint, pin-sized stars filling her vision. She was aware of Evelyn by her side, holding her, trying to get her to calm down; aware of Vernon shouting at his sister to do something. Iris felt the glorious rush of blackness as she passed out.

Were it not for Vernon's watch, Iris wouldn't have known that she was unconscious for only four minutes. It seemed like longer, much longer. When she opened her eyes, blearily taking in the horribly familiar confines of her room, she realised that she was alone with Evelyn. Vernon had gone. When Evelyn saw her eyes open, she leaned over and started to talk.

"You've got to focus on getting the map. That's all." She sounded drained from the whole thing.

"But he – you can't let me go back to Pasture Farm, can you? Not afterwards. Because I'll know!"

"Calm down." Evelyn looked back towards the door, worried that Vernon might be listening.

"You're going to kill me, aren't you?"

"I won't let him hurt you," Evelyn said, a note of fear in her own voice. "I'll tell him that we can keep you here afterwards, and let you go after we've dug it up. How does that sound?"

"So I come back and I'm a prisoner?"

"Yes, but only until I can use the map to find what we need."

"Would he agree? To keeping me here?"

"I won't let him kill you."

Iris didn't feel any more reassured. She knew she couldn't trust this woman, and even if she could, she wondered how Evelyn could stop Vernon from hurting her. With his temper, he wouldn't let anyone stand in his way. But Iris didn't have the opportunity to ask any more questions, because Evelyn left the room. Iris was left with a deep feeling of foreboding. But what could she do?

At six-thirty, the door was unlocked and Vernon entered. Without saying a word or acknowledging her existence, he walked slowly to the wardrobe and took down her suitcase. Bringing it towards the bed, Iris moved her legs to accommodate it. Vernon opened the case and took out Iris's Women's Land Army uniform, the dungarees, jumper and shirt that had become her constant companions since arriving at Pasture Farm. The shirt still had a beetroot stain on it.

"Get dressed," he said, leaving the room. She could tell he was nervous, worried about what would happen. It wasn't just her future that would be decided, his would be too. If it went wrong, he could face the gallows. If it went according to plan, he could get away. Iris didn't know how much thought they had put into their plan. If she was late back and they murdered Finch, what would they do with his body? Iris wondered if they would bury it in the garden outside.

Maybe that's what Vernon had planned for her too.

What would happen to her? Would Evelyn really make sure she was just kept at the cottage? With all the upheaval and displacement caused by the war, it was easy for people to vanish or go missing. As people could slip through the cracks, Iris knew that missing person cases were difficult for the few remaining police officers to investigate. So if she or Finch disappeared, it would be unlikely that Evelyn would be caught as no one would even start looking for her until the war was over.

Iris finished getting dressed, pushing her strapped hand through the tight armhole of her jumper. She winced as she caught some of the splinted fingers. It was agony. She was sure that her fingers were broken, but she had to put it out of her mind. That was for worrying about later.

Iris looked around for something to put on her feet and realised that the only footwear was her wellington boots. Like it or not, it looked as though she would have to run in them. As she slipped them on –

– *Black, patent-leather shoes* –

– *"Can you do it, darling?"* –

– Iris tried to shut out all the other thoughts. All the distractions and noise that were building in her head. All those yesterdays. They would only get in the way, dragging her down.

When she was dressed, Iris stood up, shakily on her feet. She glanced at the watch. It was nearly a quarter to seven. It was nearly time to run.

Margot Dawson had wanted to talk more, so Esther waited at the factory until she finished her shift and then the two of them walked together back to Stanley Street. Margot explained that Northampton had been lucky so far during the war, with only one bomb having fallen on the Duston area of the city. It was surprising, given its proximity to Birmingham that it hadn't been hit more, but Margot was thankful for small mercies. She saw Esther glance at a gaggle of children, all under 10 years old, running the other way.

"Evacuees," Margot stated. "Because we're considered a fairly safe place, we get a lot of them. Mind you, I don't trust it. My other kids are away."

They reached the door to Margot's house and she let them inside. She hadn't seemed inclined to talk about her missing daughter on the way home, but Esther assumed that she would now they were in private. Margot made a pot of tea and uncovered half a fruit cake that was in the larder. She brought them to the table, allowing Esther to fetch the cups and saucers from the kitchen. The front parlour was a small, neatly furnished room, with a large radio having pride of place on the sideboard. The single downstairs window that Esther had seen from outside served this room. She noted that there were only three dining chairs around the table, rather than the customary four, as she pulled one out to sit down.

"So what do I do? About my Iris?" Margot asked, pouring out tea that should have spent more time in the pot.

"It's an unusual situation." Esther sighed. It certainly was unusual, all right. She'd never found herself managing the search for a missing Land Girl before, and she wasn't sure what to say. She knew what she should say. The Women's Land Army treated desertion seriously and offenders would be reported to the authorities. But Margot wasn't worried about the legalities of desertion. She had lost a daughter and just wanted to know how to find her. Esther wanted to get the formal issues out of the way so they could concentrate on Iris. "I should make a formal note to my superiors, but I think we should give her more time to turn up and do the right thing."

Margot nodded, grateful for that small mercy, even though, as Esther had suspected, she hadn't been thinking about that side of things at all. "This is so unlike her. Where could she have gone?"

"I'm afraid that she wasn't at Pasture Farm when she disappeared."

"Where was she?"

"Another farm. Jordan Gate," Esther said. "I'd just written to tell you about the move, but I don't expect you've got the letter yet."

"No," Margot replied. "Do you know if she was unhappy at this new farm?"

"I don't know, I'm sorry." However, Esther guessed that Iris probably was unhappy, having been sent away.

"Why was she there? I thought she liked it at Pasture Farm."

Esther pondered whether she should tell Margot the full

story. About the drinking, about the confrontation with Finch's lady friend, about her having to send Iris away. But Esther thought that Margot didn't need to know that yet. Perhaps in time, but not right now. "Sometimes the girls are moved around, depending on the workload at various farms."

Margot nodded, accepting Esther's explanation. Esther realised that Margot had no grounds to doubt it, believing her young daughter was happy and enjoying her life on the farm. She wondered if Iris had told her mother about the whole ordeal with Vernon, but assumed she hadn't. Iris didn't contact her mother often. She had phoned only once from the farm and had spoken to Margot at a neighbour's house. Iris sometimes got Frank to write a dictated letter home, but Esther didn't think Iris would have unburdened herself about Vernon via a third party. She suspected that Iris might tell her mother, but only face to face when she came home on leave. And as she hadn't been eligible for any leave since she had joined, she thought it unlikely it had happened. Esther decided to keep quiet.

"Will she come here, do you think?"

"Maybe. You should assume she will, eventually. She may be staying with someone she met, working out her next move," Esther said, as kindly as she could manage, wanting to give Margot as much hope as possible.

On the mantelpiece was a photograph, faded from the light from the window. It showed a woman who was obviously Margot with a young girl. Esther guessed by her features that it was Iris, aged around 10 years old. Next to them was a smiling man in a dapper suit with a pocket watch. As she sipped her tea, Margot noticed that Esther was looking.

"That was us, happier times."

"Is that Mr Dawson, Iris's father?" Esther enquired.

Margot nodded with a heavy sadness that made Esther realise immediately that he wasn't around any more. She worried that she had put her foot in it. Iris had rarely spoken about her family when she had been at Pasture Farm. But despite Esther's unease, Margot seemed happy to talk. Perhaps she rarely got the chance.

"My Ivor. A wonderful man, taken too early from us, God rest his soul," she confirmed.

"I'm sorry, I really am."

"Iris was never the same after," Margot said, sighing.

"Because of the grief?"

Margot looked down at her cup, not wanting to meet the eyes of her guest. Then she looked up and said something that chilled Esther to the core.

"No. Because she thought it was her fault."

Vernon strode ahead, the ominous cawing of crows in the distance as they walked through the dead forest. The trees were tall and skeletal with no branches until the canopies a hundred feet above their heads. Iris stayed behind Vernon, not keen to talk to him. He would glance back periodically, to check she was still trudging behind him. But he knew she would be there; she had no choice. His watch spun around on her wrist.

They had waited outside the cottage, which Iris now knew was an isolated building down a dirt track. She felt small relief that she hadn't shouted for help when she thought it might have been part of a denser clump of houses. They hid behind some bushes as Fred Finch arrived, watching as he checked the smell of his breath in his cupped hand and rapped on the door. Iris had found the whole situation truly bizarre, wanting to shout out as Finch walked down the path. Wanting to warn him. But she knew too much was at stake to mess things up. She stayed silent, under the watchful gaze of Vernon Storey, until Finch was greeted by Evelyn and he went inside. Iris heard Finch's familiar chuckle as the door closed. Then, almost immediately, Vernon gave Iris a shove and told her to move off.

And now here they were walking through the creepiest forest she had ever seen. They reached a country lane and Vernon pointed to the right.

"It's just under six miles to Pasture Farm –"

"Six? I can't run that far!"

Vernon grinned. "You've got two hours to get there and back. And you'd better be back by nine on the dot."

Iris knew she couldn't argue, so she was already moving quickly away from Vernon down the muddy slope that led to the lane. He watched as she reached the road and set off immediately, running as fast as she could.

"And don't tell anyone what you're doing!" Vernon shouted as a parting shot.

But Iris couldn't hear him, she had already moved two hundred yards away. Vernon watched her go and smiled to himself. He sat down on a tree stump and took an apple out of his pocket; biting into it as he settled in for a long wait.

Chapter 18

The first mile was heavy-going, with everything feeling wrong. Iris felt her lungs bursting with the exertion, her bruised legs hurting with every footfall, and her wellington boots rubbing against her feet. But after that first mile, she started to find her stride, some sense of a rhythm to her steps, as, relentlessly, foot after foot hit the ground, driving her forward. She blocked out the pain in her feet; blisters had formed so early on that the injustice made her want to cry. Added to this, her damaged hand was throbbing as she jarred it with each footfall. She willed the terrain to become familiar so that she could recognise that she was close to Pasture Farm. But each corner only showed another unknown, seemingly identical section of lane, until that too gave way to another bend and another new section.

And so it went on. Iris carried on running.

She reached an isolated country pub, tucked into a recess in the lane. Its windows were shuttered up, but muffled voices and soft light emanated from within. Iris ran past the White Oak, mentally noting it as a marker for her return journey. She knew it would be important to catalogue every landmark as she knew she wouldn't have much time to find her way back. And also it would be dark by then.

Esther politely refused a third cup of tea and told Margot Dawson that she had better head off. She didn't want to miss her train back to Helmstead. She thanked Margot for her hospitality and asked her to inform her when Iris showed up. Esther had purposefully used the word 'when' and not 'if'. She wanted to leave Margot feeling positive and hopeful that she would see her daughter again. But Esther was beginning to wonder what had happened to Iris. They shook hands and said their goodbyes.

"I'm sorry for crying," Margot said on the doorstep. "I don't normally get like that."

"It's all right. I understand," Esther said kindly. "It must have been a difficult time."

"But I shouldn't have burdened you. You're very nice, but you are a stranger."

"Please, don't worry." Esther smiled. "Thank you for telling me. It explains a lot." And the statement was true. Now Esther understood Iris a lot more than she had before she had come to Northampton. She knew everything that had happened before she joined the Women's Land Army. And it all made sense.

Iris ran, but she had slowed to a steady pace, hoping it would enable her to run more of the distance than if she tried to sprint it. She knew she couldn't sprint the entire distance. She wasn't even sure she could run it, especially in her current state. But she had to soldier on. She had to try. Vernon's watch swung its way around her wrist, a thin sheen of perspiration beneath it, and she had to pull at it to check the time. It was nearly twenty to eight. She had been running for forty minutes. The awful and terrifying thing was that she had no way of knowing how far she had run. It might be easier on the way back to landmark the journey since it would be familiar. But for the outward run, she had no real idea. She hoped with all her heart that she was nearly there. She calculated that, roughly, she needed to complete each leg of the journey in an hour.

Otherwise Fred Finch would be –

No, don't think about that.

The evening sky was beginning to turn purple. Iris feared losing the light, hoping there might be a fairly full moon tonight to help her. She reached a bend in the road and prayed a silent prayer that something familiar would be around the corner. Instead, it was her worst nightmare. Worse than just another stretch of tarmac that she didn't recognise.

It was a junction in the road.

Ahead, veering off in a Y-shape was a lane to the left and a lane to the right. Neither had any defining features, both leading off onto near-identical country lanes. One would lead to Helmstead and one to somewhere else. Iris stopped, clasping her hands to her knees, dragging in a deep lungful of air. She could see the small, square-shaped hole in the grass at the intersection of the junction. The hole where the sign would have been. But there were no signs any more, not with a war on.

Iris felt hot tears filling her eyes. What could she do? Pick the wrong turning and that would be the end. She would have no time to make a mistake.

"Please ..." Iris howled in frustration. Which way should she go? Why had Vernon not told her about this? Did he want her to fail?

She couldn't waste time worrying. She had to pick a path and hope for the best. It would be a gamble, but one with a fifty per cent chance of being in her favour. She ran to the left to see if she could make out anything familiar in that direction, and then she repeated the process with the right fork. Both hinted at similarly unknown terrain. She ran back to the junction, desperately trying to make a decision.

With time running out, there was nothing she could do, other than take the largest gamble of her life.

Iris took the left-hand fork and ran as fast as she could.

Evelyn had laid on a lovely meal. As Finch tucked into the potatoes and rabbit stew, he tried to relax, slow down and take his time. The main thing was he wanted to avoid showering her with gravy as he spoke. So he tried to take small mouthfuls and swallow before he said anything. But the trouble was the food was so delicious and he had so much to say. Something had to give. Luckily, Evelyn seemed charming and relaxed, pleased that Finch was enjoying his food. She ate at a more sedate pace, fielding Finch's excitable questions. How long had she been here? Did the chimney work? Did she need the chimney to work because he knew a man who could clear it? Who was in that photograph on the mantel? Had she ever seen Sparrow Soprano?

"Who?" Evelyn said, genuinely baffled.

"Oh, it doesn't matter. She were an old act, couldn't sing for toffee!" Finch mopped his brow with his napkin, wishing he could take his tie off. But he knew he had to keep it on, he had to stay respectable. The ring was in his pocket and he'd already contemplated popping the question twice, firstly when Evelyn had fetched him a welcome drink and secondly when they sat down to dinner. But he forced himself to wait. It wasn't the right moment. He slurped at his drink, annoyed with himself for his lack of manners. He wasn't used to eating with proper company present. Esther and the Land Girls didn't count. They were always as ravenous as he was, and with their heads down in their plates they didn't notice what he was doing.

As Finch's mind raced, and his eyes flickered nervously, he felt a warm, slender hand on his.

"Just relax, Fred." Evelyn smiled. "Enjoy the meal."

Finch nodded. He would do his best. He went to cut a piece of potato and it flicked onto the tablecloth. He felt mortified, until Evelyn flicked a potato from her plate onto the tablecloth too. "It's all right," she said.

He relaxed and wondered how Evelyn Gray could be so perfect.

In the twilight, with the time edging towards ten to eight, Iris watched her feet as she ran and ran. As she watched footfall after footfall, it was as if she was looking at something disconnected to herself. A machine of some kind. She passed a windmill on her left and was about to continue, when she stopped dead in her tracks. She recognised it! Oh My God! The shattered blade of one of its sails. She had seen it before, but the infuriating thing was she couldn't place where she had seen it.

Think, Iris, think.

The shattered sail. Where had she seen it?

Inexplicably, she thought about Finch's son. Billy marrying the Land Girl. Why did the windmill make her think of that? Was her tired mind just playing tricks now? Iris wracked her brains, and then the answer came bubbling up from the recesses of her memory.

She'd passed it with Finch when he drove her to Jordan Gate! Yes, he'd been talking about his son at the time!

That's when they'd passed the windmill.

But which side was it on?

Iris thought quickly to try to remember. It had been on the left-hand side. Yes, on the left. That meant that now she was going towards Jordan Gate and not Helmstead. No, no, no.

Oh God, she was going the wrong way!

Immediately, Iris turned and sped off, picking up the pace. Her feet felt soaked with perspiration. At least she hoped it was perspiration and not blood. But she ignored such worrying thoughts; she ignored the pain and she reached the junction. Now she knew that she had to go the other way and take the other turning, so she ran down the right-hand fork.

Vernon's wristwatch told her it was nearly eight. She should have completed her journey to the farm by now and be preparing to turn back. She had to find Pasture Farm very soon, otherwise it would be too late. She thought of Frank's shed, where she hoped she would find the map. She hoped with all her heart that it would still be stowed in his emergency cigarette tin. But what if he'd destroyed it? Or moved it somewhere?

No, don't think about that.

Iris had to believe it was in the shed, where it had been left.

She continued running, running, running. The sound of her heavy boots padding on the road surface; the sound of her breathing, urgent and desperate.

– black patent-leather shoes running over glistening cobbles –

No, don't think about that either.

But as Iris ran around a corner, she felt suddenly elated. It couldn't be! For a moment, she didn't want to trust her own eyes. She recognised this stretch of road! It was one that led eventually to Helmstead. She knew the farm would be tucked some distance from one side of the lane as it snaked its way towards the village. Squinting as she ran, she could make out the low shape of the farmhouse set back from the lane. It was about four hundred yards away, but at least she could see it now. She knew a way to cut down the distance, leaping over a stile and running across one of the lower fields. She passed the patch of ground where the Land Girls would sometimes sit and take a tea break, the ground muddy and worn beneath the shade of some sycamore trees. Picking up the pace, Iris sprinted faster. She passed the disused barn on the outskirts of the land and soon found herself out of breath in the yard of Pasture Farm. There were a few lights on upstairs at the farmhouse, but she couldn't hear any noise. The evening meal, if there had been one, was probably long over. Iris slowed her pace so that she could walk quietly without attracting attention. Frank's shed was up ahead, in darkness. She assumed he was in the pub tonight, playing dominoes. That suited her perfectly as she didn't have time for a discussion.

Iris ducked inside the shed, lit the lamp and searched furiously through the stacks of papers. After a few minutes, she stopped being careful and started to throw the unwanted sheets and cuttings aside as she tried to find the tin. Finally, she heard it clatter to the floor. Found it!

She picked it up, opened it and, to her relief, she found a small yellowing sheet, folded in half. Iris opened it up and checked it was the map. Yes! Frank had kept it. She fought to calm herself, blew out the lamp and left the shed. She was about to run off, tucking the map in her dungaree pocket, as she went, when –

"Iris?"

The voice was soft, kind, but tinged with confusion. Iris spun around, knowing before she turned who it belonged to. Martin Reeves. He had a mug of tea in his hand and a daft smile on his face. "Where have you been? We've been worried sick. My mum's gone to –"

"I haven't got time, Martin. I've got to go." And she sped off.

But Martin threw his tea away and ran after her, catching her arm. "Wait! What's happening?"

"I can't stay, and I can't tell you," Iris said, near to tears. She needed to go. She needed to focus. This was all too much, the strain of running, the worry of not getting back in time. "I've got to get to Finch! Please!"

And she raced off. Martin looked anxiously after her as she disappeared back across the field into the darkness. He made a decision, putting his mug on the ground. He walked quickly over to the stables, opened the door and lead out Frank's pony. Martin didn't really like horses, but he did his best to pat its nose to calm it down. He'd seen Frank do that. Gently he pulled the animal across the yard, its hooves clip-clopping as it went. He moved it near to the trap, which was upended like an empty rickshaw, and tried to coax it between the harness poles. After a few failed attempts, Martin was about to give up, when Frank ambled into the yard, his face red from a good evening in the Bottle and Glass.

"What are you doing, son?" he asked.

"I've got to follow Iris," Martin replied.

"Iris? She's back?"

"Yes, but she wasn't making much sense. She ran off. That way!" Martin was grateful as Frank took the reins of the pony and led it round in a circle, before walking it between the harness poles. Martin didn't have time to contemplate how he made it look so easy. "She was talking about getting to Finch!"

"Why?" Frank fastened the leather straps around the animal. "I hope she's not going to stop him proposing."

"I don't know. It seemed more serious than that."

"Not to Finch it isn't."

"No, she seemed really worried. I've never seen her like that."

"Come on."

Martin didn't need asking twice. He jumped up in the seat. Frank clambered up beside him. He chivvied the pony with the reins and they left the yard. As soon as they got to the lane, Frank picked up the pace.

Iris ran, with little style or technique, but she reached the crossroads. She glanced at the watch. It was nearly half-past eight. Her heart sank and she struggled not to scream in frustration. It had taken her forty minutes to get to this junction on the outward journey. That meant she was ten minutes short of time to make the return journey.

Don't be late. Finch will be –

Iris had no choice but to increase her pace. Aware that she was making an involuntary whimpering noise as she ran, she soldiered on, trying to blot out everything; the stitch in her side, the soreness of her feet, the pain in her chest, the throbbing ache in her damaged fingers. She had to focus everything on what she was doing. She couldn't afford to lose concentration and think about –

– Black, patent-leather shoes, running full pelt across the cobbles –

Suddenly, Iris stumbled and fell hard onto the road, grazing her chin. She winced at the pain in her injured hand. She had tried to stop her fall by putting out her hands, but she had only succeeded in pushing her splinted fingers back, causing excruciating pain. Iris writhed on the ground. She was breathing heavily and she felt suddenly exhausted.

I can't go on. I just can't do it.

The prospect of getting back on her feet and finding the

rhythm of running again seemed a monumental effort. But she knew she had to try. Iris pushed her good hand against the road and dragged herself to her feet. She managed to stumble forward until she built up her momentum again. Clutching her bad hand as she ran, Iris could feel something wet against her knee. Glancing down, she saw the rip in her dungarees and she knew she had cut her knee open in the fall. How could she cut her knee? The thoughts came again, the thoughts from before –

– A bloody, painful gash on the girl's right knee was hampering her progress. She'd fallen over in her haste, but she knew she couldn't stop. She knew she had to keep running.

No, this wasn't the same. This was different. That was a lifetime ago. She had to shut it out.

But now it was in her mind, growing as if it was a shadow at sunset, she couldn't make it go away. Tears flooded down her face as she ran, not caused by the pain of her knee or the pain in her fingers, but from the awful memories. They were filling her thoughts, taking her back to that dark time.

The girl felt that her small chest would burst with the exertion as she ran over a wrought-iron bridge, slaloming around a mother with a large pram.

Iris gritted her teeth, dug down deep inside of herself and ran faster. Her mouth felt as dry as parchment and the sweat on her back was pulling her shirt taut with every step.

The mother turned to scold the clumsy child with the mane of red hair. But Iris Dawson was already on the other side of the bridge, running, running, running.

As Esther Reeves alighted from the last train to Helmstead, she looked up at the moonlit sky and wondered where Iris was. That poor girl. In the space of an afternoon and evening, Esther had learnt so much more about her, understanding a lot of what the seemingly happy-go-lucky 17-year-old had had to endure. Her childhood had been happy, idyllic, even, until it was taken from her in the space of an afternoon. One event had changed everything, casting a darkness over the rest of her life. Margot had broken down and told Esther the whole story.

Iris, 10 years old, was a happy, carefree child. She enjoyed playing with the other children of Stanley Street, including a boy named Brian Marley. Margot had told Esther that one day Iris had gone into Brian's house, into his bedroom. She didn't know what for, but presumed it was just another game, as the pair were close, having grown up together –

Iris had expected to feel something when she pressed her lips against Brian Marley's, but it was all very underwhelming. Why did adults like kissing? She couldn't see the attraction. Brian shrugged. He liked it, but said he didn't want to do it again. That was fine for Iris. She had tried it and didn't have to kiss anyone in the future now. Iris and Brian raced downstairs, planning a game of football before teatime –

But as they rushed outside, Iris found her mother standing in the street, moving slowly around, as if she wasn't sure what to do. What was happening? Seemingly dazed, Margot didn't seem to recognise Iris at first, but then she grasped the child by the shoulders with an urgency that alarmed the young girl –

"When they ran out of the Marley house, I was outside our front door. In a daze. A bit of a panic. I wasn't sure what to do, and at first I was surprised to see Iris," Margot had told Esther. "I said as calmly as I could, although it probably didn't sound very calm, that her father had collapsed in the kitchen."

"It's very serious what's happened. It's your dad ..."

Margot had continued the story for Esther. "Ivor had had a heart attack. One minute he was joking as we were making the sandwiches for tea, the next he was on the floor, clutching his chest, gasping for breath. I ran outside as we've never had a telephone. And then I got there, I didn't know what to do."

"I can get the doctor," Iris said, her big eyes narrowing as she contemplated the task. The doctor lived over the other side of the city, perhaps twenty minutes by foot. Brian Marley stood numbly behind Iris. All thoughts of their first (and last) kiss were forgotten.

Margot Dawson. Her eyes were large and fearful. "Iris?" she said, grabbing her daughter and pulling her towards her. Margot knelt down, her voice deliberate but brittle. "Can you really do this, darling?"

They both knew that everything was resting on this.

Iris nodded. She touched her mother lightly on the shoulder, a silent promise. A child's promise.

Then she hared off down the street. Her squeaky patent-leather shoes thundering over the cobbles as Margot watched her go. When Iris was out of sight, Margot ran back inside to her husband.

The mantelpiece clock said ten to nine. Evelyn struggled to find a warm smile for Fred as he tucked into the apple batter pudding she had made. Much as she hated the idea, she knew what she would have to do in ten minutes. That's what Vernon wanted. And she owed Vernon, didn't she? The whole sorry mess made her feel queasy, but she had to get through it, do what was expected. Then it would be over and she and Vernon would have a new beginning.

Fred was also struggling to be relaxed. He was thinking about the ring in his pocket. When should he do it? When would be the best moment? He decided that after the meal would be the best time. In about ten minutes or so.

Iris approached the White Oak. She didn't notice that the shutters were now in darkness as it had closed for the night. She didn't notice the two farmhands standing in the road, saying their goodbyes to each other. They saw her, the Land Girl running towards them, her chin bloodied, her hair drenched in perspiration, her dungarees torn and the fingers of her right hand held at a strange angle.

"Here, love, are you all right?" one of the men enquired. "Love?"

Iris couldn't speak, her tongue felt as if it had ossified on the roof of her dry mouth. She shook her head and ran past. The man went to grab her, but she batted him away. She flashed him an angry look and continued to run.

Her watch said that it was seven minutes to nine.

"Can you really do this, darling?" She heard her mother's voice, from across the years.

"She ran as fast as she could to get the doctor," Margot Dawson had told Esther. "But it was too far, and by the time they got back –" Margot struggled to continue, the memory too upsetting. "We never really spoke about what happened."

"I'm sorry," Esther said, placing her hand on Margot's. Margot started to cry. At first she tried to stop herself, for decency's sake, but she couldn't, even in front of a stranger. Esther knew that losing her husband was now compounded with losing her daughter. It would be too much for anyone to bear, and she was surprised that Margot hadn't broken down before. She let Margot cry at the dining table. And she didn't stop crying for twenty minutes.

Iris felt that her body was beyond pain now. She had pushed it so far that everything but the desperate desire to get back to the cottage had been buried. It was willpower that was keeping her going. Even the memories were only struggling to the surface, half-glimpsed rather than fully formed sequences in her head.

"Can you really do this, darling?"

Three minutes to nine.

The grazed knee of a 10-year old girl as she sat in the doctor's car. She'd got to the doctor's house and he was driving them back. Why couldn't he drive them back to their house any faster?

She ran around a corner and finally her nightmare looked as if it was over. Evelyn's cottage was up ahead, sitting alone in its valley, the downstairs lights on.

Two minutes to nine.

Her mother, crying in a neighbour's arms as the doctor's car pulled up. Iris knew she was too late as she got out. "Mum?" she said, but her mother didn't notice her.

Iris stumbled and fell, but she was too close now. Too close to give up. This time she would make it. This time she would save him. The promise would be kept. She pulled herself to her feet, ragged and broken, and ran down the dirt track to the cottage.

Evelyn stared at the dirty dishes in the sink. She heard Finch belch from the other room, followed by him uttering a hasty and embarrassed, "Oh, pardon me." Feeling resigned to the inevitability of what she had to do, but finding no joy in it, she pulled out two glass tumblers from the larder. One of them had the crushed leaves of the Deadly Nightshade plant in it. She used a teaspoon to carefully take out the leaves, leaving a drop or two of highly toxic green liquid at the bottom. You could hardly see it, but she knew it would be enough to kill him. She poured a tot of good-quality brandy into each glass. Vernon had reassured her that everything would turn out fine. Even if they had to murder bumbling Farmer Finch to get what they wanted. Vernon planned to bury Finch's body in waste ground at the back of the cottage. It was a place where no one passed by. A place no one ever came. Evelyn took a deep breath to steady her nerves. She had to trust her brother. She had to believe that he would make this turn out fine. She owed him.

"I'm getting you a brandy," Evelyn shouted to the other room. "It's good stuff that I've had since before the war."

"Oh, that sounds perfect." Finch said with a chuckle.

Evelyn picked up the two glasses and went back into the living room, ensuring she kept her eye on the one in her right hand. The poisoned chalice. She put the glasses down, the right one in front of Finch. She smiled and then went over to the mantelpiece to check the time. Finch picked up the glass, enjoying the weight of the crystal in his hand. He looked at the rich, brown liquid. It looked good stuff. And it looked just like the Dutch courage he needed at this moment in time. Surreptitiously, Finch reached into his pocket and placed the engagement ring on the table, ensuring it was covered by his meaty hand.

"Cheers," Finch said, raising up his glass in a toast.

Evelyn walked back to the table and raised her own glass. "Cheers."

"After this, there's something I want to ask you ..." Finch took a big slug of his drink and winced. It tasted a bit strange.

One minute to nine.

Iris reached the front gate. She bounded up the path and hammered on the door. There was no reply. She hammered again, finding herself making desperate half-formed words in an attempt to shout. But she couldn't find her voice. She hammered a final time on the door and then, to her surprise, found her legs buckling beneath her. She collapsed on her back on the path. Her body had finally given up on her.

"Mum?" the 10-year-old girl said as she got out of the doctor's car and approached her crying mother.

She had made it this time, surely? It was one minute to nine when she knocked. She'd made it.

Hadn't she?

A little girl looking lost on a cobbled street in Northampton as the doctor rushed into the house with her mother, the door shutting behind them, shutting her out.

This wasn't fair. Don't shut me out. Let me in. I tried to do it, I tried ...

"Mum?" She'd tried her best. She'd run as fast as she could –

Dimly, as if it was in another world, Iris heard the front door open. All she could see was the inky blackness above her and she couldn't find one iota of strength to move her head to look behind her. She heard the shuffle of footsteps, someone coming out from the cottage. She braced herself for a confrontation she couldn't win. Not in this state.

Finch's face appeared above her.

Was he dead?

Floating, like a dream above her. He looked confused.

"Iris?" he said, slowly. "What are you –?"

And then he became distracted by something further along the path. Iris could hear people running and, dimly, above the sound of her own thumping heart, she could hear familiar voices.

"Finch? You all right?"

"What's happened to Iris?"

It was Frank. And Martin. Her own special cavalry. What were they doing here?

Iris tried to grip the path with her good hand, to raise herself up. Martin was by her side, helping her, his kind, boyish face overwhelmed with relief at seeing her again. As Iris staggered to her feet, allowing herself to be supported in his arms, she managed to turn to the cottage. Frank and Finch were rushing back inside. Iris pulled away from Martin, desperate to follow, but she started to stumble. Her legs were like jelly. Martin helped her, placing his hand under her armpit. Realising she wanted to go inside, he helped her along the path. They entered the front door together, almost jamming themselves in the small opening.

The first thing Iris noticed was the tablecloth. It had been almost wrenched off the table, half of it wrapped around Evelyn Gray's wrist. She was lying, unmoving on the floor, faint gurgling noises coming from her throat. Her face was bright red, her eyes sticking out, almost like organ stops. A small amount of vomit was on the carpet next to her head.

"I think she tried to poison me," Finch said numbly. "But I thought she had more brandy than me, so I –"

He mimed switching the glasses. His old trick. The same one Iris's father had done at that Lyons Corner House on the day they missed the train. It looked as though Finch's greed had saved his life.

But why was the poison even on the table? Surely she'd made it in time. Perhaps with a minute to spare, but still she'd made it ...

She looked at the wristwatch. It was nine o'clock.

She'd made it! So why was Evelyn dying on the floor?

As her senses came back to her, Iris glanced at the mantelpiece clock and realised it said three minutes past nine. Iris had made it back in time! She had saved Finch. It wasn't her fault that Evelyn's clock was fast.

A little girl staring at the door of her family home, wishing it would open and that her mother would run to her and embrace her.

Iris forced herself to think about the memory; forcing herself to accept what had happened. History had repeated itself, in its own perverse way, and Iris had been given a second chance. Or if not a second chance, then a chance to come to terms with her past. And she realised that she had had to save Finch to do that. This time she had done it. This time she had saved him. And in doing that, perhaps she had laid the ghosts of that afternoon in Northampton to rest.

"We need to get her to Hoxley Manor," Frank announced. Martin and Finch began to untangle Evelyn from the tablecloth, cutlery clattering to the floor. The three men carried Evelyn outside towards the pony and trap. Iris would have helped, but she was too weak. She could barely walk and her breathing still hadn't returned to normal. She was in no state to help anyone, even herself. She glanced around the room of the cottage and noticed something glistening on the bare tabletop. The glint of a diamond ring wrapped in a handkerchief.

Had Finch asked Evelyn to marry him?

Finch and Frank returned. "Iris, you should come with us. Finch is going to stay here."

"Apparently the pony can't take the weight of all of us," he said, looking mildly offended that he'd been the person selected to remain behind. "And it's a good idea to get you looked at, after what you've been through."

Iris hesitated. She struggled to find the saliva to talk, but managed to get out the words. A warning.

"Vernon is here, somewhere."

This time, after all Finch had been through, there was no doubting her. He looked worried.

"What should we do?"

Frank thought of a solution. "There's a shotgun on the trap. You take that and lock yourself inside until we can get back. If he tries to break in, let him have both barrels."

"All right." Finch nodded. Iris stayed momentarily behind

to check he was okay. Finch smiled warmly at her and nodded.

"We'll be back as soon as we can," Iris said. Frank returned with the shotgun and handed it to Finch.

As Iris and Frank left the room, Finch retrieved his diamond ring from the table, popping it back into his pocket.

Once outside, Iris approached the trap. Martin was tucking Evelyn under a blanket, as Iris clambered up, her weak legs struggling to climb. Martin and Frank were up the front. She hauled herself over the lip of the trap and sat in a corner. She looked down at the unconscious figure of Evelyn Gray, covered up to the neck with a beige utility blanket. She was breathing quickly and shallowly, her face bright red and wracked with fever. Would she live? Iris was too exhausted to think. She felt her head loll as Frank took the reins and steered the pony around onto the dirt track. They set off for Hoxley Manor as fast as they could go.

Chapter 19

"You should have a cup of tea. A cup of tea always helps," Joyce said, kindly. She was dressed in her makeshift hospital uniform, complete with a white apron and nurse's hat. A dried splash of blood was on the rim of the hat. Iris smiled weakly at her friend's words. She nodded her thanks and Joyce went off to make a new pot. Iris and Frank were waiting in the main corridor of the East Wing of Hoxley Manor, sitting on the long wooden bench that stretched the entire length of the corridor. The lights were subdued and the military hospital had a feeling of eerie calm about it, with hardly any people milling about at this time of night. They could hear periodic coughing and loud snoring coming from the nearby wards. They had been waiting for nearly two hours since they arrived with Evelyn Gray. She was unconscious for the whole rickety journey on the pony and trap. Iris wondered if she was already dead, but when they arrived, the nurses burst into an activity that told her there was still hope. Iris wanted her to live so she could be punished for what she had done.

In that time, while they had been waiting for news, Iris had managed to speak about what happened. She told Frank and Martin the whole tale of how she escaped from Jordan Gate; how Vernon Storey had chased her in the night and how she had ended up imprisoned in Evelyn's cottage. As she finished telling them about the race tonight to get back to the cottage, she realised that Martin was open-mouthed with shock and Frank was shaking his head in disbelief. They sat in silence for a few minutes, taking it all in. Iris was silent, partly to give them time to digest it and partly because she was exhausted.

After some time, Frank spoke.

"Do you think you should get your hand looked at?" He nodded towards Iris's right hand. She had to keep it raised because it throbbed painfully if she kept it down at her side. "I think you broke your fingers when you fell down that quarry."

"Maybe Dr Channing can take a look later," Iris replied, shrugging off his concern.

She dreaded taking off the bandage, the prospect of seeing her fingers twisted and broken again made a chill rise from her stomach.

Joyce returned with a wooden tray of rattling crockery and handed each of them a cup of tea. She sat down on the bench with them, sparing a few minutes from her duties.

"How is Evelyn?" Iris asked.

"No news yet. It doesn't look good, though." Joyce glanced down the corridor before fixing her eyes back on Iris. "Just to say, I told Lady Hoxley what had happened and she has telephoned PC Thorne. He's got people out, volunteers mostly, at Evelyn's cottage. So Finch will be all right. Oh, and they think they've found Vernon."

"Really?" Iris enquired, feeling a wave of relief.

Joyce was about to explain, but she noticed a young doctor beckoning her back to work. "Excuse me."

As Joyce left, Iris felt a huge weight lifting from her shoulders. They'd caught Vernon. After all these weeks of anguish and torment as she first imagined he was waiting in every shadow, and then had been imprisoned by him, it was finally over. Iris got to her feet, her legs feeling shaky, as if someone else was operating them. "I just need a bit of fresh air."

"Do you want me to come with you?" Martin asked.

"No, I'm all right," Iris replied, flashing him a warm but exhausted smile.

Frank and Martin watched as she shuffled along the corridor.

Iris stood in the grand entrance of Hoxley Manor, the horseshoe-shaped driveway stretching out under the moonlight. Slowly she walked along the Tudor balustrade walkway, the windows of the hospital ward to her left illuminating her steps, and she thought about everything that had happened, everything she had been through. She wondered if there would be a trial. Would she have to give evidence against Vernon and his sister? Iris didn't mind doing that, feeling empowered by what she had survived, by what she'd done. In a strange way, she had been given a second chance. After failing to save her father, she had managed to save Finch. It wasn't the same, but it was something. It was a way of closing that chapter of her life.

On the other side of the decorative walkway was a large area that was being turned into a vegetable patch, with wheelbarrows, tools and spades waiting for tomorrow's workers. Even Hoxley Manor wasn't exempt from the Dig for Victory campaign. Lady Hoxley felt torn between her obvious patriotic duty and her sadness at seeing her beloved rose gardens dug up to grow potatoes and turnips. Still, after the war, she could put the roses back. Iris wondered if she could work on the patch here. It would be a nice environment to cultivate, away from the dreary Shallow Brook Farm. She would ask Finch tomorrow. She thought he might be receptive to making things up with her.

Iris looked at her bandaged right hand. Tentatively, she unpinned the bandage and unwound it slowly, as if it was an unwanted present. She gritted her teeth, wondering what state it would be in. She squeezed her eyes tight, so that she would only have to glimpse the damage through her eyelashes. Oh God, don't let it be worse than before.

When PC Thorne and his volunteers had arrived at Evelyn's cottage, Finch nearly blew the policeman's head off. Luckily, the farmer hesitated before firing the shotgun and lowered it as he saw the terrified face of the rotund officer.

"I've had warmer welcomes, Fred," PC Thorne said, mopping his brow.

The volunteers piled into the house and PC Thorne sent them off. "You two search upstairs, you go out the back. You – see if there's a cellar!" Then he turned to Finch, gently taking the shotgun from his hands. Finch hadn't realised that he'd had such a tight grip on the weapon and PC Thorne almost had to prise it from his fingers. The policeman took in the wrecked crockery and scattered cutlery on the floor, the tablecloth wrenched off the table top. "What's been happening here, Fred?"

"I just came round for a spot of dinner," Finch said, attempting to process what had happened with levity. But it was too shocking not to be serious. "And she tried to poison me."

"Evelyn Gray?" PC Thorne asked.

Finch nodded. "I've no idea why. We hadn't even got married yet. I can understand her bumping me off for my money if we were married."

"You always say you've got no money." Thorne smiled.

"That's only when it's my round." The two friends laughed. PC Thorne bent down to pick up Evelyn's brandy glass. He sniffed it and was about to speak when, suddenly, outside they heard a commotion. Shouts and sounds of someone being dragged against their will. PC Thorne spun around and headed for the door, followed by Finch. "I think they've got him! They've got him!"

Finch came outside to see a ruddy-faced man in an ARP Warden helmet. He was puffing from the exertion of whatever he had been doing. He confirmed that they had caught a man nearby who fitted the description of Vernon Storey. PC Thorne pushed past Finch and went back into the house. He found the telephone and started to dial the exchange. "I should tell Hoxley Manor that we've got him. Put their minds at rest."

"Iris will be relieved all right."

Finch waited while PC Thorne asked to be connected to Hoxley Manor. He listened as the policeman left a message with a nurse at the Manor House. Then he replaced the receiver and headed outside. "There, that's done."

PC Thorne and Finch walked behind the ARP man and followed him into the dead forest, the trees stretching up like skeletal fingers. Up ahead, in a clearing, Finch could make out two soldiers from the Home Guard wrestling with a thin, sallow man. They had him on the ground, trying to force his struggling hands behind his back. Finch bent down to see if he could recognise the face, but the angle of his head and the darkness of the night made it difficult. But finally, Finch caught a glimpse of the man as he raised his head. Finch motioned to the Home Guard soldiers to listen for a moment.

It wasn't Vernon Storey.

Iris examined her fingers in the moonlight. She felt quite sick. Without the splint and the bandage, she could see them in their true horror. They were in a worse state than before, glistening with blood, twisted and purple. She tried to bend them, but it was too painful. She decided that she would ask one of the doctors to treat her, after all. Gingerly supporting her damaged hand, she turned to head back inside.

She walked along the balustrade, the soft lights from the manor house playing on her face. Gentle music was wafting from somewhere in the Manor House. Was it 'Chattanooga Choo Choo'? Iris smiled. How that song was haunting her, seeming to appear at every turn in her life and –

But then she saw a figure standing up ahead. A small figure, silhouetted in the moonlight.

"Martin?"

The figure took a step forward so that the light from the ward caught the side of his face. She could see pitted skin and a coal-black eye, glistening in the amber glow.

Vernon Storey stood in front of her.

She could see now that his face was contorted with fury, eyebrows pressed down in a grimace of anger.

Iris knew she couldn't reach the entrance to the Manor without going past him. And he was blocking the way. What should she do?

She decided the best course of action was to back away. But as she took a step backwards, Vernon moved forward with surprising speed and clamped a hand over her mouth, roughly pushing her backwards over the Tudor balustrade. Iris toppled over the balcony, landing heavily on a bush below and hitting the wheelbarrow with her elbow. She felt an explosion of pain in her arm.

"Help me!" Iris shouted.

Vernon vaulted over the balcony and reached her before she had time to get up. She could see a spade that had been knocked from the wheelbarrow and she struggled to stretch out her good hand to reach it. Her fingers desperately splayed, she nearly reached the handle just as Vernon grabbed her legs and pulled her backwards, away from the weapon. Still she struggled away and managed to get a small purchase on the handle. But Vernon was on her back, ramming her face into the soil.

"Told you, I'd come back for you, Iris," he hissed.

"Not this time!" Iris shouted, arcing the spade round and catching Vernon on the side of the head.

Clunk!

He fell off her and to the side. But as Iris scrambled to her feet to get into a good position to bring it round again, Vernon punched her in the stomach. She dropped the spade and it clattered to the ground. Vernon's face was bloodied by the impact of the spade, a gash snaking down his cheek. He loomed over her, disorientated, crazed.

"Give me the map!"

Iris tried to pull herself up, fighting for breath after being winded.

"Don't you care about your sister?"

"What have you done to her?" He forced her head back onto the ground.

"I've done nothing, but –"

"Just hand the map over, girl! And I'll let you go."

"All right," Iris gasped. She knew that he was a man without remorse, without sympathy. He had come too far along the dark path, his psyche becoming twisted and psychotic since the murder of his son. Iris knew that she was in great danger, and that he had no intention of letting her go. But part of her also felt a furious, boiling anger at how this man had treated her. The fear and the drinking was because of him; her terror at every shadow had been caused by him. How dare he make her feel this scared. In some small way, she was going to make a stand. She was going to mess up his plans, even if it put her in even more peril.

Iris made a decision.

She scrambled to her feet, indicating for Vernon to give her room. Cautiously he took half a step back, watching her with his hawk-like eyes, his face glistening with blood from the gaping gash. Slowly, Iris reached into her dungarees and pulled out the piece of yellowing paper. It was folded tightly. Vernon's eyes glinted. Finally, the prize. The prize that would enable him to start again.

Iris moved her hand as if she was about to give it to Vernon.

"Good girl."

But instead of handing it over, Iris tore it quickly in half, and then ripped it again into quarters. Vernon lunged at her, but she turned her body so she could continue shredding it, finally sending a dozen pieces of paper fluttering to the ground as if it was confetti.

Vernon's face contorted in anger. He fell to his knees to try to scoop up the precious pieces, but the breeze in the garden was scattering them across the vegetable patch. Then he noticed that Iris was making a break for it, running back to the balustrade.

Iris hoped that he would concentrate on the map. She went to jump over the balustrade, but a hand grabbed her ankle, pulling her back. She fell onto the upturned wheelbarrow again, this time knocking out trowels and other small tools. She winced with the pain that bloomed in her lower back. Vernon was climbing on top of her, his yellow teeth gleaming with spittle and fury.

Iris felt the same fear as before, when she had been pinned down by him in his farmhouse.

"No," she pleaded.

"Too late, Iris," Vernon said.

Iris couldn't move. He was too heavy and his weight was pushing the wind out of her lungs. She could feel metal tools from the wheelbarrow digging into her back beneath her. A drop of his blood splashed onto her cheek. She flailed at him, but he pushed her hands away. She froze in terror, her mind becoming paralysed as it had done before. She tried to struggle, but he pinned her arms down. Finally, after her ordeal tonight, even the adrenaline couldn't give her any last burst of energy, any advantage. Iris felt her struggles diminishing as her breathing became more laboured.

Vernon grabbed her face with one hand.

With cold clarity, she knew he was going to kill her now.

As she struggled weakly, she tried to bat him off with her damaged hand. She realised that Vernon had noticed it flailing at him.

He grinned, grabbing her broken fingers in a vice-like grip. Iris silently howled in pain, tears falling from her eyes.

But the pain broke her free from her terrified stupor, driving her to find the last vestiges of strength and resistance in her body. It was her last hope.

With her good hand, Iris grabbed something from underneath her; anything. It was a small scythe. Without any warning, she plunged it hard into Vernon's side.

Now it was his turn for his face to contort in pain. Immediately he released his grip on her shattered hand and his grip on her face. Iris winced as her fingers were released, but with her other hand, she managed to push the handle of the scythe to propel Vernon off her. He fell heavily, tumbling over onto the vegetable patch. Iris noticed that the entire length of the blade of the scythe was embedded in Vernon's side.

Shakily, Iris stumbled to her feet, the wheelbarrow clattering beneath her. Tentatively, she walked over to her attacker. He was staring up at the moon, the light glinting in his eyes. The light was also glistening off the blood that was disappearing into the hungry earth.

She was dimly aware of people running towards her from the entrance to Hoxley Manor. It was Frank and Martin. They reached her side and looked down at the body of Vernon Storey. Iris could hear voices asking if she was all right, a chorus of concern, but she couldn't reply. She couldn't really hear them.

Iris stared numbly, exhausted. She dared to hope that now it really was over.

Before the sun started to rise, Iris found herself in Dr Channing's office having her fingers expertly set. He didn't try to engage her in conversation, realising that she was too exhausted to talk. Instead, he offered comforting smiles as he worked. When it was finished, Iris looked at the solid paddle of wood that was now acting as a splint for her fingers and the tight white bandage that was wrapped around her hand. It felt much less painful.

"It will heal. And you'll soon be playing the piano again," he said.

"I don't play the piano."

"It's just an expression," Channing replied, with a smile. "Now, you won't be able to do heavy farm work for a while, so I'll recommend that you help Esther with the meals for the time being. Is that all right?"

Iris nodded. She thanked him and left his room. Martin and Frank walked her back towards the farm. On the way, Frank turned to her, his voice low and serious.

"Evelyn died," he said.

Iris took this in. She felt oddly numb about everything. Even Martin smiling warmly at her as they walked didn't make her feel anything. And ordinarily, she would have felt a flutter of nerves in her stomach coupled with a warm feeling. She assumed that she was too tired to function or think properly. She needed sleep, she needed a bath, she needed to get these wellington boots off. Tomorrow she would feel better.

The cockerel failed to wake her, despite its best efforts, and Iris slept through until the next evening. She was back in her old room at Pasture Farm, Billy's room, and her suitcase had been brought back to the farm from Evelyn's cottage. After a hot bath, Esther helped her to bed. Knowing that it was over, and that she would be allowed to come back to Pasture Farm now, Iris slept deeply, with warm satisfaction. When she woke, she still felt exhausted, but she definitely felt better than she had. She couldn't feel any pain in her fingers and that had contributed to her having an unbroken night of sleep.

She reached into her suitcase and opened the small pocket inside. The rag doll was there. Iris took it out and held it. She squeezed it tightly and decided that it was time to say goodbye.

The small figure had been her companion for all these years; giving her comfort during the dark times, but it was time to stand on her own two feet. She had proved that she could take on her worst nightmares and win. Iris didn't need it any more.

She placed the rag doll on the windowsill. It could stay there as an ornament for now.

Iris wrapped a shawl around her nightie and hobbled downstairs. Her whole body ached and she had a variety of bruises fighting for attention on her face. Esther and Joyce were waiting in the kitchen, pleased to see her. They made her some food and a cup of tea. Iris was surprisingly hungry and she also happily drank a whole pot of tea. Esther seemed relieved to have her back. She promised to get a message to Iris's mother to tell her that she was safe and well.

"How was my mother when you saw her?" Iris enquired.

"She seemed well," Esther said, before looking at Joyce. "Would you give us a moment, love?"

Joyce dried her hands and trotted out into the yard.

When they were alone, Esther sat next to Iris.

"She told me about what happened with your father."

"We've never really spoken about it," Iris said, bluntly.

"I'm sorry," Esther said. "Would you like some leave? You could go back and clear the air."

"There's only one thing I want to say, and I don't think I could ever say it face to face."

"What?"

But Iris clammed up. She asked if she could make another pot of tea. Esther watched as she struggled with the kettle and the tap with one hand, and then took over. But Iris hoped that the moment had passed and that she'd made it plain that she didn't want to talk about it.

Throughout the day, Iris had a succession of visitors. Joyce brought John to say hello and welcome back. Shelley came by to tell Iris how happy she was that she was safe, and finally Frank came to see her. After they spoke for a while, the topic of conversation turned to the issue of the map.

"What do you think was buried?" Iris asked.

"Don't know." Frank shrugged. "Me and Martin had a bit of a dig, and we were going to do some more. But we didn't find anything."

"Shame I ripped it up, really," Iris said.

"Yeah," Frank said, but a mischievous smile was playing on his lips; a smile that told Iris that something was up. "Good job I made a copy, wasn't it?" Frank revealed a piece of graph paper with a copy of the map. "When we were digging, we needed some sort of scale to go by, so I copied it onto squared paper."

Iris smiled. "We can find the treasure."

"If it is treasure. Who knows what it could be?"

The following Sunday, Frank, Martin and Iris set off to the North Field in the pony and trap. They were joined there by Finch, Joyce, John and Shelley. Despite it being everyone's day off, they were pitching in together to help dig some holes. Finch, Frank and Esther had spent the previous evenings studying the map in detail, trying to decipher its vague outlines and sparse information. And now, Frank allocated different areas to each of them and they took spades and began to dig up the ground. Shelley started a sing-song in a bid to keep everyone uplifted and motivated, but hopes of a quick victory were scuppered as the treasure hunt stretched from minutes into hours. It wasn't only the lack of detail that made things difficult; they also had no idea how deep they were supposed to dig. There was the fear that they might have discovered the correct location but simply not dug deep enough. As morale started to flag, Esther brought out some packed lunches and water, and after a brief break, everyone resumed their work. Iris felt like a spare part, unable to dig because of her injury, but she spent the time talking to Martin. Everyone said she should be resting anyway.

"It's good to have you back," Martin said.

"It's good to be back," Iris replied.

"Your fella is still hanging on."

"What?"

"That GI. He's still unconscious in the hospital."

"Oh." Iris took this in. "He's not my fella."

Martin offered a small smile, relief in his eyes. Now Iris felt a warm glow.

Esther and Frank looked on at the happy youngsters, clearly bonding and enjoying their time together.

"We should really make fun of them," Frank said with a wry smile.

"Let them have a day off," Esther replied.

As work continued, Iris walked between groups, making small talk, feeling as if she was a guest at one of Lady Hoxley's cocktail parties. She found Finch, who was, unusually, taking part in the digging. Bending down, Iris kept her voice low so that no one could hear them.

"I'm sorry how things worked out, Mr Finch," she said.

Finch nodded, keeping his head down. "They said you got there in time to save me," he said.

"That's right. And if Evelyn's clock hadn't been running fast, you wouldn't even have known about the poison." Iris smiled.

There was a silence between them, neither knowing really what to say. After what seemed like an age, Finch mumbled, "Thanks." He gave her a heartfelt look. Iris knew that things would be all right between them. Things would be back to normal.

Iris looked across the field at her friends, busy trying to find a dream on a piece of paper. She felt thankful that she had these people in her life. Friends away from home, friends in time of war. Friends who would help her if she needed it. A surrogate family of kindly souls.

Suddenly, Frank shouted out. "I've found something!"

Everyone downed tools and scrambled over to where he was digging, crowding round for a look. Iris got there at the same time as Joyce and Shelley. They looked expectantly as Frank pulled a soft leather pouch from the ground. He brushed off the dirt from it on his trousers and then went to carefully unfold it in his hand.

He opened it as if it was delicate parchment. Inside was paper, folded up tightly into a coil. Iris squinted and realised that the paper was bank notes. Frank unrolled the notes, hastily counting them as he went. It took a while.

"Blimey, there's nearly eight hundred pounds here ..."

Soon, Iris, Shelley, Joyce, Frank, Finch, Martin, John and Esther were back in the farmhouse, having a well-deserved pot of tea. The bundle of money was in the centre of the table, attracting fantasies about what it would be spent on if each of them had it. But Esther had suggested what she considered the fairest plan and everyone had agreed on what to do with it. Now they waited nervously for the back door to open.

"When will she come?" Iris asked.

"In her own sweet time," Finch commented, earning a scowl from Esther.

As they finished their tea, there was a soft but insistent knock on the door. They knew it would be her. Esther opened it to admit Lady Hoxley, dressed in a pale-blue dress and matching coat, understated but expensive makeup on her porcelain features.

"Hello, Mrs Reeves."

"Hello, Lady Hoxley," Esther said, pointing to the bank notes. "We thought it might be the fairest solution."

"And you're certain that Mr Storey has no living relatives?" Lady Hoxley asked.

"Not human ones, any road!" Finch blurted out, forgetting himself.

"Fred!" Esther scolded, before turning back to Lady Hoxley. "Sorry. No, Vernon had another son, but he died on the front. There isn't anyone else, as far as we know."

"And no one knows of the existence of this money?"

There was a chorus of people saying no.

"Then I suppose I cannot see a reason why we shouldn't use the money as you suggest, Mrs Reeves."

Martin flashed a happy smile at Iris. Everyone was excited by this response. It seemed the best thing to do with the money. The best thing to extract some good from a horrible situation. It would go towards something that each and every one of them believed in and supported.

"So I will donate it to the Spitfire Fund, then," Lady Hoxley said, picking up the money. "Thank you, everyone."

She turned on her expensive heels, but she stopped for moment before leaving.

"Oh, there's a girl outside to see Iris."

Puzzled, Iris went to the door, Esther coming with her. They opened it to see a thin blonde girl standing in the yard. She was dressed in a Women's Land Army uniform that was two sizes too big for her.

"Maureen?" Iris exclaimed.

"Who's Maureen?" Esther asked.

"I may have said she could join us ..." Iris smiled sheepishly.

Chapter 20

Joyce Fisher was there when Private First Class Joe Batch opened his eyes. She had been busy checking his routine readings, his temperature and blood pressure, when he regained consciousness. Joyce flashed a panicked smile at the American, before immediately rushing out of the private room to fetch the doctor. When she found him, Dr Channing was just as speedy in his response. He ran down the corridor, got some supplies from the stock cupboard, placed them in a kidney bowl and met Joyce back at the soldier's bedside. They looked at the prone figure in front of them, his eyes half-open in his battered face.

"Do you want me to do anything, Dr Channing?"

"It's probably best if you give us some room, Mrs Fisher." Channing smiled. "I'll give you a shout if I need assistance."

"Should I fetch the guard?" Joyce asked. Since his admission, Joe had been guarded by a member of the military police. She supposed that it was mainly for his own protection, since with two broken legs, a broken back and a broken arm, he wasn't going to run off anywhere. But the guard had gone outside for a cigarette, obviously viewing his work of minding an unconscious man as less than engaging.

"Don't trouble him. I'm sure he'll be back soon," Channing said. "In fact, if you see him, tell him to wait outside for a few minutes until I finish my examination." Joyce nodded and left the room. Swiftly, Dr Channing went to the door and closed it, listening for any sounds. When he was satisfied that no one was around, he walked back to Joe's bedside. The soldier couldn't move his head, but he was watching Channing keenly.

"Life is all about making judgements. We decide something, a course of action, a person's guilt, whatever. But sometimes we're wrong in those judgements. And sometimes there's a moment when the penny drops that we're wrong, isn't there? We can believe in something adamantly, only to suddenly realise that we were wrong all along. Don't you find?" Channing didn't expect a reply. Instead he leaned in close so that he could see Joe's eyes, now filling with a look of unease.

"They said you were chasing after Frank Tucker. They said you believed that he'd heard you talking about the Panmere operation. You were going to get even with him. You adamantly believed that he'd betrayed you, didn't you? And yes, he might have overheard you, apparently. But now you might have realised something else. And if you haven't realised it yet, then I'm sure it's only a matter of time before you do."

He could see that Joe was struggling to understand.

"So that leaves me with a big problem, doesn't it?"

"What?" Joe had difficulty forming the word in his dry mouth.

"I'm very sorry." Channing smiled.

Suddenly it hit Joe like a steam train, the realisation of what had happened. A knot instantly filled his stomach, his body shivering with the rush of adrenaline, as the pieces fell into place. Frank's words in the forest came back to him.

"Because someone else must have known."

And Joe remembered talking to Chuck in the hospital, in this hospital. Chuck had mentioned the Panmere Lake operation. And Channing had been in the room too.

"You heard ..."

Channing watched as the soldier's eyes filled up with terror.

"That's right, I did hear," he said, pleasantly. "For me, it was always a risk as to when you'd realise. If you would realise. In a lot of ways, I'm grateful you didn't realise when you were able-bodied. I'm not sure I could stop you in a fair fight." He smiled as if talking to a friend.

"Get ... guard," Joe mouthed, but his words were barely more than a whisper.

"Oh, let him have his cigarette. The poor chap needs a break," Channing said. "I hope you'll take some small solace from knowing you were right in the end. It's a shame for you that you realised too late. Tragic, really."

Despite his broken body, Joe managed to move his good arm and grab Channing's wrist. The doctor looked mildly surprised at the reflexes of his patient. "Very good," Channing said. "But unfortunately you don't have the strength any more, do you?"

Channing prised open the soldier's fingers, the sweaty digits offering little resistance. He watched impassively as Joe winced.

Then Channing calmly crossed to a trolley of supplies across the room. He picked up a pillow and moved swiftly back to the soldier's side. "I'd like you to think I'm not a bad man. But this is war. And it's a more complex situation than you can imagine. But for now, all you need to know is that you are in the way. I cannot allow you to tell anyone. I'm really very sorry."

And with all his strength, Channing pushed the pillow over Joe's face, forcing it hard down over his mouth and nose. The soldier struggled for a few seconds, but Channing kept the pressure up. After a few moments, Joe Batch stopped struggling and went limp. Channing waited for a moment to be sure, and then he took the pillow away. Casually, he threw it over the room onto the trolley, exhaled deeply, and checked his patient's pulse. A small look of relief played on Channing's face.

At that moment, Joyce entered. Channing instantly retrieved his cool, detached demeanour.

"He's dead, I'm afraid," Dr Channing said, looking at his pocket watch. "Mrs Fisher? Would you record the time of death as sixteen minutes past seven?"

Joyce picked up the clipboard at the end of the soldier's bed, but hesitated. Channing noticed and stepped closer.

"He was all right a moment ago," she said, confused.

"He was very badly injured. But sometimes people can rally at the last moment, can't they?"

"I suppose."

"Let's fill in the form, then." Channing offered a consoling look. "His injuries were very severe."

"Yes, Dr Channing." Joyce noted down the time of death and replaced the clipboard at the end of the bed.

Although Lady Hoxley kept her promise and gave all the discovered money to the Spitfire Fund, she decided to spend some of her own money to host a small party for the Land Girls. They had been through so much in the last few months. So when the vegetable patches were finished around Hoxley Manor, Lady Hoxley threw a double celebration. The party would commemorate the hard work of the girls who had turned her rose gardens into vegetable patches and also the bravery of Iris Dawson. About forty people filled a small marquee that had been erected. Lady Hoxley had booked a trumpet player for the occasion. He was currently playing 'Chattanooga Choo Choo'. Iris still disliked the song as much as the first time she'd heard it.

For her part, Iris felt a little overwhelmed by all the attention, managing to clam up spectacularly whenever Lady Hoxley tried to speak to her. Instead, she found a corner of the marquee and sat down with Joyce and Shelley. She remembered the last dance they went to, the one where Evelyn Gray had engineered to meet Finch. Suddenly, Joyce cleared her throat to let Iris know that they were being watched. From across the tent, Martin was looking over towards them.

"He's plucking up courage again," Joyce whispered.

"No need," Iris replied, getting to her feet and crossing towards him.

"I was going to ask if you wanted a dance?" Martin said, a little surprised by her meeting him halfway. Iris told him that she hated 'Chattanooga Choo Choo'. She wasn't sure she wanted to dance to that.

"Could we go outside instead? My hand isn't up to dancing at that speed. It still throbs," Iris said, lifting her right hand. It was dressed in a much smaller bandage than before, with a thin splint instead of the paddle that Dr Channing had used at first. Outside, Martin and Iris looked at the stars. Iris noticed him sneaking a glance at her rosy, red lips, which came courtesy of Connie's lipstick. She wondered if he was going to kiss her. She thought of those films where the hero just grabbed the girl and planted a smacker on her. But in the end she was grateful that he tried a different approach.

"Would you mind if I kiss you?" Martin said, plucking up courage.

She looked at his boyish, handsome face, with its big, kind eyes. And she thought about Brian Marley when she was 10 years old, the stickiness of toffee on his lips. Maybe it was time to try this kissing business again?

Iris nodded and they brought their lips closer, nervously, together and kissed. She liked the softness of his lips and the slight roughness to his cheek where he hadn't shaved. At first it was chaste and barely more than a peck. But they soon realised that they both enjoyed it and within minutes they were passionately kissing. After a while, they both broke away, breathless and flushed.

"Was it all right?" Martin asked, a sudden glimmer of self-doubt in his eyes.

"I might need to check it again." Iris smiled, a pretend look of concern on her face. With her splint resting on the back of his neck, she drew him close and they kissed again. This time they didn't stop for a long, long time.

Margot Dawson was just about to leave for the factory. She wasn't relishing the prospect of another twelve-hour shift, especially as she had completed two equally long shifts over the last two days. Feeling a weariness in her bones, she opened her front door and stepped out to find the postman outside. He smiled, tipped his cap and handed her a letter. Margot was about to put the letter inside when something about it caught her eye.

The envelope was handwritten with uneasy and unevenly sized letter shapes, as if it had been written by a young child.

Margot didn't recognise the writing. Who was it from? Intrigued, she stopped a moment and opened it, not caring if she was a few minutes late for her shift.

The lilac-coloured paper felt heavy between her fingers. It was expensive. She unfolded it and squinted at the writing. It was a short letter, but as soon as she realised who it was from, it brought tears welling up in her eyes.

It was from Iris.

This was the letter that her daughter had always wanted to write. The words she had always wanted to say. Frank had helped her, the two resuming her nightly lessons in reading and writing, when her hand had healed.

And as her skills improved, Iris took the plunge and wanted to try to write a real letter home. She told Frank that it would be short. Offering encouragement, he thought that even saying hello would warm her mother's heart and make her feel proud.

But Iris said she wanted to write something different. Something she had always wanted to say, but could never say out loud. Words that had always been hidden in her relationship with her mother; words that needed to be said to clear the air between them. She knew that this was her chance. A chance to tell her mother something without the stomach-churning awkwardness of having to sit across the dining table and say it aloud, without having to see the reaction on her face. Without the risk of facing rejection.

And now, Margot stared at the letter, her shoulders heaving in a silent and primal sob. The tears fell down her cheeks, but she didn't try to catch them with her fingers. She let them come. It wasn't the joy of seeing the first letter from her daughter. It was the message, written in less than ten words, that broke her heart.

The letter said:

Dear Mum,

I'm sorry. Please forgive me.

Love

Iris xxx

Margot smiled as she cried, saddened that Iris felt the need to say those words. She wanted to hug her daughter close to her and squeeze her tightly and tell her how much she loved her, how much she had always loved her. Margot never blamed Iris for not fetching the doctor in time. She'd done her best. It was one of those things; an example of fate dealing a spectacularly cruel hand. But Margot knew that she had never spoken about it afterwards with Iris. That was her failing. She had been reluctant to open up the old wounds of that day. And maybe Iris had misconstrued that as a damning silent judgement about her efforts to save her father. For her part, Margot hadn't even remembered shutting Iris outside as she and the doctor fought to revive her father. That had been a momentary decision, done to protect the child from seeing the inevitable end. Iris viewed that as a rejection, a judgement, not realising what it really was.

Margot felt wracked with guilt of her own. She had to put Iris straight, lift this dreadful weight from the girl's shoulders.

She made a sudden, impulsive decision. She raced back into the house. She knew she would be late for her shift, but she didn't care. She could make up the time tonight. But right now, she needed to do something more than she had ever needed to do anything before. She had to put things right and heal the pain from the past.

Margot Dawson opened her bureau and took out her writing paper.

Tears rolled down her face as she started to write a letter back to her daughter.

Acknowledgements

I feel blessed to be able to tell another story, following the exploits of the Land Girls. Thank you to my family for their endless support and encouragement. Thanks too to Julia Wyatt and James Anderson for everything they do. Thank you to Charlotte Ledger and Eloisa Clegg at HarperImpulse for their enthusiasm and talent in making this a reality – and thank you to Jo Godfrey Wood and Suzy Clarke for their eagle eyes and great ideas. It's been wonderful to centre a story around Iris Dawson – and I thank Lou Broadbent for bringing the character so vividly to life in the television series, and thus inspiring her portrayal in this story. Thanks again to all the team at BBC Birmingham who worked on the television series. And last, but in no way least, I'd like to thank all the people who have enjoyed the first novel and who continue to champion the television series. Thank you to those of you who have given lovely reviews. I hope you enjoy this story.